THE HOUSE OF FLOWERS

It is 1941, and England is at its lowest ebb, undernourished, under-informed and terrified of imminent invasion. At Eden Park, where Poppy, Kate, Lily, Marjorie and her adopted brother Billy have become part of the rich tapestry that is being woven around them, confidence is at an all-time low. And that is before the authorities discover there is a double agent operating within the MI5 unit based there.

Lily volunteers to be dropped into France, only to discover that her partner is Scott, Poppy's fiancé. Meanwhile, Kate's lover Eugene is in Sicily to sabotage the bombers besieging Malta. As further agents are wiped out and even Billy's life is threatened, Jack Ward, the spymaster, is forced to take desperate measures to uncover the identity of the traitor in their midst.

As Poppy closes the wooden shutters at the House of Flowers, the old folly where she and Scott first found happiness, she realizes that they were made over a century ago to repel another invader. England survived then; she will again.

THE HOUSE OF FLOWERS

Charlotte Bingham

WINDSOR
PARAGON

First published 2004
by
Doubleday
This Large Print edition published 2004
by
BBC Audiobooks Ltd by arrangement with
Transworld Publishes Limited

ISBN 0 7540 7987 2   (Windsor Hardcover)
ISBN 0 7540 6895 1   (Paragon Softcover)

British Library Cataloguing in Publication Data available

Printed and bound in Great Britain by
Antony Rowe Ltd., Chippenham, Wiltshire

To the memory of 'Aunt Bea', the inventor of Billy's famous letter-opener. A fearless agent, one of thousands to whom we owe so much.

CB, Hardway

'Nothing was heard but the dread of Buonoparte and the French invasion! Beacons, martello towers, camps, Depots and every species of self-defence occupied all minds—and everyone trembled for the safety of old England'

Humphry Repton (*c.* 1793)

Prologue

As the driver dropped down to an even lower gear, the two men in the back stared out at the snow which had suddenly started falling in a blizzard. Sensing they might not make the rendezvous, the man tightened his grip instinctively round the butt of the revolver that lay in one pocket, warmed by his hand. The passenger next to him turned and raised his elegant eyebrows, putting two fingers of his left hand to his lips to indicate his need for a fresh cigarette. The thickset man beside him stared back at him for a moment, then slowly withdrew a treasured pack of Players from his other coat pocket, inspecting it carefully before taking out one of the two remaining cigarettes single-handed and lighting it himself before handing it over. The driver changed gear yet again, down to first now as the wheels of the large black Austin began to lose their grip on the snow. He glanced in his mirror, catching the eye of the man seated directly behind.

'Keep going,' his passenger muttered, sticking his pipe back in his mouth. 'We haven't got far to go now, and it'll be a lot easier coming back down—'

He stopped speaking abruptly as the driver over-corrected the car, preventing it from going out of control, and caught the back of the seat in front.

The younger man, smoking his freshly lit cigarette, smiled to himself at their increasing difficulties, knowing very well that whatever happened to them during the last part of this particular journey, the outcome was inevitable.

1

He turned his handsome head and stared out at the snow that now blanketed the evening landscape. He liked snow. It had always excited him, never losing that boyish delight at seeing the first large flakes falling silently from leaden skies. Now lights shone ahead, torches being swung in the gloom by invisible people standing in the middle of the deserted road, a road he knew well since it bisected a large stretch of moorland that once had been his, an autumn paradise where with gun and dog he had loved to roam. Again he smiled as he considered the irony of the moment, how this time an expert shot would extinguish the life not of some fast fleeing grouse but of a rather easier target.

'You can finish your cigarette,' the man beside him muttered, tucking his briar pipe away in the top pocket of his jacket before producing a key to unlock the handcuffs that had linked the two men on their long winter journey. In front of them the driver had already half turned round to train the long barrel of a service revolver directly at the head of the prisoner.

Once again the captive raised eyebrows that appeared to have been carefully manicured, so perfect were their shape. He took one last draw on the cigarette before extinguishing it reluctantly in the ashtray beside him.

'Goodbye,' he said to the thickset man beside him, whose gaze he had observed seemed seldom given to blinking. 'I do hope you get home safely.'

The man slowly took off his heavy-framed spectacles and nodded.

'Goodbye,' he replied, beginning to clean the lenses of his glasses slowly and carefully before turning to look at the driver, who read the signal at once.

'Time to get out,' he said to the man beside him, underlying his order with a significant nod of his head towards the snow-covered landscape.

The passenger hesitated, as if he was about to try to buy time by arguing his cause. But it soon became obvious that this was far from his intention, for he used the delay simply to smile and nod at both men. Finally, after catching the eye of the man to his right, at whom he stared without apparent emotion, he pushed the passenger door beside him open and got out to stand smartly to attention by the snow-covered automobile.

'Heil Hitler,' he said, all traces of his smile now gone.

The thickset man, who was sitting quite still in the back seat, stared up at the elegant figure standing to defiant attention in the blizzard. He put one heavy hand bearing a small crested signet ring on the driver's arm as he was just about to disembark.

'Tell them not to make a meal of it.'

The driver did not respond, simply getting quickly out of the car, slamming his door shut and disappearing into the snowstorm. His superior remained sitting in the back of the car, taking the last of the Players cigarettes from the battered pack and lighting it with a small gold lighter. He sat back, inhaling deeply, staring ahead at a windscreen now completely covered with snow.

In the bleak, dark and bitter winter evening outside, the tall, elegant man turned up the collar of his still immaculate cavalry coat.

'This is what I would call a blizzard,' he

3

remarked. 'Typical moor storm. Used to toboggan down here as a boy.'

'Rather than toboggan, why don't you take a hike, chum?' a voice to match the wintry conditions wondered from behind him. 'To make it fair, I'll give you thirty seconds' start.'

'Not the most appealing of ideas,' he replied. 'Too easy to get lost up here.'

'Go on,' he was urged. 'Be a sport.'

The man turned to try to identify the voice behind him, but thanks to the severity of the storm he could see even less than before.

'Even better,' the voice suggested, 'why not go for a little run?'

He won't run, the man still sitting in the back of the snow-covered car thought to himself. *He's not the type.*

He took another pull on his cigarette, clearing the condensation off the inside of the window beside him with the back of one gloved hand as if to try to get a sight of the events taking place somewhere in the darkness outside. A flurry of snow falling against the glass immediately deprived him of any view, so, giving a deep shiver against the cold, he pulled the collar of his overcoat up round his neck and slumped further down in his seat in an effort to keep warm.

Even if there was a chance it would save his life, he still wouldn't run, he concluded. *He wouldn't even run to save his skin.*

'At the command—run.'

'And make it easier for you?' the man wondered in return, staring up into the invisible skies above him as if at a starlit summer sky. 'No—no, I don't think I'll bother, if it's all the same to you.'

4

At the back of his mind he toyed with the thought that if he just stood his ground somehow he might be able to bluff his way out of it, until he heard the tell-tale sound of a safety catch being released, at which he changed his mind. Clearing his throat, he sunk his hands in his coat pockets and began to stroll off across the snow-swept moors for all the world like a gentleman taking an after-lunch constitutional.

They let him go a surprising distance, so far in fact that his heart gave a small leap as he realised that, given the distance he had covered in such appalling conditions, his executioner might actually have lost sight of him.

His attitude changed now that he thought he had a chance to outwit his enemies, people whom in comparision to himself, and those he admired, he considered to be stupid, slow and without imagination. The thought brought a sudden smile to his frozen features, and as he smiled he found himself running. Faster and faster away from the gunman who must surely now be marooned in an impenetrable wall of snow. As he ran he threw back his head and laughed, just as the man many yards away behind him fired several shots in quick succession.

The body fell forward into a drift of snow, the blood from it staining the white that surrounded it with surprising rapidity. The marksman went up to it, turned it over, and stared down. The cap had fallen from the head revealing thick blond hair, and such a startlingly handsome face beneath it that it seemed in death to have returned to a state of peace that was almost enviable, as if, in the ultimate mercy of its end, a life had been finally unravelled and returned to a childlike innocence.

'Fool,' the man in the back of the car remarked to himself, hearing the shots and then noting the flare the marksman put up. 'You poor misguided, stupid fool—what in heaven's name possessed you?'

Taking a last pull on his cigarette he opened the car door, and, with a sigh and a slow sorry shake of his head, walked off into the blizzard to help bring back the traitor's remains.

Part One

ENGLAND, 1941

Chapter One

Major Folkestone frowned and shuffled the papers at which he was pretending to stare so hard. On the other side of his desk Cissie Lavington stood with her trademark long cigarette holder stuck jauntily out of the side of her mouth while she regarded him with her one good eye, the other hidden as always behind her other trademark, a handmade black silk eye-patch. Even though the matter before them was of a serious nature, as always Cissie's expression was one of benign indifference, as if she had only a passing interest in what the world might throw at her.

'You'd rather I told her?' Cissie volunteered, finally growing impatient with the way Anthony Folkestone was hiding behind his paperwork.

'I don't see why you would think that,' Anthony Folkestone muttered, pretending to find the latest sheet of paper in his hand of particular interest. 'But it does have to be done.'

'I expect you feel, Major, I expect you feel that—well,' Cissie replied, tapping the end of her cigarette into the tin ashtray on the desk, 'that this sort of stuff comes a lot better from a woman.'

Cissie took one last draw on her cigarette, removed the stub and inserted a fresh smoke deftly in her holder, while never taking her eye off the man on the other side of the desk. As she had noted over the past few weeks spent training agents in H Section of what was discreetly described in Top Secret documents as 'the War Office', jobs involving the breaking of bad news always seemed

9

to come *a lot better from a woman*.

'The point is I'd do it myself if I had the time. But just at the moment, all this paperwork ...'

Folkestone shook his head sadly, at the same time collecting the loose pages up and tapping them into a tidy pile.

'I understand Lady Tetherington's in lodgings in Benton,' he added, handing Cissie a sheet of paper bearing the address. 'Taking some leave.'

'Rather well earned, considering. The top brass are very pleased with what we did—apparently it cheered the Old Man up no end. Not that we expect it to be the only attempt on his life, by any means, but there you are. One down, that's something at least. Quite apart from anything else it would have been invaluable propaganda. Although I understand the Old Man has a few doubles waiting in the wings for that moment, if it ever comes.'

Major Folkestone nodded. H Section had done brilliantly to thwart the assassination attempt on Churchill, but for the moment they had other matters on their minds.

'You could always ask the WVS,' he offered, his thoughts returning to Lady Tetherington.

Cissie shook her head, standing by his office door, already impatient to leave.

'I think not,' she replied in a firm voice. 'A factory was hit near Benton last night. We can't take anyone away from much needed work.' She opened the door. 'I'd rather do it myself, Major, since I helped train Lady Tetherington. Only right really.'

'Very well,' Folkestone agreed. 'So be it. And perhaps you'd be so good as to ask Miss Budge to

10

come back in on your way out? My wretched intercom is on the blink yet again. Thank you.'

Cissie did as asked, after a thankfully brief exchange of observations about the weather with Major Folkestone's new assistant, the plump and smiling Miss Budge, who was only too happy to bustle into Major Folkestone's office, notebook at the ready.

*   *   *

Poppy watched Cissie strolling up the garden path towards the front door of the small suburban house in the back street of Benton. Cissie's eccentric way of still dressing in the vaguely flapper style of the late nineteen twenties meant that against the drab background of the privet hedge that ran along the side of the front garden she now seemed to stand out like some exotic foreign bloom.

In the kitchen at the back of the house Poppy's landlady, all too appropriately named Mrs Bellows, was listening to a radio that crackled and boomed at full volume, so much so that if Poppy had not noticed Cissie walking up to the door it was perfectly possible that neither occupant of Number 24 The Gardens would have heard the bell.

'Shall I answer it?' Poppy wondered academically, putting her head around the kitchen door after Cissie had rung for the third or fourth time. 'I think it might be someone for me.'

'It's just as I said!' Mrs Bellows shouted back over the radio. 'What I was telling you all over breakfast! Ministry of Food says we're all to go carefully with the tin-opener!'

'I'll answer the door, Mrs Bellows,' Poppy said,

nodding backwards as she heard yet another long ring of the bell. She closed the kitchen door in order to try to shut out some of the radio's din, hoping that her visitor was coming to tell her that her leave was over, and she wasn't going to have to spend much longer under Mrs Bellows's roof eating watery oatmeal and paper-thin fried bread for breakfast, with tea so weak it might have come straight from the hot water tap. But as soon as she saw Cissie's face she knew that her visit was nothing to do with ending her leave.

'I imagine you can guess why one's here,' Cissie stated at once, when Poppy had shown her into the front room, an over-neat apartment furnished with heavy square furniture with rounded feet, and arms draped with lace antimacassars that matched the freshly washed nets at the front window.

'I would say, judging from your expression, that it has to do with my husband,' Poppy replied, sitting down on one fat arm of the chair behind her. 'And if it is, it can't be good news.'

'I'm afraid you're quite correct, and it's not, my dear,' Cissie sighed, expertly loading her cigarette holder before accepting a light from Poppy. 'Don't know how up to date you are?'

'The last I heard they were changing his hotel,' Poppy said, attempting a joke to lighten the atmosphere. 'They were sending him somewhere up north.'

'Yes, they did change his hotel. Sent him to a top security one, especially designed for the likes of him. Point is—point is someone made a gaffe of it and the blighter tried to make a run for it, d'you see?'

'That can't have been good, I imagine.'

12

'Absolutely not. Chaps with him took a very dim view, I'm afraid. An extremely dim view. Hence my visit.'

There was a short silence while Poppy stared at Cissie Lavington, searching deep to try to find her feelings which at that moment seemed to have deserted her.

'I see,' she said finally. 'That is, Basil's dead, I take it?'

' 'Fraid so. Lord Tetherington was shot while trying to escape.'

'Yes. Yes, I rather thought that might happen.'

Cissie nodded and drew on her cigarette. 'A better thing altogether, if one considers it. Better than the alternative, if you see what I mean.'

'Of course,' Poppy replied quietly, imagining that given the choice anyone would prefer the bullet to the rope.

'Absolutely no doubt,' Cissie agreed. 'Much better thing all round. Besides—it's always a major worry that blighters like that might get sprung, and then one's back to square one again.' She stared at Poppy, wondering how she would take the implication. Poppy met her gaze and nodded.

'Agreed.'

Cissie could not help feeling relieved that Poppy had obviously decided on a practical, no-nonsense approach, but as a woman she was also curious. Having known Poppy from her early days at Eden Park, when she had helped turn the shy bespectacled young ingénue into a confident, courageous and bright young woman, she was well aware that Poppy's brief marriage to Basil Tetherington had been unhappy to say the least, but this did not necessarily mean that Poppy had never loved him.

'It's quite strange, really—' Speaking quietly, Poppy stood up and walked over to the window, drawing aside the net curtain to look outside. 'Even as early on as my honeymoon I used to wonder why Basil had married me, and I realised fairly quickly that it had to be because I had money. He thought of me as a gold mine—you know, only child, American parents in the diplomatic corps, no confidence. I was an easy target really, particularly for someone like him. Yet I still hoped, still went on hoping that he might just have married me because he had some feelings for me. But of course he didn't. Not one. No—actually, that is not entirely true. I think he did have feelings for me— feelings of contempt. As a matter of fact I don't think he liked me at all. So it's all rather odd, hearing that he's dead, probably because he has been dead for me for so long already.'

'Understandable.' Cissie looked round for an ashtray but finding none got rid of her cigarette ash in the coal bucket instead.

'I know. But it doesn't seem to affect me at all because the thing is I suppose I feel as if I have been a widow already. Ever since the Fascists blew up his car in Italy—and of course I didn't really know what he was up to then, that they were just faking his death so they could smuggle him back into England—but ever since that moment I have felt—well—widowed. I lost Basil then, really, but then he came back to life again, and now he's died *again*—so the consequence of all that is that now I don't really know *how* to feel. Or what.'

'Why should you, my dear? Matter of fact I'd say it would be really quite rum if you did know how to feel. Or what. If you felt anything at all.'

'Yes,' Poppy agreed thoughtfully. 'I imagine you're right.'

Cissie glanced at Poppy, who was staring out of the window at the bleak view without, and drew slowly on her cigarette.

'When it's as quiet as this, hard to think there's a war on. One gets so used to sirens, and ambulances, bombs and all the rest of it. It's unsettling, this quiet,' she murmured, breaking the silence.

'When I first heard Basil was dead,' Poppy continued, as she remembered walking in Green Park the day Basil proposed to her, and how oddly happy she had been then, 'when they said he'd been killed in Italy, for a second I did actually think that since I'd known and seen a little bit of the nice side of Basil—possibly all there was—I did think it was my duty as a widow to try to remember him at those moments. But even though he'd seemed so kind when we first met at a really rather dull dance, it really was impossible to hang on to that sort of memory, seeing that he was a traitor. Yet I still feel guilty, because after all I married him. No one else did.'

'See what you mean. Yes.'

'I suppose what I actually feel like, to be perfectly honest, is heaving a rather large sigh of relief. I can't actually pretend to be sad, that would be hypocritical. After all, he stood for everything I hate.'

'Regret's an odd sort of thing, you know. Speaking for oneself, one finds one's memories of someone are so often more than a bit tinged with regret for what they weren't, rather than for what

15

they were.'

Poppy looked round at Cissie, intrigued as always by her observations. Many people who didn't know Cissie Lavington well, or who didn't bother to try to get to know her better, were inclined to write her off as a bit of a social butterfly, because of her upper class mannerisms and her apparent determination to take nothing in this life very seriously. But those who knew Cissie well, those who bothered to talk to her and to listen to what she really had to say, admired and respected her for the astuteness of her observations and her refusal to tell anything but the truth.

'Anyway,' Cissie said in conclusion, firmly squashing her cigarette on the inside wall of the fireplace. 'The war's still on so one had best beetle off and continue to fight the g.f.'

'Of course,' Poppy agreed, walking to the door with her. 'Besides, I think my late husband's already had far more attention than he deserves.'

'Pity we didn't pay more attention to taking people like him more seriously, and locking them away years ago,' Cissie replied, dropping her cigarette holder back into a handbag that she then snapped smartly shut. 'If people had only listened a little to the warning voices, we might not be in this pickle now.'

'I thought it was precisely because of people like Basil—'

'Not a bit,' Cissie interrupted her with a vague wave of one hand. 'If Herr Hitler hadn't got the idea that Britain in the shape of the ruling classes was sympathetic to him, people like Basil who were all too ready to embrace his perfectly dreadful philosophies . . . And as for all those upper class

16

ladies with crushes on Hitler, they gave the blighter confidence. Worse—they gave him hope. Hope that he could do what he blasted well liked and no one here would raise a finger to stop him. No one in power or authority, that is. That's the sort of damage those British Fascists did. Don't worry; I'll let myself out. By the way—if you're interested—they're missing you back at the Park. Up to you, of course.' She looked at Poppy enquiringly, imagining how bored and restless she would be in her place, sitting it out in such drab surroundings.

'I'm more than up to it—I can't wait in fact,' Poppy replied, glancing backwards over her shoulder towards the kitchen door, not because she was worried that she might have said anything indiscreet that Mrs Bellows could have overheard, but more from force of an ever increasing habit. 'Tell them I'll be at my post tomorrow.'

*   *   *

It was once more snowing heavily when Cissie set out on her return journey to Eden Park, where she was now permanently based. It forced her to drive slowly, but gave her plenty of time to reflect on the surprising qualities that had emerged in Poppy Tetherington since her training as an agent. She had not only changed in looks, becoming prettier and more vital; her whole personality too had changed. She had shown daring, invention and nerve, qualities some of those working alongside her in Eden Park had intimated might well be lacking in someone who initially had seemed almost timid. But Cissie had believed in her from the word go, otherwise she would never have taken her on in the first place. She had sensed young Poppy Tetherington's worth from the very beginning, whereas she had quite conflicting feelings about her latest recruit.

Lily Ormerod had lost her fiancé Robert Maddox only a few months before, the young naval officer having been killed in the act of rescuing a child from a bomb-site. To make matters worse her fiancé was the brother of Kate Maddox, one of the girls working in C Section at the Park. Despite everything that anyone had said it seemed that Lily was still determined to blame herself for Robert's death, and it was this that worried Cissie more than anything. Guilt did not make a good bedfellow for an agent in the field. If someone felt guilty they went out of their way to try to compensate for the harm they imagined they had done, and this was what made Cissie Lavington feel sure that Lily Ormerod was in danger of turning into the kind of agent that brings dread to the hearts of every head of section—namely the kind of agent who does not mind dying.

By the time she finally made it up Eden Park's snow-covered drive, parked her car in the stable yard and ascended to the floor that housed all the offices of H Section, Lily was already waiting for her, reading an out of date copy of *Woman and Home*.

'Sorry. The snow, doncher know. Roads back to the Park were practically impassable.'

Lily stood up, carefully replacing the magazine. Like many young women at Eden Park, she was curious about Cissie Lavington. There seemed to be fresh rumours spawned every day concerning the tall, enigmatic woman with one black-patched

18

eye, the latest being that since she was said hardly ever to sleep she possessed no nightwear, and that she never closed her one good eye in case she missed something.

Holding the door to her inner room open, Cissie requested her secretary to bring in a couple of cups of coffee before following Lily into her office.

' 'Fraid it won't be proper coffee, as usual—just that dreadful Camp stuff. One would have thought by now we'd have come up with some sort of plant of our own we could brew.' Cissie sighed, digging deep in her copious handbag for her packet of Senior Service cigarettes. 'Mind you, so saying, one did have the utter misfortune of trying some herbal tea or some such once, and all one can say is not *ever* again. Now then.'

She sat down, and glanced at Lily's file, which lay open on the desk in front of her.

'Going to be one of those gels with not a lot to learn, eh?' she said with a slow smile, looking up with her one good eye to stare at the very pretty girl seated opposite her. 'According to this you speak French and German fluently, is that correct?'

'I have a bit of a knack with languages, always have,' Lily replied, fiddling with the thin gold bracelet she wore on one wrist. 'My mother was the same. She was half French. We spoke both French and English at home. She taught me both languages before I even started school.'

'Your German?'

Lily looked at the woman sitting opposite her at her desk, then at the ceiling, then past her out of the window before she replied.

'My father moved about Europe a great deal. He had a cousin who lived in Bavaria,' she finally

19

admitted. 'We used to go on holiday there, and in turn he would come over to England sometimes. My father and he used to speak German, and I just picked it up. As I said, I seem to have an ear for it. As a matter of fact I dream in three languages. That's usually considered a good sign, isn't it?'

'Where is your father now, Miss Ormerod?' Cissie cut in, having already learned the facts but not the whereabouts of Frank Henry Ormerod from his daughter's dossier.

'I'm not altogether sure, Miss Lavington. My parents got divorced years ago. Not very amicably, and I've not heard from my father since.'

'Is he still in this country? One would rather hope so. Yes? He'd be a little too old, perhaps, to have joined up.'

'As I just said, Miss Lavington,' Lily replied almost curtly, 'I really have no idea where my father might be.'

'Understand perfectly.' Cissie lit the cigarette she had now placed in her holder and tapped the file with a long bony finger. 'The French connection is handy. We can run you under your mother's maiden name—might also help authenticate any background we care to give you. That's given that you make it that far. To becoming active.'

'I'll make it that far, Miss Lavington. You need have no worries on that score.'

Again Cissie glanced up, but this time only momentarily. She had already taken in all that was necessary for the work ahead. She had observed the light in the eyes of her latest recruit, and noted how pretty she was. Cissie's ideal agent would be much more nondescript, the sort of man or woman who could lose themselves in a crowd or be passed in the street without a second glance. Young Lily Ormerod was the very opposite. Lily was most definitely the kind of blonde that, as the saying went, could make a bishop kick a hole in a stained-glass window. If she wanted to be recruited as an agent, particularly as someone they could use as a courier, things would have to change. Before anything else they would have to *defenestrate* her, as Cissie liked to call it, and if she stood up to that, well, all to the good; if not, Cissie would drop her as being too much of a risk, whatever the present crisis.

'On the other hand,' Cissie continued, as if she had been thinking out loud.

'What other hand would that be, Miss Lavington?'

'From your character assessments here,' she continued, without looking at Lily, 'from reading these assessments of your character it would appear you have plenty of what used to be called gum.'

'Gum?'

'Gumption. You are described here as forthright, determined, and certainly not lacking in gum. You seem to keep yourself in trim, too—although I'm sure Mr Jacques will still find plenty for you to do. Mr Jacques, in case you were *not* aware, is our PT chap. As far as Mr Jacques is concerned the human body is an undiscovered continent.' Cissie sighed shortly.

'Think you can do it, do you?' she asked after a long pause. 'Think you're up to snuff? They don't mess around with one if they catch one. Being shot is the least you can expect, if you're caught, which of course we all hope you won't be.' She opened

21

the drawer of one desk and held up a cyanide pill. 'If you're caught, this is the best we can offer you.'

Cissie paused again, just where she always paused, waiting to see what, if any, effect her little homily had on the new recruit. It was hardly the most graphic of depictions, yet several of the girls who had sat opposite her and heard what she had to say had suddenly found all sorts of reasons why all in a moment they no longer considered themselves suitable agent material. Lily Ormerod, on the other hand, simply raised her eyebrows, breathed in deeply and shrugged.

'Long as I've accounted for a number of them,' she confided, 'I don't really care. That's what matters to me. Taking a few of them out.'

'Bravely said, Miss Ormerod,' Cissie replied. 'Except for one thing. One thing that's absolutely *de rigueur*. Never lose sight of the fact that too much gumption can endanger other agents, and worst of all their contacts. We know of whole villages in France where the inhabitants have been shot, because of someone else's bravado. Sometimes even a heroine goes to her grave with the blood of innocents on her hands. Always good to keep that in mind.'

Lily nodded almost absently-mindedly. Ever since December when she had been introduced by a colleague to Poppy Tetherington at the pub in the estate village, Lily had made it clear that she was longing to do something other than secretarial work, and so the die had been cast. Poppy instinctively recognised a fellow soul, and sensing her new friend might be ideal material for H Section had made discreet enquiries before meeting her again.

'What's H Section like, Poppy? Has to be more fun.'

'Oh, it's more fun all right, Lily.'

They both knew what they meant by fun. Fun spelt danger, it meant work that got you out into the field; it meant that you felt so much more alive, because you were going to flirt with death.

'The work is very different in this section, you'll find,' Cissie went on, seeming to know what Lily was thinking. 'So much so that you might find yourself wishing you were back in C Section. No shame in that if you do.'

'There'll be no chance of me wanting to go back to being a secretary, of that I am quite sure.'

Released from her interview, Lily wandered out on to the landing and stood at the huge window that overlooked the park. Now that England was at war, Eden Park's eighteenth-century garden would doubtless be unrecognisable to its owners—what with so much of the grounds turned over to allotments growing much needed fruit and vegetables, and the deer having to share their grazing with large herds of dairy cows and sheep— yet even in winter the overall vista was still remarkably beautiful, the great trees stretching their bared arms towards the pale blue winter sky as if entreating those who walked beneath them to hurry off and fight for their survival.

The blanket of snow that sparkled over the fields in the weak January sunlight reminded Lily of the silver threads in her mother's evening stoles, and of the necklaces she would wear when she came up to kiss everyone in the nursery goodnight. It recalled the stars she would take them to the nursery window to see, pointing up at the night sky and

23

teaching them the names of the mighty constellations, her pretty voice repeating with her children the names of the Great Bear and the Little Bear, of Orion, the Plough and the Heavenly Twins. All that seemed a thousand years away, in another time, but one that, for a few seconds, Lily could not help wanting back with all her heart. To be small again, and safe; not to have to be brave: that was unimaginable now. As she turned from the window a siren started up its sinister wail, and downstairs in the busy hallway someone was beginning to sound the alarm, knocking together the wooden clackers that were kept for that purpose behind the great double doors.

*   *   *

'I really do have to leave, I promise!' Kate laughed, trying to wriggle free of the hold Eugene had on her, a grip that was becoming tighter the more Kate wriggled. 'I have to go and have tea with my mother!'

'And I have to go away soon,' Eugene reminded her yet again, kissing her quickly. 'You seem to be forgetting that, madam.'

'I haven't forgotten it at all, Eugene!' Kate protested, wriggling all the more. 'You're making me late enough as it is!'

All of a sudden Eugene let her go, throwing his arms wide and at the same time widening his eyes in a look of mock innocence. 'And when I do go away—suppose I don't come back?' he wondered quietly.

'You're not to say that. You promised. We made a pact—'

'Ah, madam, I fear you're right,' Eugene interrupted with an over-large sigh. 'That was a dirty move—and an unfair one to boot. I shall return, make no mistake, my fine darling—and when I do, beware.'

He caught her up in his arms again, lifting her clean off the ground. Kate allowed herself to go absolutely limp in his embrace, welcoming his next kiss.

'The Bee's kiss,' he murmured to her. 'You remember the poem.'

'No, and I don't want you to remember it either—'

Eugene ignored her. *'Kiss me as if you entered gay—'*

'My heart at some noonday,' Kate whispered in return.

'A bud that dares not disallow'—Eugene continued—*'The claim, so all is rendered up . . .'*

He kissed her once again, this time long and passionately, then let her go. 'Go on now—off to your mammy,' he teased. 'And don't forget to brush the stardust out of your hair now.'

He stood back and smiled at her, sitting himself down on the ledge of the window that looked directly out over the stable yard, lighting a cigarette and crossing his legs. Dressed as he was in his riding breeches and thick check shirt, it seemed to Kate that he looked for all the world like a wild and dishevelled hero out of a Technicolor western. She laughed and ruffled his hair, kissed him on the cheek, and allowed him to grab her by the hand and kiss her back once more before finally pulling herself free and hurrying away. Eugene was the very devil to leave.

25

Her mother was already seated in front of a book propped against the salt and pepper set in the tea shop in Benton where they had arranged to meet when Kate arrived, frozen-cheeked, blond hair awry and blown into a positive bird's nest by the January gale.

'No hat?' her mother wondered in surprise. 'No wonder you're so windswept.'

'You know it's frowned upon at Eden Park to wear hats now, Mother,' Kate reminded her as she sat down at the table. 'It's considered unpatriotic.'

'I've never heard such nonsense,' Helen Maddox replied. 'Does that mean we're meant to burn the hats we already have? Simply not wearing a hat is not, to my mind anyway, going to make the slightest bit of difference to the war effort.'

Kate apologised for keeping Helen waiting, blaming the inadequacy of the transport rather than the reluctance of Eugene to let her go. Her mother assured her that given the conditions under which they were all expected to carry on some sort of normal life there was absolutely no need.

'Besides, I have my book,' she said, holding up a Boots Library volume. 'I never go anywhere nowadays without a book. There's always a wait somewhere or other.'

While they were waiting for their tea to be brought, they engaged in desultory small talk, as if they hardly knew each other, or as if they were avoiding getting to know each other any better, like strangers on a train, or people on a bus.

'You've lost a lot of weight, dear.'

'Have I?'

'Too much. Hope it doesn't affect the tennis.'

This was a wound, but whether it was intentional

26

or not, Kate could not know.

'I'm sure I'd manage, Mother,' Kate murmured evasively. 'Anyway, it's not the tennis season, so I've plenty of time to put on condition before summer comes.'

'Not with the way this food rationing is going, dear. I know we're meant to be tightening the belt, but soon there won't be anything to tighten it round. Someone's going to have to do something about these wretched U-boats in the North Sea or we'll all starve to death.'

'That's Jerry's general idea,' Kate stated as the waitress put down two cups of watery-looking tea in front of them. 'And they're not doing too badly from the looks of it,' she added as she stared at the contours of her cup.

Kate laughed at her own joke, hoping that by doing so she would be able to lighten the atmosphere, although she realised only too well that it was a lost cause. Ever since the death of her brother, Kate couldn't remember her mother laughing. The tragedy had left a scar on Helen Maddox that Kate doubted time would heal. Not that Helen had ever been an extrovert, always giving her daughter the impression of being a quiet and intensely private person, characteristics perhaps forced upon her by the marriage she had made to a bombastic, bullying man. But now that she had lost her son, and even though she still maintained her usual immaculate appearance, her inner self seemed to have shrunk dramatically, leaving just a tidy shell of a person, outwardly composed, inwardly absent.

Because of the despair that nowadays seemed perpetually to clothe her mother, while not

27

rejoicing in the fact there was a war on, Kate was nevertheless grateful not to have to live at home any more. She had settled to the feeling that while her own healing from the loss of her handsome, courageous and dashing brother would take a considerable amount of time, for her mother there seemed no hope in view, despite the fact that, as Kate well knew, Helen Maddox was doing everything in her power to try to appear normal.

'I don't know what I'd do without these trips to Benton,' Helen announced out of the blue. 'It's not that I'm not grateful for my work with the WVS—I am. In fact it's doing me the world of good since it reminds me constantly that there are an awful lot of people worse off than myself. But I just need to get away from home sometimes. I need to get away completely. I can't imagine what it's like for you, dear. Being cooped up in the same place night and day with the same mob of people. I couldn't stand that. Not at this time of my life. I just couldn't stand it.'

'I enjoy it, Mother. I like the people I'm working with, and although it's war work and we shall be glad when it's finally over, the job is fascinating. And exciting.'

Helen looked at her daughter briefly during the silence that invariably followed a short burst of conversation. Although Kate was not aware of it, Helen knew a great deal about the sort of work Kate might be doing. She also knew that she would be forbidden to discuss it. Nevertheless she would have loved to ask Kate details of her life at Eden Park, much as Kate might have loved to amuse her mother with them. But it was not possible, which was probably why, since the war started, their

28

conversations had become so limited.

'I have to say the skies have been quite quiet these past few nights,' Helen said, finishing her tea. 'Unnaturally so, after what seemed like almost incessant raids.'

'We've been quiet too, although we did have a bit of a scare a few days ago. It was quite funny as it happens. Some poor lad on the estate accidentally set fire to a box of fireworks. It was his birthday and the whole lot went up with a bang. The entire place went into a spin. Talk about everyone reaching for their guns. Remember I told you about Eugene Hackett, the Irishman who lives nearby on the Eden Park estate?'

'I remember you telling me something about him, yes,' Helen replied, her eyes drifting away from Kate's face and out to other people sipping tea, or pretending to enjoy their tasteless biscuits.

'He was outside our cottage before you could say knife—pistol in hand in case of emergency. And young Billy—'

'You've told me about young Billy, too.'

'He grabbed this airgun Major Folkestone had given him, thinking when he saw Eugene's silhouette in the doorway that he was the enemy. Luckily Marjorie grabbed the rifle before Billy could take a pot-shot—'

'Otherwise you might have lost Mr Hackett.'

'I'm not sure about that,' Kate laughed. 'Billy's air rifle is not the most lethal of weapons. But Eugene would have got more than a jolly good sting.'

'Is this a good idea, Kate?' Helen wondered. 'You and Eugene?'

'What do you mean, a good idea, Mother? And

what do you mean, me and Eugene exactly?'

'I know I haven't met him—'

'No you haven't,' Kate agreed with unaccustomed edge.

'But it's pretty obvious you're keen on him. Every time you talk about him—'

'What? Every time I talk about him what, Mother? He just happens to—to live in the Park—and to be great fun, that's all. He makes us all laugh. He's just—he's just a rather—he's just a great character, that's all. So I don't really know what you mean about it being a good idea.'

'You just want to be careful not to rush headlong into anything. It's very easy in wartime.'

'No one's rushing into anything, Mother. Now let's see if we can get another cup of tea, shall we?'

Kate looked round for a waitress as a necessary distraction from the way the conversation was headed. She and her mother had trodden this particular path frequently at their recent meetings, Kate always being left with the impression that since her mother had lost her own son, she was determined that Kate was not going to be allowed to fall in love with someone else's son.

'We could have something to eat, you know,' Kate added, picking up the skimpy menu hand-written on a card barely six inches in length. 'They do rissoles. We tried those before, remember? They weren't that bad. We might as well strike while the iron's hot, before they cut the meat ration again, which they're threatening to do.'

'Kate dear,' Helen announced, with a distinct change of tone that made Kate look up in alarm. 'I have to tell you something.'

Kate looked across at her mother's pale, finely

30

featured face, wondering what on earth Helen could have to tell her that imparted such a note of doom into her voice. 'Are you all right?' she asked, suddenly genuinely concerned as she stared into the eyes she knew so well.

'Not really—and I'm not sure how to tell you this. Because it's all so very unexpected really.'

'Something is the matter. I don't mean that, because obviously something's the matter. I mean is something the matter with you? Or with—with Daddy?'

'There's nothing wrong with me, Kate—and there's nothing wrong with your father either,' Helen replied. 'Other than the fact that he's left me.'

Kate stared at her mother, once again stuck for something to say. If she'd had to put money on it, she would have placed her bet on her mother's leaving her father. If anyone had a more than justifiable reason for running out on what was left of her family it was her poor benighted mother, a woman who had, over many years, been all but verbally beaten into subjection by her father's unstinting sarcasm.

'Are you sure?' she found herself wondering, still clinging on to the menu which her mother now calmly removed from her grasp to study herself. 'I mean he hasn't just taken himself off for a while, you know how people can? The way people are always doing in newspapers. You know.'

Kate's foot began to wiggle under the table as she realised she could not stop saying 'you know' while Helen shrugged her shoulders, but didn't look up, continuing to study the choice on the card in her hand.

'Not according to the note he left on the mantelpiece, Kate. And not according to the total removal of his belongings, and most of the money from our bank account. He left me the car, I have to say that for him—but only because it's laid up on bricks in the garage, and with petrol so strictly rationed it isn't much use to him. Me neither.' She paused. 'I think you're right. Let's have the rissoles. I feel quite hungry now.'

'How could he?' Kate puzzled, the reality of it all sinking in suddenly. 'I mean how *could* he? How could Daddy do this to you? And at a time like this? How could anyone do this at a time like this? Just walk out on someone in the middle of a war?'

Helen glanced up at her and when she did Kate frowned and dropped her eyes. That wasn't what she really meant and her mother knew it. What she had really meant was how could her father walk out on her mother just a matter of a few months after losing their son. If ever Helen needed help and support it was now, yet her husband had simply packed up his things and walked out on her, leaving a short note of intent on the mantelpiece, and no money in the bank.

When her mother had finished explaining the circumstances of Professor Maddox's precipitous departure from the family circle, never once taking her eyes off the menu she was holding, Kate simply stared at her, shaking her head once more before placing her hand on her mother's arm.

'What are you going to *do*?' she asked. 'How are you going to cope—if he hasn't left you any money?'

'I shall have to get a job, Kate. Like anyone else. What else am I supposed to do?'

32

Kate felt a great and sudden surge of anger as she found herself thinking quite unreasonably that her brother had sacrificed his life for nothing. Robert's tragic death had really nothing whatsoever to do with her mother's present predicament, as Kate well knew. Surely the very least her father could have done in the circumstances was to try to look after what remained of his family? His heartless desertion of her mother now appeared to Kate to be a direct affront to the memory of her brother. To relieve her feelings she searched in her handbag for a cigarette.

'There must be something you can do,' she stated, finding she only had one smoke left. 'Things like this aren't necessarily definite.'

'I wonder what you know, Kate? About things like this.'

Kate looked up in surprise. She had never heard her mother address her in that tone of voice before.

'What I don't know I suppose I can at least imagine,' she replied quickly. 'I'm not in pigtails any more.'

'Look, Kate. Your father has left me for another woman, and when a man does that there is nothing a woman can do. I'm certainly not the kind of person to chase after a man, and beg him to come back—'

'For another *woman*?'

There was a short, appalled silence as Kate, having lit her cigarette, stared in amazement at her mother through the small spiral of smoke that was escaping from her mouth. The thought of her father's leaving home had been unbelievable enough, but the idea of his running away with another woman was almost too much to accept.

'It's not that surprising. After all, your father is a man, and men do this sort of thing. Often at times like this as well. At least that's what people keep telling me.' Helen bowed her head and searched in her bag for a handkerchief.

'Are you all right?' Kate leaned forward and lowered her voice, aware that several women sitting nearby had begun to take a close interest. 'Mother—I said are you all right?'

'I'm sorry, Kate. I didn't mean to give way! But this has all been a bit of a shock.'

'Perhaps I ought to take you home,' Kate whispered, half getting up, ready to go to her mother's side, aware that people were now trying not to stare at them. 'Perhaps we really ought to go home.'

'What for? What's the point? There's nobody to go home to—nobody lives there any more. Your father's gone, Robert's dead, and you're away working. What's the point of going home?'

Her mother gave a sudden dreadful sigh and closed her eyes in an attempt to staunch her tears.

Kate summoned a waitress who was hovering in the background, and asked if she could fetch a glass of cold water, while she herself pulled her chair round to her mother's side, putting an arm round her shoulders in an attempt to try to calm her.

'After all this,' her mother whispered. 'After everything I've done. After everything that's happened—this.'

'I'm going to take you home, Mother,' Kate told her, giving her the glass of water that had now been set down on the table. 'Look—drink this, and take

34

these two aspirins.'

'I don't need aspirins, Kate.' Her mother gave a sigh of utter despair. 'Aspirins are actually the last things I need.'

'They'll help calm you down,' Kate assured her. 'Then I'll take you home and we'll talk about what we're going to do.'

'I'm sorry. I meant to be so calm, and now I've ruined our little get-together. I'm so sorry, Kate.'

*   *   *

By the time they were on the bus headed back home Helen had pulled herself together sufficiently to be able to tell Kate as much as she knew about the whole sorry business without giving way again. It seemed that the woman with whom her father had disappeared was a production secretary who worked in a department of the BBC that had just been transferred to Wales. They had met when Kate's father had been invited to take part in a broadcast and as far as Helen knew the attraction had been instant and mutual, so strong in fact that Professor Maddox had resigned his university post and taken a more menial teaching job in Wales in order that they could be together and he could help take care of the domestic side of their lives.

'If I was capable, I would laugh,' Helen said, turning sideways to look out of the window at the invisible landscape slipping slowly past them in the pitch darkness. 'I could never get Harold to do anything for me at home. In all the time we were married he never so much as washed up a cup, and now he's doing all the cooking.' She fell silent, still

35

staring out at nothing and shaking her head slowly.

'I'll tell you what, Mother,' Kate announced, although with a fast sinking heart. 'I'd better give notice and come back home. You can't possibly be expected to live at home by yourself. Not now. Not in the—not the way you're feeling now. It wouldn't be right.'

'You'll do no such thing.' Helen turned round sharply to her. 'I wouldn't hear of it.'

'Well maybe I could just get some extended leave,' Kate offered, knowing such a thing to be actually out of the question since there were all too few of them at Eden Park, and every one of them overworked. If she was going to help her mother out, she realised, she would actually have to sacrifice her job, and in sacrificing her job would probably lose something even more important to her than her work—namely, Eugene.

Even so, given what her mother had done for both her and her brother, Kate knew that the very least she could do was offer to come home and keep her company.

'What would we live on, for a start?' Helen persisted. 'One of us would have to go out to work—you most probably—so what would be the point? I'd sit there all day waiting for you to come home just like I used to wait for your father— there'd be no point in you giving up your job, Kate. No, I'll be fine. I just need a bit of time, that's all. Time to get myself organised. I'm still young enough to be able to make myself useful in this war. There are lots of things I can do—and really the more I think about it the more determined I am not to sit down under it.'

'We're here,' Kate announced, peering out into

36

the darkness as the bus slowed down. 'At least I think we are.'

'I'm sorry for giving way in the café, Kate,' Helen said as they made their way carefully from the bus stop to the front gate of the house. 'It was perfectly unforgivable. And as for you coming back home, it really is out of the question. I'll be quite all right by myself. I've spent a lot of time on my own and I've always been perfectly all right. I have no right to feel sorry for myself; I don't know what came over me. Seeing you, possibly. You know you—You know you and—' She stopped, unable to go on until she had drawn a deep breath. 'My *two* children always meant everything to me and so seeing you—I suppose it was just a little too much under the circumstances. No,' she said quickly, stopping Kate before she could speak as they reached the front door and she began to search for her key. 'No, you don't have to say a thing. If I'd just stopped to think for a moment. What I'm trying to say is this.' They were inside the front door now, standing in the darkened hall where they both took off their coats and groped for the hat rack. 'What I'm trying to say, Kate,' Helen continued, 'is I'm determined to help rather than complain. If you could see some of the wretchedness that I've seen down at the depot, whole families bombed out without a stick of furniture left, not a cup, or a photograph, everything gone except their memories and the clothes they stand up in. There's billeting work to be done, and I think that's where I'm needed most.'

Once they'd made sure the blackout blinds and curtains were in place, Helen and Kate shut themselves in the kitchen, Helen helping them both

37

to a generous glass of sherry from the bottle left over from Christmas before they sat down and talked through the best way to cope with the current crisis.

There was another alternative open to Helen, one which came more and more to mind as she and Kate talked together in the kitchen, one that she later considered as she got herself ready for bed, waiting for Kate—who was spending the night—to finish in the bathroom. It was an idea that still greatly attracted her. She had been reminded of it when Kate had begun to talk a little more frankly about Eugene Hackett with whom she was plainly infatuated, and she had been reminded of it not because of some past love, but because of what she knew all too well about affairs such as that between Kate and Eugene.

She felt she knew the kind of person he might be because of the sort of work she guessed he must be doing: work that meant that Mr Eugene Hackett, if caught, could never be a prisoner of war. There was never any mercy shown to people like Eugene Hackett. Their work was so vital and so secret that all too often even their masters disowned them. Helen knew all this because she had once worked for the same sort of person as Eugene Hackett, someone who had been involved in the same kind of difficult and dangerous work.

Helen had known Jack Ward for some years, a man known affectionately by his agents as 'the Colonel' in deference to the fact that he often said if bad sight had not prevented him, he would have liked to be a colonel in charge of a small country regiment. Of course Helen had only been a small cog in Jack Ward's machine, one of many supposedly ordinary men and women whom Jack had recruited for security work in civilian life. Her task, like the others', had been to look out for small things that would lead someone like Jack Ward on to uncover greater matters.

Taking note is the way Jack Ward described it. *Sitting up and taking note.* He was always on the lookout for people suitable to his requirements, people who lived modestly in small societies, who led the sort of existence that would not attract any undue attention. Extrovert people leading extraordinary lives were of no use to him; he wanted background people, people who felt intense loyalty to crown and country, people who were not only prepared but particularly keen to keep an eye out for anyone who showed signs of being sympathetic to Fascism, from workers on the factory floor, and those selling certain newspapers, to local gentry who considered Adolf Hitler to be a good sort, and basically one of them. Anti-Semites, republicans, Marxists, Brownshirts, Jack's little army of ordinary people were able and willing to watch out for them all—arrogant bigots who despised anyone who did not share their blinkered view of life, whose very intolerance was the perfect seedbed for Fascism.

Helen had been only too happy to keep a weather eye out for people such as these, if only because it gave her back a sense of self-worth. Her battered domestic pride was partially restored by knowing that her part-time occupation was more than just that; it was a small, secret defence against what she thought of as insidious evil, against those who sought to bring down democracy. It wasn't necessarily a very pleasant job, but it was one she had come to understand was vital if Britain was not going to succumb to its own Third Reich.

Her greatest success was to help give a lead to an investigation that finally led to the uncovering of a so-called exchange group who were in fact undercover agents for a European Fascist organisation, a body of seemingly respectable people who were meant to be spending their time in England learning English, but were in fact noting military installations, factories employed in arms production, and the addresses of leading political or liberal, social and even theatrical personalities, individuals whose names were all destined for the extermination lists that, even then, were being compiled by Hitler in preparation for his anticipated invasion of England.

Whenever Helen had needed to meet Jack to pass on information he would invariably suggest a cinema, for the very good reason that they both knew that Helen's husband Harold actively disliked going to the films. Jack Ward couldn't go enough. He took fan magazines on a regular basis, and kept a proud tally of the number of times he had seen his favourite films, which meant that he was only too glad to keep his rendezvous with Helen Maddox in some local Arcade or Odeon. His pre-war habit was to buy an abundance of chocolate and start the evening by taking Helen off for a quiet drink in an unpopular public house for what he would call a bit of a pow-wow.

'Good stuff, kid,' he would say gruffly, however seemingly trivial the piece of information Helen had brought him. 'That's the ticket.' Helen loved his droll way of using movie language, knowing that his speech patterns quite wittingly echoed the last movie he had seen.

Once war had broken out, Helen's undercover work had become necessarily more hazardous, particularly since several of the people she had been able to name as suspects had been arrested, a success which could have marked her, the common factor, out as a suspect to the other side. This meant that she had to keep more distance between Jack Ward and herself, meeting him much less frequently, always after dark, and never in the same place twice. With the amount of time and money at her disposal, even though she was given a small financial reward for her work, it very soon became all but impossible to meet the Colonel at all as they soon ran out of places that were both safe and convenient for both of them—Helen could hardly risk travelling the sorts of distances that might arouse her husband's suspicions, however much enthusiasm she showed for going to the cinema.

Finally Jack Ward had been forced to put Helen on the sidelines indefinitely, promising her that if anything did come up again for which she would be suited, he would not fail to contact her.

Helen had accepted it with her usual good grace, while privately regretting the end of this particular episode in her life. She had been disappointed because she had enjoyed the work for the strange excitement it had brought into her life, and more particularly because she had come to like Jack Ward. He was an odd-looking man, and when working his professional personality was so taciturn that his company was far from easy; yet the more she got to know him—which with hindsight she now realised was very little—the more her loyalty to him and his work had grown, as if amid the

41

accelerating collapse of her domestic life the very thought of his patriotism, his intense belief in the value of both democracy and his country, gave her something for which to hope.

Now, as she carefully rubbed some precious soap on the middle of her face flannel and ran a couple of cupfuls of warm water into the bottom of the bathroom basin, Helen looked at herself in the mirror and wondered whether she would still have the courage of her previous convictions. She still knew how to get in touch with the Colonel, always provided the number she had so carefully memorised was still in operation. She would try the number, she decided, still staring at her face in the glass, she would definitely ring it tomorrow, and if she got the usual sort of stiff and impersonal reception at the other end from the kind of woman who always seemed to man the department telephones, she would leave the usual sort of ambiguous message, and wait to see if she was still wanted. She had nothing to lose, she told herself, now carefully washing her face, her eyes still watching her reflection above the slow movement of her pink face flannel. She had nothing to lose, she could still be of help to her country, and with a bit of luck she might once again be working directly under the enigmatic Jack Ward, doing something particular, something for which she knew she was at least appreciated.

*　　*　　*

Kate had to hurry off first thing the next morning in order to get back to Eden Park in time for work. As she kissed her mother goodbye she was happy to note that Helen's mood was considerably better than it had been the night before. She seemed altogether stronger, as if she had quite made up her mind to adjust to her situation. She was certainly if anything more adamant than ever that Kate was not to even think of giving up work in order to be at home with her.

Of course they both knew that Kate's avowals to stay with Helen were truly only token, as Kate had already decided that no amount of wild horses could drag her away from her work, still less away from Eugene.

Helen watched her tall, blonde, graceful daughter make her way back up the garden path to the road. She knew she had to find her own way of mourning her only son, as all bereaved mothers had to do, but she was determined that clinging on to her remaining child was not going to be one of them.

*   *   *

When she arrived back at Eden Park, Kate found she still had a good half an hour before she had to report for duty, so, quickly taking advantage of what seemed like a huge emotional gratuity, she rushed round to the stable yard, slip-sliding on the snow and ice so that by the time she arrived at the bottom of the wooden steps that led up to Eugene's flat she knew she must look like something off the top of a Christmas cake. Smiling to herself more with excitement than in amusement, she brushed the snow off her clothes before clambering up the slippery steps and knocking on Eugene's half-glassed door.

There was no reply.

Knowing his habits and hoping against hope that he might still be in bed, Kate knocked again, but this time she pushed the door open at the same time. She knew he was gone as soon as she felt the cold of the room. There was no fire burning in the stove and no kettle gently simmering on the hob as there invariably was when Eugene was in residence. Instead there were piles of discarded clothes lying on the floor and furniture and stacks of papers now flapping off the desk and the table as Kate stood with the door still open behind her. Closing it quickly, she stepped right into the room and looked to see if he had left her any word. Sure enough, a note was stuck in the corner of a large pen and ink drawing he had done of his great and beloved grey horse, who was at this very moment munching through his first hay net of the day in his stable directly beneath where Kate was standing.

Beautiful Kate—good morning to you, darling girl. By the time you're reading this, I'll be gone. Sorry—in fact you will never know quite how sorry this makes me—sorry I'm gone, sorry I won't be seeing you before I go—sorry I didn't have time to tell you before I left that I was going at all—although you knew I must be off sometime—but that's the way it is, alas. I was hoping and praying you'd be back some time last night after I got the news I had to leave first thing this morning—but then you'd gone to see your mam and I thought as sure as eggs is eggs she'll not be back before I go away. God, I shall miss you, you darling thing. I shall miss every bit of you, every divine inch. I shall miss the sight of your beautiful blond hair, the touch of that soft skin, the brush of your lips on mine. I would take you with me if I could shrink you. So that's why I've sneaked away under the cover of night—so I'm not tempted to shrink you and put you in my top pocket. But I'll be back before you can say Googonbaragh—if you can't say that, take your time and learn it, and by the time you've learned it, I'll be back, a bit smudged, but safe in your arms—your Irishman xxxxxxxxxxxxxxxxxx (don't take these kisses all at once—ration them). PS I shall bring home Hitler. PPS Dead or alive? PPPS Dead methinks. PPPPS Don't you like me just a little bit now????? Ah go on. Go on now—you do you do so you do just a little. PPPPPS A thousand more kisses on you. All from me.

After she had read the note through two or three times, Kate sat down in Eugene's old leather chair. Wrapping her arms round herself, she began to wonder where he had gone, and then, realising there was no point, she stopped.

He had gone, and where was not important. What was important was that the room in which she sat, the place where they had loved, seemed to be not just empty, but as deserted as any clearing in a wood where you might suddenly come across a smoking bonfire, an empty packet of cigarettes, and the remains of some half-eaten meal. Eugene the Nazi-hunter had gone.

*   *   *

Marjorie stared at Billy. She'd never seen anyone

45

grow so fast. One minute he'd been little Billy, still more or less the same size boy who had turned up that Christmas years ago at Aunt Hester's house, and the next a tall, over-thin young man. Now as she sat across the cottage table from her adopted brother she saw in him the makings of a man, a tall, good-looking, mischievous young man, with eyes that widened and widened the more he tried to convince a person he was telling the truth; and a countenance he loved to keep poker-blank as he spun some poor soul a piece of his usual complete and utter fabrication.

'How old are you now, Billy?' she found herself suddenly asking.

Billy sighed, without looking up from the elaborate drawing of what looked like a small narrow-bodied aeroplane he was busily completing, and then clicked his tongue loudly.

'You know perfectly well how old I am, Marge,' he replied, before adopting his old man's voice. 'I'm three light years and four and a half fathoms come next birthday.'

'I can't believe you're fifteen,' Marjorie said. 'It just doesn't seem possible.'

'The only real possibilities, sis, are the complete and utterly impossible ones—at least that's according to Eugene. What do you think of that, then?'

Billy turned his drawing book round for Marjorie to see what he had been so busily designing every evening for the past week. Marjorie looked closely at it, seeing at once that this was no childish invention, but an authentic-looking aeroplane with short stubby wings and a high tail shaped like a large V. Appended to the drawing

46

were a set of separate illustrations of all the main working parts and a carefully annotated list of instructions for use.

'I can't see any windows,' Marjorie remarked after studying the drawing carefully. 'Not even one for a pilot.'

'Well spotted, Marge.' Billy sighed with pleasurable satisfaction. 'That's because there aren't none.'

'Any. There aren't any.'

'There aren't any,' Billy echoed in a tone mocking Marjorie's carefully modulated speech pattern. 'There aren't none and there aren't any no how.'

Marjorie looked up sharply but refused to take the bait. Over the years she had worked long and patiently to try to iron out Billy's poor grammar and his London accent, a task made all the more difficult by Billy's total lack of interest in improving himself, or *hisself*, as he would deliberately remark. She was all too aware that he was only really interested in what went on inside his head, and because Marjorie suspected that he was quite possibly more than a little bit on the brilliant side, she was all the more determined that he should present what she considered to be a proper and respectable face to the world, in every way.

'It doesn't have *any* windows, Billy . . .'

'It don't have *any* windows,' Billy continued, eyeing Marjorie slyly, ' 'cos it *isn't* an aircraft.'

'It's got wings—and a tail.'

'Course it has, 'cos it's *meant* to fly, but it ain't— it *isn't* meant to carry no one.'

'Anyone.'

'Anyone or anything. 'Cept a bomb.'

Marjorie looked up again, this time with quite a different expression.

'A bomb, Billy?' she said. 'You mean this is—what would you call it?'

'A bomb without a pilot, Marge,' Billy said, over-helpfully. 'Best way to deliver your bomb to your target is to have it self-propelled, see? No pilots, no bomb aimers, no nothing. No crew at all. So if it crashes no one gets done, and if it don't crash—*doesn't* crash—then bang! It delivers the goods. Only problem I got is how to fuel it, see?'

'What's wrong with aircraft fuel?' Marjorie wondered. 'The stuff they fly the planes on?'

'Wouldn't work. This has got to deliver a bomb that's going to weigh a whole lot more than a normal bomb, and an ordinary engine—well. Well, how you going to adjust it in flight, for instance? If you in't got no one flyin' it, see? Doing all the fine adjustments and keeping the kite in the air. No, we got to power this with some sort of new engine. It's got to fly like a rocket—straight up in the air and then fast fighters are going to have difficulty catching it, see? Point is, Marge, if we could get this to work—we'd be so ahead of the Jerries we'd pulverise them.'

Marjorie looked at Billy who was now back poring over his drawing with a serious frown. It would be quite easy to dismiss his idea as the sort of typical notion that boys of Billy's age were always coming up with, yet something about the whole idea allied to what Marjorie knew was a highly precocious mind made her consider the possibility that perhaps Billy—or someone—should take it to a higher level; to some boffin or other who might see some practicality in the concept.

48

The idea of a pilotless bomb seemed more than a pipe dream. It suddenly appealed to her as a distinct possibility.

'I'll tell you what, Billy. If you like, I'll show your drawing to Major Folkestone, and see what he has to say,' she told him, sounding even to herself like a school prefect as she extended a hand for permission to take the drawing book.

Billy stared at her, wrinkling his nose and twisting his mouth sideways, a habit he had when he was giving matters serious thought.

'I'd rather work on the idea a bit longer,' he replied. 'I don't want them just to think this is some sort of schoolboy doodle.'

'They won't, Billy. Major Folkestone will make sure of that. You know he thinks a lot of what you do nowadays; I told you that the other day. Specially with codes—he says codes are like music is for gifted people. They see things written in the notes that none of the rest of us can see, and the same goes for codes. You can see the messages straight away.'

'Yeah, I know, Marge,' Billy interrupted. 'But this is different. I mean this is something what I think could really work, see? And I know what they'll say—the blokes with the pointed heads and all the gold on their shoulders. They'll just sniff and say what's some oik of a kid know that we don't? Maybe we should wait for Eugene to come back and see what he has to say. Eugene is different, you know, Marge.'

'I don't think it's up Eugene's street, Billy. I know you think the world of him, but he's not a boffin, and I don't suppose for a moment he knows any boffins.'

'What about Mr W?' Billy demanded, frowning. 'Mr W might take this seriously, and Mr W knows everyone there is to know. The major says he even has dealings with Mr Churchill, sometimes.'

'All right, Billy,' Marjorie agreed. 'But let me talk to Major Folkestone first, because we can't get hold of Mr Ward without his help. And if he thinks we should do something else, we'll have to take his advice. Agreed?'

'I'll think about it, Marge,' Billy said, closing his drawing book up, and putting it away in the table drawer. 'But you're not to do nothing without my say-so.'

'Anything, Billy. And no, I won't do *anything* without your say-so.'

'Promise?'

'Promise.'

As it happened Marjorie was not as much enamoured of Eugene Hackett as the rest of the female population of Eden Park. While recognising what she called his originality, and having finally to agree that his part in the thwarting of an assassination attempt on Churchill had actually been nothing short of heroic, Marjorie privately considered him to be a show-off, with far too much *braggadocio* for his own good. Time and again she would say to Kate that men with Eugene's sort of looks, manner and character were not to be trusted, but were usually only out for what they could get, until finally exasperated Kate had rounded on her.

'You've never been in love, Marjorie,' she told her curtly. 'When you have, well then you can talk well off. But not until. OK?'

After which, seeing the undeniable truth in this

statement, Marjorie shut up.

*   *   *

What Marjorie could not say to Kate—and would never say to her—was that the real reason she was wary of Eugene was that she had never quite shaken off the suspicion that the Irishman was a double agent. Prior to the assassination attempt, she had not been the only one at Eden Park considering this possibility. Eugene had simply arrived unannounced in their midst, claiming that he was the nephew of Lord and Lady Dunne, the owners of Eden Park, who always let him use the flat above the stables, before disappearing at frequent intervals to locations which he would never discuss.

'He could talk himself out of a firing squad,' Marjorie had once claimed to Kate after they had all been out drinking in the local inn. 'I've never heard anyone blarney as much as Eugene Hackett.'

But Kate was not to be put off.

'All I want you to admit is that Eugene is tall, dark and handsome. You don't have to say you find him attractive, but you do have to admit that he is handsome. Beautiful, in fact.'

'I'd never call any man beautiful,' Marjorie retorted. 'Men aren't beautiful—or if they are, they're usually fey.'

'*Fey* no less.'

'You know perfectly well what I mean, Kate. They're not altogether masculine.'

'Eugene certainly isn't *fey*, Marjorie. But he certainly is what I'd call handsome.'

'Now Scott Meynell, he is handsome.'

51

'Not much good to you, Marge.' Kate stood up, determined not to rise to the bait. 'Scott is in love with Poppy Tetherington, as well you know.'

'He could always change his mind.' This was Marjorie's standard reply.

'Just as pears could grow on oak trees,' was Kate's equally standard response.

But it wasn't Scott Meynell who occupied Marjorie's private thoughts—not really. She might think that Scott was classically good-looking, which indeed he was, but he wasn't the man with whom Marjorie found herself becoming increasingly fascinated, for all sorts of reasons. Someone she found herself watching closely.

*   *   *

Jack Ward unravelled the yellow oilskin pouch that contained his pipe tobacco, thankful as always for its waterproofing since the snow had long since turned to driving sleet, and the rest of him was all but wet through.

'I'll give him another half an hour,' he muttered. 'And if he doesn't show, you can go instead.'

His younger companion stared at him for a moment in horror, not yet sufficiently familiar with Jack Ward to know when he was joking and when he wasn't.

'There's a vehicle coming now, sir,' he said with a frown. 'I think, sir.'

The two men listened as the sound of a heavily clanking engine drew nearer through the storm.

'What the devil . . . ?' Jack began to wonder, only to have his curiosity satisfied by the sight of a large tractor and trailer appearing out of the wall of frozen rain, bumping its way toward them over the airfield.

'Typical Hackett,' Jack sighed. 'Can't do anything by halves.'

The farm vehicle pulled up in front of the two men with much coughing and spluttering from the engine and finally a loud backfire from the funnel exhaust. It was driven by a small squat farmer with a fixed grin, and a passenger seated behind him on a straw bale on the trailer, sheltering under a large umbrella.

'You're goodliness personified, sir!' Eugene called to him as he hopped down from his perch clutching his knapsack. 'May your shadow never grow less!'

Still grinning, the farmer touched his forelock, and following another series of protests from his machine drove off back in the direction whence he had come.

'There being no taxis, sir!' Eugene informed Jack in French. 'And no car to greet me at the station.'

'There might have been had you been on the right train, Hackett,' Jack replied in German. 'You are two hours late.'

'If I'm a little tardy it's because they made a mess of my papers,' Eugene argued in Italian. 'I'd have been shot on landing with the set they gave me. So it was hardly my fault.'

'You always have an excuse, Hackett,' Jack growled back in Italian.

'I always have my reason, sir,' Eugene corrected him in German, before adding something quite incomprehensible in the Gaelic.

'Come again?' Jack said sarcastically. 'You know

I don't speak whatever you call it.'

'Erse, sir. Or the Gaelic to you.' Eugene grinned and slung his knapsack on one shoulder. 'Ready when you are. They'll be able to take off in this, will they?'

'If they fail, we know who to blame, don't we?' Jack nodded towards the waiting aircraft. 'Your instructions,' he added, handing Eugene an envelope.

'What's the weather like out there, I wonder?' Eugene slipped the brown envelope into his inside pocket to read on the plane. 'When it comes to holidays I'm a hopeless packer.'

'If you've forgotten your swim things, don't worry,' Jack growled, holding open the small door in the fuselage. 'You're going to be a little too busy to lie around on the beach. *Bon voyage.*'

'Keep the home fire burning, sir,' Eugene said with a wave and a smile. 'I won't be gone long.'

He disappeared into the plane, and Jack shut the door and double-checked it before stepping back to signal go to the pilot.

As the pilot revved the twin engines, the sleet stopped as suddenly as it had started, a shaft of sunlight bisecting the mist and shining directly on the plane, which was now taxiing down the runway prior to take-off.

'Typical Hackett,' Jack observed. 'Right down to the special effects.'

*   *   *

Major Folkestone called Cissie Lavington into his office late one evening, unlocked the closely guarded wall map of Europe that showed the whereabouts of their agents by way of a set of specially coloured pins, and considered the overall position.

'We're a bit thin on the ground, as you can see from these black pins, Miss Lavington,' Anthony said, indicating several areas with a thin stick. 'Sustaining more losses than is altogether acceptable. We may well need Poppy Tetherington back in action sooner than we thought. In fact we may be looking at the need for more recruits full stop.'

'Might have helped if our French friends had held out just a little bit longer, doncher think?' Cissie remarked, coming to stand at the major's shoulder and blowing a long stream of smoke past him. 'Might also have helped if they'd bothered to blow up a few of their precious bridges before Jerry crossed over on 'em as well. *C'est la vie*—or, rather more precisely, *c'est la France*. You could always send me back into the field.'

'Most kind, but we rather need you here,' Anthony replied politely. 'Thanks all the same.'

'I could work for the Russians,' Cissie persisted, solemn-faced. 'I get on frightfully well with Boris.'

'I'll bear it in mind if things get any worse in Russia.'

'*War and Peace* is quite my favourite book, doncher know . . .'

'To get back to Poppy Tetherington,' Anthony continued. 'You reckon she's back one hundred per cent?'

'Absolutely. I'd have said that hubby's behaviour would only have increased her resolve.'

'Very well.' Anthony nodded, glancing back at the map of Europe as if already thinking where he might place her. 'And what about your new recruit? The Ormerod girl. She going to make the grade?'

'I should say. Far as I can gather she's the only one so far to give the famous Monsieur Jacques a run for his money in the gymnasium. Only thing I'd keep an eye on as far as young Lily goes is what goes on out of hours. That I *would* keep an eye on. Most definitely.'

Major Folkestone frowned at her, cocking his head in a way that prompted a reply.

'Boys and girls, Major,' Cissie sighed. 'Boys will be boys. And girls will be girls. That's all I have to say on that particular matter.'

As she left, Major Folkestone's assistant, the homely Miss Budge, was waiting just outside the door, notebook and pencil in hand, ready as ever to return to the fray. Smiling at the departing Cissie, she tapped formally on the half-open door and was called to come in.

As she entered, Anthony Folkestone was still standing gazing at the map on the wall cabinet in front of him. As soon as he saw he had a visitor, albeit his private secretary, he at once swung the two heavy-wooded doors across his map and locked them with a key that he dropped into one of the two top pockets in his tunic.

'Miss Budge. Marjorie not back from lunch, yet?'

'No, Major Folkestone.' Miss Budge looked at her boss. 'But I am quite ready to take dictation.'

'Fine. Good. Thank you. And by the way, they still haven't fixed my intercom properly, Miss Budge. It still goes on the blink every so often.'

'I keep asking them to check it, sir,' Miss Budge replied. 'They assured me it was working perfectly.'

56

'Well it isn't. So get after them again, will you? If you'd be so kind. I cannot stand things that don't work properly.'

'I'll see to it myself, sir,' Miss Budge assured him. 'You're not the only one it's driving round the bend.'

Anthony Folkestone smiled. He liked Miss Budge well enough, but she was no Marjorie Hendry. Miss Budge had a lot to commend her. She was a former SOE courier who had worked on several drops in Europe, showing a lot of courage in the field before being invalided out of active service after a dust-up in Brittany. She was of a kindly disposition, diligent and attentive, a good enough typist with excellent shorthand—but her hair did not fall forward when she was taking down his memos, nor did her eyes crinkle sweetly at their corners when she smiled or open so widely in amazement when they learned something new. Miss Budge knitted very well, although her choice of colours could—in Anthony's opinion—do with a little toning down. Miss Budge was never late and always polite and willing, but she lacked that oddly defiant streak that Marjorie had—that individuality and strength of purpose, characteristics that intrigued and it had to be admitted excited him. Even in her everyday office wear, in her sensible knitted stockings and plain skirt and jumper, Marjorie appealed to him. At her most tomboyish Marjorie attracted him, and even at her most taciturn she fascinated him.

So, much as he liked and appreciated Miss Budge, it was small wonder that Anthony Folkestone would have preferred the young woman sitting the other side of his desk ready to take down his dictation to have been Miss Marjorie Hendry.

Chapter Two

It was inevitable that Poppy should have found herself falling in love with Scott Meynell when they were working alongside each other the previous year. Poppy had been trained by H section to play at being a rich and spoiled social butterfly in order to try to infiltrate the circle of highly placed Fascists that Jack Ward knew was operating in London, its aim being to persuade the Establishment to embrace appeasement; or, if that failed, then to bring the country to a standstill by the simple but highly effective means of assassinating Winston Churchill. Scott had already gained access to their inner circle, and by the time he and Poppy had helped bring that particular operation to a successful conclusion they had become lovers.

They used to joke about it afterwards, Scott teasing Poppy as to whether or not she would have had the courage to become his lover had she known her husband was still alive, Poppy riposting that it probably would have made everything more exciting. Sometimes, though, she wondered how she actually would have behaved if she had known that the reported death of her unloved husband at the hands of the Italian terrorists was only part of the European Fascist party's plot to create political mayhem.

'I don't think you would,' Scott said to her once when they were discussing the matter. 'I think you'd have been too hidebound by your upbringing.'

'You're actually making assumptions, Scott Meynell,' Poppy replied. 'I didn't really have an upbringing, at least not the one you imagine I had. First of all, although I was born in Europe, my parents were American, and they didn't bring me up, the embassy staff did. No one spoils you like servants, you know—which is why I've turned out the way I have. Oddly enough, even though my mother neglected me as I was growing up, I felt I was terribly cherished.'

'It was hardly cherishing you, marrying you off to the perfectly dreadful Basil Tetherington, was it?'

'That wasn't my mother's fault. That was mine entirely. I was really awfully naïve. And since everyone else seemed to be engaged by the end of the Season, I thought: why not? No one else had ever paid me the slightest bit of attention, and besides, Basil . . . well, not only was he terribly good-looking, you know, but he was a brilliant dancer—the Fred Astaire of Belgravia.'

Poppy eyed Scott, hoping that he would show some slight frisson of jealousy, but quickly realised from his expression that his mind was somewhere quite other.

'Hum is all I can say to that.'

'*Hum* is what you say to most things, Mr Meynell. *Hum* covers an awful lot of things for you.'

'What else can a chap say except *hum* to things like that?' Scott sighed in mock despair. 'Marrying a fellow like Tetherington because his toes twinkled. It isn't really worth anything more than a *hum*.'

They were out walking in the winter sunshine along the shore of the larger of the two lakes in the park. Poppy had been to see some possible lodgings in the stable block that housed Eugene when he was at home, since she needed somewhere to live while she was to be working for H Section and all the bedrooms in the main house were fully occupied. Fortunately the estate had various other cottages and outbuildings that had been cleaned and tidied up to make adequate accommodation for the Nosy Parkers, as those working in Eden Park had nicknamed themselves. Scott had accompanied Poppy on her visit to a pretty dismal and dreary little flat directly above the feed rooms, which Poppy being Poppy announced to be entirely acceptable without even qualifying her opinion with the rider *in the circumstances*.

'Marjorie and Kate's little cottage is only a couple of minutes' walk round the corner, and it will be perfect for George since we just have to open the door and we're in the park,' she had pointed out, unclipping George's lead so he could wander freely as Scott and Poppy took their lunchtime stroll, both of them still having a good half an hour before they had to return to their duties.

'Well, obviously, if George likes it, it is sold,' Scott had agreed. 'That was all we needed to know, wasn't it?'

Hand in hand, with George running ahead of them as fast as his short legs could carry him, the two of them walked away from the main house along the shore of the lake, a dark mirror on this almost windless day. The spring-fed waters were fascinating in their clarity, their transparency allowing Poppy and Scott to watch several large mirror carp feeding among the dormant reeds, making loud sucking noises as they did so.

'They sound like babies pulling on the teats of their feeding bottles.' Poppy stared at the broad pink lips hovering on the water's surface.

A sudden gust of winter wind caused the surface to corrugate, the tiny runs of waves shifting across the lake glinting silver in the pale sun. In a nearby patch of tall dead rushes something disturbed a pair of moorhens who left their hide with harsh throaty calls, and a sudden flap of their short black wings as they rose then landed with a splash on the water, paddling away furiously from whatever unseen menace had disturbed them.

'Come on,' Scott said with an urgency that surprised Poppy. 'Come on, or we won't have enough time.'

'Enough time for what?'

'You'll see.'

Taking her hand even more firmly, Scott helped her up a steep wooded path that led away from the lake and further and further into the leafless wintry copse, at this time of year a spot where no birds sang and no flowers bloomed. And yet there was a special atmosphere to the place, even though every hasty step they took through the woodland plunged them deeper into the still, immovable winter darkness. Poppy had no idea from where the sense of enchantment might be coming, until she stood in front of the door.

They had come upon it as if by magic, since one minute they were in deep woodland, and the next standing before a faded honey-coloured stone cottage, built deliberately it seemed on a mound in a tiny clearing where it would remain hidden from all but the most curious. There was no path from the copse, just an end to the trees followed by a swathe of grass that surrounded the hummock that supported the charming little building.

Poppy gazed up at it while George stood at her feet wagging his long dachshund tail as if in approval. Scott was silent, looking not at the house but at Poppy.

'It isn't like any cottage I've seen,' Poppy said finally. 'What I mean is that cottages in the country are usually either very plain brick and tile, or whitewash and thatch. They're not like this— smaller versions of old classical stone houses, with Georgian casements and a proper slate roof—and with such elegant design and proportions. I mean why? Why was it built? And all the way out here— at such a distance from the house? The other follies at Eden Park are all so visible, all set around the lakes, none of them hidden away like this—'

'Which is the exact point of this one I would imagine,' Scott interrupted. 'The other follies were designed to be seen. This wasn't.'

'So what was it?'

'A secret? A place of secrets?' Scott suggested. 'A very private place where two could play? I imagine from the situation, and the fact that it's properly built as a dwelling place, as you'll see . . .' He took her hand and led her up a flight of steps that had been cut in the mound, in order that visitors happening on it from the direction from which they had arrived could climb to the stone terrace above.

'How did you discover it? By sheer chance? Or did you know about it?'

'I knew nothing of it,' Scott confessed with his usual engaging honesty. 'No, it was Eugene Hackett. He spent a lot of his childhood at Eden

Park; the son was a boyhood friend from Ireland, where his parents had a holiday house. He was killed recently, poor fellow. But at any rate, Hackett thinks it's very special. They all used to come up here for picnics, and Lady Dunne would rest here when life at the Park became a trifle too hectic.'

Scott threw open the front door and stood to one side. Poppy stepped into the little building with quiet reverence, looking around her carefully, as if she was stepping into a church, or private chapel, rather than a house.

They stood, silently holding hands, George at their feet, as they took in the small octagonal hall, the stone-flagged floor below their feet and the glass-domed skylight above their heads. All about them, thanks to the dome above, was a feeling of light and space, and although the hall was furnished only with the dry leaves that had blown in that autumn, it nevertheless had a lived-in feeling, as if any minute now a servant would bring in a mahogany table upon which he would lay a sheaf of letters and a copy of the *Morning Post*.

One by one Scott opened the three doors that led off the octagon, only to discover that they all took the visitor into the reception room, a small sitting room furnished only with one dining chair, a Regency chaise longue, and a fine glass-fronted bookcase.

After this came the dining room, where there was no table, but three abandoned chairs, and finally a kitchen with an old oak table, a range and a small scullery that led to yet more service rooms. A flight of elegant stone stairs led them up to an iron-railed landing where another three doors matching those below revealed two bedrooms and a bathroom. Here there was no furniture at all, other than a three-legged wardrobe in one bedroom and an antique wooden armchair in the other, once perhaps identifiable as a Regency hall chair, but now heavily disguised under thick brown housemaid's paint.

All the windows were dressed with wooden shutters held securely by long iron bars, making the rooms seem warmer than they might otherwise have been. Poppy opened one of them and stared out across the woods. Immediately the small room became more enchanting, lit by a ray of weak winter sunlight that was sneaking its way past her and through the gap left by the shutters.

'This is a strange place, Scott,' Poppy murmured, as he took her arm. 'It has an atmosphere, as if someone is still living in it.'

'I didn't bring you here just for you to see it,' Scott replied. 'I brought you here for quite a different reason.'

'Namely?'

Scott cleared his throat, rather too loudly.

'I actually—well—I actually brought you here to ask you to marry me.'

He had taken both of her hands as he cleared his throat. Poppy frowned up at him, taken aback not by his proposal, but by the fear she could see in his eyes.

'What about getting married and the war?'

Scott frowned. 'Well let's say I don't think our marrying is going to bring about world peace,' he said, drily. 'But it would certainly make me very happy. You too, I hope.'

'What I meant was how? How are we going to

64

manage to get married when we have all this work to do? What I *mean* is—do you think it's right to get married?'

'I think it would be terribly wrong not to,' Scott replied in all seriousness. 'Particularly because there is a war on. I couldn't live for one moment longer without you as my wife. Really, I could not. So? So what do you say?'

'Of course.' Poppy smiled up at the tall handsome young man still holding both her hands. 'Of course I will marry you. You surely didn't think for a moment that I wouldn't, did you?'

'I take nothing about you for granted, I hope,' Scott told her, taking her in his arms, while relief flooded him, and his kiss echoed his gratitude at her reply. 'Particularly between cup—and lip.'

After which he kissed her again, and again.

'When?' Poppy wondered. 'When do you think we can get married? And where are we going to live? I don't really think that little flat we've just seen is going to be exactly ideal.'

'We'll get married as soon as we can arrange it. We can organise a special licence and get hitched in a couple of days, or weeks, whatever we want. And as for where to live, you mean you don't like this place?'

Poppy stared round her. 'We can't live here,' she said. 'How can we possibly live here?'

'When Eugene first showed it to me, he said all that needed to be done was for him to have a word with the owners.'

'Are you sure it'd be all right?'

'Absolutely. Now come on—let's go and see exactly what we have to do to get married.'

Poppy was the one to shut the front door behind

them. As she did so she noticed some carving above the fine lintel of the heavy panelled door.

'*Domus Florea*,' she read. 'Translate please, Mr Meynell.'

'Yes. Even I with my *horribilis Latinus*, even I know what that is. It means House of Flowers.'

*   *   *

Eugene's flight was uncomfortable and dangerous, owing to the age and flimsiness of the aircraft designated to fly him the seventy-five miles from Malta to Sicily and to the atrocious weather—a storm of such ferocity that Eugene found himself quickly accepting that they were bound to crash into the black and icy seas below them.

But somehow the little antediluvian twin-engine aircraft rose to the occasion, thanks more to the skill of its pilot rather than to the resilience of its structure, since during the worst of the storm it seemed as if the howling February gales would rip it to pieces in mid-air. At one point the engines lost all their power against the might of the wind and the plane suddenly plunged nose first for the sea. Somehow the pilot, busy screaming abuse at the gods and swearing at the top of his voice in Maltese, managed to yank the aircraft out of its death dive and level it off only a matter of a hundred or so feet above sea level, before slowly beginning to ascend once more until at long last they were seemingly out of danger.

But, miraculously, the storm abated. As suddenly as it had blown up it was over, even though as Eugene could see from his little side window the seas below them were still turbulent.

But the force of the wind had undoubtedly abated because by the time the little plane was approaching the appointed dropping zone it was back on an even keel. Turning to Eugene, the pilot made a jump and drop signal with one hand and smiled before sticking his thumb up in the air. Eugene, having run all his pre-drop checks, clambered further back in the fuselage until he was alongside the door through which he was about to launch himself.

'Gude lock, Paddy!' the Maltese pilot bellowed. 'Go keel the goddamn Chermans!'

After which Eugene gave a thumbs-up sign, unlocked the door, and, taking a deep breath, without thinking twice hurled himself out into the night. After counting to five, he pulled his ripcord and heard his parachute billow out with a whoosh behind him. Opening the eyes he had just tightly closed, he grabbed the sides of the harness above his head and began to fly himself down as best as he could to a ground that seemed to be coming up at him a great deal faster than he was descending.

The fact was that the plane was little more sophisticated than those first used in the Great War and needed to fly at a much lower altitude than was considered safe for parachuting. Not only was the risk to Eugene far higher; so inevitably was the violence of his landing. By using all his strength Eugene managed to control both his drift and his speed, so that by buckling and rolling as soon as he felt the ground under his feet he escaped with nothing more than a few knocks and was able to punch himself free of his parachute. Gathering it into as small a bundle as was possible, he hightailed it for the shelter of the woods that he could see silhouetted on one side of the plateau on to which he had dropped.

As he crouched in the scrub at the edge of the copse he looked for any sign of the signal that was supposed to welcome him to Sicily. He didn't have to wait long. Hardly a minute after he reached his hiding place, he saw a small pinpoint of light flickering only a couple of hundred yards from where he was crouching. He at once responded, and waited as instructed until he heard the faintest of movements behind him in the copse.

'*Three-a-no-tromp*,' a voice whispered, feet from where he crouched.

'*Five clubs*,' Eugene returned.

'Good. Now you wait, please.'

Eugene did as he was told, remaining motionless until he felt a tap on the shoulder.

'Now-a,' he was urged. 'Come.'

There was no moonlight. In fact as they made their careful way out of the pitch-dark woods it seemed as though there was no light at all. Eugene could just make out the shape of two men in front of him, both with rifles slung over their backs; small men, both of them, who, it became quickly clear, were enviably light on their feet.

After half an hour of slow and stealthy progress they came to a road, over which they crossed before continuing through more pitch-black woodland until finally reaching a small house silhouetted against the winter sky. Eugene's guides flattened themselves against the front wall before edging up to ease open the door. A second later they were in the house, leaving their guest outside with his back against the wall while they inspected the premises.

'*Psssst?*' A hiss indicated it was safe for Eugene to enter, which he did, closing the door behind him.

'Safe-a 'ere,' one of the men said. 'We stay-a 'ere now a while. 'Ave a smokey.'

The three of them lit cigarettes, cupping their matches tightly in hand to show the least light possible. They all leaned back against the wall to smoke in silence, the quiet outside broken only by the call of some night bird. When they finished their cigarettes they took it in turn to rest while one remained on watch.

Perhaps out of respect for his journey, Eugene was invited to be the first to sleep. He huddled himself into the nearest corner of the room, pulling his jacket round him for warmth and wrapping his arms tightly round his chest, allowing his chin finally to drop as if he was already asleep, while he examined the situation.

His mission, particularly vital at this point in the war, was to help try to sabotage the massive build-up of enemy aircraft in Sicily, designed to bolster the ongoing attacks the Luftwaffe were constantly mounting against the strategically vital little island of Malta. Somehow, miraculously, the island had held out throughout an offensive that had begun the previous June when the Italians launched wave after wave of their Savoia-Marchetti bombers in raids over the island. All the Maltese had to defend them were four biplane Gladiator fighters, which notwithstanding their obsolescence in their few weeks of heroic glory intercepted over seventy enemy formations, shooting down or badly damaging thirty-seven enemy aircraft.

But once the British supplemented the tiny fighting force with a handful of Hurricanes the

Germans and the Italians realised they had a very real fight on their hands, if they were going to conquer and occupy the tiny island that had been so strategically important since the Middle Ages. Hence the building up of Luftwaffe units in Sicily, and Eugene's mission to search out and sabotage as many planes as he could. He was to pose as a sympathetic mechanic, a role that Eugene had rehearsed with his usual dedication and attention to detail. Happily so, for it was this sense of detail, allied to that sixth sense that is so necessary to survival, that first alerted him to danger.

It was the cigarettes they were smoking. Because he was so meticulous when preparing what he liked to call a new role for himself, Eugene's studies always included a painstaking study of native habits. He took a pride in knowing everything from the fact that Italians abhorred the colour purple, associating it with prostitutes, to the manner in which they smoked and drank, or insulted each other.

It was because of this attention to the tiniest detail that he had made sure Jack Ward and his associates supplied him with the correct type of Sicilian cigarette. The tobacco in these cigarettes was black, rough and pungent, a typical peasant type of smoke. But the cigarettes his companions were smoking smelt as if they were made of Virginian tobacco. Watching them from behind half-closed eyes only confirmed his suspicions.

He sat up, indicating that he had run out of smokes. Could they possibly spare him a cigarette? Without a second thought the man nearest him opened an unmarked tin, which allowed Eugene to sit back in his corner and smoke the sort of cigarette he would have greatly enjoyed in any other circumstances than the ones in which he now found himself.

He was undoubtedly in the hands of German sympathisers, which was what Jack Ward with his usual understatement would call *a bit tricky*. He quickly ran through his options. He could shoot them both with very little difficulty since presently they seemed far more occupied in eating a lump of bread filled with some high-smelling sausage than they were in keeping an eye on him. Two shots would take them out, and he would be gone before they even hit the floor. It was regrettable, but there was really no choice, since his only real chance lay in making good an escape.

Bluff Hackett—that's your only chance, just good old Irish bluff.

The first part was a lot easier than he had reckoned. Pretending that he simply could not sleep because he was too keyed up, Eugene persuaded the younger of the two men to take his place in the corner while he and his friend would pass the time playing a gambling game Eugene would teach him. The younger one was soon fast asleep in the corner, his heavy coat pulled up nearly to his eyes and his face turned away from his companions, while Eugene began to explain in whispers how the game was played. The second Sicilian listened intently as Eugene muttered the directions.

'If you win . . .'

Eugene put his hand in his pocket and produced some of the many small gold coins without which he never travelled. As always, greed very soon overcame any common sense the Sicilian might

71

have had, as he saw the chance of winning one of the coins that were now lying on the floor in front of them, glinting faintly in the light of their cigarettes.

'Now then,' Eugene whispered to him in his carefully rural Italian. 'You can have first guess. Is that coin head up? Or head down?'

As he had anticipated the Sicilian leaned slightly forward as if to try to read how the coin lay. The moment he did, Eugene struck him hard and brutally under his chin across his windpipe with the edge of one large, strong hand. He was dead before his head struck the wall behind him.

The second man was an even easier target. He was so fast asleep he would not have heard Eugene even if he had stood up and started to dance an Irish jig on the stone floor. Eugene had no need to stand up, let alone dance a jig. He simply leaned over and knocked the man stone cold unconscious with the butt of his revolver. To make sure his suspicions were correct, Eugene at once went thoroughly through both the men's jackets. In the pockets of the man who had been asleep in the corner, the one who now lay unconscious in front of him, he found nothing more incriminating than the pack of Virginia cigarettes. But sewn inside a tobacco pouch belonging to the man with whom he had been intent on playing Spoof he found a safe pass from the SS.

He had no idea of how much time he had before his scheduled betrayal. It occurred to him as he carefully inspected the inside and then the near outside of the small abandoned farmhouse that in all probability he was not to be handed over there at all, and the intention had been to take him into the nearest town where he was meant to be finding work in a garage. It was there that the SS would be waiting for him. This meant that Eugene had two questions which he had to address. The first was how much had they known about his plans? The second, more vitally, was who had betrayed him?

*   *   *

From what he could see, there was no sign of any activity in the immediate vicinity of the house. The surrounding landscape was nothing but flat fields, winter-dead to everything other than the ever scavenging birds, with mountains rising into the still dark skies far beyond. In the enveloping darkness it was impossible to make out the lie of the land, but after a careful and what Eugene devoutly hoped was an invisible reconnaissance he returned inside the house to collect the rest of his small parcel of belongings.

Just as he was about to take his final leave, to his surprise he heard the man in the corner stir. Turning, Eugene dropped to his haunches and levelled the gun at the man's temple. The young Sicilian's eyes opened slowly. As they did, Eugene pressed the gun harder into his forehead.

The man frowned up at him and shrugged. His eyes swivelled sideways until he could take in the outline of his friend slumped on the stone floor.

'What you do?' he whispered. 'What is this? We are friends.'

Eugene eyed him, then with his free hand dangled his friend's safe pass in front of him.

'Friends of the SS. I should cut both your throats.'

'No! Please! No—no me! I am your friend—I swear! I do not know 'im—I not do this with 'im afore.'

'And I don't think he's going to be doing it again, either.'

The man frowned and shook his head in bewilderment. As soon as he did so he put his hands to his head to hold it against the sudden pain that shot through it.

Eugene stared at him, trying to assemble some sort of plan. Without help and guidance he knew he was as good as dead, since he had no knowledge of the country into which he had been dropped other than the fact that he was to be taken to a safe house and from there to a safe place of work. He was helpless without contacts. Lacking an escort it was an odds on certainty that he would walk straight into the arms of the enemy.

His only chance of survival was to trust the Sicilian, lie low for a while and during that time change his appearance. The problem was the disappearance of the traitor lying dead against the wall of the farmhouse. When he failed to show up with his expected goods, the Germans or Italian soldiers would come out looking, and when they found his dead body they would know Eugene was at large.

They're going to know that anyway, Eugene reasoned to himself as he stared down at his prisoner. Putting his gun back in the belt of his trousers, he nodded to the Sicilian and, after making known his intentions, enlisted his help to drag the dead man up the rickety stairs of the deserted building and deposit his corpse under the floorboards. As they placed the wooden board back over him, his compatriot spat in disgust.

'Now where?' Eugene wondered as they stood outside surveying a bleak wintry landscape unfolding under an ominous sky. 'What's our destination?'

'We go about ten mile,' the Sicilian replied. 'But we take the river. We go by boat. Come. Quick now.'

He hurried Eugene off in a direction away from the road, keeping low as they traversed the field between the house and the trees in the near distance. They had just made the cover of the woodland when Eugene heard the sound of motor vehicles. Glancing back over his shoulder through the undergrowth he saw a small patrol of motorbikes and an armoured car driving along the road, one soldier standing in the car behind a long-barrelled machine gun. For a second he held his breath, but the unit paid no attention to the outwardly derelict farmhouse, driving straight past it and continuing without slowing down along the winding road that finally disappeared into the hillside.

There was a boat waiting for them, moored on the near bank, a quite ordinary rowing boat with a pair of strong oars, well concealed in an inlet that ran under some large heavily bowed trees.

'If anyone spots us in this, we're sitting ducks.'

'No one will see us, my friend,' he was assured. 'This river is very small, and runs away from the roads. Where we go, believe me, this is very much the safest way.'

So it proved. After a bitterly cold but entirely uneventful voyage down a small meandering river, Eugene found himself decanted on the banks of a

75

tiny little hamlet where it would seem from his first impression time had completely forgotten to move on.

*　　　*　　　*

Back at Eden Park, Billy was staring at his plate of fish pie. Billy hated fish and even more so when it had been made into some sort of pie, particularly when covered with a thin coating of white dried potato. He fidgeted at his place at Mrs Alderman's kitchen table, pushing a piece of the offending offering around his plate so regularly that Mrs Alderman, busy studying the weekly ration allocations which were known as 'Changes in the Points Value' in her newspaper, finally looked up at him and clicked her tongue loudly.

'Billy,' she warned him. 'I can't concentrate. Not with you doing that.'

Billy, all innocence, looked back at the cook. When she had returned to her reading he transferred his gaze to the cat who was sitting as ever like Patience on her monument under the kitchen table, conveniently near to his feet. The kitchen cat and Billy were now firm friends, so much so that it seemed to know at once when there was a game on, climbing down from some cosy place near the kitchen range and slinking its way across the floor to find its new ally.

So far the score that morning stood at Billy and Cat *two*, Mrs Alderman *nought*, a long way from their best score of the previous week, which was Billy and Cat *eighteen*, Mrs Alderman *one*. That had been a golden lunchtime when the cook had been so engrossed in her reading and

76

accompanying tongue-clicking that she had only noticed one morsel of her precious stew being fed to Cat.

Today, however, she seemed more on her guard, as if news of Billy's favourite pastime had somehow come to her notice. She would keep looking up at odd moments, particularly when Billy fidgeted. The more she looked up, the more he fidgeted, and the more he fidgeted, the more she looked up, which was why after twenty minutes Billy and Cat's fish pie score stood at only two.

In order to get her back to her reading for long enough for Billy to score another goal, he had to feign eating some fish, a task that made him want to retch, so disgusting was the taste of the cold and congealing forkful. Unfortunately, as he did so Mrs Alderman looked up and awarded him another stare, forcing Billy to swallow a larger mouthful than he had intended. With eyes bulging he grabbed his water glass and swallowed half the tumbler.

'It can hardly be hot, Billy,' Mrs Alderman remarked. 'Seeing you've been sitting in front of it since before the last war.'

'Must be the pepper, Mrs A.'

'There ain't no pepper on it, young man,' the cook replied, shaking out her newspaper. 'Can't get any pepper these days, not a bit. That's why they're a-calling it *white gold*. Didn't know that, did you, Mr Smarty Pants? If you wanted to make a fortune you'd be out growing pepper, that's what you'd be doing, or whatever it is you do to make pepper, instead of sitting for half a century in front of your dinner.'

'Wonder what they're calling fish,' Billy

muttered, eyeing the cat, who was now busy swishing his tail in patent discontent. 'White muck I should imagine.'

'Fish is good for you,' Mrs Alderman replied crisply. 'And we're a lot luckier than some, here at Eden Park, I can tell you, seeing how we have the lakes and the old stew ponds. Most folks in towns they don't get no fish at all, even after queuing for it for hours and hours. So you just eat it up and be thankful.'

Mrs Alderman gave Billy one more friendly glare, then returned to her study of the food points values, pushing her glasses up her nose as she did so, unable to believe how much had changed, and how quickly, now that rationing was really beginning to be felt.

'So what other treats are we in for this week then, Mrs A?' Billy asked over-politely, as he surreptitiously dropped an extra large lump of what he deeply suspected might be carp down to the ever grateful cat. 'Anything exciting on the menu?'

'You might get some American sausage meat if you're lucky. That's come down some points, as has Spam. Almost as much as that awful Tor stuff you get in tins.'

'Oh, Gawd. I hate Tor worse than I hate Spam.'

'And you're not to swear, young man. I told you that a dozen times.'

'Gawd in't no swear word. It's a name.'

'A name you're taking in vain. The Lord's name. There's nothing wrong with gosh or golly—and you're to mind your grammar too, and all, while I'm on the subject. "In't no swear word" indeed! No such word as *in't*, Billy, and you knows it. It's ain't. It *ain't* no swear word. And finish up your fish.'

'What else are we not going to get then, Mrs A?' Billy continued, all innocence, as he saw Mrs Alderman returning to her reading. 'Nothing half decent, I'll bet.'

'You won't be getting no sugar at this rate, not according to this chart 'ere. Nor any tea. Tea's gawn through the roof so it has.'

'Gone, Mrs Alderman. No such word as gawn, don't you know.'

'I'll give those ears of yours a good clip if you don't look out, Billy Hendry.'

Mrs Alderman sighed and began to fold her paper up. Seeing her doing so, Billy's heart grew heavy as he realised that gone was his chance to get anywhere near his record score. Not only that, but if she maintained her present level of vigilance Mrs Alderman would make sure he had to eat the rest of her disgusting fish pie himself.

'I'd kill for a cup of decent tea,' she grumbled, getting slowly to her feet and pottering over to the sink to fill the kettle, giving Billy the chance of a quick hat-trick down under the table to Cat.

'*When fisher-folk are brave enough / To face mines and the foe for you / You surely can be bold enough / To try a fish that's new,*' Mrs Alderman recited with a sigh, banging the lid back on the kettle while nodding at Billy to encourage him. 'You'd do well to learn that, young man, and be thankful you got something on your plate.'

'What do you think I'm doing, Mrs A?' Billy enquired, through a pretend mouthful of food. 'Look—I nearly cleared up every scrap.'

Mrs Alderman looked round at that, and saw to her surprise that the boy's plate was almost clean.

79

She eyed him suspiciously. She knew that Billy was always up to something, and no doubt making fish pie disappear was another of his illusions. Her suspicion was always greater the more innocent his smile.

'It's not me I'm feeling sorry for,' the cook continued. 'As far as tea goes that is. It's all them poor people upstairs—'

'Isn't it *those* poor people upstairs, Mrs A?' Billy wondered, widening his eyes more than ever.

'It's them poor people upstairs I feel sorry for,' Mrs Alderman continued, as if he hadn't spoken. 'Them poor hardworking bods, doing their best to help win the war, and all I can give 'em as refreshment is a cup of near dishwater. Disgraceful, that's what I say it is. Don't know what the government can be thinking, expecting this famous war effort they're always on about when a body can't even get a half-decent cup of tea.'

During this speech, to his quiet delight, Billy was able to score another fish hat-trick, bringing the score up to Cat and Billy *nine*, Mrs Alderman *nil*. Unhappily there was neither enough left on the plate to break the existing record nor indeed enough time, as Mrs Alderman suddenly leaned over and whisked away his plate.

'And another thing I cannot abide is people sittin' in front of cold food,' she grumbled. 'Particularly ungrateful people.'

''Ow can you say such a thing, Mrs A?' Billy replied, all hurt innocence. 'Look 'ow much I've eaten. Look 'ow well I done.'

''Ow well I *have* done, Billy. And what's that funny noise—Oh, no. It's not the bloomin' cat being sick, surely?'

At the realisation that the last scrap he had dropped for the cat must have been both too large and too bony and if he wasn't careful the game would be up entirely, Billy was out of his chair in a moment.

'Thanks, Mrs A!' he called as he scrambled to the door. 'Thanks for the pie—but I suddenly remembered I got to see Major F! He said he had some news about my invention!'

'You and your inventions,' Mrs Alderman grumbled, doubling over her considerable bulk in an effort to find the still vomiting cat. 'And if I find you been feeding Maudie—'

But Billy was gone, and with him any chance Mrs Alderman had of finding out whether it was the cat, or her charge, who had been responsible for the mealtime felony.

'Blimey,' Billy said to himself as he scampered upstairs. 'If this war's worth winnin', it's worth winnin' for an end to Mrs A's fish pie for good an' all!'

'You're late,' Marjorie chided him as Billy skidded through the outer door of Major Folkestone's office.

'I'm right on time,' Billy retorted. 'Right on the blooming chiming of the church clock. Listen, Marge.' He started to feign the tolling of the old clock.

'You're still late. Too late to save me from having to say yes to a drink.'

Marjorie glared back over her shoulder at Major Folkestone's inner door, which had just closed fast behind her.

'That's not my fault, Marge. Any 'ow—'

'How. Any*how*.'

81

'That's your beeswax. You can look after yourself.'

'You don't understand,' Marjorie sighed. 'You will when you're older.'

'All you had to do was make an excuse,' Billy grimaced. 'If you don't want to go out with him, tell him something stupid.'

'I've run out of excuses, Billy! Anyway, even if I do make an excuse he always gives me the *Monday then*.' In response to Billy's puzzled stare, Marjorie went on to explain. 'If I say sorry I can't tonight, Major—or tomorrow—or Friday—he just says fine. How about *Monday* then?'

'So this time . . . ?'

'This time I found myself—because I couldn't think of anything—saying all right, tonight then. If you'd only been on time, Billy, I wouldn't have been caught, would I?'

'I was bang on time! Look! Look—it's slap bang on two o'bloomin' clock.'

'You look a complete mess, Billy. Come here.'

Marjorie frowned and pulled her self-adopted teenage brother towards her, trying to make him look a bit more respectable before he kept his appointment with her boss. His long wool socks had fallen round his ankles, his striped scarf was knotted like a hangman's noose round his throat, his tie was halfway round to the back of his neck, one side of his shirt collar stuck up towards his chin while the other was entirely invisible under his tie, and, to top it all, he had his jumper on not only inside out, but back to front.

'You're going to end up in a back room here with all the other loonies,' she grumbled. 'Inventing things totally as daft as you, and the rest of them.'

82

'Has he said anything about my pilotless bomb yet, Marge?' Billy asked, his voice dropping to a whisper as the door to the inner office opened and the figure of Miss Budge appeared, a stack of files under one arm.

'No. But then he wouldn't. Not to me anyway,' Marjorie told him, easing him towards the open door.

'So what's he want to see me for then?'

'You'll soon find out, won't you? Go on.'

With one final push Billy was inside Major Folkestone's office.

'Afternoon, sir,' Billy said, giving a more than creditable salute.

'At ease, young man,' the major replied. 'I've got something for you.'

Billy cast a quick look round the desk to see if he could spot any trace of the file on his soon-to-be-famous pilotless bomb, but to his amazement nothing was visible.

'Can I ask you something, sir?'

'Not now, Billy.' Major Folkestone cut him short. 'I have a busy afternoon and you're the very smallest part of it, I'm afraid. Here.'

'I was only going to ask—'

'Not *now*, Billy. That's an order.'

Anthony Folkestone indicated for Billy to sit down at a table and handed him a pencil and paper.

'Take a dekko at that, young man, and tell me what you make of it. Should be child's play to you, with your knack with codes.'

Billy frowned down at the sheets of paper on the table in front of him.

'Even Marge could crack this one, sir,' he told

the major loftily, after a few minutes. 'It's easy-peasy. Boring, actually.'

'I'm quite sure Marjorie could not crack it, Billy—just as I'm sure it isn't what you call easy-peasy. Or boring.'

Billy gazed up at him and as always Anthony Folkestone got the strangest feeling. It was as if the boy was possessed not just of a knack but of something else, a capacity about which he had no real understanding, but which seemed to be visible in his eyes, as if there was quite another person than young Billy Hendry looking back out at you.

He had already proved that he had a highly precocious ability to add columns of figures at a glance, and to translate basic codes as accurately as, and sometimes more quickly than, most of the professional code-breakers at Eden Park.

At first Anthony Folkestone had not given much thought to Billy's precocious ability, which was hardly surprising since Billy's vague urchin look and unmilitary manners certainly did not suggest a hidden genius, and his eternally cheerful manner would have been more suited to a delivery boy. So Anthony was inclined to put his odd talents down to general quirkiness, deciding not to look beyond what was on offer—namely the boy's innate ability to decipher codes, in exchange for which Anthony willingly put up patiently with what he considered to be Billy's wilder flights of fancy, so many of which Marjorie, with sisterly love, faithfully placed on his desk, and which still sat unexamined under a pile of Top Secret documents.

'This is just another of them triple letter do-dahs, sir,' Billy said with what he considered to be a sniff of some sophistication. 'You know—we've 'ad

84

'em before.'

'Yes, I know we've *had* them before, Billy, but I am not as able as you to work through them as quickly. If I was I wouldn't bother you with them, but the boys have their hands full enough trying to decipher stuff concerning attacks on our supply convoys. This has just come through, and since you're around . . .'

Anthony petered out, realising his reasoning was beginning to sound feeble. He knew he used Billy for this sort of decoding because he was not just on hand, but very fast, although Anthony was at pains not to tell him so.

'I told you, sir,' Billy continued, in a vaguely patronising voice, 'the Ds? And the Vs—you replace them with Gs and Hs, then you replace them again with—'

'I know, Billy, you've told me a dozen times, but it doesn't really make the slightest difference because codes are not my subject, and really I don't understand a blind word, so be a good chap and—'

'You want it in German, sir?' Billy interrupted. 'Or do you want it in King's English?'

'You don't speak German.'

'I feel I nearly do. I've been working on so many of these now, I got quite a few words in German now, sir. Want to hear?'

Anthony Folkestone stared at him, trying to conceal the astonishment he was feeling.

'It's not quite as good as my French, sir,' Billy noted modestly. 'But Mr Hackett says it's coming on.'

'Mr Hackett's been coaching you?'

'No, sir. Just criticising, if you like.'

Anthony picked a pencil out of the holder on his

85

desk and began to tap it rhythmically on his desktop.

'To get back to the message, Billy. What does it say? And I don't understand why it should be in German. It's meant to be from one of ours.'

'It is, sir. It's just been sent in German probably as a decoy—since it's from Popeye.'

'Popeye?' Now Anthony was genuinely surprised. 'I see.' He put his hand out to take the message. 'We'd better have that sent to translation at once.'

'Don't need to really, sir. Says he's landed OK—but one of his welcoming committee was a d.a.'

'A d.a.?' Anthony tried not to look surprised.

'Double agent, sir,' Billy stated, all innocence.

'I know what d.a. stands for, thank you, Billy.'

'He's all right, sir. He killed the bloke and the other one's genuine. Popeye's in his safe house now, and starts work on the cars tomorrow.'

Anthony resumed his pencil tapping feeling a little as if he was working for Billy rather than the other way round.

'I have to remind you, young man, of your position here. You are not meant to work out the full message; you're just meant to break the code, nothing more.'

'It's all right, sir. I know what would happen to me if I broke the Official Secrets Act. You really don't 'ave to worry. Not on my account. If I ever broke the Act I would be for the big drop, I know that.'

Billy ran his finger expressively across his throat before getting to his feet, already restless and bored, and looking for something else to occupy him.

'Thank you, Billy. You've been a great help, as usual.'

'Maybe you'll have a moment soon to have a dekko at that file Marge gave you? It's over there, on the cabinet.'

Anthony nodded, at the same time looking away.

'Of course. Thank you, Billy. That will be all for now.'

Billy realised that this was the moment to *skedaddle*, as he himself would put it, but he hated leaving Major Folkestone's office, always liking to hang around, feeling that while he was there he was nearer to the centre of things at Eden Park. He stopped by Miss Budge's desk.

'What you doing, Miss Budge?'

He found himself addressing her back as she was leaning forward, tidying one of her desk drawers.

'I'm sorting through the kit for our people, Billy, that's what I'm doing, passports, identity cards, cyanide pills, all that.'

Billy stared into the now quite open drawer.

'Blimey,' he breathed. 'I think I know what they are, all right, don't I? One bite and you're a gonna, yes?'

Miss Budge too stared into the drawer at the cyanide pills which were routinely doled out to all agents. 'Quite correct, Billy,' she told him factually. 'As a matter of fact, I consider these to be the kindest thing we do for our agents, quite the kindest.'

She shut the drawer and locked it, putting the key into a box on her desk.

Billy walked out of her office filled with excitement. He could not wait for the day when Miss Budge would dole him out a false passport, identity card and cyanide pill.

*   *   *

'Of course I couldn't go and fall in love with someone ordinary, like a soldier,' Kate found herself moaning later that evening after she, Marjorie and Billy had finished dinner in the kitchen of the cottage. 'Someone who might be posted to Catterick; someone to whom I could send knitted socks and mufflers. No, I couldn't do that, could I? I had to fall in love with someone in H Section. Which means I will never ever know where he is—or how he is—or what he's doing.'

'A soldier's not that much better,' Marjorie remarked, standing in front of the fireplace to check her appearance before leaving to meet Anthony Folkestone for the dreaded promised drink at the pub. 'Soldiers don't remain at Catterick, and when they're posted abroad you don't know where they are either—specially not if they're taken prisoner.'

'I know,' Kate interrupted. 'I know, but at least they're taken prisoner. If I just knew how Eugene was. It's not *where* so much, just how, really.'

She fished a cigarette out of her bag, lighting it with a spill she ignited from the wood fire burning in the grate. Billy, who was busy as usual drawing in one of his exercise books at the table, glanced at the girls, wondering if there was any way of cheering Kate up by telling her that he knew that Popeye, otherwise known as Eugene Hackett, had landed safely. Then, recalling the image he was careful to keep in his head for such times—himself lined up against the wall at the back of the stable

88

yard being executed by a firing squad under the command of Major Folkestone—he merely sighed and went on drawing.

'At least someone is in love with you, Kate,' Marjorie said, pursing her lips and wishing she had some lipstick, more for her own vanity's sake than for any effect she wished to have on that evening's date.

'You got Major Folkestone.' Billy grinned up from his place at the table. 'He's got a fantastic pash on you, Marge, you know that?'

'That's quite enough out of you, Billy,' Marjorie returned. 'I'm having a drink with him simply because he's my boss.'

'Oh yeah?' Billy teased.

'Yeah,' Marjorie replied, doing up her headscarf and coat and disappearing out into the night.

As she crossed the parkland by the light of the all too bright moon, Marjorie wondered as always whether, just as she was about to escape for the evening, the air raid siren would sound and she would have to take shelter. It wasn't so bad when she was in a party of people, and they were well out of the grounds, because then they could hide themselves away in the nearest dugout, but if they were in the house and the word was they could be either targeted or simply in line for enemy bombs being jettisoned on their return journey, they very often had to go into the elaborate procedure known as Operation GOHQ, which entailed everyone's grabbing as many of the latest Top Secret files as they could manage—chaos in other words. From that moment, all such information was their own personal responsibility while they made their way to a warren of well-equipped caves.

These hiding places ran to everything from bedrooms with bunks and knitted blankets, and living rooms fitted out with the latest radio equipment, to offices with full sets of secure filing cabinets, a small chapel, and even a makeshift emergency operating room complete with side ward.

The caves were a good mile from the main house and camouflaged from the sight of anyone approaching at land level, or spying from overhead, access being obtained by way of a series of tunnels whose entrances were again brilliantly concealed behind trapdoors hidden deep in the woodlands. Possibly an invading force would find them sooner or later, but only, so the Nosy Parkers joked, if they had a strong nose for drink and cigarettes, as well as a prior knowledge of the small underground village.

On top of that, escape tunnels had been fashioned from the complex so that if the dread day ever dawned when England was invaded and the inhabitants of Eden Park were apparently cornered below ground, some if not most of them would be given the chance to run towards the sea, where the underground caves finally finished.

Happily, the evening of Marjorie's rendezvous with Major Anthony Folkestone was uninterrupted by any air raid warnings, which made it even more strange that as Marjorie made her way to the bicycle sheds she actually found herself praying for one, just so that it would get her out of her date.

*   *   *

'Ah, there you be, Miss Hendry.' Anthony

90

Folkestone was certain his voice had risen a good octave as he stood staring at the pretty girl now standing in front of him.

Although they had been out drinking in a group before, Marjorie had never previously really bothered to dress herself up, since she had considered that having a few weak drinks in the pub hardly merited putting on her glad rags, particularly since she now only had one pair of decent stockings left to her name.

But this evening, partly out of boredom and a feeling of inner greyness induced by the notion of having to go out on a date with her boss, and partly out of a devil-may-care let's-see-what-happens attitude, she had decided to make herself look as glamorous as possible. Besides, as she had reasoned to herself while she set her hair carefully and applied the very last drop of scent out of the little blue *Evening in Paris* bottle she had been given the Christmas before by Billy, nowadays she had so little chance to dress up glamorously, she might as well dress up for Anthony Folkestone as for anyone else, even if she did have to arrive on a bicycle.

She had chosen to wear an old-fashioned frock that she had recut and resewn, adding to it a lace collar and cuffs she had found at the Clothes Exchange. Over it she put on a tight little crossover angora cardigan that her late Aunt Hester's next door neighbour had knitted for her while she and Billy were still living with Marjorie's aunt. Anthony Folkestone, who was used to seeing her dressed mostly in wool—including very often an old army forage hat pulled well down over her hair to try to prevent excessive heat loss in the freezing building, not to mention mittens and thick home-knitted stockings—could now hardly believe his eyes.

Not that Marjorie did not always look pretty in her customary office outfit of layers of woolly jumpers and lisle stockings. As a matter of fact, in his opinion, she always looked quite adorable, but she never looked remotely glamorous. Now she looked exactly that, which was probably why he found himself becoming tongue-tied.

'Is something the matter, Major?' Marjorie asked, feeling suddenly disconcerted, as she observed her boss staring at her as if he couldn't believe his luck.

'No, Miss Hendry,' Anthony replied slowly. 'No, nothing at all. Nothing at all is the matter. No. At least I don't think so. No.'

There was a short silence, which Marjorie judged really should be broken.

'You're looking very smart, sir, if I may say so.'

She smiled at him. She herself felt surprised at how different he too looked out of uniform in a sports coat, checked shirt and regimental tie, and dark trousers. She could still do without his carefully manicured moustache, which she realised must make him look much older than he possibly was, but even so, the first impression she had of her escort for the evening was altogether more favourable than she could have previously guessed.

Anthony Folkestone stood staring down at Marjorie in fascinated silence for a few seconds more before he managed to ask her what she would like to drink.

'What do you think they have, sir? Do you think they have any gin? Last week they were very short of gin, and I don't really fancy sherry. Which is all they usually have.'

'Let me see, Miss Hendry,' Anthony replied, turning to the bar.

'Perhaps you could call me Marjorie, sir. After all, we're not in the office now.'

'Of course not. In that case, please call me Anthony. Although of course when we *do* get back to work—'

'I quite understand, sir.' Marjorie laughed. 'Sorry. Anthony. It's just—it's just I've never been out for a drink with my employer before. Which is not all that surprising seeing that really you're my first employer. Anthony. It is with an H, isn't it? Your name? I'm never quite sure whether all Anthony's have H's or not.' She stopped.

'Mine does, Marjorie. But you don't have to try to pronounce it,' Anthony joked. 'I think normally it's only Americans, like Poppy Tetherington— she's American—she wouldn't have an H if she was called Anthony.'

He stopped as he saw Marjorie staring at him.

'Not that she would have ever been called Anthony, or Antony, come to think of it, would she? Seeing she's a girl, but none the less I know what I mean.' Ravaged with embarrassment, he turned quickly to the bar. 'Excuse me?' he called to the landlord and started to enquire as to the situation regarding the supply of spirits, which was much safer ground, particularly since the barman immediately drew Anthony further along the bar, which meant Anthony found himself feeling almost faint with gratitude, as it gave him time to recover a small portion of his self-esteem.

'He says if we go into the inner saloon,' he explained to Marjorie on his return, 'he'll see what he can do.'

Anthony took Marjorie through to the tiny back bar, a private room that was generally reserved for ladies or members of the gentry. Tonight it was all but empty except for one portly gentleman who had fallen asleep in the corner by the fireplace, with a newspaper folded over his face as if he was sunbathing on a beach instead of trying to find warmth and comfort on an evening in what was to turn out to be one of the coldest winters in living memory.

In the end Marjorie drank gin and orange, while Anthony preferred his gin pink. After the landlord had revived the fire with a handful of fresh logs, and the portly gentleman had suddenly woken to finish his port and stagger off half asleep and half drunk into the night, they found themselves alone, and at once fell into a dreadful silence.

'It's odd, don't you think?' Anthony said after what seemed to him to be half an hour, but was actually only about a minute. He leaned forward to throw a cinder of burning wood that the fire had spat out on to the thin carpet back into the fire. 'We work together every day. As my secretary you know everything about me. Work is very personal, particularly in our field, and yet quite impersonal in that I think we all feel we can't really get to know each other without perhaps endangering what we do.'

'I'd hate to think I was doing anything that might jeopardise someone's safety by having a drink with you.'

They both smiled briefly, knowing what the word *someone* meant. *Someone* meant an agent, someone in the field, someone risking torture and death.

'No,' Anthony replied slowly. 'No, I don't think we're going to put anyone's life in jeopardy. Most especially not you. You are the model of diligence.'

'Me?' Marjorie looked at him in surprise. 'I'm nothing more than a glorified assistant.'

'You're a great deal more than that, Marjorie. A great deal more. Now, how about another drink? I think I can persuade mine host to part with a little more of his precious gin.'

Marjorie hesitated before accepting. Normally she would never have given such an offer a second thought, since nowadays treats and luxuries were few and far between, and alcohol was not something the rest of the country was able to enjoy in any great quantities. Yet a feeling of caution overtook her. Anthony was after all her boss. She certainly could not imagine Miss Budge, his new typist, swilling gin in the pub with the major.

'Oh, come on,' Anthony urged her with polite good humour. 'I have no wicked intentions of trying to get you tipsy or anything.'

'I didn't mean to be rude. It's just—'

'I know. You can't help thinking of me as your boss. It must be very hard—and if you'd rather just have one drink and go home, I'll quite understand.'

Marjorie looked at the anxious face that was looking back at her, all of a sudden aware of the kindness in Anthony Folkestone's eyes. She had always thought of his demeanour as a study in seriousness and efficiency, but looking at him now—and it might well be owing to alcohol—she realised that he had a really very sweet expression.

'Thank you,' she finally told him, with a smile. 'I'd love another drink.'

The talk stayed small for the next drink, centred safely round the subject of whether or not they enjoyed working at Eden Park, and what a wonderful house it was, and how unimaginable it must be to live as a family in such a place.

'We used to stay here before the war,' Anthony said, resuming the conversation after he had lit them both a cigarette. 'The odd thing about it is that you don't feel as if you're staying in a great house. You'd see what I mean if it was furnished the way it was before it was requisitioned. It had that indefinable English country house style. What the French call *le désordre britannique*. You know, rugs on the floor, dogs at the fire, chintz covers, old paintings.'

'You say you used to stay here,' Marjorie asked carefully, having picked up on the *we*. 'You and— what? Your family? Your parents?'

Anthony looked at her as he smoked his cigarette, as if deciding whether or not to tell her.

'My wife and I,' he finally replied. 'Jane and I.'

'I didn't—I mean I didn't realise . . .' Marjorie stumbled, wondering why she suddenly felt let down. 'I didn't know . . .'

'No, no, Marjorie. I'm not married. Not any more. Jane died three years ago, from peritonitis. Just over, actually—three years and two months.'

Unsurprisingly, Marjorie didn't know what to say. Why should she? Outside office hours, despite the fact that they sometimes worked an eighteen-hour day, she barely knew the Anthony Folkestone at whom she was now looking.

'What a terrible thing.'

'We'd only been married six months.'

'Six months?'

'Six months.' Anthony nodded and threw his spent cigarette into the fire. 'But really that's quite enough of that. I didn't mean to mention it. It just sort of came up, because we were talking about Eden. That's what we always used to call it, you know, just "Eden". Well, still do really, at least those few of us who knew it before. I was at school with the son—with David. He and I used to spend long idyllic summers here, so when it was requisitioned by the War Office for security work it seemed the family thought of me. They knew the sort of thing I was doing, in outline anyway, so they used their influence. Which is how I found myself back here. So it's not coincidence—it was the family's wishes, which kind of doubles my responsibility. Besides looking out for foreign bogies, got to keep an eye on the place for them. Some sort of thank you, if you like, for everything they did for me before the war, parents in India and so on, quite lonely in the hols, you know the sort of thing.'

'Yes, of course,' Marjorie agreed. 'Well, I hope so far they would approve. We seem to have been pretty well behaved, haven't lit fires in the ballroom or any of that kind of thing.'

'Couldn't have asked for a better crowd. Thank heavens the army didn't take it over. They'd have completely wrecked the place. You've no idea what soldiers get up to in other folk's homes. No, it doesn't bear thinking about, the army at Eden.'

'What about your friend—David, wasn't it? The son.'

'He was killed not so long ago.' Anthony glanced away from her, remembering how the two of them had used to sit in front of the pub fire together. 'We were in the same regiment. I got invalided out—a bullet in the back on manoeuvres—which is why I was sidelined to a desk, but David got sent to North Africa, poor chap. Now, I'm going to have one for the road—taking ruthless advantage of mine host because he said he doesn't know when he's going to get his next gin delivery. And you? But of course, if you would rather not . . . ?'

'As long as you promise that if I fall off my bike on the way back you'll help me back up.'

'It's a promise.'

As he went to the bar Marjorie pretended to check her appearance in the compact she had taken out of her handbag. A drink with Major Folkestone was turning out to be a little different. He was obviously one of the many walking wounded.

'Now shall we talk about Billy and his famous design for a bomber without a pilot?'

Anthony sat down again, obviously determined to steer the conversation away from the past. Marjorie smiled as she always seemed to when Billy was mentioned.

'Oh, Billy. He is such a strange boy. No one would think, from how he is now, at Eden Park, no one could imagine how he was as a child, timid and frightened, always seeing a shadow as a ghost, and a ghost as a tiger come to eat him. And yet now look at him. He's become a sort of prodigy; never stops drawing and doodling, thinking of things, adding up figures before anyone can blink. I don't know what's going to become of him eventually, but he certainly has gone from one extreme state to another, bless his cotton socks.'

'There's some medical term or other for it,' Anthony said thoughtfully, as they finally finished their drinks and started to wrap themselves well up in preparation for their bicycle ride home to Eden Park. 'I can't remember the exact official description, but I know there's an acknowledged medical state which some children go into when they suffer shock early in life—sometimes some do say before they're even born, though I don't quite see how, but then that's as maybe.' He paused before continuing. 'Apparently the child turns in on him or herself, and because they're not say as normal in behaviour or appearance as their contemporaries, they're inclined to get sidelined. And during this period in their young lives they develop all sorts of odd gifts and abilities. Interesting, isn't it? My father's a doctor, and he told me all about it. He specialises in children's conditions, and for his sins got laughed at when he first put his theory forward, although I gather they're not holding their sides quite as much now. He had retired, but now, of course, with the war on, he's needed more than ever, alas.'

'Do you think that might have happened to Billy?'

'I think it could have done, or it might be that he was just born brilliant. Some people are, lucky devils.'

As they cycled home in the bitter cold, keeping up a good pace, since it really was too cold to hold any sensible sort of conversation, Marjorie thought about the evening.

On the one hand she knew she had spent most

of the evening feeling oddly inadequate, yet now she felt more alive than she remembered feeling for a long time, and not just because the icy wind was stinging her eyes and freezing the tiny areas of cheek still exposed above the scarf in which she had muffled her face. She thought perhaps the reason why she felt different was because an older man had not only wanted to take her out, but ended up talking to her quite simply as a friend.

In fact that was the last really cogent thought Marjorie had for the time being, for the next moment she found herself flat on her back on the heavily iced gravel driveway, having lost control of her bike as they turned into the entrance. In a moment Anthony was on his knees, his own bike discarded to lie on its side with the front wheel still spinning as he attended to his fallen companion.

'Marjorie?' He leaned over her, his expression a great deal more anxious than Marjorie could ever remember before, his breath hanging on the frozen air. 'Are you all right? That was an *awful* fall. I do hope you haven't hurt yourself—not broken anything?'

Marjorie tried to sit up, shaking her head slowly. She had given it quite a bang when she had fallen off.

'No, I'm fine, thank you, Anthony. At least I think so. Except I believe I might have hurt my wrist.' She felt her right wrist gingerly, noting an apparent sprain.

Anthony, still kneeling beside her, took her injured wrist in his hands and carefully felt for broken bones.

'I don't think there's anything broken. I think you might have sprained it—or at best given it a nasty twist.'

'I've scraped my knees, though.' Marjorie laughed, looking down at the damage. 'I don't know why I'm laughing—these were not only my best stockings, they were my very last pair. I took the corner too fast. It was entirely my fault.'

'It doesn't really matter whose fault it was.' Anthony eased her gently up to her feet. 'A nasty fall is a nasty fall. Now, do you think you can make it up the drive? Or shall I put you on my bike, and give you a push?'

Marjorie laughed again and brushed some snow off her coat in order to try to cover the embarrassment she was feeling.

'I'm fine, honestly. I just think I'll walk for a while rather than ride. Until I stop seeing stars.'

Anthony smiled back at her and together they walked slowly up the long driveway, pushing their bicycles. The wind seemed to have dropped now; it was certainly less cutting than when they had been cycling, and the parkland glimmered and glinted with frozen snow under a big pale full moon. The lakes were completely frozen over, and the great trees were still laden with heavy drapes of snow. Above them, high in the dark sky hung the real stars, millions of miles away in a heaven where there was no war raging, no death and famine, no murder and massacre—or at least none of which they knew—while underneath, shadowed in the nightlight, the outline of the great house stood in fine silhouette. There wasn't a sound to be heard, other than the faint hooting of a hunting owl somewhere in the nearby darkened woods.

'No wonder you all called it Eden,' Marjorie sighed as she took in the beautiful landscape, and she turned to Anthony, but when she saw the look in his eyes she quickly turned back to the landscape once more.

Chapter Three

'What on earth's the *matter* with you?' Marjorie snapped as Kate dropped and broke not her first teacup that morning, but her second.

'I'm sorry,' Kate replied, almost as grumpily. 'I didn't do it on purpose.'

'Of course you didn't.'

'I seem to have developed butter fingers,' Kate replied sorrowfully, bending down to clear away the debris.

'You seem to have developed an inability to concentrate,' Marjorie retorted, moving Kate out of her way as she set to with a dustpan and brush. 'Not just here, either. It seems to be affecting your work as well.'

'What does?' Kate sat back on her haunches and stared angrily at her friend. *'What does?'*

Marjorie simply looked up from her brushing, shook her head at Kate and then continued clearing up. Kate, about to pursue the matter, thought better of it. Instead of involving the two of them in an argument she took a deep breath, got to her feet, threw aside the cloth she had been using to wipe up the spill and walked off into the yard outside the cottage.

Very well, teacups mattered, because nowadays they were almost irreplaceable, but Kate knew that what Marjorie was actually referring to was not her clumsiness in the cottage, but her seemingly incurable moodiness both at work and at home. At first she had thought it was simply not knowing where Eugene was that upset her, but now whenever Eugene vanished, usually without a word of warning, with no time to say goodbye, the pit fell out of her stomach and she realised she went into what she could only describe as a state of mourning; as if she had already lost the man she loved. It became a question not of waiting for news of his return, but of waiting for the news of his non-return—to be taken aside by Cissie Lavington, or Anthony Folkestone, and gently but officially told of his loss.

Every night she lost Eugene. Every night he fell victim to treachery and death, so that she began to dread going to bed and would stay up reading anything and everything in an effort to put off the inevitable. Finally she would stumble to her bed, usually managing to wake poor Marjorie with whom she shared one of the two tiny cottage bedrooms.

Cissie Lavington called her into her office the following morning. After staring fleetingly at Kate's exhausted face, she started to hunt in her bag for a cigarette.

'Don't know whether you realise it, but you've made quite a few bishes lately, and what with one thing and another, and most particularly the way the war is going, we can't be doing with bishes, not at the moment. A bish can cost a life, many lives, and we can't have that. Files left out, mistyped memos, failing to come to work on time—it won't do.'

'I just haven't been sleeping.'

103

Cissie nodded without interest and lit her cigarette, carefully putting it into the end of her cigarette holder and lighting it with the kind of regular, practised motion that a seamstress might use when threading a needle.

'Look, dear. We know what's up. It's not easy, I know, and we don't encourage fraternisation here, because it does so often interfere with work, but we don't mind turning a blind eye to what goes on just so long as it does not lead to mistakes. You have been making too many, so I have to say . . .' She paused, staring at Kate, who found her heart sinking. 'I have to say that either you pull yourself together, or you'll have to buzz off to Baker Street, and you won't want that, not at this time. So if I were you, I'd try to catch up on your kip, and improve your concentration.'

'Yes, Miss Lavington.'

'Good.'

Cissie, cigarette holder now firmly back in her mouth, nodded for Kate to leave, picking up a file as she did so, and starting to read it. Kate remained where she was for a moment, before taking several deep breaths and turning on her heel to go back to her work.

*   *   *

In order to achieve any part of his objective Eugene realised he was going to have to grab the initiative and force the play. Ever since he had taken up residence in his safe house in the tiny village of Escanti, hidden well away in the deep Sicilian countryside over thirty miles from Palermo, he had done nothing except wait and now he was both bored and impatient, a dangerous mix when it came to himself. He tried to control his growing restlessness by journeying daily into the nearby town of Putagia on the back of a hay cart to service and repair broken down and near clapped out farm machinery, as well as one or two of the very few private cars still running on the island. But since most of the machinery brought to him was beyond repair, owing to either age and infirmity or the non-existence of any spare parts, most days Eugene sat cleaning spark plugs or rebuilding primitive starting motors that he had cleaned or rebuilt the day before.

'Patience,' his friend and saviour Gianni kept advising him, every time he saw signs of increasing tension and irritation in the Irishman. 'Things move more slowly here—we set our daily music to a slower beat, yes? If you start to move faster than the beat, they notice you.'

The island, while hardly crowded out with Germans, boasted a much larger alien population now that the Italian Marchettis had been joined by a large force of Junkers, Ju 87 and 88 bombers, so that as the remorseless build-up to the attack on Malta continued Eugene knew time was of the essence.

The stumbling block had been his initial betrayal. Whoever had informed on him would seem to have ruined his chances both of sabotaging the bombers and of escape.

'Look, Gianni,' Eugene said one evening when the two men had shut themselves in the hayloft of the barn outside the safe house. 'We will have to make some sort of contingency plan if I'm not to remain a mechanic all my life.'

Gianni glanced at Eugene briefly, shrugged his shoulders, and went back to manufacturing a hand-rolled cigarette.

'We know where the airfield is, how many aircraft there are, what sort of fences they have—how many guards.'

Gianni shrugged again. 'And there are two of us, my friend. With three guns, one grenade and two rosaries.'

'Is there no one else we can trust?'

'I can organise three others. But five cannot take on fifty-five or sixty-five Germans.' Gianni paused briefly to spit contemptuously on the floor to show precisely what he thought of those Italians who had thrown in their lot with Hitler. 'We have as much chance of getting you inside there as—as I have of becoming *il Papa*.' This time Gianni paused to cross himself before sticking the drooping cigarette into his mouth under his equally drooping moustache and, finally, lighting it.

'Then we have to think of some sort of alternative plan,' Eugene muttered. 'Apparently we have two days at most before their first trip to Malta, so I have to get into those hangars somehow—even if I only manage to take out a couple of their damn' bombers.'

'They will have little trouble in taking you out, my friend,' Gianni observed. 'Before you even manage to let down one airplane tyre. Would it not be possible to waste your life a little more profitably?'

Eugene gave Gianni his best mock glare, drank deep from a bottle of rough red wine, tore off a hunk of staling bread to eat with his cheese and sat down on a hay bale to try to think out some sort of strategy.

For once his imagination quite failed him, and had not luck decided to take a hand Eugene's destiny might well have been sealed before he had even been given a chance to strike a blow. His fate arrived in the shape first of a superbly elegant, but obviously sick, dark blue Bugatti which spluttered its way into the centre of Putagia's town square, and second in the even more elegant shape that decanted itself slowly and sinuously from the red leathered interior of the car.

Eugene saw her long before she saw him, unremarkable given the fact that he was working in the dark of the tiny garage where he was employed, and she was standing in broad daylight in the town square. But even if Eugene had been standing outside his place of work it would have been doubtful if the tall, beautiful, slim woman wrapped in fox furs would have paid the slightest attention to a dirty-faced mechanic in oil-covered overalls. Yet the moment he saw the woman, despite her suspiciously over-glamorous appearance, he knew somehow his chance had arrived.

This belief was confirmed when he picked up on the conversation she began to have with two men sitting on the edge of the broken water fountain that stood in the centre of the square. It seemed she was furious that her car had broken down at this particular moment since she was expected at the aerodrome. Since the aerodrome to which she referred was the place where the German bombers were gathered for the planned air raids on Malta, Eugene sensed this might well turn into not only a golden opportunity of gaining access to the heavily guarded airfield, but perhaps his only one.

First he must make sure their glamorous visitor was directed to the garage where he was working. Despite the fact that times were hard and the region a poor one, such was the Italian obsession with cars that there was another mechanic working in the town whose reputation was considerably higher than that of the owner of the tiny workshop in which Eugene was now busy cleaning himself up, which was why Gianni had already been despatched, cap in hand, to enquire if there was anything they could do for the poor signorina.

'You?' Gianni had wondered, almost swallowing the remains of his cigarette. 'You cannot even mend a bicycle's puncture!'

'You'd be surprised what I can do, Gianni,' Eugene assured him, desperately scrubbing at his oil-stained face and hands with a sliver of soap that felt more like sandpaper. 'My uncle had a motor car of precisely that make, believe it or not. The only Bugatti in Ireland, they said, and since that was the case there was no one to fix it when it went *phut*—which it did more often than it did not. So by sticking around the old boy—because I was dying to drive the bucket, you see—you'd be amazed and astonished at what I picked up, me boy. And even if I can't fix her motor, I shall blind the signorina with an extravagance of mechanical knowledge, most of which will be entirely fictitious.'

Minutes later Gianni was signalling Eugene urgently to come and join the two of them in the square, the signorina now perched on one highly polished mudguard carefully smoking a cigarette, the top half of her face veiled against too much uninvited inspection.

'Good day.' Eugene introduced himself in his

108

carefully rural Italian. 'Ah—and what a beautiful car! This is the very car my dear uncle drives—and oh how he loves her! He loves her like a *mistress*.'

He paid no attention to the beautiful woman, devoting his consideration to the car from under whose bonnet a steady stream of steam was still escaping. Remembering how the bonnet opened, he released the catch and gained careful access to the engine bay.

'*Mamma* . . .' he whispered in distress, putting one hand to his cheek in anguish. '*Mamma mia*— please don't let it be the gasket—please?'

With a sad shake of his handsome head, he leaned into the engine bay, cloth in hand, and began carefully to unscrew the radiator cap. As he did so, a further jet of steam escaped with a hiss from the radiator, prompting Eugene to warn everyone to stand well back in case of accident. Finally, with a dramatic flourish he released the cap fully and jumped well back himself as a geyser of scalding steam shot upwards from the water sump.

'*Mah!*' he exclaimed. 'You are very lucky, signorina, so very lucky she did not explode with you up there in the mountains!'

Of course he had been only too aware of a pair of dark eyes watching him intently from behind the half veil, but it was only now that he looked into them with his own, as he gave a remorseful shake of his head.

'The thought of you stranded up there is too sad to contemplate, signorina,' he said. 'The wolves. The bandits.'

'Why do you think I come across the mountains?' the woman asked brusquely. 'Do I *look* like a woman from the hills?'

'No—no!' Eugene protested. 'It is just that I cannot imagine there is anyone so—so beautiful in these parts, yes? So you must come from far away—the mainland even—and to do so you must come over the mountains! Yes?'

The woman pursed her lips thoughtfully as she considered the compliment, then nodded once.

'Naples,' she said, searching her bag for another cigarette, immediately prompting a crowd of matches proffered by practically every man in the small crowd that had gathered since her abrupt arrival. 'So now you stop your sweet talk, signor—'

'Marco,' Eugene said with a small modest bow of his head. 'Marco, please—Marco.'

'Very well, Marco. So—enough of your charms, and tell me if you can attend to my car. I have to get out to the areodrome by this evening. It is most urgent, and I will need the car. It is not my car, you understand. The car is a loan.'

Eugene held his hands up in an open gesture, accompanying the signal with a non-committal shrug.

'Signorina. Should she have bad gasket—should she have blown her head gasket.' He shrugged again and raised his eyebrows helplessly. 'No one will repair her in less than two days. Even if we have the parts. And we do not have the parts, as you must know, signorina! Such a thing would have to come from the mainland—and in these days?'

Eugene made his mouth into a large round O of despair and closed his eyes.

'You are not from around here, are you?' the woman suddenly asked him, standing a little back and putting her head to one side. 'So where are you from, please? You are certainly not Sicilian.' She made an odd gesture with one hand, closing her first two fingers on to her thumb and squeezing them together in some sort of special emphasis.

'I am half Milanese, signorina,' he confessed. 'But my mother was widowed and came to live on the mainland, when I was a young boy, near to Vico Equense—Amalfi.'

'Ah!' she replied, holding up one slender gloved hand. 'I thought I knew it! I said to myself—Lucia, I said. This is an Amalfi man! I knew it.'

'Yes.' Eugene smiled modestly. 'Yes, you are right—and so clever, signorina. I come to see my cousin Gianni here because he has not been so well. And because he is not so well, I stay here to help him with his work. Here in his uncle's garage.'

'So what to do with the car, Marco? When shall I know my fate, please? The person who lends it to me, he will want it returned.'

'Signorina, if I may—if we take your beautiful car into our workshop I can tell you—what? An hour? Maybe less. For you I do it as quick as God permits me.'

Once she had agreed, Eugene instructed Gianni to escort their visitor to the small café in the tiny town where he assured her that after Gianni's aunt had cooked her a most memorable *lasagne* he would be able to tell her the fate of her car.

He knew there were two possible options open to him. If there was nothing seriously wrong with the car then he could use it as his Trojan horse, smuggling himself and Gianni into the compound containing the Junkers bombers. If on the other hand there was something seriously amiss, their visitor might decide to abort her trip to the

111

aerodrome for lack of reliable transport, in which case his only chance lay in procuring a decent substitute vehicle that would satisfy the high standards obviously held by the beautiful signorina, who from her glamorous clothing he guessed was probably on her way to a tryst with a lover. It would be ideal, if this was indeed the case, for having come all this way their visitor would surely be loath to miss out on her lovemaking.

'So?' Gianni wondered, popping back from his aunt's café in order to see how events were shaping. 'How is the car?'

'Sick. It's done a head gasket.'

Gianni arched his eyebrows and widened his big brown eyes. 'A head gasket? Hey, my friend, you really do know about Bugattis!'

'I know nothing about Bugattis—but I know a thing or two about gaskets,' Eugene sighed. 'And this is one very sick motor. There's oil in the radiator water—and in case you don't know what that means, it means kaput. It has to be the head gasket, but even if we had a gasket kit I wouldn't know the first thing about how to fix it. Would you?'

'Do farm carts have gaskets? No,' he replied. 'So what are we going to do?'

'We're going to patch and pray. If my memory serves me right, I seem to remember my uncle having this sort of difficulty once when we were out on a jaunt. All he did was simply drain the radiator, change the oil and get going again—until the car began to boil, when he repeated the entire procedure. So that's all we can hope to do—change the oil and water, and keep our fingers crossed the motor holds out for as long as we need it to hold out.'

Gianni smiled as he watched Eugene go to work.

'Ah yes, motor cars—they are like beautiful women, no? They need the understanding of a man. Yes? They need the understanding and the touch of a man.'

'What this beautiful woman needs isn't a man but a car to get her to her man,' Eugene replied, getting underneath the car to find the sump plug. 'To judge from all her finery she's on her way to meet someone—someone out at the aerodrome apparently. Which will suit us just nicely.'

'You think she's going to meet her lover at the aerodrome, eh?'

From under the bonnet Eugene laughed quietly. 'If she's not, my friend, then I'm not an Irishman.'

'Then let us hope that the man who lent her this car doesn't find out,' Gianni said lugubriously, prompting Eugene to squint back up at him from ground level. 'I tell you where this car comes from. Il Padrone. This is il Padrone's—and so he lent it to her as a favour.'

'But not to go and meet her lover, you reckon?'

'No, no. I would very much doubt that.'

'This woman is known to il Padrone?' Eugene wondered. 'How so?'

'Perhaps she is not known personally, Marco. Perhaps it is just that her reputation precedes her.'

'Her reputation?'

'She is here—how we say? She is here on *business*.'

Eugene glanced at Gianni then returned his attention to the sump plug.

'OK,' he called up from the ground. 'I know this is Italy—or Sicily rather—and you do things

113

differently here—but how come a woman on the sort of business this young woman is on gets loaned a Bugatti by your Padrone?'

Having freed the plug and allowed the engine oil to drain away into the bucket he had placed ready, Eugene emerged from under the car and stood wiping his hands on a rag and staring at the café where they had deposited their guest.

'You mean to tell me il Padrone was so taken with our signorina's business acumen that he loaned her his best motor car to go gallivanting in? I doubt it, my friend.'

'Then perhaps we ask her, yes?'

'Perhaps we do just that. And maybe as a result we get to be done a favour.'

'I wouldn't say no to such a favour,' Gianni grinned happily.

'Not that sort of favour, pal. A favour in the shape of a lift,' Eugene replied, tightening the buckle on the belt of his trousers. 'Come on.'

The two men joined Lucia at her table in the café. Gianni's aunt brought them a bottle of local red wine, three glasses carried in the hook of three stubby fingers, a plate of shining olives and a hunk of goat's cheese then left them alone, disappearing back into the kitchen to continue cooking. Lucia regarded her two companions, folded her veil back over the front of her peacock blue hat, lit a cigarette and sat back on her chair, eyeing them both.

'You mend my car?' she wondered.

'Your car will be up and running in half an hour, signorina.'

'Lucia. You may call me Lucia.' She smiled. 'I shall be most grateful to you if you mend my car.'

114

'Your car?' Eugene wondered. 'You brought it over with you from Naples?'

Lucia's smile turned to frost.

'That is none of your concern,' she snapped. 'The car belongs to a friend of mine.'

'I wonder, does this friend know where you are? And what you're doing?' Eugene continued, pouring himself some wine.

Lucia stared at him, smoking her cigarette quickly and furiously.

'Maybe I haven't fixed your car at all,' Eugene said with a sigh. 'Maybe I was just kidding you.'

'You know something, signor?' Lucia said, all but spitting the words out. 'I was just beginning to like you.'

'I'll be perfectly frank with you, Lucia,' Eugene helped them all to some more of the local wine. 'You have an appointment you need to keep—and so do we. You can help us keep ours, just as we can help you keep yours. But if you don't help us—'

'Yes, yes! OK! All right!' Lucia ground her cigarette out on the floor under one high-heeled shoe and regarded Eugene with a pair of dark flashing eyes. 'So what do you want, eh? Just tell me what you want and I see what Lucia can do!'

'We need a lift—simple as that.'

'Where?'

'Same place as you. The aerodrome.'

Lucia frowned and then shrugged as she considered the favour. 'Why?'

'That's our business. Same as your business will remain your business as long as you give us a lift.'

'So. So I give you a lift as far as the aerodrome—and then what?'

'No, not as far *as* the aerodrome, Lucia. We want

115

you to take us in with you. We want to go *into* the aerodrome.'

Now the expression on Lucia's face changed. 'You are surely *mad*.'

'We'll be surely mad if we don't get into the aerodrome, sweetheart. As mad as il Padrone when he finds out what you're using his precious car for.'

'How *did* you manage to get his car, by the by, signorina?' Gianni wondered, having finished picking his teeth with a match.

'None of your business!'

'We'll ask him when we see him, Gianni,' Eugene assured his friend.

'I tell him I have to visit a sick relative!' Lucia exclaimed. 'OK? OK!'

'So?' Eugene enquired after a moment. 'Are you going to give us a lift or not?'

Lucia said nothing at first. Instead she glanced out of the windows and up at the dark forests surrounding the little town.

'OK,' she said, all but inaudibly. 'I give you a lift.'

'I knew you were on the side of the angels, sweetheart,' Eugene said with a smile. 'I could see it in your eyes. Now if you'll excuse me, I'll go and attend to your car.'

*　　　*　　　*

Poppy had long ago sold the ring that Basil had given her on their engagement, sending the money to much needed war funds. In its place she now proudly wore the much less ostentatious ring that Scott had given her, a ring that it seemed had once graced his grandmother's finger.

'What about a dress?'

Kate and Marjorie both looked up at Poppy who was looking down at them from their cottage stairs where she was sitting, while the three of them debated the wartime problem of how to be married by special licence in a matter of days.

'I could wear my blue velvet,' Poppy suggested.

'It's not a wedding dress,' Kate replied. 'You can't get married in blue velvet.'

'I'm certainly not wearing anything from my old wardrobe,' Poppy said. 'Imagine getting married in something Basil had given me. That would be too gruesome for words.'

'Nobody's suggesting that,' Marjorie told her.

Poppy nodded and tried to put all thoughts of her last wedding day out of her head—the quite beautiful dress she had worn, the borrowed tiara— and then the sensational dress she had worn for the first night of her honeymoon, which Basil had so detested and derided—although perhaps not quite as much as he had finally detested and derided her.

She shook her head as if to shake away the unhappy memories, trying to think of the happiness that she hoped lay ahead in her future with Scott. He was so different from the cold-hearted Basil— warm, funny and affectionate—so different. She sighed inwardly.

'Come on, Poppy,' Kate sighed. 'You're daydreaming again. We have to get things organised. We are not going to have some dreary wedding just because there's a war on. Hitler can go hang! We are going to make sure this is a wedding to remember—in spite of Hitler and in spite of the war. But we're not going to do it by daydreaming. So come on, one and all! Snap out of it! Now, for a start, we have to find a dress for Poppy somewhere. Somehow. Anyone got any bright ideas?'

Marjorie frowned but could come up with nothing. Poppy reminded Kate of something she had said before, leaving Kate to come up with an idea that might prove useful.

'There are some old clothes stored in our attic at home,' she said, remembering. 'Don't know what's there—or in fact if anything's still there, seeing how much my mother keeps giving to Lady Alton for the Fighting Fund. I'll have a look as soon as I get home. I seem to remember she'd kept some of Grandmother's old stuff. Keep your fingers crossed. And don't worry, Poppy—we're going to make Scott's and your wedding a day you'll always remember. War or no war.'

*   *   *

Two kilometres short of the aerodrome Lucia, who had been driving, stopped the car in order to get out and check the well-being of the two men hidden away in the boot. She had pulled the Bugatti into a clearing off the road, well protected from the view of anyone else passing by so that Eugene and Gianni could get out and stretch their legs. They started to go through what was going to happen if and when they got past the guards on the gates, what Lucia was to say and do and where she was to leave the car. If all went well, by the time she left the next morning the two men would be hidden in the boot again and Lucia would leave as seamlessly as she had arrived.

'How is the car behaving?' Eugene enquired at

one point. 'Seems to be holding up all right.'

'She is a little hot,' Lucia replied. 'As if she might want a drink.'

Eugene had taken care of that well in advance, packing two cans of water along with him in the boot of the Bugatti. Taking advantage of the halt he carefully topped the depleted radiator up, mentally crossing his fingers even harder than before when he had finished doing so.

On the road once more, within a matter of minutes they were at the gate of the aerodrome. The two men in the boot held their breath as they heard the guards questioning Lucia, only to relax as they realised that all the questions being asked in true Italian style concerned not the purpose of Lucia's visit, but the magnificence and beauty of her motor car. They could hear Lucia lying gaily about how she had come by such a fine and rare model, the gift of some rich Neapolitan benefactor it would seem who had befriended her since she lost both her parents in some terrible boating accident off Ischia. Lucia's imagination matched her looks, priceless and extraordinary, and after a few minutes of talk the Bugatti slowly moved forward again, the stowaways undiscovered.

As directed, Lucia parked the car, got out and released the boot catch. The two men waited until Lucia had been gone for a quarter of an hour, then slowly eased open the lid. They found she had parked around the corner from the building into which they assumed she had disappeared, with the rear end of the great Bugatti practically touching a brick wall that ran at right angles to another wall, thus providing perfect cover for them as they eased themselves out of the car.

Very few lights burned on the airfield now that it was dark, and as for patrols, there appeared to be none. Nevertheless, Eugene and Gianni held back until they were absolutely sure there were no sentries posted anywhere within their immediate vicinity, before following a route away from the building, and along the perimeter wall that ran directly towards the huge hangars. Eugene had imagined that there would be a certain number of armed guards posted at all the salient points in such a volatile location, but the further they penetrated enemy territory, the more they became aware that the security seemed to be confined to the gated areas only.

'This is typical,' Gianni whispered, as the two of them huddled tight in a corner, watching and listening out for the slightest movement. 'We suffer as a race from a frightening degree of confidence. It is our worst fault and our greatest asset.'

He stopped as they suddenly heard footsteps, followed by a strong smell of tobacco that suggested the presence of ordinary personnel rather than an armed guard. But it seemed they were wrong, for round the end of the wall, not ten feet from them, appeared a short, stubby soldier, his rifle slung over his shoulder, his hat pushed back and a freshly lit cigarette in his mouth. Eugene looked at Gianni and Gianni nodded. Two seconds after the guard had crossed their path he was lying dead at Eugene's feet.

They dragged the body into a nearby dark corner where they stripped it of its uniform and weapons and left it under a pile of sacking. Moments later Gianni was dressed as the guard and making his way towards the aircraft hangars.

Eugene hung behind, crossing his fingers and praying for the doors to be open.

In the weak moonlight he could still make Gianni out as he patrolled the corner of the hangar, before he disappeared out of sight round the front of the huge building. He was gone it seemed for an eternity, long enough for Eugene to reckon he had lost him and he was going to have to either go it alone, or cut and run. But as suddenly as he had disappeared Gianni reappeared, gun slung over one shoulder while with his other arm he beckoned for Eugene to join him.

Swiftly and silently Eugene ran to him, keeping tight up against the towering black wall of the hangar beside him. When he looked carefully round the edge of the open door into the dimly lit building he saw a large array of unguarded Junkers.

'You mean they've left them here for the taking?' he finally hissed at Gianni as they stood with their backs against the outside of the door. 'Without guards? No patrols anywhere?'

'Unless they are hiding to surprise us, no,' Gianni whispered back. 'They are doubtless somewhere playing cards. Somewhere nice and warm.'

Eugene stood quite still for a moment before deciding to risk running round the edge of the hangar door, his pistol in his hand in case he came face to face with an unseen guard. Happily their first impression was right. There was no one guarding the aircraft.

'I think we must just look for the odd sentry— like the one we just waylaid,' Gianni whispered. 'I keep watch at the doors, yes? And you go about the business.'

Eugene nodded, never taking his eyes off the huge bombers that towered over him. In his knapsack he had wire cutters, pliers, razor-edged knives and several small bottles of a concoction specially brewed by some back-room boys which had been designed to work as what they called a *slow-stopper*, in other words an additive that when poured into aircraft fuel did not incapacitate the plane immediately but took effect after about twenty minutes' flying. It had been tested in action already, with highly satisfactory results. At least that was what he had been told. Planes simply dropped out of the sky once the additive became active, the engines stalled so suddenly that emergency control became impossible.

He set to work at once, scaling the ladders left conveniently propped up against three bombers' engines, finding the fuel lines, which he then expertly perforated with an instrument like a small sharpened screwdriver so that the fuel would slowly leak as pressure built up after ignition, and slightly loosening small sets of nuts which were guaranteed to work fully loose under subsequent engine vibration. Having sabotaged four Junkers this method, he then set to work on two Marchettis belonging to the Regia Aeronautica, finding the fillers to their fuel tanks and dosing the contents liberally with the contents of two of his little bottles of lethal additive. In the cockpits of four other planes, two German and two Italian, he hid small but powerful magnets, designed to cause chaos to the bombers' instrumentation and navigational aids, and finally he shaved the rudder wires of two more Junkers so that, he hoped, they would snap under operational pressure long before they

122

reached Malta. All in all he managed to work on a dozen planes without interruption, although he rarely took an eye off the doorway in front of him for longer than a minute at once.

As he worked he saw Gianni half a dozen times as he patrolled what he hoped and imagined was the dead guard's beat. But just as Eugene was about to finish his work on his twelfth plane, Gianni went missing. At once Eugene abandoned the aircraft, slipping down the ladder by holding both sides of the steps, then running silently to the cover of the hangar doors. He strained to hear footsteps but could hear nothing, until just as he was about to ease himself back outside something —or somebody—fell against the door. Eugene froze, certain it was Gianni. He pulled his pistol out of the belt of his trousers as quietly as possible and slipped off the safety catch, a noise that to him seemed to echo round the entire airfield.

Just outside the door he heard someone moving, as if dragging himself along the ground with great difficulty. The next moment he was staring into the dead eyes of an enemy soldier, held up from behind by the small but immensely muscular Gianni. A knife was stuck in the side of his neck, exactly on the point of his jugular vein, and the gory results of Gianni's murderous action could be seen on both the victim and the assassin.

'Apologies,' Gianni whispered. 'I was about to hit him from behind but he must have sensed me. So I had to kill him as he turn.'

He made two clicking sounds of regret with his tongue before dragging the body over to the far corner, where Eugene covered the corpse with a heavy canvas sheet that was lying spare.

123

'The blood.' Eugene nodded. 'They're going to pick up on that blood sure as Italian hens lay eggs—and if they do before we're out of here—'

'Sand,' Gianni announced. 'It soaks up oil—so it soak up blood too, I think.'

He ran back into the building, to where there were several bags of building materials possibly left over from the construction of the hangars. The one nearest them was a half-finished bag of sand, the contents of which he proceeded to spill over the trail of blood between the door and the corpse. After this they made their way silently back to the Bugatti. The whole operation from the moment Lucia had parked the car until their return had taken just over three hours, which put the time at a little after half past one.

'The man you just killed,' Eugene whispered as they crouched down by the car. 'He'd have been the guard taking over, wouldn't you say?'

'You are right, my friend. I see him come out of a building—the guardhouse maybe, who knows? There is a sound of laughter and shouts, yes? So I imagine this was where they all are.'

'So he comes out expecting to find the first guard we killed, but he sees you instead.'

'Which is the last thing he sees, yes,' Gianni agreed.

'We have no idea how long their shifts are.'

'We have a pretty good idea. We start work at about twenty-two thirty hour—the first guard is already on duty when we kill him—the next guard come on three hour after.'

'Good,' Eugene said. 'So the shifts—the patrols if you like—can't be less than three hours. More likely four.'

'More likely four, yes,' Gianni agreed.

'Can we believe they have only posted one guard for the whole airfield?'

Gianni shrugged as he considered the possibility. 'No,' he said. 'No, of course not. But we say perhaps they have maybe four guards, one for each boundary—north, south, east and west. We have taken out the guard for one boundary—this area here.'

'They're going to miss their little chum, aren't they?' Eugene asked after a moment. 'However irregular their timings, aren't they going to notice one's gone missing as they march to and fro? You're a chatty lot, you Italians. I can't imagine they have the sort of discipline the Krauts do—no talking on duty, exact pace and length of goose-step and all that—but I can believe they're going to miss their little fat friend. They're also going to miss guard number one—in fact why haven't they missed him already?'

Gianni shrugged again. 'Who knows? Perhaps they think he go straight to bed. But they haven't come looking yet.'

Eugene stared round the darkened airfield, no longer illuminated by the light of a moon. They had to decide on a new course of action. With two guards down the chances of their being discovered were now considerably more than doubled. They would be quadrupled if they stuck to their somewhat ill-considered plan of tucking themselves back into the boot of the Bugatti to wait for the return of their driver, which was why Eugene knew they had to take their leave of the party there and then.

'But what of poor Lucia?' Gianni whispered as

they crept along the line of the wall that finally became a closely meshed wire fence. 'She will be all alone, yes?'

'She won't know that until she stops somewhere,' Eugene replied. 'And with a bit of luck—if we get out of here and get on the right road . . .'

He stopped to regard the fencing. It was a good ten to twelve feet in height with a line of barbed wire topping it off. The mesh was far too tough to be cut by any of the small tools Eugene was carrying.

'This fence runs all the way round?'

'That is so, my friend. All the way round at this height.'

'Then this is the way we escape.'

'How? We never get up that height? We sure as eggs don't get over the barbed wire.'

'They're going to think we did.'

A moment later Eugene had hoisted Gianni on to his shoulders, having handed him his sweater and instructed him to take off his own jacket. These Gianni then draped over the wire, so that to all intents and purposes it looked as though whoever had broken into the compound had escaped by somehow straddling the wire. They also rolled a half-full oil drum from the side of the nearest hangar and left it directly below the point of the wire on which they had draped the two garments.

'You sure we don't make it out like this anyway?' Gianni wondered as Eugene surveyed their work.

'One of us might,' Eugene replied. 'I flip you over—no problem. But then how do I get out? Or vice versa? We'd have to give each other a leg-up.'

'You go. I stay.'

126

'And my mother was Joan of Arc. No, we're both going to get out—and we're going to get out exactly the way we came in.'

They had left the lid of the Bugatti's boot slightly open in order to minimise the noise they made on their arrival, but they had shut themselves securely away again long before a squad of soldiers was despatched from the barracks to go to look for trouble, their officer possibly having noticed the absence of two perimeter guards. Eugene and Gianni heard them alongside the Bugatti, shouting excitedly. A moment later they felt the car rock as the doors were wrenched open and a terrible feeling of despair and disappointment washed over Eugene as he realised they were about to be discovered. Gianni had obviously come to the same conclusion. Eugene could feel his body tensing against his own, just as they both became aware of the footsteps coming round the back of the automobile. A second later someone tried to open the boot, but without any success.

'What happen?' Gianni whispered after the noise had stopped. 'Why it not open?'

'Search me,' Eugene hissed back. 'Maybe the boot is self-locking. Maybe it's just stuck. I don't know!'

They heard the footsteps recede, and not another sound was heard from the squad for the rest of the night. Praying that the soldiers were satisfied that their quarry had escaped over the wire, Eugene and Gianni managed to fall asleep, before being awakened by the sound of someone getting into the driver's seat and starting the car.

At once both men were awake, pistols drawn, safety catches off. The Bugatti drove off, slowly and smoothly as if the driver had not a problem in the world, heading, the prisoners in the boot hoped, for the main gates. Sure enough, a minute or so later the car slowed to a stop and there was a muttered conversation, which ended at last with a most joyous sound—Lucia's laugh. The car started to move forward once again, heading, they both devoutly hoped, for the open road, the countryside—and freedom.

Once she had put a considerable distance between herself and the aerodrome, Lucia pulled the now sputtering car off the road, obviously finding a lay-by out of sight of anyone passing by before she turned off the engine and alighted from the vehicle. The next minute the lid of the boot had sprung open and the two men found themselves staring up at Lucia's beautiful albeit somewhat exhausted face.

'How did you do that, Lucia?' Eugene wondered as he began to scramble out. 'The wretched thing was jammed tight shut back there.'

'Yes!' Gianni exclaimed, following his companion out. 'How you manage to open it so easy?'

'Thank Signor Bugatti's great imagination.' Lucia shrugged. 'The boot is opened by a lever in the door pillar—see?'

She took them round and showed them the security device that allowed access.

'I notice it when I first get in the car,' Lucia explained. 'I thought you boys must know all about it, seeing how much you know about cars.'

Eugene grinned as he stretched his stiff body.

'Signor Bugatti sure as hell saved our hides,' he said. 'But I don't think we quite have the time to let our hair down yet,' he added, seeing the slow smile that was creeping across her face. 'Any celebrations will have to wait until we are, as they say at the racetrack, home and hosed.'

Eugene knew it was essential that they manage to get both themselves and the Bugatti back to Putagia well in advance of any alarms being sounded at the airfield. He doubted anyone would suspect sabotage, hoping that seeing the evidence of their escape over the fencing everyone in the compound would believe that they had averted a bungled attempt to blow it up. For the present he and Gianni must get the car back to il Padrone, help Lucia get back to the mainland, and whisk themselves off the island as fast as whatever transport had been assigned to them could allow.

'We have to move,' he said. 'And now.'

'But what about the car?' Lucia interrupted. 'She is making these terrible noises again—and she lose power all the way for the last five or six kilometres.'

'She just needs another little drink,' Eugene lied, fetching the second can from the boot. 'These cars use a lot of water. I probably didn't put enough in the radiator when I drained it originally.'

Refilling it for the second time, Eugene didn't bother crossing his fingers. This time he relied on prayer. He hoped and prayed with all his might that Signor Bugatti's beautiful motor car would somehow last out the final leg of this all-important journey.

*　　　*　　　*

Helen was more interested in the boxes of old photographs she unearthed in the attic than the trunks full of old clothes Kate was sorting through.

'*Bognor beach, 1932*,' she said as if surprised. 'Would you look at me in this. And look—here's old Birdy Gardiner. Do you remember Birdy, Kate? Who always used to look after us when we went down there for the summer?'

'Of course I do, Mum—and none of these dresses are any good. They're all old cocktail frocks.'

'Try that trunk at the end, dear. I think that's the one with your grandmother's stuff in it. And do look—here's Geoffrey Partridge—he was a terrible old fussbudget. I wonder whatever happened to him?'

'Why did we always go to Bognor, Mummy? We seemed to spend every summer holiday there,' Kate wondered as she undid an old dust-covered steamer trunk.

'It was all to do with your father's work. There was some arrangement or other with the university. It worked out very well because you and Robert always had someone to play with, and the grown-ups always had someone to drink with, as your father used to say. Oh, my heavens, will you just look at that ghastly hat? How *could* I have thought that was pretty?'

'Ah—now what is *this*?' Kate wondered, producing a long white dress. 'Oh, now this is absolutely the thing! This is just perfect!'

'Perfect? What for, dear?'

'You haven't listened to anything I've been telling you.' Kate laughed. 'Too busy strolling down Memory Lane. I keep telling you we need a dress for one of the girls at Eden. For Poppy Tetherington, who's getting married on Friday. And I would say this dress is just perfect.'

130

Kate stood and held up the long white dress in front of her to show her mother.

'If you say so, dear,' Helen replied, raising her eyebrows in wonder. 'I can't pretend to be abreast of the fashions nowadays, so if you say that dress will do, far be it from me to disagree.'

'But it's perfect, Mummy! Look! What could be more perfect than what has to be Grandmother's old wedding dress?'

Helen glanced at the beautiful lace-trimmed dress.

'Nothing, darling, I suppose. If only we still had it.'

'If only we had it?' Kate echoed. 'What do you think I'm holding up here?'

'Your grandmother's old tennis dress.'

*   *   *

Kate said nothing to Poppy about the provenance of the beautiful white dress she presented to her with a flourish, holding it over one arm in the manner of the manageress of a bridal department.

'*Et voilà!*' she said with a huge smile. 'Cinderella shall go to the ball after all!'

Poppy stared at it. 'Gosh—that is beautiful, Kate.'

'Glad you like it. Told you I'd find you something. It was my grandmother's.'

Poppy and Marjorie both leaned forward simultaneously to feel the fine old linen, noting the lace at the neck and on the long sleeves, while Billy frowned at it curiously before giving them his opinion.

'A princess could get 'itched in that,' he said.

131

'Hitched, Billy,' Marjorie corrected him. 'And we prefer the term married.'

'Married then.' Billy grinned before breaking into song. *'There was I, waiting at the church . . .'*

'That'll do, thank you, Billy,' Marjorie ordered. 'We don't have the time for musical interludes.'

'Try it on, Poppy,' Katie urged. 'We have to see if it fits.'

'Of course it's going to fit,' Poppy assured her, holding the dress up before her. 'I can tell it's exactly my size. The only thing is—I don't really think I *should* wear white. Do you know what I mean? Because of being married before.'

'I don't think that matters,' Marjorie said, without being at all sure. 'I really don't think that matters at all.'

'Yes,' Billy said with a frown, staring down at the floor. 'Yes, well, even if it did—even if it did matter, *I* still think you should wear it, Poppy.'

'Why's that, Billy?' Katie said carefully, noting his sudden blush.

'Because,' Billy muttered, still looking at the floor. 'Because she'd look smashin'.'

There was a long silence while Marjorie and Kate looked first at Billy, then at Poppy, then back to Billy again.

'Good—well, that settles it then,' Kate said briskly. 'Billy's quite right, Poppy. You have to wear it because you will look smashin' in it. As he says, really smashin'. And what more could anyone want on their wedding day?'

*　　　*　　　*

As he drove down from London to Eden Park that

132

day Scott was in such a state of excitement about his forthcoming marriage that he could hardly think straight, which could well explain his forgetfulness. He had never thought about marriage until he had met Poppy, but her heady mixture of reserve and devil-may-care humour, her ability to let him be himself, and her lack of vanity combined with a ready sense of the ridiculous, had quite bowled him over. And now that this was the day they were finally to be married, every other thought went clean from his happy head.

For Scott was as sure of Poppy's love for him as he was of his love for her, even though they loved each other in quite different ways. Scott loved to adore and spoil Poppy while she preferred to keep just a little bit of distance, as if to make him wonder if he was coming quite up to the mark. Scott loved this. He knew it was a sort of game— some kind of tease—but he found it a brilliant and exciting one, which was the very reason he was so anxious to marry her: so that he could keep trying to please her. The fact that at the last minute Jack Ward had suddenly summoned him to a meeting that had, as far as Scott was concerned, gone on far too long, leaving him only just enough time to make it back to Eden Park, now did not seem to matter in the least, because he was on his way. He was on his way to get married to Poppy, and that was all that mattered. He didn't know how long a honeymoon they would have, nor did he care. That was the nature of the life they all now lived; from one moment to the next. Some people had two hours together before being separated once more, but as far as he knew they would have more than that. They had a whole day and a night at the very least, and perhaps even longer—and what they were granted they would embrace knowing as they did that even an hour together, in war, was a lifetime.

Scott was on his way to marry the beautiful and divine Poppy, and in spite of the snow flurries and the bitter cold he was so happy he sang out loud and very loudly too—but just after he started singing, his car ran out of petrol.

'What can I have been thinking of?' he wondered as he pointlessly tapped and then knocked the empty petrol gauge with one gloved fist. 'Why didn't I check on the *petrol*!'

He got out of the car and stared bleakly at the equally desolate countryside.

'And today of all days! What *can* I have been thinking!'

*   *   *

To everyone's amazement, particularly that of Kate who had found herself largely in sole charge of the wedding arrangements, somehow or other Mrs Alderman had even managed to make a wedding cake for the happy couple.

'Mrs Alderman,' Kate sighed when she saw the large, three-tiered cake sitting in the middle of the kitchen table. 'Given the circumstances that has to be the most amazing cake I have ever seen!'

Mrs Alderman nodded, an expression of justifiable pride on her face. It was. It was truly beautiful. It even had the statutory bride and groom on top of the topmost tier.

'The best I could do in the circumstances, Miss Maddox.'

'The best, Mrs Alderman? You are some sort of genius! How did you manage? Where did you get the ingredients?'

Kate now stood by the table, frowning at the huge white iced cake, at Cook's masterpiece, unable to believe that with the stringency of food rationing she had been able to make and bake such a marvel.

'I couldn't get the ingredients, dear,' Mrs Alderman confessed. 'It's not all cake at all. It's a fake. Here—look. The top lifts off, see?'

In demonstration she lifted up the top of the cake, revealing a small dark brown chocolate cake underneath. 'There's the real cake underneath, see? Proper chocolate cake, using proper chocolate for the icing that is, which isn't breaking the law, I do assure you, Miss Maddox. C Section and H Section, and all the rest of them, they all helped out, donating sugar and stuff so as at least I could manage to bake something, but we could never have done this for real. Not in a month of Sundays. Still, it's not bad for what it is, even though I do say it meself. The clever thing about it is—the real beauty of it is—seeing that chocolate isn't a bridal colour—the beauty of it is the false top. Something young Billy come up with.'

'Oh, yes.' Kate smiled. 'That's Billy. That's Billy all over. And never a word about it.'

'He's quite a lad, young Billy, and a bit of a perfectionist, too, so he is. Wasn't happy till we got the colour right for the icing, and he worked all hours to get the sheen on it—scrounged something from the chemist in the village which he rubbed over the paint to make it look just so—and a dashed fine job he made of it, too, even though I say it meself. It looks just the job, until you get right up close, that is.'

'Put the top back on, Mrs A., before I'm tempted.' Kate laughed. 'I was up so early I'm starving. I've still got a thousand things to do, so I'd better run anyway—got to collect some butterfly cakes for the wedding feast from the estate bakery and then some lettuces from the vicar's wife. Everybody's been quite wonderful. You should see what everyone has donated. Even people who can't come to the wedding have given us things—it's absolutely marvellous.'

The end result, when it was laid out on the large table in the entrance of the Dunne Arms, was certainly marvellous in as much as it was the strangest collection of foodstuffs anyone was likely to see. Plates of sandwiches made from dried eggs, bottles of children's orange juice to go with dusty half-bottles of gin, marble-stoppered flagons of home-made ginger beer, obscure pudding wines, tins of custard, bottles of jam, even priceless boxes of chocolates had been taken out of cupboards and hidey-holes and brought reverently to the reception hall to be placed on the antique lace tablecloth.

'Scott's been held up,' a breathless Miss Budge reported as she hurried downstairs from her office to break the news to the wedding party that was beginning to congregate in the main hall of the house. 'He's only just managed to get to a telephone that's working, and it seems he's run out of petrol.'

'He *what*?' Marjorie echoed in disbelief. 'He's run out of petrol on his *wedding day*?'

'It's a borrowed car, apparently,' Miss Budge continued. 'From the Ministry pool, and the one thing he forgot to check—thinking there'd be a full tank—was the petrol.'

'So where is he now?' Kate wondered, realising Poppy would have to be informed.

'Somewhere the other side of Framlington.'

'But that's over thirty miles away!' Marjorie cried. 'How's he going to get here in time?'

'He's not,' Kate sighed. 'I'd better go and tell Poppy.'

*   *   *

The sky was fast becoming overcast, the weak winter sun disappearing behind a bank of clouds laden with snow.

Wandering disconsolately along what seemed to be a totally deserted road, Scott was just about to give up hope when he heard the backfire of a car in the near distance. Moments later a dark green Ford 8 chugged slowly round the bend and into sight, to be immediately flagged down by Scott.

'Got a problem, chum?' the driver asked out of his half-opened window.

Scott resisted the temptation to reply that actually he only flagged down cars for fun and explained that he had run out of petrol.

'Not a clever thing to do,' the driver replied, with a sage-like shake of his grey head. 'Not seeing what old Mother Nature has in store for us.' He nodded up at the darkening sky, then leaned across to open the passenger door. 'Hop in, chum. I can take you as far as Shamley if that's any good to you.'

Scott hesitated, looking back the way he had come. 'What about my car?'

'If there's no petrol in it, no need to worry.

Gallon of juice is more valuable than a car nowadays.'

Scott climbed in beside the driver. The man was quite right. There was no point in worrying about the car because it wasn't any use to anyone without petrol. And it was now beginning to snow quite heavily. Staying with your sinking ship was one thing, but Scott considered that staying with a War Office motor car in freezing conditions was quite another.

'Sorry I can't take you any further than Shamley,' the driver said as they drove slowly off. 'How far are you going?'

'Eden Park,' Scott replied. 'Other side of Benton.'

'Bit of a hike, eh? Maybe you'll get lucky in Shamley. Never know—maybe you'll get lucky twice.'

Scott got lucky three times, particularly when the two ladies who gave him his last lift found out he was getting married and squandered the last of their month's petrol allowance driving Scott all the way to the Park.

'I can't thank you enough,' he said to the two women as he disembarked.

'Nonsense! It was a pleasure!' the one driving barked. 'Now hurry along with you! She won't wait for ever!'

By now twilight had fallen, as well as a good three inches of snow that had made the last part of the journey slow going. Scott had invited the two intrepid ladies who had given him his last lift to come to the wedding, but they were determined to reach their own destination, which was only a couple of miles back, before they got completely

138

snowed in, so he made his own way as quickly as he could along the snow-covered path that led to the heavily studded oak door of the little church that lay to the east of the main house, fully expecting to find that the wedding party had long since gone home. Instead the door was opened to him by Anthony Folkestone, who was waiting to greet him with the kind of calm smile for which the British military are justifiably famed.

'Well done, Scott,' he said. 'Jolly good show. Given the weather I'd say you've got a jolly lucky thumb.'

'You haven't been waiting in here all the time, I hope?' Scott said cautiously, looking round the little candlelit nave.

'Not a bit of it.' Anthony laughed. 'Chap who gave you your lift to East Wisley telephoned the pub to say you were only an hour away, so we went on to standby immediately. Very decent of him. Seems weddings bring out the romantic in us all. Billy? You'd better go and tell the bride her groom has finally made it.'

'Yes sir!' Billy said in great delight, giving a smart salute in return. 'I'm on my way!'

Five minutes later Poppy duly arrived up the aisle to the strains of the Wedding March played on the church harmonium, wearing a long fur coat over Kate's grandmother's tennis dress, and holding a posy made up of a bunch of paper flowers and a sprig of holly, which had been Mrs Alderman's idea, and one she was almost as proud of as she was of her wedding cake.

The wedding service was followed by the best reception everyone thought they had ever attended. It was certainly the most original, thanks to the inventiveness and generosity of the guests, and the wonderful music supplied by the local brass band and a string quartet from the local music school. The celebration was well fuelled by a seemingly endless supply of assorted liquor that kept materialising from everywhere all evening. It mattered not that the egg sandwiches were made from dried eggs, that what should have been ham was Spam, and that the wedding cake was a fake. All that mattered was what always mattered at happy weddings—that two people so obviously in love were getting happily married surrounded by people they loved who obviously loved them too.

Finally, there being no confetti available, the newly-weds were showered with little white pieces of paper that the ever inventive Billy had collected from the hole-punchers in the Park offices. Everyone cheered the happy couple, wishing them every happiness, not to mention love and joy, all of which was certainly theirs for the first night of their honeymoon—a bliss that lasted until a dawn telephone call informed the bridegroom that he was to leave that morning on his new mission.

'A little peremptory, wouldn't you say?' Poppy wondered as she followed Scott into the kitchen, doing up her dressing gown. 'They could have given you a little longer, surely.'

'There's a war on, Pop,' Scott said with a sigh, making them both some tea. 'We've got to think ourselves lucky we at least had last night together.'

'I shall never forget last night, Scott,' Poppy admitted quietly, putting her arms round him from behind. 'Not ever.'

'Nor me,' Scott replied, turning round to face his young wife. 'And because of that I shall love you for ever too.'

'Do you really have to go?' Poppy sighed. 'I mean right now?'

Her arms were round his neck and the scent of her hair was wonderful, the feel of her skin so soft that for a second he felt dizzy.

'Don't do this to me. You know I have to go. Right now, too.'

'Not five minutes.'

'Not even two, Pop. You know how it is. Orders are orders.'

He smiled at her, kissed her once, then, firmly removing her arms from round his neck, moved one step away from her.

'It only makes it even harder,' he said.

'Nothing's harder than the fact you're going to be away,' Poppy replied. 'Somewhere in Europe, where the women will all be beautiful and all the handsome men away fighting.'

'Don't be silly, Pop. There is no one more beautiful than you. Not anywhere.'

'Then hurry back to me.'

'I'm on my way back already.'

He took her in his arms and kissed her passionately, then left.

*   *   *

Even after his initial briefing, Scott had no idea with whom he was being sent to France. All he had been told so far was that he was being dropped in for what they called a *quickie*—a short but important mission followed hopefully by a quick and equally efficient departure, the purpose of which was to set up a number of locations to be

141

fitted out with radio communication equipment through which could be broadcast information about enemy fortifications along the French sea coast and all relevant troop movements. As he made his way to the car that he had been told would be waiting for him at the foot of the long drive—now clear of snow thanks to the rain that had fallen overnight—all Scott hoped was that the agent with whom he was being dropped into France was up to snuff.

He saw the familiar figure of Jack Ward in the front of the large black Austin, pipe in mouth as usual, gloved hands drumming patiently on the steering wheel as he waited for Scott. There was someone sitting up front beside him, someone whose face he could not as yet make out in the early morning gloom.

'You're Monsieur Doncourt, young man,' Jack said to him as he climbed into the back. 'Here are your papers, and allow me to introduce you to your wife, Madame Doncourt.'

'*Bonjour, Hervé,*' the woman in the passenger seat said in perfect French. '*Ça va?*'

Scott stared at his new 'wife', into the pretty face that was smiling back at him over one shoulder.

'I'm looking forward to this trip,' she continued. 'I hear there are absolutely no food shortages in France—so here's to *la bonne cuisine et le bon vin. N'est-ce pas, cheri?*'

Scott just smiled politely and sat back with a sinking heart as the car moved off. Of all the people to be dropped into France with it couldn't be anyone else. It had to be the flirt of the Park. It had to be Lily blasted Ormerod.

Late one afternoon, the sort of fine March day when Kate could almost feel the buds on the trees getting ready to burst into new life, she took herself off for a brisk walk as soon as she finished her shift, and soon found herself headed for Poppy and Scott's little house in the woods. Poppy had told her that whenever she wanted time to herself, to think or just to relax, she could take herself off there and stay as long as she needed, even if Poppy herself wasn't there.

'I don't know what it is about the place,' Poppy had said. 'But I've found that whenever I get sort of edgy or anxious it takes it all away. It's such a special place—it's quite extraordinary. There's something in the atmosphere there that just seems to unwind one. Takes all one's cares away. It's probably because it's absurdly peaceful, I don't know. It's so quiet there it's like being in a little bit of heaven.'

Kate hadn't really intended to call on Poppy, yet she now found herself being irretrievably drawn to visiting the house. She had no idea whether or not she would find Poppy there; nor was she even certain that it was Poppy she wished to see. Part of her hoped in fact that the house would be empty and she would be able to take a closer look at the enchanting little place. So when there was no answer to her knock, she carefully eased the unlocked front door open and called Poppy's name, in case she might have missed hearing her.

There being no reply from anywhere within the house, Kate stepped into the hall where she stood for a long moment in silence, not looking round her, but just experiencing the sense of extraordinary calm that seemed to prevail. Strangely there was not a sound to be heard anywhere, within or without. Even the birds it seemed had fallen to silence. Inevitably she felt as if she had stepped into an entirely different world, a world that was at peace; where love and goodness reigned instead of murder and mayhem.

After letting the stillness settle around her Kate wandered into the little sitting room. Wherever Poppy was—and whatever the reason for her absence—the place was as immaculate as always, a fire for the evening already set in the hearth, piles of books ready on a table by the sofa, and a vase of freshly picked wild daffodils on top of the upright piano. Even though the fire was as yet unlit, the house was as warm as it might be on a late spring day, rather than a bright and windy March one. With a feeling of sudden contentment, Kate sat on the old but still comfortable sofa that stood to one side of the fireplace, kicked her shoes off and tucking her legs up under her sat staring out of the window opposite.

She knew she must have been asleep because the light had changed. As she last remembered it the sun had been shining straight into the south-facing room. But now it was shining from the southwest, slanting its rays across the floor and leaving Kate in shadow. Yet she had no recollection of even feeling drowsy, let alone falling asleep. She must have dropped off quite suddenly.

Nor could she remember dreaming. In fact as she sat up slowly, staring out through the window and listening to the birdsong that now seemed to fill the woodlands, she tried as hard as she could to

144

recall some sort of image or memory from her sleep, so sure was she that she had in fact dreamed. But none was forthcoming.

Yet she was certain that Eugene was safe.

How she knew this she had absolutely no idea, since the more she concentrated the more she seemed unable to retrieve anything from her subconscious memory. But the fact was etched firmly in her mind. Eugene was alive and on his way back to her. That much was certain. It wasn't a belief, nor a hope—it was an absolute conviction.

She sat there in the shadows for a long time, at ease for the first time in days. Finally she closed her eyes, breathed in deeply and called his name out silently in her mind, time and time again.

*   *   *

Crouched under a heavy tarpaulin on a heaving fishing boat headed south across the Mediterranean from Sicily to Malta, Eugene felt far from safe. There was still this last leg of his dangerous journey to be safely negotiated, so rather than think of what might be were he to survive, he simply concentrated on staying alive. Gianni, Lucia and he now lay hidden on board a trawler to which they had been transferred from the tiny fishing smack the Resistance had organised to transport them away from a half-hidden cove on the Pássero coastline, hopefully on their way back to Valletta and safety.

The Maltese crew had hidden the three of them—much to Lucia's disgust—in empty crates stinking of fish which they then covered with other crates full of fresh fish. They draped their cargo under huge, heavy oilcloths in the prow of the boat before turning round to head back to their beleaguered island, showing no lights and sailing the craft by a mixture of ancient nautical skills and sheer derring-do.

On arrival and disembarkation in Malta, he and Gianni were at once whisked off to a safe house high in the hills and away from the beleaguered port of Valletta. Lucia bid them a fond and tearful farewell before being escorted away by a young fisherman who could not believe his luck when she gratefully accepted his offer of a hot bath and a change of clothes to be borrowed from his sister.

'You will come and see me in Naples!' she called after the departing Eugene. 'After the stinking war is finished!'

'I shall, I shall!' Eugene shouted back, with all fingers tightly crossed. 'You are a magnificent woman. And a very brave one too!'

'You will not go, of course,' Gianni sighed as the van taking them to their safe house chugged up the hillside.

'Of course I won't.' Eugene smiled in return. 'But you will.'

For some reason Gianni found this hilarious, and slapped Eugene on the knee in delight.

'What's so funny, Gianni?' Eugene wondered, usually the first to see the humour of any situation.

'Nothing is funny, my friend!' Gianni replied, shaking his head. 'Not with a mother like mine!'

Eugene smiled back, wondering how it was that a man as brave and as resolute as Gianni could deny himself the pleasure of paying a visit to the luscious Lucia for fear of a smack round the ears from his *mamma*.

Kate tried to tell Poppy of the strange sensations she had experienced at the House of Flowers when she called there on the morning that Eugene landed safely in Valletta.

'It was this odd feeling of *assurance*. Of certainty if you like. And the more I think of it, the more convinced I am that I wasn't dreaming.'

'If you weren't dreaming,' Poppy wondered, 'then what?'

'I don't know, Poppy. I really don't know.' Kate sighed and shook her head. 'Yet I must have been asleep because it was suddenly so much later in the day. A good two hours or so, judging from the sun. I know this sounds silly, but I had the sort of feeling that I wasn't there. Or rather that I hadn't *been* there—not during the time I was meant to be asleep.'

'I'm sure you were, Kate.' Poppy smiled. 'I must tell you, it's that sort of place. I often find myself suddenly dropping off for no reason at all, then waking up just as suddenly a couple of hours later.'

'Do you dream during those times?'

'I really can't say. I never seem to be able to manage to remember what I've dreamed.'

'I had this feeling I'd been in another place. Another world almost. Or—better—another time.'

'Old houses are funny places. They seem to retain something of the past, don't you think?'

'Maybe that's what it is, Poppy. Or maybe your lovely home has just got magic.' Kate smiled and shrugged as they climbed the stairs of the great house on their way to work. When they reached the top, they went their separate ways, Kate to her office and Poppy in to see Major Folkestone.

But when she was invited by Miss Budge to go into the inner office, Poppy was surprised to find the major in the company of Jack Ward.

He was standing with his back to her, staring out of the main window, smoking his favourite briar pipe thoughtfully, legs slightly apart and hands clasped behind him. After the greetings were over, Jack Ward simply nodding his acknowledgement without turning round, Major Folkestone invited Poppy to sit down opposite him.

'I'll come to the point,' he said. 'Straight to the point, in fact. We need to talk to you about you and your husband.'

'Is something wrong, sir?' Poppy enquired. 'Nothing's happened to Scott, has it?'

'Not at all,' Jack said from the window, staring out at something in the far distance. 'Other than him getting married.'

'I understood there were no objections on that score, sir.'

'There weren't,' Jack replied. 'Still aren't. But there are reservations now, I'm afraid.'

Poppy frowned at Anthony, hopeful of some explanation.

'It's rather put the kibosh on any further work in the field,' Anthony explained. 'At least as far as you and Scott go.'

'I thought you were quite happy with us as a team, sir.'

'Absolutely. You and Scott work very well together,' Anthony replied carefully, holding a freshly sharpened pencil between his two index fingers. 'You're absolutely first rate as a team.'

148

'Were,' Jack said. 'You were absolutely first rate as a team.'

'We can't send you out in the field together any more,' Anthony continued with a glance at his superior, who was still staring out of the window. 'In circumstances such as these, we do not use married agents, or even agents who are emotionally involved with one another.'

'I see, sir, of course,' Poppy said. 'Of course.'

'That is why we didn't send you off together on the mission your husband has been sent on,' Jack said, turning round at last and looking at Poppy over his spectacles. 'It wouldn't have been sensible to put a couple of agents into the field who have such a close personal affiliation. Your feelings for each other would obviously affect your mutual judgement.'

'In no way does this affect the perception we have of the two of you individually,' Anthony interposed hurriedly, seeing the look of obvious disappointment in Poppy's eyes.

'Of course not,' Jack agreed, relighting his pipe. 'It isn't just for our sake either. It's for your own good. You know as well as I do—you drop your guard for one moment—just one . . .' He looked up again at Poppy over the flame of his match. 'You know perfectly well what I mean, young lady.'

'Of course, sir. Will that be all?'

'Not quite,' Anthony said, consulting the file on his desk. 'We're as anxious to get you back into play, as it were, as you are. So you're to go along now to see Miss Lavington who will go through your new briefing with you.'

'Thank you, sir,' Poppy replied, preparing to leave. 'Thank you for letting me know about Scott

149

and me.'

Once she had left the room Jack turned to Anthony Folkestone.

'God help young Scott if she ever finds out who he has been dropped into France with.'

'I don't think it would worry young Poppy, sir. Poppy Tetherington isn't that sort of girl.'

'Poppy Meynell, you mean,' Jack muttered. 'And as for her not worrying about it, I wouldn't put money on it, Tony. Not if I were you.'

Jack turned back to stare out of the window. Anthony Folkestone was a first rate officer in every way. But one thing he obviously didn't know much about was women.

Chapter Four

Poppy stood in front of Cissie Lavington's desk, having politely refused the offer of a seat. She had been told during her training that far from putting you on an equal status during an interview, sitting down more often than not put you at a disadvantage, particularly since the chair offered to the interviewee was generally and deliberately lower than the chair of the interviewer. So she had remained politely at ease in front of her superior's desk until she heard what was to be on offer.

'What you're really saying, then, Miss Lavington,' Poppy recapped, 'is that Scott and I should have waited to get married.'

'Entirely your own business, my dear,' Cissie replied. 'What I'm saying is, if you wanted to go on working as a *team*—'

'We should have waited to get married.'

'There's nothing I can say on the matter, doncher know,' Cissie observed, lighting a fresh cigarette. 'Course, one's sorry it's happened because you were a dashed good duo—but I'm sure you don't really regret that you're married. Not to such a nice chap as Scott Meynell. However, dare say you don't like to be idle, so we'd best find you something interesting, eh?'

'Thank you. I'd appreciate that. I don't want to sit around Eden twiddling my thumbs.'

'Or filing files, I'll be bound.'

'Not really.'

Cissie glanced up at Poppy, then returned to consulting the papers on her desk.

'Might have to for a while, just as a stopgap, you see,' she muttered, having reread the salient memos. 'It appears C Section could use you.'

'C Section? Isn't that rather like being buried alive?'

'A bit.' Cissie chuckled. 'Except I can't see anyone burying you alive. It would only be for a short while. Till they come up with something a little more intoxicatin', doncher know. Trouble is they can't use you in London in case anyone would recognise you after your last op. Shame, but there it is—common sense has to prevail, and you made a pretty distinct mark during the Churchill business. Then of course, now you're hitched—' Cissie stopped, took a long drag on her cigarette and eyed Poppy with her one good eye. 'There's always this thing of gels getting pregnant, do you see. Married gels, of course.'

'Scott and I only had one night together.'

'All it took my parents,' Cissie remarked, tapping

151

her ash into her tin wastebasket. 'Point is, these things happen, and if an agent gets preggers, bye-bye agent.'

'So it really wasn't a good idea,' Poppy concluded. 'Us getting married. Does this mean I'll be deskbound for the rest of the war?'

'Not necessarily, me dear,' Cissie replied. 'Certainly not if I can help it. You're far too good an agent to fester away in C Section. Don't you worry—I won't let it go.'

After an interview with the woman in charge of C Section, Poppy wandered back through the woods to her house. The weather had suddenly changed, the promise of spring being replaced by a reminder of winter as the wind shifted, bringing snow showers in from the east. As soon as she got home, she lit the fire and, pulling her chair round in front of it, sat staring into the pile of burning logs as she tried to sort herself out.

First she wondered when she would see her beloved Scott again, and then if she would ever in fact do so. Since being married, she had found herself thinking more and more about the chances of something happening to either Scott or herself, most particularly Scott. Somehow she felt that as long as they were together they would be able to protect each other, just as they had done on their first famous mission. Prodding the logs into brighter life with a long poker, she remembered how clever Scott had been with his feints and his disguises, how seemingly fearless he was. Then, remembering so much of his careless courage, her spirits sank, knowing that his tremendous nerve and dash would always lessen the likelihood of her ever seeing him again. Scott never played safe and for that very reason he might never be safe.

Realising more clearly than ever before how easy it would be to lose him, Poppy's feelings turned from wistfulness to sudden anger. She found herself wishing to God she had never married him, because by doing so she seemed to have killed for ever the chance of their being sent out on an assignment together. Because they were married her Section would keep choosing someone else instead of her. They might even send other young, unmarried women out with him, and as she realised this for the first time her spirits sank to zero. She had imagined almost every kind of exigency in war, but not exclusion from the work they both knew to be vital. She knew it had been wrong to agree to marry him; she should have refused so that they could stay together as agents. They could have been lovers without ever marrying, and as long as they had kept their affair secret, as long as the Colonel and Major Folkestone had not been aware of their intimacy, they could have waited till after the war was over to get married. Marriage was only a certificate, Poppy told herself. People could still be *married* without any ceremony, civil or religious. So damn marriage—damn marriage, damn weddings, most of all damn Scott for insisting on marrying her in the first place. She should have refused, made him wait—and by doing so stayed where she would be most needed, namely by his side, so that together they could accomplish something, they could help defeat Hitler and win the war.

After which another thought occurred to her, one that gave her a sudden feeling of hope. Perhaps Scott had insisted on marrying her in order to keep her out of the firing line. Maybe he loved her that much—enough to want to make sure that her life was out of immediate danger.

She pushed her chair back from the fire, realising that while lost in her thoughts she had slowly begun to roast. Rising, she collapsed on to the sofa away from the fire and tried to take fresh stock and make sense of the confusion of thoughts running through her head.

A small table to the side of the sofa held a pretty mahogany box which Poppy had not yet opened. Idly, she reached out and lifted the lid. There was still some sewing in it, a half-finished tapestry cushion with still loaded needle stuck neatly in one side, the piece itself folded carefully so as not to crease the work. She picked it up and looked at it, seeing a picture of a spaniel. For some reason she showed it to George who was sitting patient as ever by her feet.

'Look, George,' she told him, sounding ridiculous even to herself. 'A little spaniel.'

She looked into the box once again. Originally the piece was obviously not intended to be a sewing box, for although it was stacked with skeins of silk and wool its sides were obviously made to hold wine bottles, or perhaps tea caddies. She removed the skeins and looked below them, and noticed something else. Reaching down she picked the object out with a sense of sudden excitement.

'There's something else here too, George,' she muttered to the dog. 'A book. No—no, it's a diary of some sort. A journal.'

Poppy sat back and began to read. As she read she got the oddest feeling that somehow she knew the writer, so familiar was the voice coming off the pages, as if she was actually eavesdropping on someone still alive rather than a woman who had lived over a century before.

First the writer described her feelings of love for the younger son of the Eden estate—how he had ridden by her father's cottage door, stopped to talk to them all, and caught her eye. Then she told how he had returned to the house by invitation, and taken tea with them. How her mother had embarrassed her profoundly by remarking on his having asked to be allowed to return yet again, and saying it was perfectly apparent that he was taken with the youngest of her daughters; and how it seemed no time at all before they were married.

And so we are married, against the wishes of his mother, but with the final blessing of his father, who is a dear. His mother does not approve of me because I am from a different background, but has told Edward that she will not stand in his way, and that at least I have grown up on the estate! Edward says she will come round to the idea, particularly once we have children, and I am sure he is right. She sent her maid to fill the house with flowers on our return, so many of them that Edward has renamed the old place the House of Flowers and intends to carve a stone above the door saying as much. My dear husband has bought me a fine new mare, so that we can ride out together of a morning. Up every day, before even the light, and my heart pounds with excitement at the idea that Pretty Lady is being got ready for me! After all the hirelings I have ridden the idea that I have a mount of my own is truly wondrous. The estate is quite beautiful in the early morning light, and sometimes we stop by Father's cottage, and Mother and he insist we sit down to breakfast with them. The lakes are Arthurian in their beauty in the early morning. The mist rises from them in such a mysterious way that I almost think I can see the king and his knights rowing towards me, and certainly I would not be surprised, so romantic is the light, so ethereal the feeling of the estate at that hour, with the trees dripping quietly into the waters, and only the sound of water fowl moving in the reeds.

Poppy put the book down, and turned, as George ran from beside her feet, barking at the sound of knocking at the front door, disturbing the gentle whispers inside the house, the hissing of the fire, the movement of the flames in the fireplace.

Poppy picked up the long-haired dachshund, and went to the front door. She peered out. There was no one there. There was not a soul to be seen anywhere. She closed the door again, guiltily returning the journal to its original hiding place among the skeins of wool in the mahogany box.

*   *   *

In spite of Kate's assurance regarding his safety, Eugene was still a long way from home. Due to the increasingly heavy bombardment of Malta he had been unable to get an airlift out of the tiny island, forced to travel by sea instead, as far as the port of Marseille where he had managed to collect a new set of papers, and begun the long haul of getting

156

himself from the south to the north of France where he hoped by some miracle to utilise one of the tried and true escape routes. On his travels he learned two things—first that France is a very large country, particularly when one has no transport of one's own and is forced to rely on the goodwill of farmers and the like when cadging lifts in hay wagons and market lorries, and second that if he was given the opportunity to come back in another life as someone else, that someone else would definitely not be a plumber.

It had been the idea of his contact in Marseille that he should travel disguised as a plumber.

'It doesn't matter if you know nothing about plumbing!' the man had assured him. 'My brother-in-law is a real plumber and he knows less than I! Just stick a few pipes together—unblock the odd drain—change the washer on a tap—but above all stink! All plumbers stink, which is why no one wants to go near them! Since very few people want to know more about the plumbing than whether it can be mended they will leave you alone! *Voyez-vous?* They want a plumber, sure! But they do not want to know what he does or how he does it! They just want him to plumb and go—*comprenez?* That is why it is always so safe to be a plumber, because plumbers—pooh! You will have no friends, but you will also have no trouble!'

So far his friend had proved to be right. Thanks to the ever present smell of plumbing that hung about the clothes borrowed from his contact's brother-in-law, everyone gave Eugene a very wide berth, including the Germans he encountered before and on reaching Paris.

Having found the rue de Rivoli, Eugene now

checked the exact address he had in his hand. The famous fashion house of Blès had finally been closed down by order of Goebbels, owing to Madame's habit of opening her doors to anyone and everyone unsympathetic to or on the run from the Nazis. Following the fall of France, when Goebbels had actually called at her salon in the hope of socialising with the celebrated couturier, she had sent him away with a flea in his ear, something to which the propaganda minister had not taken kindly. The following afternoon Madame had hoisted the Tricolour outside her Maison, at which point it was immediately closed down by the Germans, although for some reason—perhaps out of respect for her great artistry—they did not actually imprison Madame herself. The result was that Madame Blès immediately set up new escape routes and help lines for any enemy of the Third Reich who might be passing through the occupied capital of France.

Thanks to his most convincing disguise and ever present odour, Eugene was ignored by the two Nazi soldiers on patrol in the street outside Madame's house, leaving him free to ring the old bell on the equally old door.

'Enter!' a man's voice commanded from within in impeccable French. 'And close the door behind you!'

Eugene found himself in semi-darkness in the hallway, able only vaguely to make out the figure standing in the doorway to one side.

'My God,' the man drawled. 'That is a really frightful smell.'

'Forgive me, monsieur,' Eugene answered, the humble plumber relaying the message he had been instructed to give. 'But I understand you requested a plumber. For the kitchen, I believe. There is a blockage under the sink.'

'Ah,' the man replied, with a nod, standing to one side. 'The plumber. Of course.'

As Eugene passed him he could see the man was both handsome and extremely elegant, dressed perfectly from head to toe and sensibly holding a canary yellow silk handkerchief to his nose as he indicated which way Eugene was to proceed, along the corridor to a room at the back of the house, well away from the front door. Eugene found himself in the ante-room of the kitchens, a small apartment with shutters at the windows, furnished with a plain wooden table and chairs set in the middle of the room, where an extremely elegant woman sat drinking black coffee.

'*Ah, mon dieu!* But what a truly terrible stink!' she cried, in an equally elegant voice, before leaning forward to stare at Eugene. 'Eugene?' she said. 'No! No! I can't believe it! You? *Enfin!*' She roared with laughter. 'You rascal! You came here just to stink me out, no?'

They embraced, laughing.

'Pooh! But I have more courage than you, Harvey!' she said to her companion. 'To embrace such a *mauvais*! Even so, you had best take him away and allow him to bath and change. Get him some fresh clothes, for God's sake. It doesn't matter whose. Yours! Anyone's! Just get him out of those frightful garments!'

'Ah, madame—no,' Eugene sighed. 'Not yet, anyway. The Germans have seen me come in so they will wish to see me go out again.'

'Whatever you say,' Madame agreed. 'I just do

not know how long we can put up with this smell. This is Harvey Constable, by the way,' she added, waving a beautifully manicured hand in the direction of the elegant gentleman who had shown Eugene in. 'He comes in and out by the back door and no one says anything. They are far too nervous I might fly the Tricolour out of the window again and arouse more local feeling, which is intense as it is. To occupy Paris is worse than to conquer it, as they are finding out. Only the prostitutes and the nightclub owners are sympathetic to the Germans—the concierges are running rings around them, but then the concierges run rings round everyone, *n'est-ce pas?*'

She went on to describe relevant moments of insurrection by the locals, the courage of her own concierge, and the hatred she felt for the women of easy virtue who were busy fraternising with the occupying forces. Eugene listened to her attentively, laughed at the right moments, but finally indicated that it was time for him to go. Madame agreed, telling him the procedure whereby he might return in safety later that evening.

Under cover of darkness and at the agreed time, Eugene emerged from his given hidey-hole and slipped up the back stairs of Madame's mansion, where he was finally able to bath himself thoroughly, removing all traces of his malodorous former self before changing into fresh clean clothes, albeit those of a railway worker.

When he emerged from his room, he found himself in the company of another railway worker.

'Are you travelling with me as well?' he asked the transformed Harvey. 'Won't it be a bit rough for someone like you?'

'I have been summoned back to England,' Harvey replied. 'And don't worry—I can cut the mustard. In spite of my usual appearance I was not brought up by nannies and maids, I do assure you, nor educated at Eton. My mother brought me up herself, I sewed and cleaned in her workrooms as a nipper. So please don't worry about me, my friend. I can look after myself.'

'Any particular reason for your sudden return to England? Old boy?'

'Yes,' Harvey replied. 'Not that it's any business of yours. I'm going back to see an old friend of mine who needs my help.'

'That so?' Eugene persisted. 'Well, well.'

'You might know him as it happens,' Harvey continued, with a tight little smile. 'Jack Ward?'

Eugene frowned then shrugged. The Colonel was the last person he would have guessed to have called the dapper and elegant Harvey Constable back to England.

*   *   *

Madame Blès sent them on their way—after a delicious dinner of homemade fish soup, beef casserole and apple tart—with knapsacks containing small bottles of brandy, tartines, and some pieces of garlic.

'Chew on those once you get outside,' she advised. 'The more French you smell the better. And may God speed you, and let you reach England before that bastard Hitler.'

As he took his first step on what he hoped would be the last leg of his long journey home, as always

161

Eugene felt in his pocket to rub Kate's lucky stone. For a split second he could have sworn he heard her voice and that wonderful laugh of hers, the one that thrilled him and drove him mad with love. It was only for a moment, but the sound of it inspired him and gave him the necessary spring in his step to help him cover those last long miles towards the French coastline.

Naturally they conversed in French from the moment they left Madame. Eugene was immediately taken with Harvey's assumed singsong country accent, which he gathered was typical of certain regions around Brittany.

'Yours,' Harvey said after listening to Eugene speak, 'yours definitely belongs behind a bar in the roughest part of Marseille.'

'Good.' Eugene laughed. 'Seeing that's where my papers claim I'm from.'

'It might not be important to any German who stopped us in the street,' Harvey commented. 'But it would certainly be significant to any Nazi sympathiser on the lookout for bounty money. The price of turning in blokes such as us has gone sky high.'

'I'm not sure I quite like all the French at this moment,' Eugene remarked, lighting a smoke.

'I'm quite sure I don't like some of the French,' Harvey replied, taking a cigarette out for himself. 'I'm also quite sure I like an awful lot more.'

'Papers, please!'

Yet again they were stopped for a routine check, and yet again they were sent quickly on their way as soon as the guards had taken a peremptory look at their beautifully forged documents.

'Funny thing about smell,' Eugene mused as they

took a zigzag route out of the city, making first for the outlying suburban districts and thence the open countryside beyond. 'I happen to think that there is safety in smell, and always have done. People don't seem to see through smell the way they see through disguises, through what they suspect are iffy signatures, or phoney accents. It's a most emotive thing, smell—more perhaps than any other of our senses if you think about it.'

'Absolutely,' Harvey agreed. 'I can't stand the smell of marigolds, or geraniums, but I couldn't tell you why.'

'I can't stand the smell of petrol, and I know exactly why. It reminds me of my father taking me back to my terrible prep school in England. The smell of petrol reminds me of being parted from my horses and dogs in Ireland, and my parents of course—but them a bit less since it was their idea to send me to the wretched school in the first place.'

'I hardly went to school,' Harvey returned, his voice taking on a tone of some satisfaction. 'Just enough, but not too much—like the vermouth in a good dry martini. Oh, God—how I wish I hadn't said that.'

'How I too wish you hadn't, pal.'

They walked on through the night, keeping near the railroads on which they were meant to be working, until dawn granted them sight of their first green fields.

'Danger's quite exciting, though, don't you think?' Harvey wondered, stopping to drink in the view before them. 'I quite enjoy all this—and of course you enjoy it a whole lot more if you hate the Nazis. My mother clothed a lot of Fascist women, as it happens. She fitted them out in their glad rags, which is indirectly how I came to be brought into the Service. She listened to their conversations while she was fitting them, to everything they had to say, and passed it on to me to pass on to a certain gentleman who lived in a certain block of flats in Victoria. Finally I came to meet Madame Blès, again through my mother. They'd started out in the same cutting room as young girls, crossed the Channel several times in pursuit of their careers, and in doing so grew to loathe the international Nazi set as much as we all did, and still do—bad cess to them all. Quite satisfactory when you think about it.'

Before moving off on what they hoped really was the very last leg of their journey, they ate their last tartines and drank the last of their brandy. Eugene looked towards the horizon and took a deep breath.

'Yes,' he said in deep satisfaction. 'I was right, Harvey. Take a good deep breath. You *can* smell the sea.'

*   *   *

'You trust people too easily, Lily,' Scott said crossly as they left a small, dimly lit café on the outskirts of the tiny village of Gesore some ten miles inland from St-Valery where they had just made initial contact with the man who was supposed to be the first in a line of Free French who had promised to help them find the necessary locations for a small but all important number of radio transmitters, apparently all ready assembled and waiting to be collected. 'You use your charms, and when they fall for them—which the French are bound to do—'

'Thank you,' Lily said tartly. 'Compliments always welcome.'

'You think that's fine—you can trust them, because they can't take their eyes off your—off your assets.'

Lily eyed him from under her plain French beret, said nothing and went on walking down the road that finally led back to the small *pension* where they were staying, ostensibly as a newly-wed couple up from the country on honeymoon. Lily was finding it as hard as Scott to share not only the same roof but also the same bedroom, but for different reasons. While Scott found Lily nothing but a quite specific pain in the neck with her openly flirtatious manner and her deliberate emphasis on her sexuality, which Scott was convinced would and could only finally get them into deep waters, Lily was finding Scott oddly attractive—oddly because he was one of the few men she had met who seemed totally immune to her charms. She knew of course that he had just got married and no doubt sworn his undying love to Poppy, a choice Lily found strange since she had always thought Poppy both reserved and more than what Lily considered a little eccentric in her manner and her attitudes. Why the dashing, debonair, and undoubtedly courageous Scott should have thrown his cap into her particular ring Lily could not imagine, since to her way of thinking women who did not exude their sexual persona had to be by rote rather dull. For the life of her she could not imagine Poppy in bed with Scott, let alone being inventive enough between the sheets to keep Scott's interest alive— at least not for very long. Even though what they were actually on was a highly dangerous mission rather than a quiet and private little honeymoon, Lily had fondly imagined that once they had been flown out of England and dropped into France things would change. Thrown together in a highly dangerous situation, the adrenalin would rush, and past associations—however recent or serious—would be set to one side while they concentrated on doing their work and, most important, on surviving. And to Lily the best way of guaranteeing one's safety would seem to be to have a strong, handsome and courageous man, while not necessarily in your bed, at least in your pocket.

Sadly, so far the only signs of interest in Lily shown by Scott had been the very opposite of what she had hoped. Ever since they had arrived he had done nothing but criticise and order her about. The ordering about Lily did not object to so much since she found it rather exciting, but the constant criticism of her attitudes and behaviour was beginning to irk her. She had flirted quite deliberately with the somewhat coarse but really quite handsome young Frenchman who was their contact, less to arouse the Frenchman's passions than in the hope of igniting some sort of jealous flame in the heart of her companion. But it seemed she had failed, since the moment they were out of earshot of the café Lily found herself the target for yet more of Scott's somewhat acid criticism.

'You're behaving as though this is some sort of holiday,' Scott snapped when he had caught up with her.

'Isn't that how we're meant to be behaving? Or would you rather I started behaving like a spy?'

'You are meant to be behaving as if we have just

got married. And girls who have just got married do not go round flirting with every bloody Frenchman they meet.'

'Language.'

'So just try and behave.'

'The girl I'm pretending to be likes to flirt,' Lily said with a sideways look and smiled at the handsome man striding alongside her. 'That's how I've decided to play her.'

'You're not in a play, Lily. You're in a war. This is a war you're in—we're both in—so perhaps rather than thinking of it as some sort of light comedy—'

'I didn't say it was a comedy,' Lily retorted, dropping her voice as they arrived at their *pension*. 'Of course it isn't a comedy. It's a drama. A huge drama. I don't see the harm in thinking of it as that.'

'If you'll perhaps let me finish? I would rather you dealt with it as a hard reality, rather than play-acting. In my estimation—'

'Look—'

'In my estimation it would be safer all round if you came to your senses. I certainly don't want to be taken out because of your determination to play-act.'

'You won't be,' Lily assured him. 'I may have a fondness for *play-acting* as you call it, but I certainly don't have a death wish.'

Scott gave her one last glare, then knocked on the rough wooden door that was closed against all comers at this time of night.

A peephole slid open, an eye regarded them from the other side and then the door was silently unbolted.

167

'My dears.' Madame Daumier sighed sentimentally as she carefully rebolted her front door. 'I was becoming concerned for my little lovebirds. Ah.' She pinched and squeezed Lily's cheek, hard enough to make Lily's eyes water, then winked at Scott. 'It is so *late*, I was afraid for you. There was a convoy through the town only half an hour ago and of course you are well after the curfew.'

'It seems no one pays much attention to the curfew at the moment, madame,' Scott replied. 'There are cafés and bars open all over the place.'

'Not for long, monsieur. My husband tells me we shall have troops garrisoned here maybe this week—certainly next. All this coast here—well. I have never seen such activity. Maybe the invasion, yes? Although may the Lord forbid it—but every day more troops, more guns, more everything. Not really an ideal place for your honeymoon, perhaps?'

Scott wasn't quite sure how to read the look he was getting from his landlady. He wondered if she already suspected that a couple such as Lily and he would hardly choose this tiny village outside Trouville on the Normandy coast as the ideal place for their honeymoon unless they had perhaps some other reason. Or had she already detected flaws in what they both hoped were their perfect accents? Scott was confident that because of his family background he could pass as a Frenchman, but privately he had worried about Lily, even though he had been assured by Jack Ward and Anthony Folkestone that she too had the right credentials to pass as an authentic Frenchwoman. Not that he could fault her accent for a moment; to his very well tuned ear it sounded as if she spoke perfect French, fitting the region she avowed she was from both by her accent and her use of *argot*. Neither could he fault her manner. Lily seemed to have adopted an entirely new character to fit her assumed identity, even though the character she had chosen to play was not one Scott would have sanctioned had he known about it in advance.

Madame Daumier was still staring at him as he made his excuses and prepared to climb the stairs to bed.

'Is there something wrong, madame?' he asked, believing as always that it was much the best to wrong-foot any possible opponent by pre-guessing them.

'No, monsieur, no—far from it,' she replied with a smile, putting a heavy hand on his forearm. 'You are such a good-looking couple—and such a charming pair. I just hope and I pray . . .' She stopped for a moment, closed her eyes briefly, then clasped her well-worn hands at her waist and shook her head. 'I lost my own son, monsieur. He was killed in the Ardennes. The so-called impassable Ardennes. *Puh.*' Madame Daumier shrugged and puffed in contempt. 'He was in the Light Cavalry. Imagine—with no anti-tank guns—without a decent tank—how are they meant to stop the might of a Panzer division? They couldn't even slow their progress. That wretch Gamelin.'

Lily frowned at Scott for illumination.

'General Gamelin,' Scott repeated. 'Perhaps a little too old for the game as it is played now.'

'Too old?' Madame Daumier opened her big brown eyes to the full. 'He is the sort of soldier who should only fight in peacetime. Too old? He

169

charges like a bull into the Low Countries, sacrificing our lambs everywhere—then as soon as he sees a German he holds up his hands. What a waste. What a waste.'

She shook her head, tightened her mouth, then put her hands back on to Scott's forearm. 'I look at you, monsieur, and I see my son. Shall I tell you why? He had the same look in his eyes. He had just that look you have in your eyes when he went away. He had the very same look.'

In their room, Scott stood with his back resolutely to the bed, staring out of the window and smoking a cigarette while behind him Lily undressed herself as was the routine, accompanied by an ever increasing number of sighs.

'You know this really isn't necessary, Scott?' she remarked as she pulled her sweater over her head. 'I know you don't fancy me—that you don't like me in fact—so this charade really isn't necessary.'

'So you say each and every night, Lily. And while I agree that it might not be necessary, it's altogether sensible.'

Lily smiled as she dropped her skirt from trim waist to pretty ankles, reckoning that Scott at least was beginning to admit that she had some sort of allure, otherwise he would never have made that remark. All she had to do, she figured as she slipped into the bed dressed in just her silk French knickers and matching brassiere, was see it out. Married Scott may be. In love even, she admitted. But that love and that marriage were a long way away right now, and if she was going to risk her life, or perhaps even lose it, then she was going to enjoy it right up to the last moment.

'Aren't you coming to bed, Scott?' she asked as

170

factually as she could, not wishing in any way to pre-empt her game. 'You must be as tired as I am after all that excitement.'

'In a while, Lily,' Scott murmured, still with his back turned. 'I'm going to smoke another cigarette first. You go to sleep.'

'Sure thing, boss,' Lily replied, lying on her back and letting her long hair fall either side of her face. 'Just try not to wake me when you do finally climb in.'

Little chance of that, Scott thought to himself as he lit a fresh cigarette. *I shall as usual doze in the armchair until I am absolutely sure you are asleep, and then and only then shall I crawl quietly under the eiderdown—but not under the sheet.*

'Good night,' Lily sighed from behind him. 'Sleep tight.'

Scott said nothing. He just stood smoking his cigarette and looking out into the dark night.

While below him, hidden in the untended shrubbery, Madame Daumier watched him for as long as he remained at the window, before she too disappeared into the darkness.

*   *   *

The first inkling Marjorie had that something was up was when the air raid siren sounded at the Park and everyone vacated the building to take to the caves in the woods—everyone except Major Folkestone, who remained at his desk; and Marjorie, who was detained by Major Folkestone; and Jack Ward who suddenly and almost silently appeared from an adjacent room.

As soon as the building was empty, Anthony

171

Folkestone and Jack Ward hurried out of the room, summoning Marjorie to follow.

'Might I ask what's up, sir?' she wondered. 'Is there some emergency?'

'Not your business, young woman,' Jack growled at her as they hurried along a corridor. 'Yours to do and die, get it? Not ask questions.'

'Just do as we say, Marjorie,' Anthony Folkestone said. 'And you're to say nothing about this at all. Understood?'

'Not a word, young woman,' Jack muttered. 'Or we'll have you in the Tower.'

'Take all these files—here,' Anthony said to her, handing her folder after folder from a filing cabinet in the first office they entered. 'Take them back to my desk and put them in the bottom drawer. Then come back here.'

There had to be a security leak, Marjorie concluded as she hurried back along the corridor. There had to be a leak and this was obviously an Emergency with a very large E.

When she got back the two men were still working their way systematically through the filing cabinets, checking and double-checking heavily numbered and marked files before putting them in a pile for Marjorie to collect. Some of the files were so old they made Marjorie sneeze as she carried them back to Anthony's office, while others were so flat it was obvious that there was nothing in them of note. Yet Marjorie realised, like the old dusty ones they all had to be checked, because if there was a leak the vital facts could well have been disguised and buried in some old folder somewhere.

As she set down yet another set of records on

172

Major Folkestone's desk, Marjorie suddenly gave a shiver as she took in the reality of the situation. If what she thought was true, then there was a traitor within the gates of Eden. One of the Nosy Parkers was an enemy agent.

*　　　*　　　*

After all the necessary files had been stowed away in Anthony's office, a signal was given to sound the All Clear. Fifteen minutes later the place was back to normal, the rooms echoing to the clatter of typewriters and telephone bells and the corridors to the clacking of heels. Some four hours elapsed before Jack Ward came back into Anthony's office and carefully laid a file down in front of his junior.

'Thank you,' he said to Marjorie. 'That will be all.'

After Marjorie had gone, Jack nodded to the file, and began to relight his pipe.

'Let me know your thoughts,' he said. 'I know mine.'

It was one of the older files, dating back to before the war, and from the details on the front there must have been some sort of muddle up between departments because the file actually belonged to Baker Street and not to Eden Park at all. Theoretically no one from Baker Street would be employed at Eden Park, but none the less all the information contained in the file pointed to the named girl as the number one suspect.

Anthony read the details not once but four times, to make sure he understood the matter absolutely. Then he closed the file and shut his eyes tightly while he took it all in. The matter was even worse than he thought, because not only had someone infiltrated their security at a critical level, but if what he had read was correct then the young woman responsible had not only been placed in the Service by Jack Ward, but worse—she was his god-daughter.

*   *   *

Several days later Anthony Folkestone was surprised by the sound of direct knocking on his office door.

'Not now, please,' he called back sharply, barely looking up from his paperwork. 'Busy!'

'It's only me, sir!' came an all too familiar voice.

'Billy,' Anthony sighed, clucking his tongue as the boy pushed open his door. 'How did you get past Miss Budge? Though knowing you there's not a lot of point in asking that.'

'Miss Budge isn't out there, sir,' Billy replied, standing in the doorway, one-legged, removing something sticky from the sole of one shoe.

Major Folkestone looked up, frowning slightly.

'Probably gone to powder her nose. Although she usually tells me when she's leaving her post.'

'Why's it called that, sir? Powdering your nose? Why do girls always say they're going to powder their noses when—'

'Billy.' Anthony Folkestone stopped him in his tracks, amplifying his authority with a sharp tap on his desk with the pencil he had in his hand. 'If you have something on your mind. I have a lot of work to do.'

' 'S all right, sir, I don't mind.'

Billy wandered round to the front of the major's

174

desk, picked some pencils out of a mug and began carefully to sharpen them to perfect points with his pocket knife, leaving the wood shavings to fall where they may.

'I was just wondering, sir, if you haven't heard nothing about my pilotless bomb thing, that's all.'

'If I have heard anything.'

'That's it, sir. If you in't heard *anything*.'

Anthony avoided looking at the young man, instead leaning over and carefully brushing the shredded pencil shavings into the adjacent waste bin.

'Not exactly, Billy,' he replied. 'Not as such.'

'I saw the folder out on Miss Budge's desk, sir—'

'You had absolutely no right to be looking at anything on my assistant's desk, young man.'

'I weren't, sir. I was passing by and I saw it, right on the top of the In pile. On top of all today's stuff. Stuff that's just come in.'

'You still had no right, Billy.'

'I couldn't help it, sir. It was as clear as mud, sittin' there like. Right slap bang on the top.'

Anthony glared at him, then went to the door to call for his assistant who appeared almost at once in response, as if she had been ready for the summons.

'Today's files, please, Miss Budge. Anything new that's just arrived if you'd be so kind. Good. Thank you.'

Having finished sharpening the major's pencils, Billy now turned his attention to attending to the wick on the desk lighter, pulling it up to make it longer then carefully cleaning and trimming it with a small pair of scissors he had just made appear from the other end of his knife.

'I bin thinkin' about the desert, sir,' Billy said, as if to fill in the silence that had fallen. 'You know— what it must be like to fight in the desert and all that.'

'Interesting,' Anthony replied without any actual interest, reading some documentation that was now in his hand.

'Bloomin' big, the desert, in't it?'

'Are you referring to any particular desert? Or just "the desert" in general, I wonder?'

'The Western Desert, sir. Where we're fighting.'

'No doubt you have thoughts on that matter as well, I suppose.'

'Not really, sir.' Billy shrugged. ''Cept it's bloomin' big—and supply lines must be more important than ever.'

'Look, Billy,' Anthony said in exasperation. 'Why don't you just run along and join up, eh? The army won't be able to carry on till you do.'

Billy eyed the major, whom he happened to rather admire, but said nothing. He hadn't meant to irritate him, but as Marjorie was forever telling him, he seemed to have the ability to get under people's fingernails just at the wrong moment. So rather than infuriate one of his heroes even more, he fell to silence, looking down at his shoes, turning his toes inwards as he did so and pulling his mouth to one side.

'Sorry, Billy,' Anthony muttered. 'Got some problems. Didn't mean to snap.'

'That's all right, sir,' Billy said with one of his sudden grins that had the ability to lighten anyone's mood. 'I didn't mean to irk you.'

'*Irk?*' Anthony smiled in return, amused by the odd choice of word. 'You weren't *irking* me. I've just got a few things on my mind.'

'Yeah.' Billy nodded. 'I bet.'

Anthony frowned, and stared at Billy, wondering what he meant by his reply. But the boy was just looking back at him quite ingenuously, as if his remark had been meant as nothing more than sympathetic. Any further thoughts fled, however, as after a brief tap on his door Miss Budge appeared holding a small clutch of files which she handed over to her boss. As Anthony took them and began to sort through them, Miss Budge turned and smiled her usual kindly smile at Billy, putting a hand out to ruffle his hair. Seeing it coming, Billy stepped smartly back, at the same time lowering his eyes to regard the plump, kindly figure with what he hoped was his best 'ere *leave off* look, a look which seemed to leave Miss Budge, as always, unruffled.

'Yes,' Anthony said after a short space of time that seemed the length of a light year to young Billy. Anthony closed the file, having first removed a covering letter which he slid into his top drawer. 'Good,' he continued. 'It appears the boffins were most impressed by your ideas, Billy, but I'm afraid it also appears that you're a bit too smart for them. They say that while the idea is absolutely first class, they just don't have the science.'

The look on Billy's face was such that Anthony quickly tried to make up for the disappointment the boy was obviously feeling.

'Ahead of the field yet again it would seem, Billy Hendry. Jolly good.'

'Could I see what they say, sir? Please?' Billy held out one hand carefully. 'If that's all right.'

'No can do, Billy, alas. Not just comments about

177

your idea, but a lot more stuff. All HC. Sorry about that.'

'Understood, sir. Absolutely. Still. Want to hear my ideas 'bout the desert now?'

'Not right now, Billy. As I keep saying—got work to do.'

'As I see it, what they've got to do—'

'Some other time, Billy.'

'They got to shore up Tobruk proper, that's what they got to do, sir.'

'Some other time. Billy? Now tell Miss Budge I need her again, would you? On your way out.'

'Honest, sir—'

'On your way out, Billy—which is *now*.'

Billy pulled a face and ambled out, one of his socks falling down round his ankles. He stopped to pull it back up in front of Miss Budge's desk. She had for once failed to notice him, so busy was she sorting through the letters and business on her desk. After he had pulled up his sock Billy glanced down at her desk, but seeing nothing of interest he closed the office door behind him, only to bump into a tired and unshaven Eugene.

'Hey, Billy Hendry. The very man I wanted to see.'

Eugene stopped to pretend-box the boy, and Billy at once tucked his right hand under his chin and led quickly with a series of left jabs that Eugene parried easily, before feigning hurt.

'Haven't lost your touch, eh? My little gossoon.' He laughed. 'Getting faster by the minute, too, I'll swear.'

'Where've you been?' Billy wondered, still dancing round the big man. 'Where've you been *now*?'

'Ah-ha! And wouldn't you like to know, me little spy?' Eugene replied. 'I been to London to see the king.'

'They've turned down my plans for a bomb without a pilot,' Billy said, stopping his boxing now, and standing with a heavily wrinkled nose. 'Said they in't got the science.'

'Knowing how far advanced you are technically, Billy boy, sure they're probably bang on the mark. Maybe they should just enlist you straight into the Department of Pointy Heads and have done with it.'

'My plan'd work, Mr Hackett,' Billy insisted. 'All they got to do is make a fuel.'

'Tell you what, Billy boy,' Eugene said, pretending to land a couple of rights to Billy's head. 'We'll work on it ourselves, just the two of us, in the evenings. I got plenty of lighter fuel and paraffin, and you have a head full of ideas. We'll be a matchless pair.' He put out a hand to ruffle his hair.

'Don't,' Billy warned. 'I really got to hate that.'

'I know. I used to hate that too.'

Eugene waved a farewell, and ambled into Anthony Folkestone's office where the major was ready for him, standing behind his desk holding a long ruler behind his back as if it was a swagger stick.

'Welcome home, Hackett,' he said, with a nod. 'Mission accomplished, I imagine.'

'You tell me, Major,' Eugene replied, relighting the half a cheroot he still had to smoke. 'I did my bit. *We* did our bit—Gianni and I.'

'We've had reports of three bombers down in the Med between Sicily and Malta. Not shot down,

179

down, straight after take-off, so that is something. Damned good show.'

'Ta,' Eugene replied with a glance over a plume of smoke from his cheroot. 'But it wasn't without a certain amount of difficulty.'

'No, always the same, I'm afraid. The best laid plans et cetera.'

'As you know, Major, they were expecting us. One of the two-man welcoming committee was a double agent. I found papers on him.'

Anthony gazed at him steadily, before sighing deeply and sitting down behind his desk with an air of doom and resignation. He indicated for Eugene to sit opposite, which Eugene did, stretching his long legs out in front of him.

'You and I know there's always that risk, Hackett. But with this operation . . .' Anthony stopped to shake his head and then light a cigarette. 'I'd have said security was as watertight as it could possibly be on this one. A small but vital op, nursed through from inception by the Colonel and myself, but as you know there is always a chance of a leak. These things happen. Double agents are the bane of our work. I sometimes think we can cope with everything, except them.'

'These things happen, they most certainly do,' Eugene agreed with a nod. 'They happen in the most organised families. But it isn't a good thing. Not if it's coming from inside. Had I not despatched the fellow, God knows how many of our contacts in that region would have gone down.'

'My thoughts entirely.' Anthony tapped some ash into his tin ashtray and then, rising, went to unlock and open the map on his wall, the one that contained the precise locations of dropped agents,

180

which was always kept locked except in the most confidential of meetings.

'See here, Hackett,' Anthony continued. 'These black pins. Ten of them all told. They're agents—all down. Fine—we all know you win some, you lose some. But six of those went down within the last three weeks. And they were all briefed and despatched from here. From Eden Park.'

'So.' Eugene looked at the end of his cheroot, blew it back into a brighter form of life and then regarded Anthony Folkestone with a narrowing of his large eyes. 'So that means we have—what shall we call it, d'you think, Major? Yes—I'd say somewhere or other we have to smoke out a rat here, wouldn't you say? Which reminds me—did I ever tell you about the time my cousin in Kerry put a blowtorch to the bottom of a pipe to smoke out a rat and the flame shot out the top, caught his haystack on fire and burned down the barn? No. Well, never mind, eh? Let's just hope that it doesn't happen to us.'

*   *   *

Even though Kate had known Eugene was safe she was still overcome by his homecoming; so much so that for the first few days following his return she had become so shy with him she had found herself actually having to think up things to say to him.

In what seemed like the vast amount of time they had been separated she had rehearsed many conversations they might have when she saw him again, including discussions on various suitable topics, vague debates concerning the future ambitions of them both—although not anything

181

that smacked of a joint future just in case it might sound too forward—and, naturally, exchanges of views about subjects of general interest to both of them. She had some of these imagined conversations off pat, only to discover to her consternation that they all fled from her memory the moment she saw Eugene, and she was left feeling as wordless as any ingénue.

She could not imagine the disappointment that she must be causing him, but then Kate had forgotten the man with whom she was in love. She had quite forgotten how wonderfully voluble he was, how excitingly outspoken; how much he loved to talk, and when he wasn't talking how much he loved to hold and kiss her, seeming oblivious of her sudden shyness, and more than making up for her own awkwardness by his gaiety and observations. It made everything better and also a whole lot worse—better in that he was back and they were together once more, but also worse, because the longer they were together the more the dread of their inevitable parting seemed to hang over their every moment.

'I'll tell you what, Eugene,' she suggested in desperation one balmy evening as she sat at his feet on the far bank of the great lake. 'Let's defect to Ireland.'

'Shame on you for the good Englishwoman you are,' Eugene mock-scolded her. 'That is tantamount to treason.'

'A tantalising idea, do admit.'

'The best idea I've ever heard. Come on—we'll saddle up and away. They'll never catch us if we take the byways.'

Kate sat between his legs and leaned back

against his chest.

'Wouldn't it be wonderful if we could, though?' she said wistfully. 'Blasted war. We could escape it all—if we just took off. They'd never find us. Never in a million years.'

'Good heavens no,' Eugene replied lightly. 'The last place they'd look for me would be the bogs— and the last person they'd think you'd run off with would be that rascal Eugene Hackett. Let's hear your next grand idea for our future.'

'You could suddenly develop a limp. Or short sight.'

'And you could turn round and kiss me.'

What made it worse for Kate was that Eugene always seemed to be in such indomitable high spirits. Nothing ever seemed to get to him, rattle him or depress him. Sometimes he might fall to silence, but his silences were short and usually well rationalised. He would carefully explain what he had been thinking and why, and such was his plausibility that Kate never doubted him for a moment—until a week or so after his return when they were out walking one evening he fell into the longest silence she had known from him.

'OK,' she said, finally tiring of skimming stones across the placid waters of the lake while Eugene sat on a bench some little distance from her. 'Enough is enough. Have you finally taken a vow of silence?'

'What?' Eugene looked round at her in genuine surprise, as if he had forgotten all about her presence. 'I'm sorry, Katie—what was it you said?'

'Eugene.' Kate threw her last flat stone in a perfect duck and drake across the glassy lake, put her hands on her hips and turned to him with a shake of her blonde head. 'You haven't said a word for what seems like weeks.'

'Fine. So I've been thinking. I like to give the old brain a workout now and then. Keeps it ticking over.'

'No point in offering you a penny for them, I suppose?'

'None at all, darling one—none at all.'

Eugene got up from the bench, threw away the end of the cheroot he had been smoking so thoughtfully, and wandered off along the path past Kate, for once without taking her arm or her hand. Kate called after him, finally having to break into a trot to catch him up.

'Is it something I said, Eugene?' she managed to get out, as she caught his arm.

'You? Never.' Eugene turned and looked at her but didn't stop walking for a moment. 'You could never say anything to upset me. Other than you didn't love me any more. It's got nothing to do with you.'

'I thought there might be someone else—'

Eugene kept on walking. 'It's worse than that. Much, much worse.'

'What could be worse?' Kate persisted, trying to keep the tone that was in danger of growing sombre as light as she could. 'I can't think of anything worse.'

Eugene suddenly stopped and, taking her by both her hands, confronted her.

'Yes you can, Katie,' he said quietly. 'Don't think of us for once. Put us to one side and think carefully of what could be worse. Of what could be worse here—that could affect not just us.'

Kate was there in one. She had got it even

184

before Eugene had clued her in. Something that would affect everyone—something that would affect Eugene and her—something that might *already* have affected them. She knew what it was. Something they all dreaded.

Treachery.

Chapter Five

Scott was beginning to get worried. Since they had established themselves and their alibi, he and Lily had more or less drawn a blank with the people they had been designated to contact. From experience he knew that he could not pursue the two men with whom he had so far talked, albeit only briefly, about the purpose of their visit, but he also knew that he was running out of time fast. As predicted by their amiable landlady, German troops had arrived in their thousands over the past few days, convoys of lorries packed with infantry and gunners, followed by heavy vehicles drawing artillery, stores and supplies.

The little village in which they were staying had up until then escaped direct occupation since the army seemed more intent on heading directly for the coastline of the Somme from St-Valery west to le Tréport, a part of France that still showed horrifying signs of devastation from the previous war. None the less, a small platoon of surly German foot soldiers had been garrisoned in each of a long line of neighbouring villages, and so inevitably a small troop arrived in the nearby square, bringing with them their own particular whiff of arrogance and churlishness. Fortunately the soldiers were unaware of Madame Daumier's *pension*, and they chose to billet themselves on the luckless proprietor of the village café.

Naturally the presence of the enemy in the village added a further sense of urgency to Scott and Lily's mission. Whatever else was going to happen, the Germans had obviously been ordered to turn their attention to examining the population of the towns and villages they were set on occupying. Scott quickly realised that he and Lily had to consolidate their local contacts and literally take to the hills, or, preferably, the caves they had already earmarked for their project. Just as they were beginning to realise they were out of luck, and that they would have to abort their mission, help came from an unexpected source.

'I have a visitor for you, monsieur,' Madame Daumier informed Scott one night when he and Lily returned ahead of the curfew that was now being strictly enforced. 'He's waiting for you in the kitchen.'

Leading the way through, their landlady opened the door of the kitchen at the back of the house: a small room lit by a well-trimmed oil lamp and shrouded in the heavy pungent smoke of Gitanes cigarettes. At the scrubbed wooden table drinking coffee and brandy sat a thickset man, with a head of hair that looked as if it were made of compacted wire and the sort of rough and weather-beaten countenance that can only be earned from a life spent permanently out of doors.

Everything about their visitor was big—his hands, his forearms, his thighs, his chest and his massive shoulders. He was also immensely ugly,

186

with a large broken nose, one half-closed eye and a deep scar that ran from the bottom of his left cheek in a cut right across his mouth, ending in what appeared to be a hastily stitched lump on the right-hand side of his chin.

Scott observed all this as he shook hands with the man and sat down opposite him, Lily seating herself beside him. The man said nothing other than grunting an all but incomprehensible return to Scott and Lily's salutations, barely even sparing them more than a glance. As Scott and Lily settled at the table he remained silent, lighting another Gitanes from the end of his current smoke and casually dropping the latter on the stone kitchen floor having first extinguished it on his thumb.

'Some coffee, monsieur? Madame?' Madame Daumier asked. 'And some armagnac? It's the last of our home-made.'

Scott accepted with thanks, Lily declining the armagnac while lighting up one of her own cigarettes. Through the heavy fug that surrounded him, the man wrinkled his nose in distaste at the smell of her tobacco and waved it away from his face with one enormous hand.

'You object to my smoking, monsieur?' Lily asked, unable to keep the surprise out of her voice.

'No. To your smoke, madame. It smells so sickly.'

He continued to wave his hand in front of his face in the manner of a demented dowager with a fan, even though Lily by now was making sure to hold and to smoke her cigarette in the opposite direction.

'This is Rolande,' Madame Daumier said,

putting her hands on the man's shoulders as she stood behind him. 'He is a very close friend—not only of my family and myself, but of France. And because he is such a friend of France, he is therefore your friend—*monsieur*.'

Scott knew by the little gap Madame had left before pronouncing *monsieur* that *she* knew, just as he had always suspected. His hackles rose. His immediate worry, however, was that she might not be Free French but a woman alone who, because of her precarious situation, might feel obliged to report to the occupying forces the presence of people in her little community whom she obviously deemed suspect.

As if reading his thoughts, Madame Daumier threw back her head and gave a shout of humourless laughter, slapping Rolande on the back before making her way to lift the coffee pot from the top of the black range of ovens that lined one wall.

'I can see that Monsieur here is worried that I have rumbled him—and that I will inform on him.' Her expression changed. 'Me? Who has lost her son? I think not, *enfin*.'

Rolande turned his attention to Scott, fixing him with a pair of eyes that from where Scott was sitting looked completely black, saying nothing but just staring until he finally shook his head in despair and spat on the floor.

'Is that a mark of contempt, monsieur?' Scott wondered. 'Or simply a lifelong habit?'

Again Rolande fixed him with a look. Suddenly he banged one of his great fists on the table, making cups and glasses leap in the air, and he too gave a great roar of laughter.

188

'It is habitual, my friend!' he cried. 'It is nothing personal! Suspicion, since the Occupation, is habitual.'

Leaning across the table he grabbed one of Scott's hands and shook it, Scott's long-fingered, elegant hand disappearing entirely into the centre of the bone-crushing grasp as he did so.

'You are very brave coming here, monsieur,' he continued, with a smile of appreciation in Lily's direction. 'Very brave and foolish—like all your countrymen.'

Scott nodded, realising that the time to stop pretending to be entirely French had undoubtedly arrived. 'I think you probably mean foolhardy.' He smiled. 'At least I hope you do.'

'You do not consider it foolish to come here? To occupied France? And try to work for their defeat? This is not your fight—this is ours, monsieur. We too shall defeat them. We shall drive the pigs from our land. They do not know what they have done, invading la France.' He shook his head slowly and menacingly. 'They can have no idea at all, monsieur. None whatsoever.'

'I don't think they can, monsieur.'

Scott smiled politely, still feeling wary, for he knew nothing of this man, and less of his allegiances.

'We are a race of fools. We should have blown up the bridges—we should have blown them in the Nazis' faces.'

'I don't think you are a race of fools, monsieur. Misguided, perhaps, but fools—never!'

Rolande eyed him then grinned, his disfigured mouth twisting into an affecting and infectious smile.

'Nor do I think this is your fight alone, either, much as you would want it to be—and rightly so.' Scott held up one hand in appeasement, although Monsieur Rolande had given no indication that he was going to take offence. 'Had it not been for some fools in England—as well as some fools in France—you would not be in this terrible position. We have a duty to dig you out of this hole.'

'And so say all of us,' Lily agreed, putting out her cigarette in her saucer. 'And for the sake of *entente*, Rolande, I shall even take to smoking your sort of cigarette.'

'Good.'

Rolande solemnly offered her a Gitanes, but one so loosely packed that the black tobacco spilt out of it as he handed it to her.

'How kind,' Lily said sweetly. 'But might I save it till later, perhaps? I'm not really a very heavy smoker.'

With a small shrug Rolande laid the fat cigarette by her cup. 'For when you have your next cup of coffee,' he said.

Lily did her best to avoid having any more coffee, but since there was so much to be discussed and Madame Daumier's coffee was so good, finally she could hold out no longer. As soon as her cup was full, and despite Rolande's being now deep in conversation with Scott about the logistics of what was henceforward their mutual enterprise, Lily found a lighted match being waved under her nose.

She tried to ignore it, but her new friend was having none of it. To emphasise the point he now picked up the Gitanes and offered it to Lily in such a pointed fashion that she knew she could do nothing to get out of smoking the loathsome-looking offering. As she started to draw on the foul-smelling smoke, neither Rolande nor Scott paid her the least attention, continuing their earnest conversation, while Madame Daumier sat down by Lily to enjoy the last of her armagnac with her coffee and to talk to her guest in her usual animated way.

'Something the matter, my little one?' she finally enquired with concern as she saw Lily slowly turning very pale.

'No, no,' Lily muttered, swallowing hard. 'At least . . . yes. Would you excuse me just for a moment please?'

Lily made it just in time to the back door that mercifully opened directly on to a patch of garden.

'A little armagnac now, my dear,' Madame insisted as Lily took her place again. 'It is a very fine *digestif* after such discomfort.'

As for Rolande, he merely continued talking to Scott as if he had noticed nothing.

*   *   *

The following morning, just as the cock in Madame Daumier's chicken coop began to crow, Scott and Lily crept out of the house to meet Rolande, who was waiting for them a mile up the lane that led to his farm. As soon as they caught up with him he hurried them into a nearby outbuilding where there was a change of clothes set out, and so it was that in a matter of minutes Scott and Lily had changed from neatly dressed honeymooners to working peasants. Scott wore a loose blue canvas jacket and trousers, a rough white undershirt, traditional Norman footwear and an equally traditional beret, while Lily had tucked her hair under a dull red headscarf and donned a plain blue crew-necked jersey, canvas skirt and sandals. Following Rolande's example, they took the bicycles that stood propped up against the stone wall and fell in line behind the huge man, who was now sitting astride an old but tremendously sturdy tricycle that he somehow managed to ride with great élan.

'Hard to believe, eh?' he called to them. 'But I could never master the two-wheeler! I can swim like a porpoise! I play football like a lightweight! I can even walk a tightrope! But *bah*! The bicycle she defeats me! One day, perhaps—one day!'

They cycled through a whole stretch of green and verdant countryside, bathed in sunlight, the air seemingly full of birdsong. Alongside the road a small clear river dashed and rushed over rock and stone, sparkling in the bright sunshine until it disappeared in a torrent over a huge dark slab of granite, eventually to run away from them into deep woodlands that stretched as far as the eye could see. There was no sight of the war and no sound of it, just the natural music of the countryside.

'I feel as though I'm going on a picnic,' Lily laughed as she cycled alongside Scott. 'I could even start worrying about whether or not I packed a bottle opener.'

'Don't mention bottles,' Scott called back. 'I could murder the contents of a dozen of 'em.'

And of course a bottle was the last thing a Frenchman would forget on such a day as this, even though, far from being out on a picnic the trio were intent on sabotage. Nevertheless, at the appropriate moment Rolande steered his tricycle over to a gateway that led into acres of perfect pasture. The three of them were careful to keep both their varied conveyances and themselves out of sight of the road, by sitting with their backs to the inside of the hedgerow to enjoy a simple and traditional repast of baguette and cheese washed down with rough local wine.

'When the war's over, Scott,' Lily announced, lying back to enjoy a cigarette, 'let's all come back here for a holiday.'

'After the war *you* can do as you please, Lily,' Scott replied, also lighting up a smoke.

'You know what I mean,' Lily replied casually, seemingly unperturbed by his put-down. 'It was actually meant as a fantasy, if you like. Something to aim for, rather than a proposition.'

'Sorry. I didn't mean to be rude—and I know exactly what you mean. It's rather why we're here. What we're fighting for.'

'Put out your cigarettes!' Rolande commanded suddenly. 'And don't move!'

Happily he had heard the convoy seconds before them, because unlike them he had been listening out. By the time the cigarettes were extinguished and bodies flattened against the hedgerow the noise and rumble of the passing vehicles, not to mention the feeling that the earth beneath them was shaking, all suggested that the Germans had to be passing within inches of them.

Scott found himself closing his eyes and praying that there were no foot soldiers following, that the convoy was all vehicular and there were no stragglers who might be tempted into the field for any reason, the most likely being to answer the call of nature. But as the lorries and smaller vehicles rumbled off into the distance, silence fell once more, unbroken by the sound of any footfalls.

'There's certainly a lot of activity round here,' Scott murmured to Rolande as the noise eventually faded away. 'It doesn't bode well if they're building up reserves along the coast here. The sooner we get some transmitters in place, the better we'll all feel.'

'We already have some detailed information about the placement of the heavy artillery, the troop movements and the new defences that are being constructed. My cousin waits for us ahead. When we get there you will learn all this—and perhaps more.'

If we get there, Scott thought as he made ready to take to the road again, checking the inside pocket of his jacket to make sure his forged papers were still in place. With the amount of German activity in the region he felt sure that they were bound to be stopped at some checkpoint, and frankly he was dreading it, for the one thing that he and Lily lacked between them was a plausible reason for their travels. According to their papers their current work was many miles inland, and even their honeymoon destination was a long cycle ride from the Somme coastline that was their final objective.

However, it seemed that Rolande had already foreseen that exigency, guiding his charges away from even the minor roads on which they were travelling and up a series of unmade paths that grew more nearly impassable the further into the hills they went. Finally, the way became so rough that even pushing their bicycles became too much of an effort, but apparently Rolande had already thought of that as well, for just as Lily was convinced that her legs were beginning to give way, their guide diverted them to a track that finally led to a small stone barn where they concealed their priceless transport under the rubble and rubbish of the obviously deserted shelter.

From there they made their way by foot along the side of a cliff line, keeping a good fifty yards inland and well away from the ridge itself, where they could have easily been spotted by any guard or casual lookout, until at last they found themselves a couple of hundred feet above a tiny fishing village which they could see outlined below them.

Rolande nodded to another stone shelter where they waited until darkness had fallen. As soon as it was safe Rolande disappeared, leaving Scott and Lily behind as had been agreed. Rolande had deemed it both wiser and safer for him to make his contact alone, rather than risk all three being stopped and cross-examined.

'At least if they stop me, my friends,' he argued, 'I have genuine relations in the village who will vouch for me. As well as a woman who is prepared to swear that my reason for such a long journey is because we are enjoying a little liaison.'

He grinned mischievously at them both and winked before disappearing into the twilight, leaving Scott and Lily to wonder at his aplomb. Only a Frenchman it seemed would come up with such a wonderful and totally plausible alibi. The French were so justifiably famous for their love of *amours* that no one—not even the most suspicious—would doubt that Rolande was intent on the pursuit of Cupid.

'I'm cold,' Lily complained, after the first hour alone.

'It's spring. You can't be cold,' Scott replied. 'For God's sake it's been the warmest day of the year so far.'

'It may have been a warm day, but we're a lot of feet above sea level, it's night, and I happen to be cold.'

'Here.' Scott had taken off his jacket and was now offering it to her. Lily stared at it.

'You'll get cold now.'

'I'll survive. I don't feel the cold.'

Lily shrugged her shoulders and wrapped the canvas jacket round them, tucking her legs up under her as she sat in one corner of the shelter, while Scott stood opposite her, his back to the wall, smoking a cigarette and looking up at the ceiling, if at anything at all.

'Why don't you come and sit down? You'll get tired standing there. Rolande is going to be gone some time.'

'You know that for a fact?'

'Look how far he has to descend,' Lily retorted with a nod of her pretty head. 'That's one hour gone before he even reaches the village. Then another hour if not more while he makes contact without arousing suspicions, then another hour at least to climb back up here. If you insist on remaining standing all that time, you're not going to be of much use when it comes to us getting going.'

Scott gave her a brief look then nodded.

'After I finish my cigarette,' he said, 'I'll take a pew—but only after.'

His smoke finished, he seated himself opposite Lily rather than beside her. Lily sighed loudly.

'We'd both be not only more comfortable if you

came and sat beside me,' she said, 'but also a whole lot warmer.'

Scott said nothing, refusing to admit that by now even he was feeling not just foolish, but chilled in the night air, high up as they were above the sea. Finally, after a brief struggle with his pride, he went over, and sat down beside Lily in the darkness.

'It's OK, Scott,' she murmured. 'I don't bite.'

Scott sat stiffly with his back to the wall, leaving about a foot of space between him and the woman who he was sure was smiling to herself in the darkness. Next thing he knew Lily had shuffled herself up close to him, so close that he could feel the immediate warmth from her body.

'*Huh*,' she whispered, breathing warm breath straight on to him as she took one of his hands. 'You're half frozen. You loony.'

She breathed on his hand again, holding it up to her mouth and warming it the way Scott remembered his mother warming his hands in winter-time. All at once he was back by the family fireside, fresh in from tobogganing on a tin tray down the steep lawns outside the house, sitting on his beloved mother's knees while she blew warmth back into his hands, before settling him down between their two sleeping red setters in front of a blazing fire. He swallowed hard, and was trying to remember when he had last been as suddenly homesick as he was now, when right out of the blue he found himself longing for a fireside back in another house, a small house up in the woods in Eden Park where he imagined Poppy might even now be sitting in front of a log fire with her little dog, asleep in the warmth of the glow. He closed his eyes and tried to banish the desperate longing, knowing that it would only weaken him, diminish his sense of dedication, but the sickness in his throat would not subside. It was just as if he was a small boy again, sent away for the first time to school, alone in a darkened dormitory full of strange boys all as miserable as he was, his heart and mind awash with unhappiness and despair as he lay in the dark longing for the love of his home and family.

He was so engrossed with his memories he was hardly aware of Lily's head on his shoulder, or of her arm round his waist as she cuddled him to her, until it was too late.

'It's OK,' she whispered, trying to reassure him. 'I'm only keeping us warm. It's OK.'

Scott sat as still as a mouse, not daring even to take a breath for fear of inhaling one of his favourite scents, the warmth of a woman's hair, let alone another, the sweetness of a woman's skin under her clothes. Yet even though he was still holding his breath, the delicate fragrance of Lily's body was already in his being, and the warmth of her was in his arms. He closed his eyes again and thought of cold, and rain, pain, discomfort and unhappiness, but the warmth was still there. Alone and in danger, there was nothing he wanted more than affection. But he refused to respond.

He stayed as still as the rock he was trying so hard to be, thinking only of the person who waited for him on the other side of the narrow channel of sea that lay between them. At long last, Lily fell asleep, her breath rising and falling in a gentle steady rhythm, and her head sliding forward off his shoulder. Instinctively Scott put up an arm to prevent her from jolting herself awake, and the next thing he knew she was folded up in his arms, her head on his chest, the warmth of their bodies fused into one.

* * *

Rolande did not return until morning. When he arrived he was accompanied by a younger man, not much shorter than he but of an entirely different physique. Where Rolande was big this man was slender, where Rolande was hefty, he was nimble, and where Rolande was heavy-featured, his face was almost classical—almost but not quite, since both Scott and Lily could see at once that there was too much of the agricultural in him to be classically framed. His mouth was a little too full, his eyebrows slightly too thick, and his chin a touch too square. It was his eyes that were compelling—and it was to his eyes that both Scott and Lily were immediately drawn, so much so that the first impression they got of the stranger was that he was in fact immensely good-looking, mesmerised as they were by the pair of brilliant green eyes that examined them so intently. For his part Scott thought he had never seen a pair of eyes more full of mischief, while Lily thought she had never met a gaze so hypnotic. They were both fascinated at his arrival, failing initially to take in the formal introduction Rolande was busy making as he established his cousin's credentials. Scott asked his forgiveness at once, pretending he was still dozy from sleep when in fact he had been fully awake for at least two hours, while Lily just smiled.

'My cousin Yves,' Rolande repeated gruffly, as if to show his irritation at the seeming indifference of his companions in arms to his all important cousin, when in fact he was simply reliving the experience that befell him practically every time he introduced the mesmerising Yves into company. What infuriated Rolande even more was that his cousin seemed to be totally unaware of both his good looks and the immediate and often catastrophic effect his appearance had on people. Most famous of all had been the time when Rolande had taken the reluctant Yves to the wedding of an old flame of his own, only for the bride to desert her husband-to-be at the altar and run off with Yves for a passionate affair which, although it only lasted a little under two months, left the community astounded and the runaways exhausted, if finally apart.

'We are late back here,' Rolande was explaining, 'because we were stopped—rather I was stopped, as we thought I might be. I spent a couple of hours in the company of the Boche, who were only dissuaded from putting me up against a wall and shooting me by the arrival—thank the Lord—'

'Oh yes,' Yves chipped in, raising his startling eyes heavenwards, crossing himself as he did so. 'Thank the Lord indeed.'

'By the arrival of my supposed mistress, who talked the pigs out of shooting me.'

'Tut-tut,' Yves sighed, making an over-innocent face. 'Cousin, that is not why you are *so* late. You must tell our friends why we are this late—and why we are now late for our work.'

Rolande glowered at his cousin in return, furrowing his huge black eyebrows until they met in the middle and narrowing his dark eyes to their most fierce.

'Rolande,' Yves scolded lightly. 'You must tell our friends—or would you rather I did?'

'You can go to hell, cousin!' Rolande retorted, turning on his heel and striding out of the shelter. 'You can go straight to hell!'

Yves winked at Scott and Lily. 'He became partial to the lady who says she is his mistress,' he said, keeping his face straight while raising his eyebrows quickly just once. 'They fell into *deep* conversation—which lasted most of the night. My cousin is very interested in philosophy, you understand?'

'Yves!' came a mighty roar from outside the barn. 'If you do not shut up this moment I shall break your head in two!'

Yves shrugged, raised his eyebrows again and took the pack off his back, crouching down on his haunches to unpack a quantity of food and drink.

'The success my cousin has with women is phenomenal,' he said quietly, with a conspiratorial grin. 'I think they suppose if they kiss him he will turn into a prince.'

Rolande had returned just in time to pick up the last part of this comment, an aside that was rewarded with a smack on the back of Yves's head.

'While when they kiss you they find out just what a toad you are, cousin!' he roared. 'Now give our *copains* their *petit déjeuner*, because we all have work to do.'

*   *   *

By late morning they had climbed down to the village and Scott and Lily had been introduced to the local grocer, who took them into the back of his store, locked the door behind them, and produced three small but fully assembled radio transmitters from the bottom of three sacks of corn. It appeared he had made and fitted them out himself, radio being not just a pastime but a complete obsession. Yves further assured them that although they had not dared run a full test yet for fear of discovery, the sets would work because Monsieur l'Epicier was a genius, and once the transmitters were installed in the caves they were about to visit the war would be over in no time, and they could all return to a full and proper contemplation of the serious things in life, wine, *pétanque*, and the fair sex, strictly in that order.

'Aerials,' Scott said. 'We shall need aerials. We can't transmit without aerials.'

Yves looked at Rolande, who in return shrugged and pulled a non-committal face.

'So?' Yves said. 'We rig up aerials once we have the transmitters in place, yes?'

'Where?' Scott wondered. 'We shall have to see where we're transmitting from first.'

Again Yves looked to his cousin, who nodded agreement that they were about to enter the next phase of their activities, and possibly so far the most dangerous one. Now they had to hide the priceless transmitters away somehow in some form of transport and ferry them to the chosen destination under the noses of the Germans, who it seemed were now everywhere.

It was finally agreed that the transmitters should be hidden once again in their bags of corn and loaded on to the grocer's delivery cart, which Yves volunteered to drive as far as he could into the surrounding countryside before meeting up with the others in order to carry their precious equipment into the caves that lay deep in the high cliffs.

'No. I don't think so. I think I should drive the cart.'

The three men stared at Lily, as if unable to believe their ears.

'You do not know the way, for a start,' Rolande growled, after a small pause. 'And you're hardly going to be able to stop and ask a friendly German.'

'One of you, Yves I imagine, can hide in the back and direct me,' Lily replied. 'It's better that I drive. If I get stopped, I can—as a last resort—flirt my way out, perhaps.'

'She's right there, boys,' Scott interrupted with a smile. 'If anyone can flirt her way out of danger, Lily's the number one choice.'

'Hmmm,' Rolande said, eyeing the pretty young woman as he lit another Gitanes. 'Hmmm.'

'And if she doesn't succeed,' Yves added, 'which I have to say I greatly doubt, then I shall kill the offending Kraut.'

'Krauts,' Scott said, pluralising the noun. 'If it's a patrol, two at the very least—possibly more. If it's a squad, the best of British to you is all I can say.'

'Pardon?' Yves frowned. 'The best of British . . . ?'

'Luck, chum. Particularly since our arms at the moment run to a couple of knives between us.'

'I don't see the alternative,' Rolande said finally. 'We have to go by daylight because at night we are even more certain to be stopped—after curfew.'

'And the corn has to be delivered, as always,' Yves added. 'So naturally it must be delivered during the day.'

The grocer had volunteered to deliver it himself, but since he was elderly and more than a little infirm no one considered it fair that he should be put at risk, Rolande assuring him that he had done more than enough by assembling and hiding the transmitters. Finally it was agreed that Lily should drive the cart with Yves well hidden below all the bags of grain and feedstuffs and Rolande and Scott following on foot at a more than discreet distance. The directions were in fact much simpler than Rolande had at first indicated, since there was only one road out of the village. After three kilometres it forked into two, at which juncture Lily was directed to take the right fork and drive the cart as far up into the hills as she could, a matter of another kilometre and a half before she finally came to a point of no return, the farm to which she was meant to be delivering the feedstuff.

After only three hundred or so yards, she saw two Germans, rifles slung over their shoulders, patrolling the road. They had their backs to her but as soon as they heard the sound of the cart they turned to look.

'Good day, boys!' Lily smiled at them as she approached, gesturing with one hand to the blue sky above. 'Some day for April, yes? Bet you'd rather be out of those uniforms and on the beach, yes?'

One soldier stared at her, not understanding a word of her French, and seemed about to challenge her. But his companion put an arm on his to stop him, stepping forward to take control and smiling up at the beautiful peasant girl sitting smiling back down at him from her driving seat.

'Slowly, mademoiselle, if you would,' he

requested in schoolboy French. 'My French is not so good.'

Lily bent over towards him, allowing him a good view of her breasts through the open neck of her shirt as she did so. Repeating what she had just said carefully and slowly, she remained in that position until a more than visible blush had begun to rise from the young soldier's throat to suffuse his face.

'It is certainly warm today, mademoiselle,' he said in halting French, running a finger round the back of the collar of his heavy shirt. 'I said just now to my friend here that we would like to swim.'

'I'm going to swim as soon as I have delivered this wretched corn,' Lily replied, broadening her smile. 'When are you boys off duty? I know a lovely part of the beach.'

The two soldiers looked at each other, the French-speaking one translating for his friend, who immediately opened his eyes wide to stare with wonder at Lily.

'We have some time this afternoon, late, mademoiselle,' the first soldier finally replied. 'We were thinking of going to the—what is the word?'

'Beach? Well, if you are, let me show you the best place. It's very private too.' Lily let the implication hang in the air as she continued to smile at the young men.

'First I have to ask you where you are headed,' the French-speaker said, trying to hide his own smile. 'We have to ask everyone their business.'

Lily explained what she described as her boring task for the day, a job that was keeping her from the beach, which was why she was so anxious to get it done as quickly as possible. As she kept the soldiers so well occupied, Scott and Rolande slipped unnoticed into adjacent fields and took to the woods, headed fast now for their objective.

'So, boys,' Lily smiled, picking her reins back up. 'Maybe we'll see each other later on the beach? I'll look out for you and take you to my little cove. OK?'

She left the two soldiers grinning like the schoolboys they had been only a handful of months before, smacking the rump of the old pony between the shafts of the cart with a limp whip and smiling to herself at her sangfroid. She had known no fear whatsoever during the exchange, only a sense of purpose and confidence, which she knew would give Miss Lavington twin fits. Unlike herself, Cissie Lavington felt that agents should not be fearless, that to be fearless was actually to play the most dangerous game anyone could perhaps play, but according to the way Lily saw things their work had to be viewed in terms of game-playing. As long as it was, and reality was kept at bay, then she could indulge herself to the full.

When the two German soldiers had stopped her in the road she had assumed the role of the character she had decided to play with zest. She *was* a peasant girl delivering a load of animal feed to a farm, and she *was* already bored by the task, having previously determined to spend a lazy day on the beach. She was also a flirtatious miss, and one not averse to toying with the emotions of the enemy as much as she did with the local boys, although the character Lily had created for herself was already bored with the local lads, and excited by the thought of fresh young and energetic blood being infused into her dull little fishing village.

That was why she had succeeded so

convincingly, she told herself, as she drove the cart up the long incline towards the farm at the top. She had succeeded in convincing the Germans she was bona fide because that was what *she* believed—and therefore to survive that was all she had to do: continue to believe in whatever fantasy she created.

*   *   *

The rest of the initial part of the mission went according to plan. The four of them rendezvoused at the end of the track, at a holding owned by another Resistance worker who led them to an entrance concealed in the rocks behind his family farm, which in turn led them down to the warren of caves that had been chosen as ideal hiding places for the transmitters and their operators.

The caves were a genuine labyrinth, smaller and more tortuous than those that Lily had grown to know so well at Eden Park, although fortunately well marked with white chalked-up directional signs for the benefit of the newcomers, ending in three large caves approximately fifty feet above sea level, each with tiny apertures in their sea walls, allowing a restricted view of both the Channel and the beach below.

They had already been equipped with plain tables and chairs, as well as two camp beds in case anyone had to spend any length of time in hiding there and a simple camping stove on which the operators could make a hot drink or heat a can of beans or stew. Heavy batteries had been put in place ready to power the transmitters once they were set up, which they were within two hours of the party's arrival underground. Each set worked to

perfection, other than the fact that they were
unable as yet to transmit because of the lack of
vital aerial wires.

Scott pronounced the caves perfect as far as
security went but not so the set-up, considering the
rock walls to be too thick for successful
transmission even if they did manage somehow to
rig up the necessary aerials. He further considered
that in order to maximise the power of the
homemade transmitters, whose signals had to be
picked up by receivers at Beachy Head, they
needed to be higher or they would never finally
reach HQ.

'You've all done a wonderful job so far,' he
declared as they sat down at the table to drink
some wine and smoke cigarettes. 'But the problem
is these transmitters are weaker than one had
hoped for. No fault of your grocer friend, who has
made a great job of assembling them—but from
here we have a good fifty or sixty miles to carry
across, and unless we erect a socking great aerial
we're not going to reach our destination.'

A long discussion then followed concerning how
best to erect an aerial tall enough to do the job, but
not tall enough to be noticed by curious German
eyes. The farm owner suggested they transmit from
his house instead, erecting some sort of aerial on
the roof, which seemed to be a sensible idea until
Scott pointed out that it could only be a short-term
solution as the Germans were known to have
sophisticated monitoring devices that could readily
pick up radio signals within their vicinity. It was
why the caves had been suggested in the first place;
they were rumoured to be impenetrable to enemy
listening devices.

'It doesn't have to go up in the air, does it?' Lily suddenly enquired, looking up from her nails, which she had been carefully cleaning with a sharpened match. 'This aerial. It doesn't have to go straight up in the air, does it? Or does it?'

'That's what aerials usually do, Lily,' Scott replied, using a deliberately over-patient voice. 'Remember seeing them? They're like little beacons—and sometimes rather larger beacons.'

'Yes, yes, mein Führer,' Lily interrupted, getting to her feet and carefully brushing herself down as if she was in her best party clothes rather than borrowed peasant garments. 'I know what they look like—but that wasn't my question. Is that the only way aerials work is my question. Vertically?'

All the men looked at her as they realised a little late that it was a question they had not really considered before. They also all, to a man, remained silent, as if finally reluctant to take up the challenge.

'Let me put it another way,' Lily continued ruthlessly, realising at once that none of them had ever thought of using aerials any way except straight up. 'Could an aerial work horizontally? If it was off the ground, and long enough?'

Scott frowned. 'I don't see why not,' he said at last, reluctantly. 'But then I don't actually see why either.'

'No, no!' Yves exclaimed, jumping to his feet. 'Lily is perhaps right! There is no reason, so long as the aerial wire is long enough and is raised sufficiently, why it should not work! No—I see no reason why it should not! Why? What are you suggesting, my little one?'

'I take it that's a compliment in your language,

209

Yves? To be called a little one?'

'But of course! Of course! So? Then?'

Lily looked round at them, mischievous as always, before finally beginning to expound her idea. It was so simple it was astounding, and of course, always provided it remained undiscovered, there was no reason why it should not work.

'You *are* married, monsieur?' Lily asked the farmer, to reassure herself.

'But yes, mademoiselle. I have a wife and four children, three of them under the age of conscription, thank God.'

'So you will have plenty of washing?'

'There is always plenty of washing in our household, m'moiselle. My wife—even with the restrictions, she is a very strict housekeeper.'

'Then all we have to make sure is that your new washing line is always well hung.'

* * *

It seemed it was as simple as that. Monsieur Rochard, the farmer, acquired a brand new washing line behind his farmstead, along the top line of the cliff but not particularly noticeable from below. To be sure it was a little longer than the normal domestic line and made of an entirely different material, but that would only become apparent to anyone standing beside it, and since it was determined that he should keep as much washing hanging out to dry on the line as possible, whatever the weather, given the remoteness of the farm, and the fact that visitors were few and far between, there was only the remotest of chances that any foot soldiers would bother to come and inspect the Rochard family's line. Nor would the transmitters give their positions away, left as they were far below ground and wired securely up to the washing line above them. The only difficulty facing the Resistance now, given the sizeable German presence in the area, would be gaining regular access to the caves without being spotted by the enemy patrols.

'Perhaps not for much longer,' Rolande remarked, as they sat drinking marc in the farmhouse late that night, their day's work finally done. 'We hear only the other day that Herr Hitler is turning serious attention to Russia. And if this proves to be the case, my friends, I think we may see many of these troops being withdrawn. After all, they were sent here to invade England, not Russia.'

'Let's hope,' said Scott, raising his glass. 'It would certainly make life a lot easier for you.'

'Not for us?' Yves enquired. 'You are leaving us?'

'Not yet, comrade,' Scott replied. 'We're going to make sure all this is up and running first and that we get the first all important bulletins back home. Tomorrow we shall transmit all the information you, my comrades, have gleaned about the fortifications being built along this stretch, as well as all troop movements so far and any new ones— just in case the forecast about Russia is wrong. No, no, we're not going to ship out just yet—though we are ordered to return by the end of the month provided everything is running smoothly by then.'

Yves nodded his understanding, all the time looking at Lily, who, although she was perfectly well aware of his attention, chose to ignore it.

211

'I'm out of cigarettes,' she announced. 'Has anyone got a cigarette that *isn't* made out of sheep droppings?'

The three Frenchmen shrugged and sighed their regrets.

'Here,' said Scott, offering her a Players.

'It's your last one,' Lily said with feeling, looking up at him.

'Then I shall have to learn to smoke sheep droppings.' He nodded to her to take it.

'Thank you,' she said finally. 'Ta very much.'

'Ta to you too, Lily,' he said. 'That was actually quite a bright idea about the aerial.'

'Shucks,' Lily returned in mock American.

'I mean it,' Scott insisted. 'But in future if I were you I'd forgo the manicures. If you're stopped, some bright-eyed Kraut might wonder what a peasant girl like you is doing with such dainty manicured mitts.'

So attractive was her laugh and so gay her smile that Scott felt like kissing her instantly. Instead he cadged a Gitanes from Rolande and poured himself another glass of marc. They were nowhere near safe yet. In fact they were only just beginning the business of their mission, and now that the transmitters were ready to work, the danger they were in was all the greater. Any false sense of celebration must be put aside.

'God,' Lily suddenly thought aloud. 'Listen—do you think they'll have reported the cart? The Germans who stopped me this morning. If they've put the cart down in their reports—'

'Which they well might do,' Scott agreed.

'Then whoever takes over their duty might notice my non-return. Mightn't they?'

They just managed to hide everything away in time. While Madame Rochard cleared the kitchen of all traces of the visitors, emptying cigarette ends into the stove and washing and drying the brandy glasses and coffee cups, Monsieur Rochard pulled his bewildered seventeen-year-old son out of bed and dragged him over to the hay barn where he was introduced to an already half undressed Lily, who got up from in between the hay bales to greet him.

'Now you behave yourself, young man,' Monsieur Rochard warned his still utterly bewildered son. 'This is for France, understand? You are not to think of *anything* other than la belle France! You do and I will see to you myself!'

'It's all right, monsieur,' Lily whispered to the distracted farmer. 'I'll take good care of him.'

'You had better not, m'moiselle,' Rochard growled back. 'He is barely seventeen!'

'I meant I will make sure he comes to no harm. We shall only be pretending. Please don't worry.'

Monsieur Rochard regarded her with deep suspicion, smacked his son lightly about the head with one hand as an advance warning of what might befall him should he get carried away, then hurried back to bed in his house. Two minutes later, when Scott, Yves and Rolande were all safely on their way down to the labyrinth, the Germans arrived.

They turned the place over, much to the well-acted consternation of the Rochards whom they yelled at to get out of their beds, along with two of their children.

213

'There is another child!' one of the soldiers barked in half-acceptable French. 'There is an empty bed in this room! Where is this one? Well?'

Monsieur Rochard frowned deeply and shrugged, turning to his wife, who simply raised her eyebrows to the heavens.

'Should this child be in bed, madame?'

'But of course, sir. It is very late, and even though he is the oldest—'

The German captain cut her off with a nod of his head to the men behind him and a barked order. The four soldiers who had followed him up the rickety staircase swung themselves back down with a great heavy clatter of boots and clank of equipment as they left the farmhouse to instigate a further search.

It didn't take them long. The door of the hay barn was swinging open and within minutes two of the soldiers, aided by their powerful spotlights, had found the so-called lovers in their bed of hay. At once Lily grabbed the short top she had discarded to make herself decent, holding it over her breasts, while the unfortunate young Rochard tried to hide himself under the hay, mortified with embarrassment and shaking with terror.

The two German soldiers stood looking at them, the younger one smiling helplessly while the older one looked at Lily in a quite different way. Seeing the look, for once Lily put all ideas of flirtation out of her head and began to cough as deeply and unpleasantly as she could, before seemingly trying to control the fit.

'Forgive me, sir,' she muttered, wiping one hand slowly across her mouth while biting hard at the inside of her lip at the same time, successfully

214

drawing blood which she carefully made evident on her hand as she stopped coughing. 'Forgive me, please—it's my chest.'

At once the older soldier's expression changed from one of patent lust to one of equally obvious fear and revulsion.

'Come!' he ordered them, with a wave of his rifle. 'Move!'

Grabbing their clothes, the two fake lovers covered themselves and hurried as best they could down the ladder. At the bottom the young German captain waited with his other two men, tapping his leg with his baton. He looked from Lily to the young Rochard boy and shook his head, laughing. Then he clicked his tongue at the boy.

'You're a bad boy,' he said. 'I wonder what your father is going to say.'

'No, no! Please, sir, no!' young Rochard pleaded, as he had been instructed by Lily. 'No, please, sir— do anything but tell Papa! Please!'

The captain regarded him, as if uncertain whether to take him in and punish him himself or to hand him over to be reprimanded by his father. When he saw how violently the boy's knees were knocking he smiled broadly and indicated the house.

'Go on,' he ordered. 'Off with you! Take him inside, Corporal! And tell Papa what his little boy has been up to! And now, mademoiselle—to you.' The captain had that same look in his eyes as he moved towards the beautiful half-dressed young woman who stood before him, hair entangled with hay, only her canvas shirt held tight to her breasts protecting her decency.

'You may go, men,' he ordered in German. 'I

wish to have words with this young lady here.'

'Excuse me, sir,' the older soldier said, stepping forward. 'If I may make so bold, Captain . . .' He dropped his voice before continuing, having given a sideways glance to Lily.

Lily knew what he was whispering from the expression on the captain's face, a look that also turned from lust to loathing.

'Filth,' he said, slapping her hard round the face. 'Filth. Disgusting disease.'

Then turning on his heel he stalked out of the barn, leaving his men temporarily behind him. The younger two smiled shyly at Lily, and left ahead of their older companion, who stared at her before spitting his contempt on the floor.

After he too had gone, and despite the fact that the aftermath of the slap was hurting her more than she could believe, Lily managed to smile. She had, after all, convinced them. At that moment, like many an actress, she felt the pain was nothing compared to the triumph of her performance.

Chapter Six

The first part of their work done, with reports of troop movements and recent fortifications successfully transmitted to HQ via Lily's washing line aerial, Scott and Lily now had to effect their escape from France and back to England as ordered. Getting in was one thing, Scott kept remarking to Lily during time spent in the waiting room, but getting out was quite another.

Lily remained blissfully unperturbed by the

thought that there was a very real possibility that they might be stuck in France should no escape route be organised for them, intent it seemed on practising her deceptions on whoever crossed her path. She even went bathing with the two soldiers whom she had let down the night they were setting up the transmitters, spending one long sun-kissed Saturday first on the main part of the sandy beach that lay west of the tiny harbour, and then in the tiny cove she had discovered that lay out of reach and out of sight to all but those in the know, accessible only by boat or by strong swimmers.

Lily was an exceptionally good swimmer and loved to show off in the water, deciding to swim round the Point with a strong easy crawl while her two tame Germans wallowed behind her, doing their best to cope with the current with their basic breaststroke and finally being forced to give up and return to the safety of the home strand where they waited in frustration, unable to reach the young, nubile woman on whom both their minds were firmly set.

After which Lily took great delight in stripping off, quite alone and unseen by anyone, and soaking up sun and sea air. Finally, as the sun began to sink, she swam back with as much ease as she had swum round, finding her two forlorn soldiers still waiting for her, stripped down to the waist and reddened like lobsters from sunburn, their shoulders already painful to look at. She put an arm round them both, making them wince instantly, and exhorted them to improve on their swimming, so that they could all three of them enjoy the joys of their own private beach.

'Having a nice holiday?' Scott wondered when

he met up with her later at the Rochard farmhouse where he was still awaiting news of any escape plans.

'What do you think of my tan?' Lily dropped both straps of her dress.

'Looks to me as if that is going to cause you a bit of pain, Miss Ormerod,' Scott remarked, turning away to stare out to the sunset over the Channel, visible through the open windows of the farmhouse kitchen.

'I don't burn. I have that sort of skin.'

Scott tried to put the thought of her golden body out of his mind as he stared stupidly out to sea, but found finally he was unable to do so. Lily had a perfect figure, firm and round in all the right places, and now, enhanced by several days spent in the late spring sunshine, she looked as if she'd stepped right off the silver screen. Scott closed his eyes and prayed that he would soon be delivered from temptation by way of an escape route, because although Lily had made no more direct advances to him, he knew—just as she did—that it wasn't necessary. The message had been transmitted and had been received loud and clear, and Scott knew perfectly well that if he had to spend many more days in such proximity to Lily he might well succumb to her all but irresistible charms.

In the event he was saved at the eleventh hour. That very evening, to celebrate the successful establishment of the radio stations, Monsieur Rochard opened yet another bottle of fine homemade marc, Madame Rochard baked a game pie, Rolande conjured wine from nowhere as always and Yves produced his harmonica, an

218

instrument which he played expertly. Pretty soon after they had eaten everyone was dancing and singing, including the children, who were allowed to join the party, the boy who had shared the hayrick with Lily proving himself a fine singer of local songs. Lily finally persuaded Scott to dance, much to the delight of the assembled company, all except Yves whose eyebrows grew lower and lower the more they danced and the more he had to play.

The party was finally broken up by the arrival of one of the radio operators who had been working down in the labyrinth all evening with another trusted volunteer from the village. He brought the news Scott and Lily had been hoping for—there was a ship a couple of miles out to sea waiting to transport them back to England.

They had to leave at once, the two of them hurrying down the long, narrow, winding path that ran down to the tiny cove where a rowing boat with muffled oars riding the high but fast turning tide was ready and waiting to take them out to sea. An hour later they were aboard the unlit vessel that had arrived out of the darkness, the rowing boat moving off almost before Scott's and Lily's feet had hit the deck.

Once on board they looked around them in surprise, both of them having half expected to be collected by an ordinary fishing boat. However, this was no ordinary fishing boat, but a craft that not even Scott had seen before, a Motor Torpedo Boat, developed specifically to target the U-boats that were wreaking such terrible damage on convoys crossing the North Sea or trying to make their way up or down the Channel with vital supplies. On this fast and superbly crafted boat, the crew, in their white knitted headguards and dark blue uniforms, went about their business briskly and efficiently, two sailors ushering Scott and Lily below decks before returning to their duties topside. Lily at once complained that she didn't want to be stuck below, and asked to be allowed back on deck in case they engaged the enemy on the run home to Portsmouth. She was immediately refused, and this despite using all her charms on the officer on watch.

'Oh well,' Lily sighed, sitting down on the bench in the little cabin. 'We'll have to find some other way of amusing ourselves on the home run.'

'Why don't you just try and get some sleep like any other normal human being?' Scott grumbled, attempting to make himself comfortable.

'Because I'm not normal, that's why,' Lily retorted, kicking her shoes off and plonking her feet in Scott's lap. 'And because I'm still too damn' excited.'

Scott glanced round at her, before trying to lift her feet out of his lap.

'Come on, Scott,' Lily sighed. 'Admit it—this really has been quite an adventure.'

'It's been a job well done, that's what it's been.'

Scott tried again to remove her bare and shapely feet, but Lily was digging them well in to him.

'Stop being so stuffy.' She half smiled at him, catching his eye. 'You're not at all stuffy, I know— so stop behaving like a school prefect. And admit you found it exciting.'

'OK.' Scott shrugged, unable to break the look between them. 'Of course it was exciting. We did damned well and I'm really quite proud of us both—'

'Good,' Lily said, losing her smile. 'So let's celebrate.'

Next thing Scott knew he was being firmly and expertly kissed. He also knew that for far too long he made no effort at all to resist, aware of Lily's warmth and softness and welcoming it after the hard reality of the dangers they had both been through.

'Lily,' he said, gently easing her away from him.

'It's OK, Scott.' She smiled mischievously at him. 'All's fair, remember? In love and war. Or as an uncle of mine always used to say—it don't count on tour or in war.'

'On tour?'

'As in the theatre. He was an actor. And stop looking so worried—once we land, that's that. Don't *worry*.'

'I'm not worried. Concerned, maybe.'

'You don't have any reason to be. I'm not that sort of person.'

'I know. You're pretty terrific. And if I may say so—you're also brilliant.'

'Thank you. I'm pretty good at kissing, but I'm even better in—'

'That wasn't what I meant,' Scott interrupted. 'I meant you were brilliant at what you did—back there.' He nodded backwards at the country that was fast disappearing behind them in the night. 'You're a bit unorthodox, but I really like that. I admire your sense of invention and your ability to think on your feet.'

'Thank you, boss. That means a lot. Specially coming from you, Captain Stuffy.'

Scott smiled before falling silent. He *was* concerned, there was no geting away from it. He realised he had grown to trust her in an odd sort of way. She was after all brave and inventive. What Scott was worried about was a quite different anxiety. His concern was in case Lily might actually be having some effect on him.

* * *

'No problems then?' Anthony Folkestone asked Scott as soon as Miss Budge shepherded him into H Section. 'You didn't encounter any unforeseen circumstances? Other than those that we have to take for granted on this type of sortie?'

'Went like clockwork, sir,' Scott replied. 'Amazingly so—for this type of sortie. In fact we actually accomplished more than I expected. I'll write it all up for you, and Marjorie can . . .' He stopped suddenly, seeing Anthony Folkestone's uneasy expression. 'Sorry, sir. Have you heard something different? Or . . . I mean, you look as though you think we *should* have encountered something else.'

Anthony Folkestone regarded him from his side of the desk, tapping his pencil steadily on the top of it, as was his habit, while he considered the wisdom of informing his agent of the present danger surrounding all combined sorties from Eden Park and SOE in Baker Street.

'We appear to have a double agent. Here.' He sighed. 'Someone inside is working against us. It's the only explanation, do you see? The only possible explanation for all the agents we have lost. Out of Brussels—forty down. In the south of France, reprisals. A whole village wiped out. In revenge.'

Anthony stood up and unlocked his wall map,

222

indicating the black pins.

'Fifty-six all told, in fact,' he said. 'And in far too short a space of time. That's why I was enquiring if anything—er, untoward had occurred.'

Scott thought again and shook his head.

'Not that you would know,' Anthony went on. 'That at least is good. Unfortunately, it's not so good for some other people, although we have to allow of course for coincidence. Your first contact—the man in the café who never came back to you—we think either he was a double agent or else they have picked him up. They certainly picked up Madame Daumier.'

Scott looked at Anthony sharply. One of the last people he would wish to fall into the hands of the Gestapo was their kindly landlady.

'Don't tell me that,' he said, turning away and reaching for a cigarette from Folkestone's box. 'For God's sake not her.'

'I haven't anything further on that, alas. Just that the Gestapo paid her a call and she hasn't returned as yet to her house. Soon as I hear anything, of course—'

'We have to get a mesage to the Seagull—and the Cockerel,' Scott interrupted urgently, his heart stopping as he thought of the farming family on the top of their cliff, of Rolande and Yves. 'They mustn't go back home. Not in any circumstances.'

'It might be too late, Scott.'

'Try, please, Major. Just try and get through to the stations. I know they're not meant to be transmitting tonight, but they're so damn' keen over there, and I should imagine the little Sparrow will be wedded to his post as always.'

Anthony nodded.

'Any complaints about your wife-on-the-mission?' he asked, lowering his voice, since he took care never to refer to agents by name.

'No, sir—none whatsoever. She's very resolute, certainly doesn't lack courage, and has tons of initiative.'

'Thought she might have. Miss Lavington was worried—probably still is for all I know—that she might prove a little too headstrong. But you didn't find her so.'

'She's extremely headstrong, sir. Utterly impulsive. But then on the other hand she thinks on her feet so fast . . .' Scott stopped and nodded. 'I can do nothing but give her a full recommendation, sir.'

'You'd be perfectly happy for her to work alongside you again?'

'Yes, sir,' Scott replied after a momentary hesitation. 'Of course.'

Anthony looked up, taking heed of the fractional indecision.

'Not if you're not happy.'

'I'm perfectly happy, sir. Anyway—it's not really up to me, is it?'

Anthony shook his head. 'The Colonel thought you might make a good team,' he said. 'Seems he's been proved right. And you know Mr Ward. Once he's proved right.' Anthony smiled and nodded for Scott to leave. 'Well done anyway, Scott. Good work.'

'Thank you, sir.'

'Enjoy your leave.'

'I will, sir. Make no mistake.' He walked off back through the section.

'Goodnight, Mr Meynell,' Miss Budge called

224

after him.

Scott smiled and waved, preparing to run, not walk, through the woods to the House of Flowers and Poppy, for whom he found he was now quite literally aching.

'Good night, Budgie,' he called back. 'And hurry up and finish my scarf, will you?'

Miss Budge smiled and called after him. 'Nearly finished.' She watched him hurry away down the corridor, then break into a run, knowing that he was running back to the arms of his new wife—and then she cleared her throat, pulled her knitting bag shut, and wound a fresh sheet of crisp white paper into her typewriter.

*   *   *

Having procured some extra petrol rations from the best of his local black market sources, Scott dusted off his Sunbeam sports car and prepared to take Poppy away for the weekend, in an effort to make up for their truncated honeymoon.

'Are you sure you wouldn't rather stay here, Scott?' Poppy stopped in the middle of packing one of their suitcases. 'It's such lovely weather, I've got the house all ready for us—and—well. We've been so looking forward to this, George and I, having you home, all to ourselves.'

As if in complete agreement the dachshund obliged Poppy by climbing carefully into one of the open suitcases.

'I thought you might like to go away,' Scott said, bending over from the bed on which he was sitting to tickle the dachshund.

'It's not that I don't want to go away, Scott. It's

225

just—it's just that everything's so perfect here, really. We could just shut up shop and stay here all by ourselves—in the woods.'

Scott stared at Poppy, knowing exactly how she was feeling, and suddenly realising that his plan for a second honeymoon was perhaps not what was wanted. As soon as he had set foot over the threshold once again all he himself had wanted to do was shut the door, lock it, carry Poppy upstairs to the bedroom and make love to her.

Of course, this is precisely what he had done, and then, after they had slept for a couple of hours in the afternoon, he had woken Poppy to make love to her all over again. After that he had discussed his plans with her, his idea for a weekend away, hurried off to ensure he had enough petrol to make the round trip and then returned to find Poppy still in two minds.

But Scott had persisted with his idea of going on a belated honeymoon, although the truth of the matter was that he had quite another reason for wishing to get away from Eden Park that weekend, a reason that unbeknownst to him was at that moment walking up the narrow woodland path to the House of Flowers.

'Don't you think we're cosy here, Scott?' Poppy wondered, looking half pleading, half humorous.

'Of course, sweetie. No, I only wanted to make it up to you, because we didn't have a proper honeymoon. We could just go away for a couple of nights, then come back here. Anthony Folkestone more or less indicated I could put my feet up for a few days; you know, a little rest between sorties can be good, stops you going back in and making what he calls *bishes*.'

226

Poppy looked at her handsome husband and much as she wanted to stay in their enchanting new home she immediately relented.

'Very well then,' she agreed, kissing him. 'Where are you taking me?'

'Mystery trip, my darling. I think I might blindfold you with one of your scarves. In fact I may even make you keep it on after we've arrived so you can't see quite how badly I will be behaving.'

Poppy laughed and kissed him again, just as there was a knock on the front door downstairs.

'Hello?' called out an instantly recognisable voice. 'Anyone at home? Can I come up? Or are you coming down? Or should I go away again?'

Poppy immediately looked mock-grumpy at Scott, hands on her hips and mouth pursed.

'This your idea? To ask Lily up here?' she whispered. 'If so, it's not one of your best, Scott Meynell.'

'Of course it wasn't my idea!' Scott protested, dropping his voice. 'Why should it be my idea?'

'Come on down, you two. You've surely had enough of each other by now? I'm only calling with a belated wedding present, not a bomb!'

Scott sighed, shrugged his shoulders, and went downstairs, leaving Poppy to finish their packing.

'Good morning, Mr Meynell,' Lily said cheerfully, holding up a gift-wrapped oblong box. 'It's a little late, I'm afraid. But I didn't get a chance to shop before you two dashed off and got spliced. It's a wedding present. Belated, but a present all the same. Hope I haven't called at a bad time.'

'Not at all,' Scott said, rather stiffly taking the box as if it might indeed contain a bomb.

'Not that there's ever been a good time to call on newly-weds,' Lily said, rolling her eyes and laughing mischievously. 'Ah, here's the blushing bride—with a suitcase, I see. Good morning, Mrs Meynell. Gosh, but you have lost weight—and it really suits you. And I love that dress. That new?'

'Hardly new, Lily.' Poppy smiled. 'I made it from a couple of old ones.'

'It's terrific. *Très chic*. Don't you think so, Captain Stuffy?' She didn't look at Scott, even though she used a familiarity. '*Très, très chic*. Going somewhere nice?'

'I don't know,' Poppy replied. 'I'm being taken on a mystery tour, apparently.'

'How exciting. Lucky you.'

'It all depends. Might be unlucky her if she doesn't like where I'm taking her.' Scott started to undo the present.

'It's *champagne*,' Lily put in quickly before he could finish unwrapping. 'Premier cru. We all shared another bottle last night, mixed it with brandy and heaven only knows what else.'

'Champagne. But that's incredible.'

'Well, we are near the coast, Scott, things do suddenly appear overnight where they never were before. I found this with the milk bottles this morning. Heaven only knows who it's from.'

She took out a packet of Gitanes from her handbag and lit one. Scott stared at her and she started to laugh, waving the cigarette about.

'It's all right, I'm not going to be sick, Scott. Shall we open the champagne now?'

Scott looked appreciatively at the label on the bottle. 'Why not? A treat like this doesn't come along every day. Like to get some glasses, Poppy darling?'

'I thought we were in a hurry to get going?'

'I am—but *un tout petit coup* before we go off will only add to the gaiety.'

Poppy shrugged her shoulders and collected three glasses from the corner cupboard.

'What is the toast?' she asked, facing them both now from one end of the room, and perhaps because of that, for some reason she could not understand, feeling strangely wrong-footed, as if she was no longer in her own house.

'Your marriage. Remember?' Lily smiled, pouring the wine. 'Oh, and *Scott's* safe return. Cheerio!'

'In thanksgiving for Scott's safe return,' Poppy agreed, with a smile to Scott. 'Hear hear.'

'You know *Lily*.' Scott laughed, turning half apologetically to Poppy, knowing that this interruption was the last thing either of them wanted. 'Everything and anything's an excuse for a celebration.'

'Not *quite* true—'

'You know, we really should get going, Scott,' Poppy interrupted. 'We're late already.'

'Don't be a spoilsport, Poppy!' Lily said, taking the bottle from Scott and topping up both their glasses. 'It's not every day the hero is returned to the arms of his loved one by the heroine.'

'Is there something I don't know?'

'Tell her, Scott! Tell her how I snatched you from the very jaws of death!'

'I don't think so, do you?' Scott replied firmly. 'Not if we don't all want to end up in the Tower of London. Come on, Lily, time to go.'

'Oh, but I so want to stay and celebrate. After all,' she turned to Poppy smiling over-gaily, 'I've

229

now been married to Scott even longer than you have Poppy, although only in the most professional way, of course.'

Poppy put down her glass and stared at both Scott and Lily.

'I see,' she said slowly. 'By that am I to understand you two—that the two of you have just returned—from a drop?'—she turned to her husband, eyeing him carefully. 'Was Lily—was she—your new partner?'

'Nothing to do with me, sweetie!' Scott found himself protesting. 'You know as well as I do we have to go where we're sent, and no arguing. You don't get to choose your partners in arms!'

'I see,' Poppy muttered, dropping her eyes.

'Scott would never have chosen me over you, Poppy.'

Poppy went to the door, Scott following her, still protesting.

'I wasn't in a position to tell you. Lily shouldn't have said anything either—'

Poppy left the room without a backward glance at Lily who was now standing smiling foolishly, the glass of champagne in her hand tipping dangerously at a right angle. Scott walked over to her and promptly confiscated her glass.

'Go on, Lily, hop it,' he said tetchily. 'I imagine you must still be a bit tight from last night to have behaved so stupidly. But most of all I reckon it is time you *went*.'

'I'm not drunk, Scott, not in the slightest,' Lily retorted, resisting his push towards the door. 'I'm just glad to be alive. You must tell Poppy how brilliant we both were. And how when the war is won we shall have our statues in Parliament

230

Square.'

'You *are* still tight. So go on—take your bottle of champagne and get out—go back to your party or wherever, but I want you out of here.'

'Don't be boring. Everything's so *boring* after France. You can't pretend otherwise. You can't tell me you didn't feel more *alive* in France? Because I simply won't believe you.'

'I feel a great deal more alive now that I'm home, Lily, and *still* alive, thank God.'

'Oh, there you go, being Captain Stuffy again. Did you know he had this stuffy side, Poppy?' she called up the stairs, having been helped out of the room and into the hall by a further push from Scott. 'Do you know your husband can be extremely stuffy at times?'

By now, Poppy was coming back downstairs with the second suitcase, her coat folded over one arm.

'I think we ought to go now, Scott,' she said, ignoring Lily. 'Or we really are going to be late.'

'How do you know you're going to be late? If you don't know where you're going?' Lily persisted as Scott opened the front door and eased her out. 'You can't possibly know you're late if you don't know where you're going.'

'Go, Lily, go, *please*,' Scott ordered. 'Go and drink the rest of the champagne with your friends. Celebrate your safe return with everyone else, but please leave us alone now.'

'Spoilsport.'

'You too,' Scott said, closing the front door firmly.

'Spoilsport!' Lily shouted from outside. 'Stuffy pants!'

'She's tight,' Scott said to Poppy. 'Extremely

tight.'

'It's quite understandable,' Poppy replied. 'Remember how tight we got after our first sortie? We were tight for days.'

'Look, sweetheart—I'm sorry about this. Really I am. I had no idea Lily was going to—'

Poppy smiled, then bent down to put George on his lead.

'It's all right, I understand perfectly. You don't have to say another word.'

'Very well.' Scott shrugged.

He shut the front door behind them and they walked off down the wooded path to where Scott had parked the car, George happily trotting beside his mistress and Poppy with her composure regained, determined to put the whole incident behind her. She knew what a strain being undercover could be, just as she knew that people were often thrown together in difficult situations. She also knew that if those people happened to be attractive members of the opposite sex then temptation could enter the equation all too readily. However, what she could not deny was that the heart that only moments ago had been young, happy and carefree now felt as if it was made of stone. Whatever else she might or might not have done Lily had quite ruined Scott's homecoming.

*   *   *

'Could be someone close to the throne,' Jack Ward said. 'In a way it has to be.'

Anthony stood staring at his wall chart, the number of black pins seeming to outnumber the red and green ones. It wasn't so, of course; Eden had many more active agents in the field than inactive ones, yet the choice of the mortal colour of black suggested a far greater number were down than up.

'What about the girl, sir?' Anthony wondered, having as yet received no update on what if anything had been learned about his senior's goddaughter.

'Bit of a blank so far,' Jack replied. 'They're still interrogating her, and she still keeps swearing the file was a plant and the whole thing a deliberate red herring.'

'She would, wouldn't she, sir?'

'Of course. But then she could also be telling the truth. We'll soon see.'

'By further interrogation?'

'By seeing whether or not the leak has been stopped. If she's right, and she is a patsy, then it's back to square one—and if it's back to square one then I'm as out of ideas as I am of tobacco.' Jack stared gloomily into the oilskin tobacco pouch he had just pulled from his pocket and attempted to fill his pipe with enough tobacco dust to get some sort of smoke. 'Trouble with this sort of thing is you don't know where to start looking. Under the bed or in it.'

Anthony frowned at him, not quite understanding the reference.

'Is it one of ours—someone in the bed?' Jack explained with a brief look over his spectacles. 'Or one of theirs—hiding underneath it?'

'For the life of me, sir, I simply can't even begin to get into the minds of people who can play both sides of the net.'

'Doesn't mean to say there aren't plenty of them

233

about. My gut feeling, for what it's worth, is that we have a difficult one here. Very difficult,' he added factually.

Anthony looked at his notepad to check the Gaelic word Eugene Hackett had recently used to describe someone working from the inside.

'Hackett calls it a *caochán*, sir. Apparently it's come sort of Irish creature—Gaelic for a small animal of some kind. Celtic, anyway.'

'Spare me Celtic folklore. I get the picture. So.' Jack lit the little tobacco he had managed to pack into his pipe, puffed away at it while regarding Anthony over the bowl, then stuck the lit pipe in the side of his mouth before continuing. 'So. We had best initiate a covert operation. See what we can unearth. We'll need some sort of framework. I'll see to all that side of things and meanwhile I'll do a bit of truffling myself. Might as well call it Operation—What was that word again?'

'*Caochán*, sir.'

'Operation *Caochán*. And the sooner we catch the damn thing the better for us all.'

*   *   *

Some few months later, Marjorie saw him completely by chance. She was out walking George for Poppy, who was confined to bed with a heavy cold, when she saw him in the distance on his horse. There was nothing unusual about that at all, since when he was on leave Eugene spent the time he wasn't with Kate riding his seventeen-hand great grey horse. She was however surprised to see him this morning because she was well out of the parkland proper, having decided since it was such a

234

fine late October morning and the autumnal colours were still so vivid to walk the countryside around the park, an area she had always meant to explore but somehow had never got round to as yet. She knew George would enjoy it, for in spite of his short legs he was a very fit little dog and being a hound he loved to run for hours.

And so it was that Marjorie found herself breasting a ridge that rose well above Eden Park, which she could see lying far below her in the distance when she turned to draw breath. George was hot on the trail of a rabbit and had half disappeared into the hedge when Marjorie first caught sight of him—or, rather, of them.

For Eugene was not riding alone. There was someone riding after him on a bright chestnut horse, a woman wearing a coloured headscarf and dun-coloured rat-catcher who sat to her horse with perfect ease. Instinctively Marjorie sought cover for herself, bending over first to put George on his lead and then slipping back into the shadow of the small copse in front of which she had been standing. The two riders were headed in a course not quite towards Marjorie's but not quite parallel either, which meant that if they stayed on that track they would pass her by with a good hundred feet or so to spare. But then as the woman caught up with Eugene she called him to a halt in a sandy clearing right at the bottom of the hill on top of which Marjorie stood hidden. Eugene reined his horse in at once, and as his mount came to a neat stop he looked round in order it would seem to ensure they were not being overlooked before turning his attention to his new riding companion.

Nothing odd in that, Marjorie sought to reassure

235

herself. *People run into each other all the time when they're out walking, or riding, or cycling. So there's nothing odd in this so far—and yet somehow—somehow it still doesn't look quite right . . .*

They were deep in conversation now, the woman seeming to do most of the talking while Eugene took something from his pocket, a piece of paper that Marjorie saw him unfold, check and then hand over to the woman. She glanced at it briefly, then looked about her before folding it and slipping it into her own inside jacket pocket. A few more words were exchanged, before the woman picked up her reins, only to drop them again as she leaned forward and raised herself out of the saddle to put her arms round Eugene's neck and hug him.

A peal of Eugene's unmistakable laughter floated up to Marjorie's perch above them before the riders, with a gathering up of reins and a couple of gentle taps on their horses' flanks, spun away from each other, breaking into a slow canter, and finally disappeared from Marjorie's view in a swirling curl of dust thrown up from the track.

Marjorie stared at where they had just been, but were no longer. It had been like watching a scene from a film, or reading a particularly vivid passage in a book. Dramatic, odd, enthralling and yet ominous, for what else could Eugene be doing but betraying someone; or *something*. She could not believe what she had seen. It did not seem possible that the magical, enchanting and rambunctious Irishman, so beloved by all, could not be above suspicion in every way. Not that there had not been rumours about him before, especially when he had mysteriously vanished to Ireland, it was said at the time, suspected of making contact with the enemy on the west coast, where U-boats were meant to be finding shelter in certain famous bays. How the rumours had started no one knew, but nor did they know whether they were based on fact.

So what was he up to this time? Was this an act of treachery? Had he been passing classified information? Or was it perhaps part of one of his covert manoeuvres, part of an Eden commissioned *dodge*—Eden slang for an operation—the woman either part of the ground force or even an enemy agent whom Eugene was *codding*, as he called it. Such was the difficulty of working in Security that everything had to be suspect, and yet nothing could be discussed, except with one's superior officer. Marjorie knew it was her duty to report the incident, and yet she could not but shrink from doing so.

Should she be right she could hardly bear the thought of Kate's discovering that her lover was in fact a double agent; should she be wrong, and Kate learn from the gossipmongers who had blown the whistle on Eugene, it was equally unbearable to imagine what Kate would think of her then, let alone what Eugene would make of it. And if it turned out that all Eugene was actually doing was two-timing Kate, then that too would be something for which Kate would never forgive Marjorie.

All the way up the drive Marjorie wrestled with her conscience, while George ran alongside her, happy but exhausted, his long pink tongue hanging out more and more the nearer they got to home. Marjorie found herself wishing that she was anywhere except at Eden Park; so much so that she started fantasising about handing in her notice to Anthony Folkestone and taking up some other

237

occupation, in a factory perhaps. Normally she would have gone straight to the cottage behind the stable yard and made herself some tea, waiting for Kate to come off duty and for Billy to get back from school, but today she had to return one exhausted dachshund. So she bypassed the house, cut through the first set of woods, walked round the top end of the great lake and took the short cut through the second area of woodland that led her finally to the House of Flowers.

Someone was waiting for her. But it wasn't Poppy. Marjorie didn't even get as far as the door of the house before she was held by a large firm hand on one shoulder, a hand that turned her round until she was face to face with the person who had been to the forefront of all her thoughts.

'Not a word now, Marjorie Marjoram,' Eugene said quietly and seriously. 'One word of what you saw and I swear I'll kill you with my own bare hands.'

*   *   *

Kate sensed there was something up, but couldn't put a finger on it. First of all there was an atmosphere in the cottage that was more than uneasy, it was claustrophobic; and second it was perfectly obvious that Marjorie was doing her best to avoid her. If Marjorie had not been such a gregarious personality it might not have been so obvious. Yet now she seemed to be avoiding not only Kate and Billy, but also everyone in H Section. She went about her work wordlessly, as if deeply preoccupied, and although it was obvious to everyone involved with her that she was in fact

238

working even longer hours than usual, instead of joining her usual large table of friends at lunch or supper whenever possible she would either sit with people she didn't know at all or skip eating altogether, leaving the dining room the moment she thought she might have to sit with someone she knew. She also absented herself from drinking in the local pub in the evenings, choosing instead to work late, take other people's shifts—anything rather than mix with her friends. Kate teased her, trying to joke her out of it, but to no avail.

Once or twice Kate confronted her and asked her if anything was the matter, only to be told in Marjorie's newly gruff way that she was perfectly all right—just a little tired. When she was out, Kate and Billy discussed Marjorie's change in attitude, Kate suspecting it was probably some emotional disturbance and therefore possibly to do with Marjorie's growing relationship with Major Folkestone, while Billy had his own theory, as always.

'It's 'er glands. Glandular disorders account for a really high percentage of mental instability, Kate,' he told her seriously. 'I mean it—don't laugh. I betcha your glands played you up as you was growing up. I know mine did and all.'

'As I was growing up,' Kate corrected him.

'That's what I said,' Billy replied.

'No you didn't. You said as you was growing up—' Kate stopped when she saw Billy grinning impishly at her. 'You just do it to trick people, don't you?' She laughed. 'You're a sausage.'

'Well if I am, then you're a sport. And listen—'cos you're a sport—I want you to give us a hand with somethin'.'

                    *   *   *

Even Anthony Folkestone was beginning to get
worried about Marjorie, in spite of the fact that
because of Operation *Caochán* he had been so
busy he had barely had time to sit down, let alone
sleep, or pay much attention to someone with
whom he now realised he was possibly hopelessly in
love. As soon as he could find a moment he took
time out to consider what could be wrong. His list
of possibilities included feelings for someone other
than himself, some sort of light ailment, or perhaps
one of those things about which he had absolutely
no idea but which he recalled his father referring to
as *women's palaver*. Other than the fact that they
were not in any way the same as men, and despite
having been married, Anthony was still blissfully
ignorant on the subject of the opposite sex, and
knew it. But this did not stop him trying to unravel
that most complicated of creatures and make some
sense of at least one.

'Marjorie?' he asked one morning as she put his
papers on the desk in front of him. 'I'm afraid I
have to ask you something. That is if you don't
mind?'

'Of course, sir,' Marjorie replied, rechecking
carefully that she had put all his correspondence in
the correct order, and that the files that had been
delivered by messenger that morning were still all
sealed in their envelopes. Ever since she had
observed Eugene's mysterious meeting with the
lady on the bright chestnut horse, Marjorie's life
had become utterly miserable, particularly since
the wretched man had followed her back to

240

Poppy's house.

'Ask me anything you like, sir,' Marjorie continued, once more checking the seals on a series of large buff envelopes. 'After all, that's your privilege.'

'I've noticed you're not quite yourself, Marjorie. At least, you don't appear to be; that is the impression I have been getting these past few days. Now of course if it's something personal then it's absolutely no business of mine—'

'I'm afraid it is.' Marjorie stopped him as politely as she could. 'It is personal, so I'd rather you didn't continue. If it's all the same to you.'

'Oh.' For a moment Anthony Folkestone looked hurt. 'Of course. If it's something personal, Marjorie, then it's absolutely no affair of mine. Just as long as you're all right.'

'I'm fine, sir. Now if there isn't anything else? I have an absolute mound of work.'

'Thank you, Marjorie. That will be all. Except—'

Marjorie stopped at the door and turned back.

'Might you be free for a drink tonight? My spies in the shape of mine host tell me a new consignment of gin has just arrived in.'

'I'd love to, sir,' Marjorie replied carefully. 'But I'm afraid I'm otherwise engaged.'

'I see. Jolly good,' Anthony said as bravely as he could. 'Some other time, eh? Some other time and soon as you can, eh?'

He turned away, trying to hide his disappointment, and lit a cigarette.

'Absolutely, sir. Now if you'll excuse me?'

On her way back to the cottage that evening Marjorie passed Kate and Eugene leaving to go out, walking hand in hand down the path and

241

laughing and joking.

'Top of the evening to you, Marjorie Marjoram!' Eugene called to her with a wave.

'We're off to the village!' Kate cried. 'Why don't you come and join us?'

'I'd love to!' Marjorie called back. 'But I promised I'd help Billy.'

Billy's project had given Marjorie another perfect excuse for remaining as uninvolved in the off-duty life at Eden Park as possible. It had been a terrible year as far as the war had gone, and much as everyone tried to keep smiling, privately few could deny how bad everything looked as the year began to draw to a close. The Germans had begun bombing London heavily again, the U-boats were blowing the merchant ship convoys out of the water all but unopposed, Coventry had been blitzed and its wonderful cathedral bombed and burned, a disaster that shocked the British spiritually as well as physically, HMS *Hood* and *Ark Royal* had been sunk, the Germans had overrun Crete as well as staging a mighty counter-offensive in North Africa and were apparently taking a winter stroll into Russia, blowing any resistance out of their path. Like most other people in the land Marjorie often went to her bed thinking all was just about to be lost if not lost already, and though the bulldog spirit was still alive in the British, everyone suddenly felt alone, as if their little island was fighting the might of Nazi Germany and her allies all by itself.

Possibly this was why Billy had decided on what he called a *distraction* for Christmas. He had written and designed his version of *Cinderella* which with the help of Kate and Marjorie he was now getting ready to rehearse—with the full co-operation and consent of those willing to take part. Kate had agreed to play Cinderella after Marjorie had turned it down, protesting that she was in no way pretty or talented enough to play the leading role, as well as being blessed with a tin ear and a voice to match; Anthony Folkestone and Corporal Duckworth were to play the Ugly Sisters, Cissie Lavington, much to everyone's delight, was to appear as the Fairy Godmother, Eugene was to play Prince Charming and Scott Meynell would be the Dame. Billy had done his research as thoroughly as he did everything, finding old copies of traditional pantomimes and rewriting and reworking them to make his show topical for Eden Park and its inhabitants.

* * *

'Not you again?'

Anthony Folkestone looked up as a familiar knock sounded at his office door.

'Sorry, sir. Just wanted to check something,' Billy said, poking his head round the door. 'If that's all right.'

'Long as you're quick. I'm very busy.'

'I just wanted to check you were all right for this evening's rehearsal, sir. And that you weren't thinkin' of shavin' off your moustache.'

'I'm fine for the rehearsal, Billy, and I have absolutely no intention of shaving my moustache off. Why?'

'Nothin', sir. Just that an Ugly Sister's goin' to be a whole lot funnier with a moustache, sir.'

'Moustache in place, young man. And ditto for

said moustache owner at rehearsals.'

Anthony Folkestone looked up and smiled at the ever-anxious Billy, wondering what the boy's adopted sister would make of seeing him dressed up as an Ugly Sister, before concluding that since it seemed she had no intention of even going out for a drink with him at the moment it perhaps didn't matter one whit.

'I've left the full rehearsal times with Miss Budge, sir. She's going to make sure you know when you got to attend. She's also going to play the piano for us, which is ace. Didn't know she could play the joanna. Did you, sir?'

'Not something I thought of asking her, Billy. But then I've got a lot on my plate at the moment.'

'Probably why you in't noticed there's somethin' not quite right with Marjorie then.'

Anthony looked up sharply.

'Sorry? Meaning?'

'You in't noticed Marge has been a bit off lately then? We all have—and I know why. I think she's got a secret, sir. She's always been the same. Soon as someone tells her a secret she goes all stiff. Thought you might have noticed somethin' was up. Anyway—thank you, sir. Sorry to trouble you, sir. TTFN.'

'TTFN?'

'Ta ta for now, sir.'

And with one last grin Billy disappeared, leaving a bemused Anthony to stare after him.

*　　　*　　　*

Billy and his band of helpers were already hard at work making the costumes and building the

244

scenery. One of their stalwarts was Eugene, who set about using his carpentry skills to help build a rock-solid set, work that he carried out while singing Irish ballads at the top of his voice as he sawed and hammered away in his workshop at the back of the stage that had been erected in the ballroom, while a gang of the Nosy Parkers painted the scenery and sewed the costumes.

Now and then Billy observed how little notice Marjorie took of Eugene whenever he came out of his workshop to put up another piece of his scenery, but said nothing. He had always suspected that his adopted sister did not think Eugene was as wonderful as everyone else did, yet now he noticed they barely spoke. However, since there was nothing he could do about it, he concentrated instead on rehearsing and directing his pantomime, in which he himself was playing Buttons.

'Mum's the word, eh, Marjorie, me auld segotia?' Eugene would whisper now and then as he passed Marjorie. 'Mum's the auld word, isn't that right now? We don't want to go letting no little kitty cats out of the bag now, do we?'

After which he would wink at her, blow her a mock kiss and disappear back to his workshop, whistling or singing as he went.

At these moments Marjorie found herself detesting Eugene. For as the days passed she became more and more frightened that she would suddenly blurt out her secret, if not in conversation—at night in her sleep. So anxious did she become that she took to sleeping on the sofa in the cottage living room, pretending that Kate talked in her sleep and was keeping her awake. Unsurprisingly her neurotic routine began to take a

245

visible toll on her appearance, so that soon it seemed everyone had a theory.

*   *   *

'Perhaps Marjorie's our *caochán*,' Jack Ward suggested, only half jokingly, at one point. 'If we're talking about someone near to the throne.'

'You don't really believe that, do you, sir?' Anthony replied. 'Not with her background? After all, her aunt was one of your people, and the reason Marjorie is here in the first place is because of her Aunt Hester—'

'Of course not,' Jack cut in, standing as always staring out of the window at the park beyond, his back to Folkestone. 'I'm just saying anything's possible, and because it is, we must examine everything—and everyone. I'm quite sure that Marjorie could no more be our *caochán* than I could be a film star. But that is how wide our thinking has to be.'

Anthony Folkestone nodded automatically, praying with all his might that their traitor did not turn out to be the object of his affections, his beloved Marjorie. Yet he could not get Billy's words out of his head. *I think she's got a secret, sir.*

'I know what you mean, sir,' he said after a moment's reflection. 'But I really cannot believe young Marjorie is our man, or rather our woman.' He smiled briefly, and bleakly.

'Nor do I, Tony,' Jack replied. 'But we have to keep everyone in the frame. That's all I'm saying. Everyone.'

*   *   *

Billy stared at the vicar, and the vicar, obviously feeling this, looked round at him from under his tall, tight-curled wig.

'Do I look all right, young Billy?'

'Yes, sir, you look fine, truly you do.'

'I don't know what my parishioners will say when they see me. I expect they *will* understand.'

'Yes, of course, sir. And it's really decent of you, really it is. There's a bit of a run on men at the moment, see, because of the war, obviously, and none of the girls was at all suitable for the role.'

'There has to be a first time for everything, I suppose,' the vicar continued doubtfully, turning yet again to see how he looked in the long dressing mirror: carrot-coloured wig, red knickerbockers and purple stockings. 'God help us anyway.'

'You're the perfect Baron Hardup, Vicar, 'onest.'

Having reassured him one more time, Billy then darted off, considering the Reverend Morris was making an awful fuss about nothing.

I mean, he said to himself. *I mean it's not as if he in't called on to wear what amounts to a frock most days anyway.*

*　　　*　　　*

Yet somehow in spite of all the alarms and excursions everything was ready in time for the night of the pantomime, largely thanks to Eugene's great ability to plan everything down to the last detail. The dress rehearsal had gone as badly as it should, yet in spite of the traditional spate of unrehearsed disasters Billy stood in the wings ready to signal curtain up confident that equally traditionally everything was going to be all right on the night.

The moment Miss Budge finished playing her overture, a medley of the tunes about to be sung on the stage, Billy cued the spotlight and stepped out in front of the curtain.

'Welcome, ladies and gentlemen all,' he announced with a flourishing and well-practised bow. 'Tonight we tell the tale of the poor English maiden Cinderella, and her two beastly Nazi Fräulein cousins, her ugly relations who are fat, ugly, beastly and ever so cruel. In fact they thrives on being beastly to others.'

Billy was proud of this piece of propaganda; as well he should be for upon the announcement a cheer of approval shot up from the audience.

'The two Ugly Fräuleins steal Cinderella's invitation to the ball—but as you will see, good ladies and gentlemen all, thanks to Cinderella's Fairy Godmother, Queen Britannia—well, no—I must stop, gentlefolk, or I shall spoil the story for you all! So please—let our curtain rise on the story of Cinderella which we hopes you will enjoy one and all!'

From the moment Billy introduced the notion of his two ugly Fräuleins the audience was with him and his wonderfully inventive pantomime. Everyone gathered in the ballroom of Eden Park that night joined in the fun, cheering, booing, clapping, and singing their hearts out during the memorable performance, the greatest laughs of all being reserved for Billy who stopped the show with his performance as Buttons, whom he portrayed as the village simpleton. He played the character for sympathy rather than mockery, yet still managed to get laugh after genuine laugh at the wonder of the lovelorn lad's simple innocence.

'D'you know, I'm really enjoying myself!' the Reverend Morris said as he scampered off followed closely by the Ugly Sisters. 'Can't recall when I last had as much fun. Maybe I made the wrong choice. Maybe I should have gone into the theatre after all, rather than the Church . . .'

'And for the life of me I don't know how women cope with these things, do you, Major?' Scott asked Anthony as he yet again hitched up his brassiere and pushed his falsies back into place.

But before Anthony could answer, and with a good half an hour of the panto still to run, the wail of the air raid siren broke the spell.

'I don't believe it!' Scott moaned. 'Blasted Jerries!'

Everyone gave one great sigh before going straight into their evacuation drill. Whatever the moment, whatever the occasion, the regime was the same—all personnel to the shelters, Home Guard back on duty, sentries posted and C and H Sections off to the caves with their boxes of Top Secret files. And of course nothing could dispel the overwhelming feeling of disappointment which was engulfing everyone, a feeling of utter dejection which was all of a sudden overcome by one of intense mirth when those hurrying to their posts and dugouts were suddenly aware of the farcical events happening around them.

However serious the threat might be from overhead, no one's sense of the absurd could resist the sight of Major Folkestone running across the lawns with his huge pantomime falsies bumping up and down, followed by the heroic Scott Meynell,

249

hoisting up long silk skirts while also trying to cope with an overlarge bosom and flying red wig, and pursued by the Reverend Baron Hardup who lost his comedy drawers halfway across the drive, underwear that was swiftly and skilfully gathered up by the leader of the pack of white rats following closely behind him. Finally along the path that led to the woods and thence the underground caves could be seen Cinderella, her Fairy Godmother, Prince Charming and a stream of none too stately courtiers, whipped in by Buttons who was all but helpless with mirth.

By the time they reached the caves and had collapsed on to various beds and pieces of furniture they were still all prostrate with laughter.

'Only hope Jerry got a view of that through his bombsight,' Corporal Duckworth said. 'Might put him off his stroke a bit.'

'Just as it was all going so well,' someone sighed. 'What a shame.'

'We can pick up again, don't worry,' Billy reassured them. 'Soon as the raid's over—the show will go on.'

'That's the spirit, Billy,' Scott said, before turning to Eugene. 'Talking of which, I seem to remember the last time we were down here a certain party hiding away a bottle of the homemade somewhere.'

'You'll find it filed under P,' Eugene replied, pointing to a large grey cabinet. 'P as in poteen.'

They needed the refreshment as the raid was a long one, too long in fact to allow the pantomime to be concluded that night. But before everyone dispersed back to their beds in the house some two hours later, it had been unanimously agreed that the second act should be played the following evening, the Luftwaffe permitting.

'Great stuff,' Eugene remarked, raising his bottle of homemade moonshine. 'Here's to Act Two tomorrow, everyone!'

But neither did the performance of Act Two of the pantomime pass by without its share of high drama. This time, however, the unscheduled event was nothing to do with the enemy, but all to do with one of Eden Park's inhabitants. Halfway through the act Billy found himself hijacked and whisked off into the back of the wings by Eugene, who whispered him an urgent message. Billy's eyes all but started out of his head when he heard, but Eugene's great hand was clapped over his mouth in order to prevent any audible expression of amazement.

'Not a word, gossoon! I'm warning you now!' Eugene hissed. 'Or you'll end up at the bottom of that lake out there! Understand?'

Billy nodded his complete compliance with Eugene's great hand still gagging him.

'Mmmmph!' he said. 'Mmmmmmph!'

Eugene nodded in satisfaction then let him go, pushing him off and away to set about the task he had given the lad, while he himself, also free from any acting duties for the moment, disappeared altogether from the stage to vanish out of one of the side doors of the ballroom and into the winter night.

He had just enough time to complete his secret mission before he was required back on stage. The last thing he wanted was for attention to be drawn to his absence, or, worst of all, to miss his all important last scene with Cinderella Kate. But

Eugene was nothing if not hyper-efficient when needs be, and so was back in the wings and then onstage as Prince Charming in plenty of time to play his final scene.

Kneeling by Cinderella, Prince Charming found that the satin slipper fitted her dainty foot, and at once proposed marriage to his Cinderella—except that he called her Kate.

Imagining that he had simply made a mistake, Kate continued as scripted in her role as Cinderella, accepting the Prince's proposal with modest delight, whereupon Eugene suddenly leapt to his feet, pulled off his silver wig and made his astonishing declaration.

'My own, my true love, my darling Kate!' he proclaimed, by now well off the script. 'Now that you have agreed to be mine, I have a present for you! A present to celebrate our engagement! Something you have wanted for a very long time, and I have now found for you! Billy?'

With a grin which must have been at least as broad as the mouth of the River Liffey, Eugene gestured grandly to the wings, whence Billy came forward, leading the prettiest black pony pulling a beautiful hand-painted trap behind it. The audience gasped and fell to stunned silence, then roared its approval, cheers that in no way worried the little pony, which thanks to the perfection of its early training stood obediently on the stage with ears pricked and eyes bright while Eugene took the leading rein from Billy and handed it to a totally astonished Kate.

'Now all is met!' Billy proclaimed, back in character. 'Now all is most happily resolved, and our tale is ended! So let us give three hearty cheers for Prince Charming and his Cinderella—and may they live happily ever after!'

'Not too loud a cheer!' Eugene cautioned with a grin. 'We don't want to go frightening the pony here!'

Again, thanks to its training, the young animal stood as still as a circus horse while the audience cheered and the makeshift velvet curtains were pulled across by the stage staff. Eugene nodded to Billy to lead the pony and its trap back outside, and was about to follow him when a hand grabbing the back of his doublet stopped him.

'Eugene Hackett,' Kate said, turning him round to her. 'You're the very devil.'

'Isn't it just what you've always wanted?' Eugene smiled, putting one hand under her pretty chin. 'Aren't you always longing out loud for a pony and trap to go about in? Well now you have one.'

'Eugene—'

'Later, my darling girl! I have to make sure he doesn't suddenly decide to bolt round the ballroom!'

But the pony was as good as Eugene had hoped he would be, allowing himself to be quietly led back out of doors where Eugene's friend from the stables took charge, throwing a rug over the animal's back before leading him back to his box.

'You'd best have this, if you meant what you said,' Eugene said as Kate and he stood in the wings after taking their curtain calls, producing a ring box from one pocket.

'What are you talking about?' Kate asked crossly. 'Meant what exactly?'

'Didn't I hear you saying that you would marry me just now?' Eugene replied. 'And in front of a

253

goodly number of witnesses, too.'

'Eugene . . .' Kate tried to warn him, but, failing to keep her straight face any longer, burst into a peal of laughter and threw herself in his arms. 'Yes of course I'll marry you, you barmy great idiot! You don't do things by halves, do you?'

'We're only this way once, Katie my love. So we might as well try and make it as special as we can.'

After the audience had finally vacated their seats and the actors had taken off their make-up and costumes, Scott invited the cast up to his and Poppy's house in the woods for a party. They had managed to get hold of a couple of crates of light ale, as well as some whisky and gin, through one of Eugene's usual contacts, and persuaded Mrs Alderman to make a few extra sausage meat rolls as well as some of her famous stovies, rissoles made from potatoes, onions and dripping.

They also managed to coax the reticent Miss Budge, who had accompanied the pantomime so expertly from the grand piano in the ballroom, to come and play on the little upright piano Scott had installed in the drawing room of the House of Flowers, since he loved nothing better than to sit and sing to his young wife when they were alone in the evening.

'But you're a pianist,' Miss Budge had protested. 'You surely don't need me.'

'We want you to come to the party anyway, Miss Budge,' Poppy assured her. 'And if you feel like playing that's entirely up to you.'

As soon as she'd had her first stiff gin, Miss Budge threw inhibition to the wind and sat down at once to play for the party, since everyone seemed anxious to get to the dancing as soon as possible.

'It's an extraordinary place this, you know,' Eugene remarked as he danced with Kate. 'Soon as I set foot in here I always feel like singing. Don't ask me why.'

'I hope you're going to sing tonight, Eugene,' Kate said. 'I want nothing more than to hear you sing.'

'And so I shall, darling girl. I shall probably sing all night, so full is my heart. Let's see the music our Miss Budge has brought up with her.'

Eugene wandered over to the piano and started to leaf through Miss Budge's song sheets. When he found her shyly looking at him, he smiled, which immediately disconcerted Miss Budge so much that she reddened and began to fiddle agitatedly with the pretty locket she always wore round her neck.

'That's a very pretty locket, Budgie,' he stated. 'What's in it? Someone special's picture?'

'Someone very special's picture,' Miss Budge muttered in reply, dropping her eyes. 'My dog actually.'

'May I see?'

Miss Budge hesitated, her hand still on the locket.

'Of course,' she said. 'But will you just excuse me first for a moment? I have to discover the geography.' She smiled back at Eugene as she set off to find the bathroom, leaving him to continue sorting through the music, while Kate and Marjorie settled themselves down on the sofa nearby, Kate having just replenished their glasses.

'You really had no idea at all?' Marjorie asked Kate as she was handed her drink. 'You honestly had no idea what Eugene was up to?'

'Of course not! Why should I? You say things

like that off the top of your head. But you never think for a moment someone is going to act on them.'

'You actually said you wanted a pony and trap?'

'It's not so daft.' Kate laughed. 'Ponies don't run on petrol and we can also use it for salvage drives. I thought I might manage to buy some broken-down old pony, so can you imagine? When I looked up and saw what Eugene had gone and got?'

Marjorie laid her head back on her chair and sighed deeply.

'Great,' she said. 'So let's just hope you don't get any more funny whims.'

'Why, Marge?' Billy wondered in mock innocence, sitting on the arm of Marjorie's chair and finishing off a particularly delicious-looking stovie. 'What's it to you?'

'Never you mind and don't you dare get any of that greasy food on Poppy's lovely furniture,' Marjorie warned him. 'You make sure you wipe your hands before you do anything else.'

'Why do you hope Kate don't get no more funny whims then, I wonder?' Billy persisted, stuffing the last of the fried rissole in his mouth before wiping his hands on a grey-looking handkerchief.

'Because as you may recall, Billy, I'm not that hot at keeping secrets.'

'You knew?' Kate frowned. 'How?'

'I saw Eugene meet this woman,' Marjorie said, beginning to blush. 'I thought all sorts of things, I have to say—'

'You would,' Billy interrupted. 'It's all those awful books you read.'

'First I thought he was seeing someone else—'

'Oh, poor Marjorie!' Kate exclaimed

sympathetically.

'Then when I saw Eugene passing something to this woman, I thought—well . . .' Marjorie petered out, too ashamed to continue.

'You thought he was passing information!' Billy suddenly burst out, before realising what he had said.

'You thought I was what?' Eugene wondered idly, having strolled by in time to pick up on the last bit of the conversation. *'Passing information, Marjorie?'*

Marjorie looked up at Eugene, blushing deeply. 'I'm sorry, Eugene,' she said. 'Billy's right. I read too much cheap literature.'

'Don't be daft, Marjorie Marjoram.' Eugene smiled. 'I'd have thought the very same thing meself. Anyway—isn't it what we're all trained to do? The lot of us here? We may all be friends, and some of us more than that, but we must never drop our defences. Walls—as they keep reminding us—have ears.'

'So what was on the piece of paper you passed to this mysterious woman?' Kate wondered. 'And who is she anyway?'

'You obviously didn't get a very good look, Marjorie.' Eugene's smile now turned to a mischievous grin. 'Or you'd have seen the mysterious lady is a lot older than I. The mysterious lady is my mother's sister, my lovely Aunt Maude—a great horsewoman and breeder. It was she who both bred and broke Kate's lovely little pony. She lives ten miles from here—married to a major-general—breeds ponies and trains ponies for the shafts, and is little short of a saint.'

'And the piece of paper?' Kate insisted on

257

knowing.

'Why, an IOU!' Eugene laughed. 'What else? Where would I get the money to pay for a handsome creature like that? Sure I'm stitched!'

'You wanted to see the picture in my locket,' the newly returned Miss Budge said to Eugene, bending forward and holding the now opened locket for him to see. 'That's Tansy. My dog.'

'Ah, and isn't he?' Eugene nodded. 'Isn't he beautiful? What a beautiful boy he is to be sure.'

'He's also a very good boy,' Miss Budge said proudly. 'And a clever one. He knows the names of all his toys—and brings them to command.'

'Look,' Eugene said to Kate and Marjorie. 'Budgie's beautiful boy. Isn't he lovely?'

Marjorie and Kate both looked at the picture in the locket and made the right sort of approving noises.

'I didn't know you had a dog, Budgie,' Marjorie said as Miss Budge looked longingly at the photograph herself. 'Do you keep him at home?'

Miss Budge glanced at her quickly and shook her head.

'No,' she said. 'Because of the hours I work, I can't. It—it wouldn't be fair to leave him for so long.'

'So who looks after him for you, Budgie?' Eugene asked. 'I trust he's well cared for.'

'A friend looks after him for me,' Miss Budge replied. 'Naturally I'm just dying for the war to be over so we can be together again.'

She clipped her locket shut, dropped it back round her neck and cleared her throat.

'Now then.' She smiled. 'I'm neglecting my duty. I'd say some more music is the order of the day,

258

wouldn't you?'

She sat at the piano and began to play a medley of the most popular tunes of the moment, well enough to have almost everyone up on their feet in no time. Anthony danced with Marjorie, happy to see her good spirits apparently quite restored.

'One thing I've always dreaded,' she confessed. 'That's being asked to keep a secret.'

'Perhaps you shouldn't be working here, in that case,' Anthony said, then seeing the look on her face added: 'That was meant as a joke, Marjorie. Sorry.'

'I never thought of that.' Marjorie looked at him and suddenly laughed. 'You know—you know, I never thought of that.'

Everyone danced, not only that, everyone danced with everyone else, or so it seemed. In fact so it was, with one exception. Poppy made quite sure that Lily did not get to dance with Scott.

Finally, when everyone's feet were sore and legs were tired, people sat on the floor and sang. They sang old favourites, and new ones, starting with 'Pennies From Heaven' and ending with 'You Are My Sunshine'—at least that was meant to be the last song.

It wasn't, of course, for Eugene had yet to give them what he called a one-voice-only song. There were many requests, but he surprised them all by refusing to sing the Irish favourites they begged for, choosing instead to sing unaccompanied one of the best-loved songs of the year before in his lyrical tenor voice—'When You Wish Upon A Star'.

When he finished, all was silence, within and without the little house high in the woods. The wood fire crackled its last and began slowly to self-

259

extinguish, while around it everyone fell to thinking and to wishing, hoping that the new year about to dawn would bring them hope and above all peace, and outside, far to the east, a star high in the firmament shone with a sudden and peculiar intensity.

Interim

CHRISTMAS

Now that America had entered the war everyone's spirits rose. Not that people began to believe that the war was going to be over in a matter of a few months; the British had become too well versed in political bromides to believe once again the sorts of fairy tales those who remembered the outbreak of the First World War had believed in—that it would all be over before Christmas. This was the third wartime Christmas the people of the British Isles had endured since Chamberlain had declared war on Germany in September 1939, and they knew it wouldn't be the last. Yet since the entrance of the Americans, people had begun to look ahead with hope. Britain no longer stood alone. Fighting by their side was the mightiest nation in the world, and as the military were at pains to explain to anyone who had time to listen to them, wars were inevitably and invariably finally won by the side which had the most soldiers. Even Anthony Folkestone, a man not given to pontificating, began to let it be known that it was now only a question of time before the Germans were defeated.

'It's going to cost lives, of course,' he told Marjorie one evening as they discussed the prospect of an end to the war over a drink, Marjorie being once again happy to go out with him now that she had been relieved of the burden of carrying her secret. 'And I'm not saying it's going to happen tomorrow, Marjorie. But with rumours coming back that the Germans are already finding the Russian winter just as bad as Napoleon did when he decided to invade Russia . . . not a good plan, by the way.'

263

'It's all right, Anthony,' Marjorie replied with a sigh. 'It's not something I'm planning to do. At least not in the foreseeable future.'

'I'm being a bore. Sorry. Tell you what—let's go to the cinema. Tonight in Benton they're playing something rather good. Are you on?'

Marjorie put a hand over Anthony's and smiled. 'You're not being a bore, and yes I would love to go to the movies. It's some film with Rex Harrison in, isn't it?'

They had become so close since the night of the pantomime that Marjorie did not even mind Billy teasing her, morning, noon and night, by whistling or singing 'The Galloping Major' under his breath whenever he saw her. As for Billy, he was concentrating all his hopes on Christmas, particularly since he had been invited to join Mrs Alderman's small circle of conspirators, specially recruited to help prepare a surprise feast for those who were unable to leave Eden Park over the holiday.

'Of course, given the fact we 'aven't won the war quite as yet, in spite of young Billy here's Victory Dance he keeps giving us,' Mrs Alderman told her select body of helpers, 'they'll be thinking they'll be lucky if they get sausages and mash. They're going to get a lot more than sausages and mash, I'm a-telling you, but you're not going to be a-telling them that. We're going to make 'em believe, because of all these further rationing whatsits, they'll be lucky to get *a* sausage and mash, let alone in the plural.'

'So what you goin' to be givin' them then, Mrs A?' Billy wanted to know, biting a fingernail in a mixture of anxiety and excitement. 'I mean you're not plannin' on a proper Christmas feast, are you? 'Cos where we goin' to get the stuff from?'

Mrs Alderman nodded portentously rubbing the side of her bulbous nose. 'Never you mind exactly where, young man. All I'm saying is they're in for a few surprises. When folks work as hard as this lot does, and when they does work as important as this, God 'elp 'em, then if Cook can't do a bit of rustling up, she ain't worth her name. I'm going to have to rustle, too, 'cos I've given up on my points system. It's gone totally haywire now—what with the local paper down to only one page—I don't know what we're allowed and what we're not any more. Or what's on ration and what's not.'

' 'Ow many we goin' to be catering for, Mrs A?' Billy asked. 'I can't see you doin' enough rustling for the amount of mouths you normally has to feed.'

'There'll be thirty-six sitting down to Christmas lunch all told, I gather, young man. That's us included and all, so we got a fair bit of rustling to do, mark my words.'

Billy widened his eyes and sighed, trying to imagine what a Christmas dinner might taste like again. He could still remember his adoptive aunt's Christmas feast but held out little hope of Mrs Alderman's being able to reproduce anything like it, seeing how stringent food rationing had become. With a bit of luck there would be sausages, real butcher's sausages too, because Mrs A had a good relationship with the local butcher and he was always keeping this and that aside for her. There'd be roast potatoes too—with gravy. He was certain of that because he had caught a brief glimpse of one of Cook's lists, and those two items had been

265

there as clear as anything at the top of it. He reckoned there might even be Christmas pudding, with custard, and a sprig of holly on top of it just like there had been on the very first Christmas card he could remember seeing—a big steaming plum duff covered in custard with a huge green sprig of bright red-berried holly sticking up from it, borne to the table by a jolly red-cheeked woman surrounded by her family, all with faces shiny with happiness and excitement. He could remember the scents of Christmas as well, those very special smells of crêpe paper, oranges, sugared almonds, sherry wine, new soaps and talcum powders opened as presents, spices and crackling log fires, although when it came to it Billy couldn't actually remember any big log fires. The memory of them had to come from Christmas cards or pictures as well, yet somehow that didn't make the pungency of a burning Yule log any less sharp in Billy's fine imagination. Christmas, although something he had rarely celebrated as a child, was perhaps the firmest of fixtures in his young mind, owing no doubt to the fact that it was at Christmas time that he had first discovered what happiness meant, when Marjorie's wonderful aunt had adopted him into her small but very special family of two.

So he was doubly excited when he chanced upon the wine cellars because he had discovered them at Christmas. There they were, running the length it seemed of the entire house, accessed by a long flight of stone steps that he happened to find behind a hidden door in one of the very back sculleries, a room no longer in use but where, according to Mrs A, pot boys and kitchen maids might well have slept on beds little wider than shelves, in Victorian times when the Great House had been at its busiest. In his ignorance he imagined that he was the first of the new incumbents at Eden Park to have found the cellars, because, given how everyone was always complaining about how little what they called *proper drink* there was anywhere, he reckoned that had anyone else found the stairway before him there wouldn't have been a bottle left on the racks.

Instead he found dozens and dozens of bottles stacked neatly on top of each other in two of the caves, covered in dust and so obviously untouched for ages. Meaning to rush upstairs and tell Mrs Alderman about his discovery, Billy picked up one of the long slender bottles and began to dust it off with his handkerchief. That was when he realised that what he thought was his original find might not be as original as he had thought. Under the main layer of dust were labels that showed that all the wines left behind in the cellar by the owners of Eden Park had been left behind for a very good reason. They were all German.

Pretty sure now of the reason why the wines had escaped consumption by the officers and men billeted in Eden, Billy was also certain that wines from regions around the Rhone would not be a popular choice for their Christmas tipple. Yet it seemed a crying shame to let them go to waste, particularly since he had heard that the only drink likely to adorn the festive table was a crate of Watney's Pale Ale.

'I need some of them big glass things, Mrs Alderman,' he announced when he had decided what he must do. 'I shall need about a dozen.'

'Shall you indeed?' Mrs Alderman wondered in

return, her sleeves rolled up to her elbows and her hands covered in flour as she rolled out what seemed to Billy to be square yards of pastry. 'And what shall you be needin' 'em for precisely, Billy boy?'

'To put the wines in, Mrs A. I read about it in one of your cookbooks. There's a whole bit on it in *The Proper Presentation of Table Wines*.'

'Decanters is what you want—and they're in that cupboard there. But you don't want to go decanting no wine yet, young man. It'll get aeriated, so it will.'

'Aeriated, Mrs A?'

'That's what I said, Billy. You don't want to go decanting nothing till a couple of hours before the meal. Not 'less it's port you're decanting.'

'What colour is port, Mrs A?'

'What colour is port indeed. What colour do you think it is, you noddy? It's port wine colour! Sort of claret!'

'Claret?' Billy pulled an equally baffled face.

'Brown, you noddy! Port wine's always a sort of claret brown. Now go on, get out of it and get on with it—unless you want to help me pluck a chicken.'

'You bet!' Billy cried. 'Chicken? We goin' to 'ave chicken, Mrs A, are we?'

'You won't be getting nothing, young man—not until you watch your grammar. Your grammar isn't half shocking still. It don't matter how I correct you, it don't really.'

Billy smiled happily and set about taking the decanters down from the indicated cupboard, dusting them off and washing them. So they were going to have chicken after all! The thought of it was enough to set his saliva buds tingling, particularly when he married the image of roast chicken to that of nut brown sausages done to a crisp, stuffing, and a rich thick gravy covering the entire roast, golden potatoes included. It was too much to think of. It was as if the war was over already.

Knowing the sort of enthusiasm that would be aroused by the thought of a proper Christmas feast, Mrs Alderman made her small band of helpers swear her version of the Official Secrets Act, the pain of death clause being replaced with a pain of starvation one, namely that anyone betraying their secret would be deprived of their share of the feast. Billy got a particular finger wagging from Cook, since according to Mrs Alderman he could give away information just by looking at people with his big tell-tale eyes.

But Billy was utterly tight-lipped and completely discreet. No one suspected anything unusual was happening in the kitchens downstairs, mostly because nothing unusual ever emerged from the kitchens now that all the home-grown produce had been commandeered by the government for the general welfare and good, leaving the Nosy Parkers to subsist on the sort of plain, and by and large pretty distasteful, diet the rest of the country was having to endure. Occasionally some sort of treat would surface in the shape of a pie or a pudding, when Mrs Alderman could call in a favour from one of her contacts, or someone granted her a favour in the hope of being able to call one in in return at a later date. But as far as Christmas went, they all saw the menu pinned on the board and what they read was what they thought they were going to get.

269

Home-made broth with pearl barley
Sausage and mash
Gravy
Apple Flan
Custard
The Loyal Toast

Wines
Watneys Ales

The real problem was keeping people from straying into the kitchen, usually in search of an extra cup of Camp coffee or tea that was known as Dishmop Cha, or in the case of Kate and Marjorie using the kitchen as a short cut through to their offices from their cottage, something that had to be stopped as soon as the preparations began in earnest.

Billy saw to this, telling them the kitchen and environs were out of bounds to all Nosy Parkers until further notice, due to an outbreak of *botularism* in one of the kitchen staff.

'Mrs A is very determined that there won't be no epidemic and have Christmas ruined and all,' Billy told them solemnly. 'But it's highly infectious, being based in and affecting the gut, so if I was you—'

'Were you, Billy,' Marjorie corrected him. 'If I were you.'

'You wouldn't like it.' Billy grinned. 'Not one bit. So as I was saying before I was so crudely interrupted—if I was you two I'd give the kitchens a wide berth. You don't want to spend the whole of Christmas—'

270

'All right, Billy!' Kate and Marjorie carolled. 'That's quite enough, thank you!'

And so it was—quite enough to keep Marjorie and Kate well away from what was going on below stairs: the plucking of half a dozen plump hens, the roasting of one hundred and twenty potatoes, the gentle boiling of home-grown Brussels sprouts, the washing off and cooking of the salted French beans stowed away under the stairs in huge earthenware pots since the summer, the thickening of Mrs Alderman's special gravy, the stuffing of the roasting fowls, the careful making of fresh bread sauce, the filling of sixty-six home-made sausage rolls and mince pies, the pricking and cooking of three dozen fat sausages, and the gentle simmering of four huge plum duffs. All doors into the rest of the house were kept shut, locked and sealed lest the smells of the cooking should pervade the rooms where the innocent were still at work, or spending their leisure time—which was little enough—decking the place with home-made paper chains, bells and streamers, and clumps of freshly picked holly and mistletoe, all dominated by a magnificent spruce Christmas tree lovingly decorated by all the girls of all the various Sections working in the house.

'It even smells just like Christmas!' Billy exclaimed on Christmas Eve when Mrs Alderman led her little gang up through the all but silent house, their work nearly done, only the final cooking and presentation to be completed the following morning, before and after church.

On Christmas morning everyone left behind on duty at the Park put on their bravest faces, wishing to a man and a woman they could be home with

271

their loved ones, but knowing there were literally hundreds and thousands of men and women in the armed forces who were far further away from home than they were, trying not just to celebrate Christmas but to manage to stay alive to enjoy it, so much more dangerous were their circumstances. Some friends filled stockings for each other, as did some lovers, while Scott and Poppy made sure that at the foot of their bed in their little house in the woods hung two white pillowcases full of little presents wrapped tight in red crêpe paper done up with thin green ribbons.

'Happy Christmas, darling girl,' Scott said quietly as he woke his warm, soft and still sleepy Poppy.

'Happy Christmas, you great beast,' Kate laughed after Eugene had climbed in through the bedroom window in the cottage to kiss her awake on Christmas morning, dressed as a makeshift Santa Claus, but somehow still managing to look more like an overgrown leprechaun.

'Happy Christmas to you too, Marjorie my love!' Eugene called, leaning over the bed and tickling Marjorie out of her slumbers, the party finally being joined by Billy, dragging in a pillowcase stuffed full of oranges, nuts, chocolate bars (negotiated by Eugene), second-hand board games of snakes and ladders and Ludo, and two almost new comic books from America, their purchases also negotiated by Eugene, even though there were as yet no Americans in England.

'I have my ways,' Eugene said seriously, tapping his nose. 'I have contacts you could only dream of.'

Billy bet his last penny that although many of them might have dreamed of what was going to happen at midday, few of them would ever have believed it was actually going to happen.

Once everyone was seated, happily waiting for their home-made broth and sausages and mash, Billy rushed off to the kitchens to give the signal, whereupon—just like something out of an old Victorian Christmas illustration—Cook led the way into the dining hall with a huge platter bearing the first of the roast chickens held high over her head, her loyal band of followers carrying the rest of the feast on large trays or pushing it in on trolleys, and the rear being brought up by Billy, also pushing a trolley but very slowly, since on the top and bottom shelves were balanced twelve decanters of the finest Rhone wines, chilled as cold as the cellars would allow.

'I say,' said Jack Ward, who had made a special effort to be able to attend this Christmas lunch, in order, as he thought, to keep up morale. 'I say, Billy,' he repeated, sniffing the exquisite wine carefully after the first glass had been poured. 'Where did you unearth this little beauty from, hmm?'

'That would be saying, sir,' Billy grinned. 'Cook made us sign her version of the OS Act.'

'Contraband, no doubt,' Anthony Folkestone remarked with a poker face. 'Knowing young Billy, he hijacked a boat and went to France specially for it.'

'You got it, sir,' Billy agreed. 'All the way to France and back I went.'

'What happened to the bottles?' Jack wondered, sipping with equal care at the wine. 'Not usual to have white decanted, is it?'

He looked kindly at Billy over the top of his

273

glasses, not challenging the boy but genuinely curious.

'No, sir, you're quite right there. But it was in the cellars, see. Under the house. And there must have been a flood at some time 'cos none of the bottles had labels, and I din't think that looked so hot—so I decanted it. It hasn't done it no harm, has it, sir?'

'It hasn't done it no harm whatsoever, Billy,' Jack assured him. 'In fact it is one of the finest Rhones I think I have tasted in many a long year.'

Billy looked at him appalled, hoping against hope that no one else had heard, sure that if they had there might be an immediate repudiation of the wines. But no one seemed to be bothered in the slightest, even those people close at hand who Billy thought must surely have heard. All he could think, as he swallowed hard, was that their geography wasn't as hot as his and they hadn't a clue where the Rhone Valley might be.

'It's all right, Billy,' Jack murmured, one strong hand on his arm guiding him quietly to the side of his chair. 'Wines as great as this have no enemies. But well done, you. And a jolly happy Christmas, too.'

Jack winked at him to reassure him, and Billy, feeling six inches taller, hurried back to take his seat alongside Marjorie, who was sitting next to Anthony Folkestone.

'Well done, Billy,' Anthony said. 'Cook has told us what a sterling role you played.'

'Yes, well done, Billy,' Marjorie said, turning to kiss him on the top of his head the way she had always done since she first took him under her wing all those years ago when they were both orphaned. 'Really well done. You're a smasher. Know that?

274

Happy Christmas.'

Billy started to eat his wonderful Christmas dinner, his whole being aglow with happiness. After the first delicious mouthful of tender chicken breast, carefully speared on to his fork with a slice of perfectly roasted sausage and the corner of a matchless roast potato, he looked round the huge dining hall, lit gently by the light of fifty odd candles in jam jars, and beamed a beam of pure delight and joy.

Yes, he thought to himself. *Yes, you bet. This is certainly worth fighting for. You bet your life it is.*

Part Two

JULY 1943

Chapter Seven

In preparation for the planned landing by the Allies in Sicily, Eugene once again found himself dropped in the mountainous and volcanic island that lies southwest of the foot of Italy, his job this time to make contact with a fierce Resistance group led by one of the most notorious of the Sicilian bandits and subsequently to help plan a series of sabotages that would weaken vital enemy supply lines as well as jeopardise any possible escape routes. It was a commission that had sounded quite straightforward when explained to those about to undertake it, but Eugene was now far too skilled an agent to be fooled by the apparent simplicity of the enterprise. When commissioned he knew at once that this was far and away the most difficult *dodge* he had been requested to do.

To the once again deserted Kate, however, his absence was no different from the last. She knew that once he was gone there was nothing she could do about it. They were at war and this was what happened when a country was fighting not only for its own survival but possibly for the survival of the entire free world. Terrible risks had to be taken and they had to be taken generally speaking by people who were dearly loved by other people. So in order to cushion the shock and avoid worrying herself to death she had invented an emotional bolster for herself, considering herself twice blessed to have fallen in love with and to be loved in return by someone as heroic as Eugene. This didn't mean that Kate either took Eugene for granted or simply put him out of her mind until his prayed-for safe return; it simply put her plight and anxiety into a better perspective, allowing her the chance to try to equate her own situation with the much more important universal one, and to put her own private suffering into a context that she was then able to contain and control.

She and Poppy called themselves the WGWs— the War Grass Widows—doing their best in a typically English way to make light of a possibly dreadful situation. And with every day Kate grew more glad of Poppy's friendship and her companionship. Although Marjorie would never be replaced as her oldest and dearest friend, Kate grew very close to Poppy because of the similarity of their situations, the only difference being that Eugene acted as a solo operator, working in tandem when he had to with people on site, as he called it, while, although it was not said aloud, Scott was known to be working as part of a home-based duo.

Scott's partnership was never discussed specifically between Kate and Poppy; both were too well trained, too fiercely loyal and far too professional ever to discuss the possible details of their partners' commissions. The only thing that was talked about regularly between them was the problem of how to deal with the absences and how best to cope with their own daily lives while their lovers were gone. Poppy duly confessed that she would find it much easier if she was back in the field herself, even though she understood the reasons why she was not going to be allowed to work with Scott again now they were married.

'I simply itch to get back in the saddle,' she would tell Kate time and time again when the matter was aired. 'And what I can't understand is why they won't make use of me, instead of just letting me fester away in H Section. After all, I didn't do a bad job on the Churchill thing.'

'You most certainly did not,' Kate had assured her. 'You were brilliant apparently—according to what I heard. Perhaps they're saving you for something special?'

As it happens Kate was absolutely right. Jack Ward, who had been very impressed by the part Poppy had played in the Churchill Incident, as it had become known, was also mindful of how the incident had affected Poppy who had taken a considerable time to level out—as Jack called it—after playing such a pivotal part in saving the life of the man who was now saving the life of a nation. Jack had several important prospective missions—albeit still in embryonic stages—on his drawing board, but since they were set in what was at this moment the future, he thought it best not only to rest Poppy by putting her behind a desk, but also to rekindle what he knew to be her fervent desire to help fight in her country's corner by seeming to ignore her. Jack viewed his agents in much the same way as a trainer might view his best thoroughbreds—keep them in steady work but never allow them out of anything more than a steady working canter, so that when the tapes finally went up the horses were more than ready to run their hearts out.

Even so, in spite of Jack's great skills as an officer in MI5, in Poppy's case he very nearly made a serious miscalculation.

It was Mrs Alderman who first noticed the effect Poppy's enforced inactivity, allied to her constant separations from her beloved husband, was having on one of Eden Park's favourite heroines.

'You need feeding up, young lady,' Cook remarked one afternoon when she was surprised in the kitchens by a pale-faced Poppy. 'Aren't you eating properly?'

'No one's eating properly, Cookie,' Poppy laughed in return, accepting one of Mrs Alderman's home-made biscuits but then only toying with it. 'I've never been a great eater anyway, so don't worry. You do wonderfully, the way you feed us all here. We don't know how you do it, any of us. You're really some sort of miracle worker, given the perfectly dreadful ingredients you have to work with.'

'So if it's not a few extra titbits you're after,' Mrs Alderman said carefully, eyeing a young woman who in her opinion was now simply wasting away, 'to what do I owe the pleasure?'

Poppy shrugged, and nibbled a tiny bite of biscuit.

'Kate's got some leave, and everyone else is busy. And I was at a loose end, so I felt like a chat.' She smiled. 'And you're always good for a wonderful chat, so I thought I'd dip on down to the kitchen.'

'I could fix you a nice bacon and egg,' Cook said as if it was nothing. 'I keep a few eggs aside and a little portion of rashers for anyone I consider needs a bit of bolstering. So why don't you let me do you a nice plateful?'

'Because I wouldn't eat it. It's jolly kind of you, so don't think I don't appreciate it, but it would be

282

wasted on me. I'm not hungry—and before you go pulling any more tragic faces, the reason I'm not hungry is that I ate a jolly good lunch of rabbit stew, cabbage and potatoes. Why don't you treat yourself for once? You're always worrying about everyone else, and the last person ever to come into your consideration is you.'

'Nonsense,' Cook replied with a wave of a work-worn hand. 'Tell you what I could do with, though—that's putting the old feet up for a while. It's the one thing that gets you about this job. Standing for hours on stone floors, I can't tell you what it does to my feet. There,' she exclaimed as she sat down opposite Poppy at the table. 'Lord, that's better, I can tell you.'

She poured herself a cup of tea that looked a little more reasonable than usual and held the pot up on offer to Poppy, who raised an appreciative eyebrow and nodded.

'This is the one perk I do allow myself,' Cook said, pouring another cup. 'When I get an ounce or so of decent tea—and I'm not saying from where'—a statement she embellished with a wink—'I keep it for myself. After all, it's only going to make a couple of pots, and that's no use to all them upstairs. Only thing we're short of is sugar today, dear. I'm afraid I'm having to save it for Sunday's pudding.'

'Any more news from John?' Poppy wondered, sipping her tea.

'Funny as you should ask,' Mrs Alderman said, pulling a letter from her flowered apron pocket. 'I haven't heard from my boy since this last letter. Did I read you this one? When they were moving him to another camp?'

283

Poppy frowned and shook her head. In all probability she had heard it not once but twice, such was the shortage of letters from Cook's captured son, but then, such was the shortage of any direct news from abroad, Poppy was as happy to hear it reread as John's mother was to reread it.

'I just hope he's not been taken sick,' Mrs Alderman continued. 'As he says in this letter here, he's been lucky so far, but who's to say his luck will hold? Particularly when winter comes round again. Last winter he said was atrocious, remember? The snow and frosts were something 'orrible—never known it so cold, he said—and some of his pals in the camp, they was so sick some of them they didn't make it through. Proper epidemic it was, according to John. He says he's still strong enough to survive anything—least that's what he says here. "Don't you go worrying yourself, Mum—I'm still strong enough to do two men's work, and you won't catch me going down with no flu or nothing. All you'll catch me doing is hoping and praying this thing'll be over soon and I can come home again and have a great big bowl of that smashing steak and kidney pie you does so well."' Cook stopped and smiled down at the letter in her hand. 'His grammar's as bad as young Billy's,' she said. 'Mind you, the conditions he's living under, last thing you'd worry about is the state of your grammar. Wouldn't you say, dear?'

'Absolutely,' Poppy nodded. 'Couldn't agree more.'

'Even so, you have to wonder. He says here the hut he's living and sleeping in measures only fifteen foot by fifteen, which don't seem too blooming commodious to me—not once you realise there's ten of 'em sharing. Fifteen be fifteen? Hardly bigger than his granddad's garden shed, that is, and they go and pack ten men in it. Disgraceful I say. So much for the Genoa Convention.'

'Absolutely,' Poppy agreed again. 'Except I think it's the Geneva Convention.'

'You're probably right, dear—not that it would make any difference to Jerry what it's called, they're so busy ignoring it.'

Poppy smiled at Mrs Alderman as she watched her staring at the precious letter from her son, her finger moving slowly across the page as if the paper might carry some small reminder of her son's very essence.

'They got a vegetable patch, mind,' she added. 'So things can't be all bad. John just says he wishes Jerry'd thought of throwing in a bit of manure and all, because the ground's so bad, of course. Taking all their will and ways to grow anything at all.'

She sighed and looked up from a letter Poppy knew she could recite by heart, and shook her head slowly.

'Least we know how to treat our POWs. Them that came here only last week, we haven't put them behind barbed wire, have we? No—they're out free as birds helping in the gardens here. They got a uniform, of course they have, but that's all. We put our POWs on trust—give 'em the same food we're having ourselves and don't go crushing them into no huts fifteen by fifteen.'

'Someone said there might be a bunch of Italians going to be housed in the old dairy house, and in some of the flats above the garages.'

Mrs Alderman nodded. 'No hut fifteen by fifteen for them neither,' she noted. 'Mind you, the way they've been carrying on I'd say the Eye-Ties need locking up more than the Germans. Mr Hackett was down here the other evening—he's a funny man, Mr Hackett. Always manages to raise a laugh somehow, so he does. Anyway, he was saying—and it did make us all laugh. He was saying the Italians build their tanks with one gear. Reverse!'

Mrs Alderman shook her head once more but this time with joy as she laughed all over again. Having finished her tea she glanced at the big kitchen clock hanging on the wall before getting up with a sigh to resume her duties.

'I'd better get going as well,' Poppy said, letting George down off her knee. 'I didn't realise it was that late.'

'Not working you too hard, are they?'

'Not hard enough.' Poppy smiled. 'No, I've got to get back to the house—because I was in such a rush this morning I didn't manage to clean through.'

'Off you pop then, dear—and you drop in any time for a cup of something. I'll try and save you some tea when I gets some more—or maybe next time I'll get you to eat some bacon and eggs.'

'Absolutely,' Poppy said, without much conviction, the very thought of a fry-up making her feel queasy immediately. 'And here's hoping the post brings you another letter from John very soon.'

Poppy wandered back across the sun-bathed parkland towards her house high up in the woodlands, in no real hurry to get back and start her housework, a task that had become an all but compulsive one, so obsessed had she grown with keeping their precious home spotless and tidy until Scott's return. She knew perfectly well that she had allowed it to become an obsession simply to keep her mind off her main and very real anxieties, namely what was happening to Scott, where and with whom—but this late summer afternoon, as she made her way slowly home with her ever faithful dog at her heel, her mind was dwelling on quite different things.

As always, when she had spent time with people as down to earth, and what she would term utterly decent, as Mrs Alderman, she immediately took stock of herself and her own problems, and as always she found herself coming up short. Scott was doing what he had chosen to do. She had married Scott in the full knowledge that this would be their life for the foreseeable future, and once she had been parted from him professionally she knew that he might well be working with someone else. Scott liked to work if not in a team then at the very least in tandem, so Poppy could not pretend that this had come as much of a surprise either. So in one way she had absolutely no reason to feel hard done by, let alone sorry for herself. Mrs Alderman's son was a prisoner of war, living in the most atrocious conditions, not knowing whether he was even going to survive until the end of hostilities, let alone get home again. If the war continued the way it had been going the year before, with Germany running rings round the Allied armies in North Africa and the Japanese seemingly doing as they willed in the East and the Pacific, then not only might John Alderman never get home but no one might any longer have anything they could call a home, let alone their own.

So the more Poppy walked the more determined

she became to keep both her body and her soul together, yet the more she tried the more she watched herself slowly but surely beginning to disappear before her own eyes. She tried to eat everything that was put in front of her in the canteen, and she tried to cook herself small but nourishing meals at home, but her appetite had gone—and not, she discovered, just for food and drink. It seemed increasingly obvious the longer Scott was away from her, doing his bit for the country in tandem with whoever it was who was working alongside him, that Poppy had lost her appetite for life itself.

*　　　*　　　*

Cissie Lavington was surprised to find herself face to face again with Harvey Constable, her old acquaintance and partner in arms—or rather *partner in crime, ducky*, as Harvey liked to say— since she had imagined him still to be working for Special Ops/Europe, which meant dropping regularly and frequently into Europe to set up contacts in Brussels and lines of communication across France. The last place she would have expected to see him was in the semi-wild of Eden Park, for Harvey was anything but a countryman. Harvey Constable claimed to have been born in Brook Street—which all his friends knew was a whopper—but there was no doubt that the way he lived and dressed for his life thereafter was designed to be seen at its best in a Mayfair environment. Harvey Constable was not happy to get mud on his spats—yet here he was, immaculate in his army uniform and sitting on a plain and uncomfortable little wooden office chair in front of Cissie's famously untidy desk deep in the very heart of the English countryside.

'You're going to stick out a bit here, Harvey darling,' she said, getting straight to the point as usual. 'You are going to appear—shall we say? As a little bit of a wild flower.'

'Then I should repair to the meadows at once, ducky,' Harvey sighed, brushing a tiny and totally imaginary piece of lint off his immaculately pressed khaki trousers. 'My appearance will do them nothing but good. Even the buttercups look as though they're rationed.'

Cissie smiled and lit yet another cigarette. 'Thank you for these, by the way,' she said, tapping the tin of Markowitz Black and White cigarettes he had brought her as a present. 'One had no idea one could still obtain such luxuries.'

'If one knows under which stone to look, one can obtain absolutely one's heart's desire. This is a dullish hellhole, is it not? And as for your Major Folkestone—bit of a school prefect, isn't he?'

'I will not hear a word said against our gallant major,' Cissie retorted. 'If it's possible for a major to do so, he runs a very tight ship. And you still haven't told me what on *earth* you are doing here.'

'Sustained a little ding to the right knee, alas,' Harvey replied, arching his eyebrows. 'Jumping out of a plane. Makes certain pastimes of mine a little difficult, as you can imagine. Thus came down the decree from on high that Harvey Constable is to do no more bobbing and weaving in the name of his country until said small ding is quite better. As a result, and oh so very sweetly of the Head Prefects, they bought me a desk to sit behind, where I am

289

ordered to stay until the knee is himself again. Unfortunately, they would not let me choose *where* to put said desk, which is how I came to end up here in Deadwood Gulch. I just hope there is a good and regular supply of whoopee water, otherwise I might take to wearing green orchids and very funny clothes.'

Cissie drew on her cigarette and did her best to keep her face straight. In return, holding her dead-pan look, Harvey smiled his usual smile, a mixture of arrogance and insouciance, of mockery and defiance, chin stuck slightly out, and the corners of his mouth curled very slightly upwards. He had first known Cissie when he was a small boy running errands for his mother from her workrooms above the shop in Bond Street, his mother at that time being a couturier and hat maker to the gentry, aristocracy and minor royalty.

'I have to say you look really quite passable in uniform, Harvey.'

'Passable?' Harvey opened his eyes wide in mock horror. 'I trust I look more than *passable*, Duchess. I took the whole damn' thing to pieces and remade it, so that, unlike most of the military, my uniform actually *fits*. Have you seen the Yanks in theirs? They look positively *gorgeous*—so why oh why cannot *we*?' He lit a cigarette, inhaling deeply. 'Did you know I helped Digby design the WVS uniform?'

'No, I didn't,' Cissie replied, having never given the matter the slightest thought.

'Well I did, indeed.' Harvey blew a perfect smoke ring and watched it lazily drifting towards the heavily blacked-out window behind Cissie. 'I do think that the success of the WVS is in great part due to the design of that uniform, and the colour. So flattering, that deep cherry colour, wouldn't you agree? Unlike yakky khaki that makes everyone look jaundiced. I have yet to see anyone wearing the WVS jersey whom it makes look ugly—and that is the absolute truth.'

Cissie sat back and also attempted to blow a smoke ring, which she succeeded in doing, although on a much smaller scale than Harvey. He, noticing the size of it, stuck one hand slowly up and pierced her effort with one long elegant index finger.

'You want to leave that sort of thing to the men, ducky,' he said. 'We do that sort of thing *so* much better.'

Cissie, while sometimes wishing that Harvey didn't make her laugh inside so much, was usually very glad that he did, since whatever her front, and her apparently unflappable manner, Cissie needed cheering up like the rest and the best of them. He really was such an odd mix, she thought to herself, as she stubbed out her cigarette. If she hadn't known him as well as she did, she would never possibly have guessed that he was held in high esteem both at Baker Street and at other Intelligence HQs. Harvey Constable was a contradiction in anybody's terms: effete, artistic and immensely intelligent, capable of speaking three languages fluently, he was also a tremendous athlete, and therefore both extremely fit and strong, a top ranking skier, horseman and swimmer of near Olympic standards.

Even so, she could not help wondering what kind of ill-assorted pair Eugene Hackett and Harvey Constable must have made wandering

291

across France together disguised as first one thing and then another. It could have been a laughing matter, until one looked into Harvey's eyes and saw the steel in the bright blue orbs, and the look of utter determination behind them. These were the times when those who did not know him would suddenly feel a surge of gratitude that he was on their side and not in opposition. It would always be a far, far better thing to have Harvey Constable on your side than fighting against you. Harvey Constable was, in essence, the very best and most brilliant of secret weapons, a piece of lethal armament most beautifully concealed, the classic iron fist in a velvet glove, even though the glove might not be quite the colour required by the Establishment.

'Now then,' Cissie said, pretending to rifle through some papers on her desk as she realised yet again how absurd it was that she should still find Harvey so attractive. 'This famous new desk of yours. Have they put anything of interest on it as yet?'

'I'll say,' Harvey mocked. 'It would appear you have someone working away *within*. This is what I'm doing sitting here the other side of your desk, Duchess. I'm to work with you in H Section to ferret out what I understand is called a *caochán*.' Harvey stopped and frowned over-deliberately. 'I imagine that is some sort of bogspeak, yes? Ye Gaelic or some such?'

'It's the Gaelic, Harvey. For whatever. For this mythical creature that—'

'Go no further.' Harvey held up a perfectly manicured hand as if to stop traffic. 'I cannot abide Celtic whimsy. They always—all of them—have these quite unpronounceable creatures, sprites and spirits bansheeing all over the place stealing your shoes and putting crocks of gold in their place. I shall have none of it.'

'You've no doubt heard about our wild-goose chase? That's not too Celtic for you, I hope?'

Harvey carefully cut the end of his nearly finished cigarette with a pair of nail scissors he produced from his breast pocket, letting the hot end fall into the ashtray before the rest.

'I'd forgotten that little habit of yours,' Cissie said.

'You shouldn't. It avoids all horrible ashtray smells if one follows my procedure. As well as avoiding that awful-looking mess of squished up smokies. To get back to your wild goose,' he said in a stage Irish voice. 'Am I right in thinking someone planted what I understand some people call a *falsie* about the wretched girl? The Colonel's godchild?'

'A totally false file. Very well done, too. Had the Colonel running round in circles, doncher know.'

'No I don't, ducky. Can't begin to imagine the Colonel running anywhere, let alone round in circles.'

Harvey raised his eyebrows once again at Cissie, as if to pull rank and remind her that he had known Jack Ward even longer than she. They were in fact the closest of friends, if Jack Ward could ever be said to have close friends, that is. But whatever the differences in their characters, they each appreciated the other in a way that only true originals can.

'Yes, I know what you mean about the Colonel,' Cissie said edgily, getting the nuance. 'But the truth of the matter is it got under his skin. And, for him,

293

he raised quite a stink—because quite simply he was furious when he realised he'd been taken in. Don't blame him either—what a waste of precious time. And then of course the knowledge of what the poor wretched innocent girl had gone through.'

'She is still *on leave*, I take it?'

'Compassionate leave, of course. Not a whole lot of fun thinking one might well be shot for something one didn't do. Fair enough if one did— but not at all if one did not.'

'Hanged, Cissie old thing,' Harvey corrected her. 'We don't shoot traitors here—we hang 'em. Is she near recovered? Someone like that, given that sort of jolt, they often turn into v. useful material. Even if they are the wrong sex. She could be of use to yours very truly, et cetera, now that the pushing in the back is about to become a kick up *la derrière.'*

'We could always ask. She was pencilled in for a soft posting,' Cissie replied, consulting her files. 'Meant to be going to the Bahamas to work as a housekeeper and keep an eye on the Duke and Duchess of Windsor.'

'Not soft—dull. Deadly dull. Not my most favourite duo. Not that she'd be needed out there either. Hear the American Secret Service is all over them. They can hardly open a letter without our cousins across the water wiring us its contents. Anyway—as far as the girl goes I have to say *not* a good business at all, finally.'

'Meaning?'

'Meaning arresting the wrong girl. Gives the opposition time to continue with their nefarious deeds, old thing—puts bone in their meat, too, gives 'em the impression they're top dogs. Won't do—not in my book. We've had God knows how

294

many agents across Europe blown in the past two months as you know, and that is *not* good for us, and I'll bet those who do not love us as much as we love ourselves are feeling quite gooey with pleasure—and we cannot have that, we really, really cannot. Extraordinary what makes people cross the floor, you know. I remember one bloke changing his loyalties simply because his expenses were three months late. And there was I thinking it was all about patriotism when in fact it's all about accountancy.'

'I don't have one idea as to where would be best for you to start,' Cissie said carefully, allowing him the initiative.

Harvey stood up, stretching his long elegant legs.

'Don't worry about it, Cicely old thing,' he said, checking the knife-edge creases in his trousers were still just that. 'Softly, softly catchee bastard, as always. I shall sit and look and listen. Always best to concentrate on characters, keeping the weather eye out for those all bitter and twisted. Sit, look and listen and wait until you hear Nana's bark.'

'Nana's bark?' Cissie laughed. 'Harvey—you are more than one guinea a minute.'

'Don't laugh, old thing. I shall prevail. I shall ferret out this whatever—'

'*Caochán.*'

'I shall find him. Or her. Or *it*. Nor shall I shed one little teardrop when he, she or *it* swings from the end of a rope. I recruited a lot of those agents who have gone down, as you know.'

Cissie nodded her agreement, and walked across the room with him to the door.

'So wish me all the luck of the chase, old pal, won't you?' Harvey said.

'I shall,' Cissie replied. 'And I do.'

There was one more flash of steel from the blue eyes and then he was gone, leaving Cissie Lavington startled and bewildered at the odd surge of emotions stirring within her as she realised that Harvey Constable was about to become part of the Eden Park fabric.

Chapter Eight

Marjorie had watched him go, and now sat waiting for him to come back. The day she had dreaded more than any other had finally dawned, the day Billy was old enough to volunteer, and no sooner it seemed had the candles been blown out on the birthday cake specially baked by Mrs Alderman than Billy had been off, as fast as he could bicycle, to the nearest recruitment centre. Marjorie had long ago given up trying to persuade him to wait until his call-up papers came. Her assurances that they inevitably would arrive, fell on deaf ears.

'I don't wanna be called up, Marge!' Billy would protest by way of reply. 'That looks like you're not willing! But I am, see? I'm dead willing—and I'm not going to hang about waiting. Some blokes I heard of, they don't ever get their papers.'

'Probably because they're on some sort of fiddle. A lot of people buy their way out of getting conscripted, you know.'

'Yeah, I'll bet, Marge. But I'm not going to sit and wait for my papers. I'm going to make sure I get in the army—and the way I'm going to do that is blooming well go and blooming well volunteer.'

So off he had gone that morning, waved farewell by Marjorie and Kate after an extra early breakfast, since Billy faced a fifteen-mile ride to the nearest town with an enlistment centre and was determined to be first in the queue.

Kate had given Marjorie the warmest of hugs before they went their separate ways, knowing exactly how she felt, remembering only too well the day her own brother had gone off and enlisted and how heavy her heart had been that morning. But as so many thousands of women all over the country were finding out, mothers, sisters, wives and sweethearts, when their man was determined on fighting for his country, there was nothing that could be said to stop them. And like every other woman who felt the terrible pain of separation Kate had known the secret pride that went with it as well, that someone they loved obviously loved them back so much that he was willing to risk paying the final price for that love.

Marjorie had not yet reached that emotional point. All she could think of was Billy as she had first known him, a tiny, half-starved little boy in the terrible school where they both had been abandoned, a child who would hardly speak he was so deeply unhappy and so deeply hurt, who would have been a lost soul by now if Marjorie had not befriended him as if he was her brother, and if her wonderful Aunt Hester had not surprised them both quite utterly by adopting Billy into her little household.

They had grown up together, although Marjorie, being so much the older of the two, had always been the responsible one, the one who once Aunt Hester had been killed looked after Billy's welfare and tried to make sure he was going to grow up in the right way. Privately she thought there was no need for him to fight. She felt sure the war was about to turn in the Allies' favour, as most people did, and with America providing most of the troops there no longer seemed the terrible need for volunteer soldiers that there had been when Britain stood alone. No one would think less of Billy for not volunteering, she had argued, only for Kate to tell her gently that one person would, that was the person who mattered most—Billy.

And so she had sat at the window of the cottage as Billy cycled fast and furiously out of her sight. She had gone to work that morning feeling more miserable than she had for an age, hardly able to concentrate on anything that was put in front of her. Anthony tried to comfort her, but she was in her way inconsolable, for nothing could convince her otherwise than that the moment Billy put on a uniform he would be killed. That was what would happen. That was the way of war.

By lunchtime she expected him back, as promised, both of them having worked out how long the ride would take him, approximately how long the interview and subsequent medical would last, and finally how long the ride back, both of them concluding that if everything went well Billy would be back in time for a canteen lunch. But at half past one, nearly an hour after the predicted time, there was still no sign of Billy, and Marjorie was beginning to become concerned. Everyone in the know assured her that if anything had happened to him, she would have been informed, but Marjorie dismissed such notions as fallacious, reminding everyone there was a war on, and that the Germans had recently resumed their heavy bombing of key British towns and cities, one of which was being visited by her adopted brother that very day.

The afternoon seemed to drag by, with each second lasting a minute and each hour worth a day. When it was finally time to go home, Marjorie ran all the way to the cottage, half expecting the ever-cheerful Billy to fling open the door and behave as if nothing had happened, other than the usual half a dozen scrapes he had got into on his travels.

But there was no Billy, nor was there any news.

Then at nearly half past eight Marjorie heard something and leaped to her feet. Alone, with Kate away visiting Poppy in the house in the woods, at first she feared for her life, so loud and sudden was the noise, before she recognised it as the sound of a bicycle crashing to the ground. A moment later the door burst open and Billy fell in, trying to clutch at the doorpost to stop his fall, but failing to do so and tripping heavily to the floor.

Marjorie was by his side in a second, convinced that he had been the victim of some terrible accident, only to be greeted with an overpowering smell of drink.

'Billy?' she said in deep bewilderment. 'Billy—Billy, have you been *drinking*?'

The young man on the floor did his best to look round, trying to focus the bleariest pair of eyes Marjorie had seen in a very long time, before collapsing at her feet once again.

'Oh, Billy,' Marjorie sighed tetchily. 'You're drunk.'

'Yes,' Billy muttered, face down. 'I know. Sorry, sis. Sorry.'

'But why, Billy? Why are you drunk? No—not just drunk—why are you *so* drunk?'

Billy lay still as a corpse for a moment then turned his head again to try to focus on Marjorie.

'' 'Cos they wouldn't ruddy well have me, sis,' he muttered thickly. 'I failed the ruddy medical.'

* * *

Marjorie couldn't help but feel intense relief. Billy wouldn't be joining up after all, which meant that all they both had to do now was survive the war raging overhead. And since Eden Park was a long way from any likely targets their chances of survival were fairly high.

It was young Billy's chest apparently that was at fault, something to do with an irregular heartbeat, much to Billy's disgust and dismay. Everything else about him had been absolutely A1, he told Marjorie the next morning when, sobered up but suffering from his first hangover ever, he recounted the events of the day before.

'Mind you,' he said, 'I had to get me skates on, sis. We'd miscalculated how long it was going to take me by bike—'

'You'd miscalculated, you mean. You're the one who knows how fast you can ride your bike.'

'Yeah—well, we didn't take no account of the hills, did we?'

'*Any* account of the hills, if you don't mind, Billy—and *you*, not *we*,' Marjorie corrected him as ever.

'Point is it took a sight longer than I thought so I had to cycle like I never cycled before—and the last bit was all hill. About a one in five I reckon, and that's not funny when you're pushin' on. So anyway, I get there OK—and I'm pretty much at the top of the line, and everything's in perfect working order according to the MO. Fine physical specimen's what he called me, till he checked the old ticker one more time, saying there was something he thought he'd heard but wasn't too sure about.'

Marjorie nodded attentively, spreading a thin layer of margarine on a curling piece of stale toast and wondering whether the extra effort required by all the pedalling uphill might have exacerbated whatever condition it was the inspecting doctor thought Billy might have.

'You got—I don't know the exact words he used, Marge,' Billy continued. 'Sounded as if it had something to do with rhythm or something. Anyway, he said I got this heartbeat that in't altogether regular. It sort of misses a beat now and then, and he said though it won't kill me—least he didn't think it would—he said he couldn't pass me fit for active service as all the training and route marches and all that might well do me some harm.'

'So that's that, is it?' Marjorie wondered, trying to look as disappointed as her adopted brother. 'No second goes or anything like that?'

'Nah.' Billy shook his head and pulled a cross face. 'All goes down on your record, don't it? Dicky ticker—NGFA. No good for active service. A bloke afterwards said if I was still keen I could always apply for a desk job, or join the NAAFI or something, but that's not what I want to do. I don't want to sit behind no desk or serve in no canteen when I could be out doing something useful.'

'These things are useful in war, Billy. Someone

has to do them.'

'Not me, Marge. Over my d.b.'

'So what *are* you going to do then?'

'I'll think of something. Don't you worry.'

With a look of sudden determination Billy then removed himself to go and try to walk off his hangover in the park. Marjorie watched him go from the door of the cottage. He was a young man now and whatever he chose to do next there was little she could do to stop him. Even so, the fact that he had failed his medical made her jump on her own bike and speed off to the main house whistling as merrily as any errand boy.

*   *   *

It was Anthony Folkestone who came to Billy's rescue. With the amount of work on his desk he possibly would never have given the young man's quandary a second thought had it not been for Marjorie, to whom Anthony found himself more and more attracted. Knowing that she had her superior's total support, Marjorie now felt confident enough occasionally to discuss domestic or private matters whenever there was a slight lull in their office proceedings, which was how she came to tell Anthony of Billy's disappointment. At first Anthony considered the possibility of getting him re-examined in case there had been an error on the part of the doctor, but since Marjorie much preferred the notion of Billy's not being a member of the armed forces she did not encourage that suggestion, telling Anthony instead that a second disappointment following another failed medical could really break Billy's heart.

302

'Poor Billy,' he said, although he was finding it difficult to concentrate on Billy's difficulties because Marjorie was looking so pretty. The lace of her blouse showed off the small brooch he had given her at Christmas, and the line of her neck was emphasised by the fact that she had put up her hair, while the few stray curls which had fallen out made his heart turn a small somersault.

'He's so cut up you wouldn't believe it, Anthony. As cut up as all sorts of other lads all over the country will be to receive their call-up papers and be passed fit. But that's Billy all over.'

Anthony's concentration reverted to the matter in hand.

'Billy's such a bright spark, he would be wasted in a normal wartime occupation. I mean—can you imagine Billy turning out rissoles in a NAAFI canteen? He would be getting the chef to try some new recipe or trying out some new way of increasing the heat, or how to make the hens lay faster or more furiously, or working out how to feed five hundred men in five minutes rather than twenty. It doesn't bear thinking of. No, I know that Billy has to find something he can be good at, and useful. Something where he could make the best use of his inventions, and all the rest of his nonsense.'

'I love the idea of Billy in a NAAFI canteen.' Anthony smiled, but as he did so he was also looking thoughtful. Billy was a cracker, a one off, one of those bright sparks that the Colonel always liked to collar and make his own. He looked across at Marjorie. The only trouble was, he reckoned that if Marjorie knew which way he was thinking of using young Billy's gifts it might well spell the end

303

to romance.

*   *   *

Jack had his initial meeting with Harvey Constable out of sight of anyone, instructing Harvey to make his way up to a small suite of rooms in the attics that were reserved for the Colonel's use only.

It was the first time since he had known Jack that Harvey saw him visibly disconcerted. Jack pretended he was in a bad mood because the stem of his favourite Dunhill pipe had broken, and being unable to get it repaired anywhere locally he was having to make do with keeping the pipe held together by a band of thick medical adhesive wound around the offending part.

'Damned war,' Jack growled, trying yet again without success to keep his pipe alight. 'Can't get any decent tobacco and now a chap can't even get his best pipe repaired.'

'Could you possibly smoke another pipe out of your vast collection, sir?' Harvey wondered as idly as he could. 'After all, every time I see you you're wearing a different one.'

'I don't happen to have another pipe with me, chum,' Jack replied, flashing Harvey one of his darkest looks. 'You imagine I'd be putting up with this for a smoke if I did?'

Harvey had guessed of course at what was really disconcerting his friend. The same matter that was occupying his own mind: the loss of all those good agents, and the sabotaging of all the fine and brave work they had been doing. No one liked the thought of dealing with double agents in the field, but what was even worse was the thought of one at work *within*, as Jack put it. Harvey also knew that the wild-goose chase on which he had been sent by way of the false file had embarrassed the Colonel, who did not appreciate being made a fool of.

But Jack Ward was not one to waste time or energy on self-blame, nor on too much self-analysis. Jack Ward, although known never to rush into anything, did on the other hand like to get on with the job, preferring to dispense with formalities and small talk so that problems could be readily faced and hopefully soon surmounted.

'We know now it has to be someone inside,' he said, once the subject had been broached. 'No one else would have been able to pass off such a good personal file from before the war. I swear to God even the dust was regulation Ministry dust, and the whole damn thing was so authentic anyone would have been fooled by it. I shouldn't have, but I was, dammit, and so a lot of valuable time was wasted.'

'Mmm,' Harvey said with a tight smile. 'And now we're licking our wounds, are we?'

'You know me better than that, Constable.'

'I hope we're still on the god-daughter's parents' Christmas card list.'

Jack eyed him while putting another match to his recalcitrant pipe, deciding not to dignify Harvey's needling with any reply.

'Got a plan of action yet, chum?' he wondered instead, gently fanning the match to extinction. 'You're going to have to get cracking, you know. If we're going to have any agents left.'

'Need to know what I'm going to be first, sir,' Harvey replied. 'This is obviously not a uniform job. So what's the plot and which character am I?'

'Decommissioned,' Jack replied. 'You've got

a visible wound—at least, a visible list—so temporarily DC and doing a bit of office work to keep the mind active.'

'When I get to interview level?'

'In camera, and strictly confidential. No relating chapter and verse afterwards. You'll be covered by the OS Act anyway, so you'll be able to work that phase in complete confidence. So what's your starting point?'

'I'm going through everyone's file first, naturally,' Harvey replied, carefully examining his fingernails. 'Not that I expect to find the bastard that way—I doubt very much if that sort of information leaps off the page at one. But what I might find is some interconnection somewhere, or some lapse, some interruption in someone's daily round and trivial task. Then I shall do what I like to think of as a house to house.'

'Going to take some time, interviewing all and sundry.'

'Has to be done. And I'm a fast worker. Always been known for it, know what I mean?'

'We have to consider the possibility that it might not be someone within,' Jack said, carefully and slowly as always in his beautifully modulated voice. 'That is to say not actually here in the Park. It *could* be someone in another branch of the firm, but somehow I doubt it because so many of the disastrous missions were ordered up from here.'

'And it's much more likely too, old man, that it's someone behind a desk rather than in the field. As we know, agents don't have much access to HC info—they know who's who often enough, and who's meant to be doing what—although even that is pretty well classified—but not the really confidential stuff.'

'Agreed.' Jack nodded then narrowed his eyes as he regarded the bowl of his pipe, which had once more gone out. 'Anyway—in order to get the ball rolling, so to speak, some of my bogies are busy laying false trails across Europe. Starting here, of course, then across and down through France. False drops, phoney names, dead post boxes, safe houses that aren't—that sort of thing. Don't know what it's going to throw up. Point is it'll distract 'em. If we can get 'em to take their eye off the ball for a second . . .'

'Then they might drop it. Hear hear! The very thing. I need to buy a bit of time while I plough through the Social and Personals.'

'The agents that have been blown out cover quite a territory. They're not just in France—we've lost agents and contacts in Belgium and the Low Countries. Worse, quite a few of the escape routes organised by Black Wing have been blown as well. Which suggests that whoever is doing this is determined to do a good and proper job.'

'That it?' Harvey enquired, looking at his watch. 'I'm as anxious as you to kick on—so if that's it.'

Jack nodded and tapped the unsmoked tobacco out of his pipe and back into his pouch. 'I'm back off to town,' he growled. 'You know how to get hold of me.'

'I do indeed,' Harvey said, getting up and adjusting the cuffs of his uniform. 'And for heaven's sake while you're up there, get yourself one of your spare pipes. Talk about a bear with a sore bonce. I mean to say.'

'Hmmm,' Jack murmured, gazing ruefully at his damaged briar. 'One should never have a favourite.

Never have a favourite anything. You always end up disappointed that way. Never does to get too attached to any one thing. Or any one body, now I come to think of it.'

Harvey half closed his eyes and nodded his agreement.

'Arm's length,' Jack added. 'Minimum distance for anything—or anybody. Keep it all at arm's length,' he finished, half to himself.

*　　*　　*

Unable to sleep the hours she had slept in the old days, Poppy found herself getting up earlier and earlier each morning, and automatically cleaning her little house from top to toe, even though that was, all too often, the last thing she had done before she had gone to bed the night before.

'You're going mad, Poppy Meynell,' she told herself one morning when she found herself rearranging a perfectly well arranged set of silver ornaments. 'George?' she called to her dog who was having a blissful roll on his back in the middle of the room. 'George, I think I am perhaps going round the bend.'

There were still two and a half hours to go before she had to leave for work, and once again Poppy was at a loss to know what to do with her time. After she had taken a long bath, drunk a cup of terrible coffee and smoked a cigarette there was still an hour and a half to kill, half an hour of which could be taken up with walking George, although this was a complete waste of time since she took George to work with her. The distance to the house was a good half a mile, so George got plenty of exercise without being forced to take more.

Before, when Scott had gone on his first mission without her, Poppy had filled her spare time with reading, playing the piano and gardening. Now she found she had neither the inclination nor indeed the energy to do any of the things she had so enjoyed previously. She was quite enervated, lacking enthusiasm for anything other than seeing her husband again, and even that filled her with a sense of dread lest Scott had in any way changed towards her as a result of his adventures—or, worse, as a result of his continuing intimacy with Lily, his now long-established partner.

It was eating her up, this jealousy, she decided, a jealousy which was becoming obsessive and was without any real foundation. She had absolutely no reason to believe that Scott would be unfaithful—until she remembered the thrill of the chase, as he had called it, the intense excitement they had mutually experienced when working together to try to thwart those intent on assassinating the Prime Minister. When she thought about it, which she often did, Poppy swore she could feel the adrenalin rushing through her system all over again, just the way it had when she and Scott had found themselves face to face with the putative assassins, and most particularly when she had to see down her very own husband as the leader of the traitors. So, she thought, she could after all have real and very good grounds for her growing anxiety, since there was no reason to believe that Scott and Lily wouldn't be sharing exactly the same sort of thrill, the kind of excitement that can well and truly open up a relationship.

'Stop torturing yourself,' Kate advised her.

'People can just work together, you know, without anything like that happening.'

'I know, Kate. But being in the field with another woman—an attractive woman—makes the chances of that something happening a little higher, particularly if the woman happens to be Lily Ormerod.'

Worst of all, to add to anxieties that were already acute enough, Poppy found herself first resenting the officers in Eden Park and then actively disliking them, her old friend Jack Ward in particular, since she held him personally responsible first for separating her from Scott and then for sending him out in the field with another woman. Being Poppy she kept her feelings well under wraps, but possibly the fact that she was bottling everything up added to her physical deterioration.

'Come along will you,' Mrs Alderman said to her one morning as she caught her taking a short cut with George along one of the corridors in the staff quarters. 'I don't care what you say nor what you're a-going to say, but we're going to get some food into you if I have to sit you in a chair and hold your nose.'

Privately appalled by Poppy's pallor and wraith-like figure, Mrs Alderman marched her straight into the kitchen where sitting her down like a child at the table she immediately busied herself cooking a plate of bacon, eggs and sausages with provisions taken from what she called her emergency store. Poppy tried to make some feeble protest about being late for work, which Cook dismissed at once as poppycock, saying she had a good twenty minutes before she had to be in her office and even if she was late, Mrs Alderman would testify that getting food into Poppy had now become a medical necessity.

Finally—and all too easily once the delicious smell of grilling bacon filled her nostrils—Poppy submitted and waited patiently for the breakfast being so lovingly prepared for her.

'I got another letter,' Mrs Alderman said over her shoulder as she busied herself at the range. 'At long last too. Like to read it?'

Fishing the crumpled envelope out of her apron pocket, Mrs Alderman handed it backwards to Poppy as she skilfully flipped the fried egg over in the frying pan.

'Tell you what, dear,' she suggested. 'Why don't you read it out loud? I can never hear it too often.'

Poppy unfolded the letter, pencil-written on thin lined paper, and laid it on the kitchen table in front of her.

'"Dear Ma,"' she read. '"Not much to tell except it was turnips and cabbage for lunch and supper most of last week. But nine thirty is the time we get up—I say, don't tell old Bushell, will you? When I get back and start work for him again he will think I'm a rite lazy bones! The Red Cross do us proud, really, and we have some good things from them. Well, that's all for now. All the lads send you best wishes and all that. Can't wait to taste your steak and kidney pie. I told them all about it. They think I'm the luckiest devil alive having you for a mum. That's all for now. Your son John."'

'Good, eh?' Mrs Alderman said as she put down the plate of food in front of Poppy. But she was referring more to the letter than to the fried

311

breakfast. After all, Mrs Alderman saw food every day in some shape or another, but it was only every so often that she got a letter from her adored and captive son.

'You'd never have thought it if you knew John to think he was such a good letter writer. But there you are. Appearances can be very deceptive. He's got a good hand, too, see? Well taught he was at his writing. I always made sure of that. A good hand makes the man, I always say, and John's got a very good hand.'

'He certainly has,' Poppy agreed, looking at the large, heavily looped handwriting. 'It's a whole lot easier to read than mine.'

'We've always paid the greatest attention to handwriting in my family. My father used to make sure we all had a good hand. Gives you a proper start in life he used to maintain. And how about that?' Mrs Alderman picked up the letter and tapped the relevant bit. 'Not getting up till nine thirty, if you please. And there was I thinking he was slaving from dawn to dusk. Nine thirty, indeed. What a laugh I had over that, I can say.'

As Poppy ate her way through a breakfast that she could only describe as delicious, Cook stood at her shoulder reading through her son's latest letter all over again, saying the words over in a barely audible whisper. Poppy smiled to herself, suddenly feeling better about life than she had for a long time.

'I think I've just discovered what's meant by someone saving your bacon, Mrs A,' she said, setting her knife and fork down on a perfectly clean plate.

'I should think so too,' Mrs Alderman said,

removing the plate with a told-you-so nod. 'Can't imagine what you've been doing to yourself these past weeks. Trying to starve yourself, were you?'

'Not trying to, Mrs A, not really. Succeeding though, I suppose. Silly, really. Can't think what came over me.'

'It's the war, dear,' Cook said, putting the plate in the sink. 'Does funny things to us all. Personally speaking I haven't been able to think straight since September—what is it? Goodness gracious—since September four years ago! Who'd credit it? Four years ago come September. No wonder we're all going a bit doolally.'

*   *   *

Cissie Lavington wanted to see Poppy the moment she arrived up in the office.

'Now then, my dear,' she said, shutting the door behind them. 'Come in and sit down. I have some news for you.'

'Good, I hope?' Poppy said as she did as bidden, glancing quickly but anxiously at her superior.

'I think so,' Cissie replied, lighting a cigarette. 'Looks as though your grounding is about to come to an end. Not that you've been sidelined for any reason, y'understand me, but you have been inactive for a good while now, through no fault of your own—'

'You mean—' Poppy interrupted, retracting as soon as she caught the look in Cissie's eyes. 'Sorry.'

'Word has it that things are falling into place where they were not falling into place before. Plan is to send you off to meddle with some of Jerry's toys—but 'fore you do, goin' to have to go and get

313

a few lessons in the noble art of sabotage. Learn a thing or three about finding your way round engines and the like. Aero engines, that sort of thing. We've been having a great deal of fun grounding Jerry at certain prime times, and what we've learned is they're planning a bit of a special party for us—London especially—and we'd quite like to get in first. There'll be a group of you— small but select—but when it comes to it, the sharp end of the business will be done by singletons. So.'

'Good,' Poppy said with a deep sigh. 'I can't tell you how I needed this.'

'You make it sound as if we're sending you on hols, dearie!' Cissie laughed through a cloud of cigarette smoke. 'Not going to be much of a holiday, I assure you. Anyway—here's all you need to know for the moment. Pack your bag this evening and toddle off there tomorrow. And by the way, you're allowed to take the doggie. Seems dogs are more than tolerated.'

*   *   *

The train journey Poppy had to make up to the Midlands was one of the longest she remembered, not for distance but for the time it consumed. The train kept stopping, or being shunted back and forth, or parked in a siding without apparent reason, full of weary passengers packed like sardines into the carriages without the relief of food or water until night finally fell and still they had not reached their destination. Then, during the later part of the evening, when darkness had finally fallen, everyone was ordered off the train at an unidentified railway station from where they were expected to travel onward, either by waiting for another as yet unscheduled train or by taking one of the buses that occasionally turned up at the blacked-out halt on its way into the nearest town, which might still be miles from their final target.

Poppy was one of the unlucky ones, forced to find a bed for the night in a small, characterless town where about fifty or so other people were looking for accommodation, many of them not averse to following those in the know to their lodgings and immediately jumping the queue by use of elbows and shoulders in order to make sure of a place. Having suffered at the shoulders and elbows of two lots of queue-bargers, Poppy was about to give in when a kindly soul took pity on the pretty young woman traipsing down the street with her little dog at her heels. Hurrying after her, the woman took her by the arm with a finger to her own lips, and led Poppy back to a small but immaculately kept terraced house.

Here Poppy managed to get her bearings, discovered she was still a good fifteen miles from her final destination, a large complex that stood in the middle of an even larger patch of seemingly uninhabited countryside in the flatlands. The woman who had taken her in knew of it only vaguely, hinting that it was some sort of place where a lot of hush-hush work went on. More to the point was that she did know a way of getting Poppy out there since one of her neighbours made deliveries to its aerodrome, which was used for training pilots, and she was quite sure that tomorrow was the day when he normally went. By the time Poppy had turned in, her hostess had even gone and checked with her neighbour, returning with the news that Poppy indeed had a lift to where she was required to go.

* * *

Far from being surrounded by security fences and guards, as she was half expecting, as soon as Poppy was decanted from the van that had ferried her out she was faced with a range of ramshackle buildings, a couple of what looked as if they had once been runways, but had now been reduced to a series of bomb craters, and a large tower above which blew a ragged windsock.

Clutching her letter of introduction in her hand, Poppy looked around the desolate landscape, seeing nothing but fens and flatlands for miles. Then she made her way to the building that looked the most likely to be offices of some sort. A notice on the door that announced *No point in knocking— just barge straight on in* indicated that she had made the correct choice, so as requested Poppy and George made their way inside the glorified Nissen hut, passing through a series of deserted rooms with the odd item of broken furniture until finally they reached a room at the end with a glass door and a light on within. She could hear the sound of men talking and laughing, so, after taking a deep breath, Poppy knocked on the door and waited.

A curly-haired blond man wearing a dirty fur-lined flying jacket and with a cigarette stuck between his teeth flung open the door.

'Yes?' he asked rudely, checking himself the moment he saw the apparition in front of him. 'Hey—sorry!' he said, mending his manners. 'I had no idea they were making a film up here!'

At once three or four other young men appeared behind him to stare wide-eyed at their visitor.

'Down, boys!' the blond young man cried, in what Poppy now recognised as an Australian accent. 'I saw her first!'

'I wonder if you could help me actually,' Poppy said coolly. 'I'm looking for . . .' She consulted the piece of paper in her hand. 'I'm looking for a Mr Perkins.'

'Mr Perkins?' the young man said with a quick look at his friends.

'A Mr Trafford Perkins. He's expecting me.'

'I doubt that very much, Miss . . . er?'

'Meynell. Mrs actually. Mrs Scott Meynell.'

'Beg your pard, Mrs Meynell,' the flier grinned, managing to make Poppy's name rhyme with kennel. 'So you're expecting to see a Mr Perkins, mmm? Then we had better take you to the right place, because one thing *Mr* Perkins don't like is people being late.'

'I'm not late. In fact I'm early if anything.'

'In that case you shall live to see another day. Come along, sweetheart—let me show you the way.'

As he began to lead Poppy away all his friends surged forward to accompany him, only to be prevented from doing so by the flier's shutting the office door in their faces and locking it from the outside.

'Rough types,' the flier said with a grin. 'The name's Mark, by the way. How do.' He extended a hand that Poppy shook with a slightly quizzical look. This was not the sort of place and certainly not the sort of reception she had been expecting.

'Mr Perkins doesn't work in here?' she

wondered. 'I couldn't see what else might be occupied as offices or you know—'

Mark nodded to the control tower.

'That's where *Mr* Perkins works, Ma'am,' he replied. 'We're a bit short of proper working offices here and hereabouts. Thanks to the attentions of Jerry.'

'It certainly looks as though you've taken a bit of a hammering.'

'Too right. Hasn't been much of a party of late, I can tell you. OK—in you go—all the way to the top.' Mark opened the door at the foot of the control tower. 'Top floor—you can't miss it. And the best of British to you. But I wouldn't go in for too much of the Mr business if I were you. You might get a clout.'

With a wink and a grin, Mark turned and trotted away back to his friends, leaving Poppy to climb up the stone steps to the top of the tower.

The heavy wood door was closed so Poppy knocked firmly and stood back, waiting to be asked in. She didn't have to wait long.

'Come!' a voice hollered almost immediately. 'Come!'

Poppy pushed the door open and went in. Far from being confronted by the man in overalls whom she had been expecting to see, she found herself staring at a tall, elegant middle-aged woman in a spotless white motor racing suit, with a head of jet black hair and a full and beautifully painted red mouth, seated with her feet up on her desk fondling a small black pug dog that was sitting on her knee.

'Good,' the woman said, turning round in her swivel chair. 'Young Poppy Meynell, I take it. Yes?

Jolly good—come in then, come in. Survived the Antipodes, did you? They're a good crowd of lads, don't worry—in fact they're a damn' sight more than that. They're an exceptional bunch of young men altogether, as you'll see. This your dog? What a grand little fellow. Bring him over here at once so that he can meet Ron. This is Ron—he loves other dogs and I imagine from the way your chap is wagging his tail he likes a bit of company too. Why don't you let him off his lead and I'll put Ron here down and they can get to know each other while I put you in the picture. Have a good journey? Bet it was hell. Don't go anywhere by train now if I can help it—best to fly where you can. Anyway, that's neither here nor there, is it? Want a drink or something? Or still a bit early, is it? I've got some half decent whisky, or some totally decent French brandy—you choose. Tell you what—I'll make us some coffee and we'll lace it up a bit and get the old blood running, that's the ticket. Now what have they told you about me? About this place? B-, knowing them. I'm Trafford Perkins, we know who you are, and you're here to learn about budgering up engines and the like. Know anything about engines? From the look of you I should think you know not a thing. I certainly didn't know a solitary thing about engines when I was a gel—all I knew was you turned a key, pressed a button and hoped it fired. Now I can strip a six cylinder in my sleep *and* put it back together. Nothing to it—you'll see. Where's the damn' kettle gone? See? Told you they'd hit it off mmm? Told you.'

She pointed to the two dogs who were now busy playing together as if they had known each other all their lives, the way dogs can do, with George

319

allowing Ron to best him since he was the newcomer and Ron was the boss.

'How do you like your coffee? This is the real stuff, you know. Smuggled all the way from Holland. One of the *good* things about having an airfield is what sometimes comes in. You won't find yourself going short of much up here. Flown, have you? Ever been up? Left the ground at all? I don't imagine so. What chance? Unless you did any flying before the war—but I doubt that. You'd have been in pigtails and white socks still. I started flying in the Twenties, when I imagine I was possibly even younger than you are—no, I'd have been quite a lot younger. Considerably so. What age was I, in fact? Yes—nineteen. I was nineteen, of course I was. Still—that's not what you're here for, mmm? You are here to learn about engines. And how to budger 'em up.' She gave a huge but not unattractive laugh, banged the tin kettle on a small gas ring, lit it, then sat back down in her swivel chair, thumping the desk that was set in front of her. 'That's part of a de Havilland engine,' she continued, indicating a selection of oily bits and pieces that littered her worktop. 'When you're ready—because you certainly can't work in those clothes—I'll show you what goes where and what don't. I'll fix you up with some sort of boiler suit or some such—unless you fancy a set of these? Like mine? This is my old motor racing suit—not that I don't or won't still race, because as soon as this fudging war is over, yours truly'll be back behind the wheel of her ERA before you can say Adolf's dead, and pray God that will be tomorrow, if not sooner. Yes, the sooner I can get back behind the wheel the happier I shall be—like motor racing, do

320

you? Sport of the gods, I tell you. I was in Italy for two years before all this nonsense started—thought I could drive until I met Signor Fabio. There was a driver. I have never seen a man handle a car the way Paulo Fabio handled a car. He's dead now, sadly—great loss, crying shame. Shunted off by guess what—a German in the Italian Grand Prix. Took his line and shunted him into the trees. Boom. End of one of the world's great drivers. Taught me everything I know about driving—we even got married for a while. Didn't last—how could it? We both wanted to drive. Divine man, quite the best driver I have ever met. Not a bad lover either. Terrible husband, not a bad lover. Coffee. Let's have that coffee, and a lace of the old French—then we must have a good chat and get to know each other. Mmm?'

That was Poppy's introduction to a person she would come to consider to be the most astonishing character she had so far met. Previously she had put Cissie Lavington, Eugene Hackett and Jack Ward top of her list of People She Would Never Forget, but after meeting Mrs Trafford Perkins in an all but deserted aerodrome in the middle of the flatlands one misty September morning a new star was in the ascendancy. Even as she stood there for those first few breathtaking minutes of their newly formed acquaintance, Poppy knew she had just met someone who would have a profound influence on her life.

More than that, Poppy felt a sense of personal liberation, as if she was about to discover something entirely new about herself that would drive her life forward in a totally new direction. She was also all at once aware that she didn't have to go on worrying herself half to death about Scott because there was simply no point. By doing so she was denying herself any sort of life and therefore the chance to help fight for the country she had grown to love so much. It was not a question of losing her affection for her absent husband. She still loved Scott, in fact as a result of her rediscovered determination probably more than she had ever loved him before, but she also had a duty to herself. You might give your heart to a man, she thought as she looked into the clear blue skies through the control tower window, but your soul had always to remain your own.

*   *   *

For a while Helen Maddox had some difficulty locating Jack, but then, as she thought to herself, working her way steadily through the crowded bar, when had it ever been otherwise? Jack Ward had the ability to disappear. As the chameleon blends with the greatest subtlety into its background, so too did Jack Ward have the knack of melting into whatever landscape he might be in. Like many before her and those yet to come, Helen had very soon appreciated this facet of Jack's character, an ability he used to the full by never drawing attention to himself by his clothes, his mannerisms, or most of all his voice. Jack Ward never raised his voice. In one way he had no need to do so, since there was enough implicit authority in the way he spoke to bring anyone to heel. All he had to do to add some persuasion was to remove any trace of warmth from his famously melodic tones. Helen had seen him do it on occasion—a change of key

322

very often accompanied by the slow removal of his spectacles and a subsequent steady gaze at the object of his attentions, and when she had seen the effect it had on the victim Helen had hoped and prayed that he would never turn such a power on to her.

But just at that particular moment she found herself wishing her friend and mentor wouldn't make himself *quite* so invisible since she couldn't see his familiar stocky figure anywhere. The saloon bar was packed with office workers like herself who had clocked off, all dying for some sort of refreshment before making their various journeys home.

'Hiya, kid,' an unmistakable voice said from behind her. 'Of all the gin joints in the world, you had to pick this one.'

'Jack?' Helen said, turning round to see a familiar moon face staring at her over the top of an equally familiar and now happily mended briar pipe. 'What was that you said?'

'From *Casablanca*,' he said, steering her to the bar. 'Great flick with Ingrid Bergman and what's his name. Humphrey Bogart. Saw it last night—and I wouldn't mind seeing it again, it's so good. We could go tonight. The usual?'

Helen nodded, thoughtfully chewing her bottom lip. There was nothing she'd love more than to go to the pictures with Jack that evening, but she had another appointment, one she couldn't and mustn't break. She didn't know how to put it to Jack because even though he wouldn't show any emotion at all she knew how disappointed he would be, yet she had to refuse.

'One ever so luvverly gin and lime,' he said,

323

handing Helen her glass. 'We could just catch the last house, if we hurry.' He checked his wristwatch to make sure. 'It really is one heck of a good flick. You'll enjoy it.'

'Could we make it another night, Jack? It's a bit short notice.'

'Short notice never did no one no harm, didn't you know that?' Jack mused, looking at her over his spectacles as he relit his pipe. '*Carpe diem.*'

'I never know what that means.'

'Seize the moment. Live the day. Something like that. How's life in Baker Street?'

'Much as I thought it might be,' Helen replied. 'Dull. All filing.'

'Things have to take their course,' Jack murmured. 'Good things come to those who wait. Shallow end first and all that. So. What about the flick? Are you on?'

'I have to get home Jack. As I said, it's a bit short notice.'

'You don't have anyone to get home to,' Jack said bluntly but with a slight smile. 'Unless there's something you're not telling me.'

'You'll only laugh,' Helen replied a little sadly. 'It's my cat. She hasn't been at all well.'

'Why should I laugh? You know I like cats. What's wrong with her?'

'She's not eating. And she was sick all last night.'

'Then you must get home at once, Helen. You shouldn't even have bothered meeting me for a drink.'

'I couldn't get hold of you.'

'When people don't show, in this job, it's my job to understand.'

'But I'm not active, Jack,' she laughed, but

keeping her voice down. 'I'm desk-bound.'

'Mmm,' Jack mused. 'I might have some news for you on that front. You might have to go visiting some of your relations.'

Helen looked at him, widening her eyes slightly, a thrill of pleasure running through her at the thought of the possible chance of another mission.

'So go on,' Jack urged her. 'Finish your drink and off you go to your cat. Hope she's OK—and I'll be in touch.'

He was gone by the time Helen finished her drink and put her glass down. She gave a long, slow look round but he had vanished as expertly as he had arrived. Helen pulled the belt on her raincoat tight, picked up her bag and went out into the fogbound evening.

She had not been walking very long before she became certain that she could hear a regular footfall behind her, as if someone was close on her tail, so she quickened her pace, crossing the road backwards and forwards in the ever thickening fog, so that by the time she had crossed the Marylebone road and was heading north to Swiss Cottage the streets directly behind her had fallen oddly silent.

Chapter Nine

'Billy?' Marjorie called over the sound of the siren. '*Billy?*'

The door under the cottage stairs opened and Billy's face peered out.

'I might have known it,' Marjorie sighed. 'You spend all your time in there.'

325

'I have to have somewhere quiet to think, sis.'

'It's not going to be very quiet for a while now—in case you haven't heard it, there's the siren.'

Billy listened, head cocked, just managing to hear the distant wail from the air raid siren positioned on top of the fire station in the village.

'You'd best come in here then, sis, as usual,' Billy said, opening the cupboard door a little wider.

'Ta muchly I don't think,' Marjorie said, squeezing herself in. 'Oh, Lord—it's even more cluttered than usual. What have you been up to now?'

Marjorie pretended to be irritated by Billy's mess and jumble but secretly she was pleased that he had become so preoccupied with what he called his *notions*, since his disappointment over his enlistment. He seemed to spend every free moment in the place he had now made his den, the tiny little cupboard tucked away under the stairs that he had rigged up like a miniature workshop, with a worktop fitted across under the lower part of the stairs and a board fixed to the wall on which were pinned lists of tasks done and various agendas for things yet to be invented. He had even rigged himself a working light that could be turned on and off at a neck switch.

'If you pull that blackout curtain a bit tighter, Marge, we could have the light on. We'll be perfectly all right. I double-checked the security.'

With another exaggerated sigh Marjorie made sure the dark velveteen drape was covering the cracks in the door while Billy reached up and turned on his light.

'Right,' Marjorie whispered. 'So what have you got for us tonight?'

'There's no need to whisper, Marge,' Billy replied, clicking his tongue at her apparent stupidity. 'Jerry's hardly going to hear us hid away under the stairs, is he? And you wait till you see this.'

'I don't think I can,' Marjorie replied facetiously. 'The excitement is overcoming me fast.'

'I got the idea the other day in Major F's office. I was helping Miss Budge sort out the envelopes—all the TS ones that had come in by bike—'

'You shouldn't be doing that,' Marjorie interrupted. 'You're not meant to go near anything Top Secret.'

'I was only sorting 'em out, Marge. I weren't reading the bloomin' things.'

'I should think not. Not that you could anyway—but even so, if any of them had come open . . .'

'I don't need 'em to be open,' Billy said slyly. 'Not with this.'

'What's that?' Marjorie stared closely at the hyper-thin length of what looked like silvered wire inserted in the wooden handle of a small screwdriver instead of the usual blade. 'What on earth is it?'

'Just you wait,' Billy replied with relish. 'You just wait and see. 'Cos what I was thinking about, up in Major F's office, was there's always a space at the sides of every envelope you care to think of, right?'

'I don't know,' Marjorie shrugged. 'You tell me.'

'Yeah. Well, there is. Envelopes seal in the middle, or as far as they can go cross the back like, but there's always a gap. You think about it. Better still, have a butcher's.'

Billy handed her a large brown foolscap envelope, officially sealed.

327

'Where did you get this? It's Top Secret!'

'Where d'you think? 'Ere—give it back.' Billy took the envelope and held it up in front of him.

'They'll send you to the Tower if you're not careful, Billy.'

'It's a fake, sis.' Billy grinned. 'You don't think I'm daft enough to steal a real TS, do you? This is an old envelope I rescued, and resealed with a phoney letter in it. For demonstration porpoises only. Right.'

Biting his lip hard with his upper teeth, Billy inserted the end of the long needle-like probe in the gap between the unsealed end of the flap and the envelope itself.

'Right,' Billy said quietly. 'Now if I twist this round and round—ever so carefully, and ever so slowly—I can remove the contents without disturbing the seal on the envelope, read 'em, and then—if I'm really clever—put 'em back again.'

As he spoke Billy was doing exactly what he was describing, until he had produced a letter from inside the envelope, wrapped around his invention.

'Good heavens above,' Marjorie murmured, genuinely astonished. 'Well I never did.'

'There are all sorts of ways you can use this—as I'm sure Major F will be the first to appreciate.'

'I wonder about you sometimes, Billy, you know. Where it all came from. I wonder who your parents were, and whether or not one of them was some sort of wizard like you. You must have got it from somewhere.'

Billy grinned at her and tapped the front of his head, to indicate that in his estimation that's where everything sprang from, before proceeding to re-insert the letter by way of a reverse of his procedure.

'Suppose I learned a lot of stuff from when I was doing conjuring,' he observed. 'A lot of sleight of hand and that sort of dexterity comes in dead useful later on, you know. As you just seen.'

In the distance there was a thump and a crumping noise as a bomb landed somewhere within their vicinity. Suddenly frightened, Marjorie hugged Billy to her, only for Billy to adjust the position so that he was protecting her. With a private smile Marjorie appreciated the readjustment, realising that even though Billy had failed to be enlisted, there was no doubt that he was no longer her adopted baby brother.

'Are you going to tell the major about your invention?' she wondered, after a silence while they both waited hopefully for the All Clear to sound. 'I think you should.'

'OK,' Billy replied, putting his paraphernalia back on his worktop. 'I got one or two other notions that might be of interest as well.'

'I'll get you an appointment tomorrow,' Marjorie said. 'I think you should go and see him.'

'I don't need no appointment, Marge.'

'Yes you do. There's been a tightening of security all round—no one's allowed any freedom to roam any more, or to drop into each other's caves if and when they feel like it. Not that it was ever easy street exactly, but things have become a whole lot stricter.'

'It's the new bloke, I bet,' Billy said, considering the matter. 'You know.'

'Which new bloke precisely?'

'Dapper Dan, I call him. I don't know his name and number, but that good-looking bloke who's always dressed to the nines and always checking himself in the mirror.'

'Dapper Dan.' Marjorie laughed. 'I like that—but I don't think it's him. He's a rester, apparently. Got dented recently and has been grounded for a while. Anthony said he was helping out round the place just to pass the time.'

'Yeah—well he would, wouldn't he?' Billy grinned. 'No one here's ever doing exactly what they say they're doing, are they?'

*　　　*　　　*

On her way to keep her appointment, she had been forced to take shelter from an air raid, her quarter of an hour underground delaying her meeting so that she was quite out of breath from hurrying when she arrived at the rendezvous.

At first she thought she was too late as there was no one sitting waiting for her as arranged, nor could she see anyone in the immediate vicinity. She looked round, trying not to appear as hopeless as she felt, before picking up the menu and pretending to examine it. A waitress came over to ask if she was ready to order, but she shook her head, explaining she had only just arrived.

Five minutes later someone came to her table and drew out the chair opposite her to sit down.

'I hear the pilchards on toast are good,' he said.

'I prefer bacon and egg,' she replied as casually as she could, only half glancing at her companion.

'Then perhaps today I shall try the bacon and egg too,' the man replied. 'It's always good to try new things.'

Proud as Punch, Billy now worked directly for Major Folkestone, having been enlisted not into the army but to Billy's way of thinking into an even finer force, the Secret Service. He could hardly keep the smile off his cheery face, unable to believe his good fortune, a childhood dream come true. So often at home, before he and Marjorie had been moved to Eden Park, and even after they had taken up residence there, he had lain in bed reading stories about the derring-do of spies and secret agents. Like every boy his age he had fantasised solidly about being such a hero, and now here it was, all come true, all come to pass. He really could hardly believe his luck.

Anthony had always been intrigued by Marjorie's adopted brother, and the closer he got to Marjorie the more he learned about the lad and the more he began to understand him. To Anthony, the boy who had always been such a bright and inventive spark had now turned into an exceptionally gifted young man, a young man with an ability now to decipher even the most complex of codes, to plan stratagems that made more sense than a lot of the more senior officers', and to read and analyse actions both in advance and retrospectively, as had proved to be the case over Tobruk.

'Yes, well, I appreciate that, sir,' Billy had said when Anthony was commending him for his comments on the all-important fall of the desert stronghold. 'But it's quite easy from a chair and desk. To see the mistakes being made.'

'You said all along we were leaving a weak

fourth wall, in fact a non-existent one as I remember. Everything up front and on the two sides, and a fully exposed rear.'

'The whole Gazala line was weak, that was the point. Everyone thought it would hold, that it was strong enough, but 'cos it had to sort of do a double job, it was never going to hold.'

'And it certainly didn't take Rommel long to find that out.'

'Daft really, sir. We had him outnumbered both in men and tanks.'

'He had the aircraft.'

'I know, sir, but he won it by cunning.'

'That's why they call him the Desert Fox, Billy.'

'Hell of a general, sir. Took a bit of seeing off.'

'But we did that at El Alamein, didn't we, Billy? We sent the Desert Fox scuttling off back to his den.'

'Masters of the North African shores we are, sir. Fantastic it was too. And what with Jerry surrendering at Stalingrad in February, it's been quite a year, sir, in't it? I like what Mr Churchill said—it's not the end of the war . . .' Billy quoted, in a more than passable Churchill imitation. 'It is not even the beginning of the end. But it is, perhaps the end of the beginning.'

But much as Anthony liked and admired the young man, it was the Colonel who thought up the *dodge* that was to make young Billy Hendry a hero in his own right.

* * *

Eugene was lucky to get out of Sicily in one piece, let alone escape unscathed from further escapades in Calabria following the capture of Sicily in August after a series of nightmare battles. He had been working closely with cells of the Resistance on the island, successfully sabotaging German supply lines as well as armoured cars, mechanised gun carriers and even the odd Panzer tank. He was hit twice, once by a sniper's bullet that quite literally creased his temple and once by a piece of shrapnel that removed several inches of one side of his waist, leaving him to joke that fighting a war was the quickest way to lose weight. Fortunately it was only a flesh wound, and he was patched up and back in underground action again within the week.

The Germans thought so highly of their unknown saboteur that a large ransom was placed on his head, leading to several near betrayals of the unsuspecting Irishman. It wasn't until one of his more dependable colleagues pointed out how much he was worth to a poor Sicilian that Eugene found himself suddenly wishing that the Sicilian campaign would finish and he could escape to the mainland, with victorious troops, and from there quickly back to England for a well-earned rest.

It was of course not to be as easy as that. When Sicily finally fell and the action moved to the mainland, with the Allies landing in Salerno and Taranto in early September, it seemed that Rome would soon be recaptured and a victorious highway forged northwards. But the Germans put up a valiant resistance, and with winter not far off Eugene found himself once more in the thick of things, being sent ahead of the Allies to blow up certain key bridges before the enemy crossed them and blew them up themselves as they retreated. The campaign was hard fought all the way by both the advancing armies and the retreating ones, and in spite of the heroic efforts of undercover agents such as Eugene every kilometre of ground had to be battled for.

Finally, after a particularly close run incident just east of Gaeta where Eugene and his small band of brothers were all but successfully ambushed by a small corps of elite German sharpshooters, with Eugene losing two of his comrades and collecting another flesh wound in his right arm, the three survivors had to make a run for it, finding themselves virtually surrounded by the riflemen. Thanks to a sudden rainfall of monsoon proportions, they managed to escape over the hills and along the eastern Mediterranean coast, past the massif of Monte Cassino that was about to become the scene of one of the bloodiest battles of the war, along the valley of the River Liri, over the mountainous spine of Central Italy—with the invaluable help of local guides and climbers—and finally on to the Adriatic coast near Termoli. The three of them walked all the way, in all sorts of weathers, nearly freezing to death as they crossed the Apennines, in spite of the thick extra clothing with which they had been generously supplied by villagers in the foothills, and nearly drowned by continuous near-tropical rain along the Liri valley. But they not only made the trek, they survived it, resting up in a tiny village where they were welcomed in true Italian style, now that the natives had decided it was time for a change of coat; hidden away, fed and watered until they were strong enough to try to arrange their safe passage home.

Helped by a family of fisherfolk, they were

shipped out to a cargo boat bearing the neutral flag of Sweden on which—after a lengthy negotiation with the captain and the handing over of the last of Eugene's precious emergency gold coins—they were stowed away and shipped to Lisbon where they changed boats, managing to scrounge a free ride in a broken-down Irish tramp steamer that all but sank in the rough seas encountered in the notorious Bay of Biscay. Nine weeks to the day from when they started their escape, Eugene and his companions found themselves disembarking in Cork, where after three nights spent in alcoholic celebration, and consequently in worse shape than when they had finished the most exhausting part of their trek, they boarded the ferry for Fishguard.

'That'll do for the moment, I think, Eugene,' Kate stated, as if he'd just come in from riding. 'I think you can retire now and take up growing tomatoes.' He had taken her by surprise in the House of Flowers, where she was staying in Poppy's absence, walking up through the woods and bursting into the little sitting room without a word of warning.

'God forbid it, Kate darling!' he cried, lifting her up bodily and whirling her round in the air. 'When I go it's with me boots on!'

He kissed her as he swung her, then he put her down on the ground and kissed her again.

'Not here,' she whispered, understanding the strength of his passion and his longing. 'I wouldn't feel comfortable.'

'Poppy wouldn't mind.' Eugene smiled. 'And Scott certainly wouldn't.'

'I would,' Kate said. 'I know your place isn't quite as comfortable as this, but at least it's yours.'

Shutting the House of Flowers up behind them and blowing it a kiss, Kate led Eugene off back to the jumbled but cosy place that was his flat in the stable yard, where they retired to the bedroom for the rest of the day and all of the night.

'I never doubted for a moment you'd come back,' Kate whispered to him in the twilight. 'Not for a moment. Particularly when I was up in the house. I used to sit there for hours sometimes and I could see you. I could literally see you.'

'Where, Katie? Where did you see me? What was I doing?'

'You weren't anywhere. It's hard to explain really. You were just you. You were just you and you were just there—but you were coming home. I just felt it. It was almost as if I was being told.'

'I was telling you. I used to call to you over the mountains and the seas—all the way from Sicily and all the way up through Italy, all I did was call your name. In the middle of the darkest night, the wettest day, the coldest evening, I'd call to you. In my heart. All the time. Now come here—come here to me, my darling love, for we've a heck of a lot of that time to make up.'

Kate had never been happier. Somehow it seemed now that Eugene was home and the fortunes of the war had changed so dramatically in favour of the Allies that she was not alone in believing hostilities were all but over. She began to hope and then to think that perhaps the need for agents to go on quite so many highly dangerous missions was diminishing, and she could almost start looking forward to a future spent with her beloved wild Irishman. And it wasn't only Kate who was thinking of their future life, for now when they

336

sat down in front of the fires they would lay in the House of Flowers—where they spent every evening but never the night—Eugene would begin to paint a spell-binding picture of the sort of life they would live together when the war had finally come to an end. Not that he was counting his chickens yet, as he kept assuring Kate. It was just that the time had come to stop dreaming so much and to discuss a little bit of reality. Kate was only too happy to discuss that little bit of reality with him, for ever since she had met and fallen in love with Eugene she had spent far too much time daydreaming, never really daring to give any credence to her daydreams lest her lover failed to come home. Yet here he was by her side with another Christmas close at hand and the Germans it would seem not only on the back foot, but on the run.

A week or so after Eugene's safe return to England's shores, the winter weather turned bright and sunny, a fine enough day for a good ride, Eugene declared when he rose that morning, standing at the window of his flat looking out over the roofs of the stables at the park beyond, tucking the tail of a heavy white wool shirt into the waist of the breeches he had already pulled on.

'I have to go to work, unfortunately,' Kate said, climbing out of bed with a happy yawn. 'Otherwise I'd follow behind in the trap.'

'Watch for me from your window,' Eugene commanded as he sat to pull on his riding boots. 'I'll blow you one of my devastating kisses.'

'I shall watch for you all morning,' Kate replied. 'And probably get sacked for inattention.'

She saw him leave all right. Everyone in her office did, their attention drawn by hers as she stood at the big window that directly overlooked the park to wave at the horseman standing up in his irons in the middle of the main lawn, blowing as promised the mightiest of kisses to his love. Then with a theatrical wave, his hand circling the top of his bare head, he sat to his fine horse and galloped off along the track between the great lake and the smaller one, up the hill that led to the country beyond and away out of sight. Kate watched for a moment after he was gone, imagining herself behind him on the horse, her arms clasped tight round his waist and her hair flowing out behind her in the wind as he carried her to their home high in the hills above the lakes in the west of Ireland, about which he had already spun her thrilling, romantic tales; their little whitewashed house that stood at the foot of Mount Nephin, surrounded by the wild and wonderful countryside of Mayo.

That was more or less where Eugene was himself in his own mind, as he galloped fast over the perfect turf that lay beneath his horse's pounding hooves. He was a boy again back home in the west, bareback on his pony, with a cabbage stalk for a whip and the big stone walls of the Blazer country rising up before him. Coming up was one of his favourite leaps in the park, five foot of drystone wall whose landing side fell away another three feet below the five to carry horse and rider down in a breathtaking sweep on to a fine gallop that rose gently up away from the wall for a good quarter of a mile. Eugene loved this jump with all his heart, for there was nothing better to his way of thinking than to be on a fine strong horse on a bright sunny day with the winds of winter in your face and the thought of landing running so that horse and man were one as they accelerated away along the ride ahead of them.

They were into the wall just perfect, the horse setting himself up for the right stride and Eugene finding and feeling it at once beneath him. He barely had to ask the animal—all he had to do was tip and balance, hands like silk in the ribbons so as not to catch the horse in the mouth as they landed, firm at the knees and light on the toes in the stirrups. He almost shouted as he felt the leap they were making, his horse rising higher than he ever had before at the wall, yet not ballooning it— simply flying it, back arched, neck stretched—and then they were down.

There was no way either horse or rider could have seen the hole on the other side of the wall, no way at all. It looked to those who saw it later like the beginning of a den or a set, dug by a fox or even perhaps a badger, although the countrymen among the party who found him doubted very much if any badger would wish to build a set so close to an exposed wall. Whatever its origin, what the horse put his near fore in was a hole of big enough dimensions to bring him down, shooting his rider straight over his head at a lethal speed before Eugene could know what had happened.

He landed on the very top of his head, buckling over straight on to his back, unconscious from the moment his unprotected skull hit the ground. Miraculously, the falling horse missed him by inches, crashing onto its side parallel to where its rider lay supine, lying there winded for fully two or three minutes before slowly clambering to its feet, groggy and disorientated, treading on one of its rider's arms as it stood and crushing the bone into splinters as it did so. With reins flapping and saddle slipping down one side, the animal began to run, still too winded and frightened to gallop. The ever loosening saddle would have been enough to make any other horse panic, but not Eugene's. As if realising the enormity of their joint calamity, the creature stopped a hundred yards from where its master lay and, instead of disappearing into the beyond, turned its head for home, running steadily parallel to the wall until it came to an open gate through which it immediately turned, quickening its pace now as it anticipated the warmth and security of its box, cantering at a steady but sensible pace back down the track past the lakes and towards the great house itself.

* * *

Cissie Lavington was the first person to see it, standing at the window smoking one of her interminable cigarettes as she reviewed certain vital matters in her mind. She was immediately distracted by the sight of the riderless horse, a horse she recognised at once, as did everyone else who gathered at the window in response to her gasp of dismay and look of horror.

Hurrying to find Kate, Cissie nearly knocked Marjorie over in her haste to take the corner in the corridor.

'It doesn't necessarily mean he's hurt though, does it?' Marjorie wondered a little breathlessly as she hurried along the corridor behind Cissie, who had explained her mission in a few brief words.

'Of course not, my dear,' Cissie replied. 'Only thing is, riders as good as Eugene don't fall off without damn' good reason.'

Kate ran into them, rather than the other way round, on her way out of the washroom. Seeing her, Cissie backtracked and, taking her by one arm, told her what had happened.

'We'll need to organise a search party,' she announced, deputising the young woman nearest her. 'Go along and tell Major Folkestone, there's a good girl. Tell him we're taking a party off to look for the fallen hero.'

Micky, who acted as Eugene's groom among other things, was already on the case as the search party fanned out of the front door of the house, arriving in the battered old pick-up truck that was used as the all purpose vehicle for the estate. The youngest of the party clambered up into the back to sit among a jumble of uncleared bits and pieces while Cissie and Miss Budge, who had also volunteered her services, sat up alongside Micky in the cab.

'I know next to nothing about horses,' Miss Budge announced. 'Other than that according to my mother they shy on the way out and do the other thing on the way home.'

'I take it that's intended to relieve the atmosphere, Budge dear, is it?' Cissie asked with a look of disdain. 'Because if so it hasn't.'

'Horses frighten me,' Miss Budge continued, taking absolutely no notice. 'I'm a dog person myself. I only really like dogs.'

She fell quiet then, staring out of the front window with a deep frown on her face as if remembering something. Cissie regarded her, decided she could make nothing of her whatsoever, lit a fresh cigarette and turned her attention to scouring the landscape for the fallen rider.

They found him within five minutes of leaving the house, Micky having seen which way Eugene had ridden away from the house, and knowing almost as well as his employer the best rides in the parkland. As soon as the great wall came into sight, Micky nodded at it and spun the wheel to the right to head for the adjacent gate.

'His favourite jump,' he said. 'Or rather *lepp* as he calls it. His and his horse's.'

Seeing the gate open, Micky was sure now where they would find him, long before they saw the fallen body.

Eugene heard their approach. He had come back to consciousness a few minutes earlier and he knew that the only thing he mustn't do was move. It was ingrained in him, from the moment he had begun riding to the time when he had gone into training as an agent. If you fall forward from a horse or a moving vehicle, or even hit your head diving into the sea, and you lose consciousness, when you awake *you do not move*. It wasn't a conscious decision—it was instinctive, going back to the time he was a gossoon in Ireland and seeing them fall out hunting. *Don't move 'em!* the Master would bark. *Don't touch 'em—just make sure they don't move and no one moves 'em till we get the quack!*

So Eugene lay still, noting that the sky above him, which had been that particular shade of pale winter blue, was now a jaundiced yellow—and that everything around and about him seemed very far away, including the rest of himself, including his very being.

He was aware of someone beside him but they

342

were drawn in pale yellow too, besides being well out of focus. He could also hear the clamour of distant voices, although the people to whom those voices belonged were standing no more than a foot or so from him.

'Don't move me,' he whispered. 'No one touch me even. Fetch a stretcher, splints, thick bandages —and a doctor. I think it's my neck. I think I've broken me damn' neck.'

*   *   *

He was quite right. The X-rays showed his neck to be broken in two places, one fracture worse than the other, the damaged vertebra missing the spinal cord by the tiniest of possible fractions.

'He's lucky in two ways,' Dr Brooke said at the hospital when Kate was finally allowed to visit, with Cissie and Anthony Folkestone also in attendance. 'He's lucky to be alive at all—he's a strong man, and also a very sensible one because he didn't move. If he'd moved an inch before a doctor had got there he'd be dead for sure. He's also lucky in that it appears—and I use the word advisedly because there's still an awful lot we don't know about neck fractures—he's lucky in that there seems to be no paralysis either. He has feelings in all limbs and extensions, so if we can keep him on an even keel there's every chance of a recovery. A full recovery, just as long as we can first of all keep him immobilised and then he behaves himself once he leaves hospital.'

'How long will that be?' Kate asked. 'Or don't you know?'

'We'll know more in a week. But I don't think

he'll be home in time for Christmas.'

She was allowed five minutes, no more, and she was not to ask him anything that needed an answer. Kate had simply to sit by his bedside and do her best to smile at a man who could not look at her. After the first thirty seconds the smile was replaced by two lines of tears that ran silently down her face until, drying them away with her handkerchief, she stood at the end of Eugene's bed and blew him a kiss of farewell.

*   *   *

'Anything to report?' Jack wondered, seating himself in the taxi that had stopped for him on the instructions of its passenger at the bottom of Wigmore Street.

'I think I might have,' Helen replied, as the taxi moved off.

'Where to now, missis?' the cabbie called backwards through the intercommunicating window.

Jack took charge, leaning forward and giving the driver the address of a small, insignificant hotel that was in fact a safe house.

'So, good lady—tell me all,' Jack said, with a sideways smile at Helen, tapping a Players cigarette on his old silver case. 'I trust your living has not been in vain and all that.'

He had taken Helen out of Baker Street for a while, allotting her the job of working behind the tea bar at Charing Cross Station, the terminus for all lines from the southeast including the line that served Eden Park. He had long ago become convinced that railway stations were not only the epicentres of illicit love affairs but also places where classified information might easily and often be exchanged. The idea had become fixed in his mind when in the middle Thirties he had been in the same railway carriage as two German tourists, who were busy noting down military installations along the route the train was taking. He had also learned another useful fact at the same time, that however hard Germans tried to disguise themselves they still looked like Germans.

'I have to confess, sir,' Helen said, always careful to use formalities in working situations, regardless of the state of any relationship. 'I have to say I did not think this was one of your best ideas—working behind the bar in the hotel. But I'm beginning to see what you mean. People don't ever just come and go—there's always some set purpose that only becomes obvious if you start looking for it.'

Jack was sitting with his back to the driver, having made sure the intercommunicating window was tightly shut.

'What in particular have you been looking at?'

'I have one or two regulars that might be worth a second glance.'

'Jolly good.' Jack drew on his cigarette, then looked out of the window to see where they were. 'Let's save that for that drink we're both looking forward to, shall we?'

He half smiled and nodded at her, then produced an early edition of the *Evening News* and began to read, blotting out Helen's existence all but completely.

Jack was very good at blotting things out. He had learned how to do this for himself some five years previously when Juliet, his wife, died giving birth to

345

a son. He never understood the full medical reasons. Something had gone wrong at the moment of delivery and both lives were lost in a matter of a few seconds. He seemed to remember one of the nurses trying to explain about umbilical cords and strangulation, but what he couldn't understand was why Juliet had died as well, and so suddenly. Jack being Jack he had more than a suspicion that the doctors didn't know either, or else they were covering up someone's atrocious error, because the cause of death on his wife's certificate was *massive haemorrhaging*, and to the best of Jack Ward's knowledge no one died from *massive haemorrhaging* without due cause.

But he had not pursued the matter. There was no bringing Juliet and their dead son back. They were lost and gone for ever, and whatever Jack might have unearthed—and he suspected there was plenty there to be unearthed—it would be an academic and pointless exercise. Juliet, his adored Juliet, his childhood sweetheart, the romance of his life, his wonderfully funny, adorable and bouncy young wife was removed from his existence in one terrible sweeping moment, along with the child they had both so wanted—and that was the moment when Jack Ward learned, as he called it, to blot stuff out. He knew Helen had a life, and because he knew Helen so well, he knew the sort of life she had once enjoyed and the sort of life she was living now. But he didn't go up that path. He stayed at the gate, occasionally waving at the woman in the house before passing on by. What he must do—and most particularly now—was not cross the line. Helen, attractive woman though she might be, was to stay one side of that gate and Jack

Ward firmly the other.

Helen knew nothing about Jack's past life. All she knew was that he had always been nothing but kind to her, and she appreciated more than she could say his offer that she should come back and work for him. Sometimes she tried to guess at his past life, but found herself getting absolutely nowhere since there were no clues on the particular patch of ground he was occupying. Sometimes she would try to ease some information out of him, but she was dealing with an expert, as she soon realised. Jack was gone and running long before she got round to asking the first leading question.

She smiled at the newspaper that was facing her, wondering what he might think of her; how much he knew, and how much he had guessed. She reckoned that because of the way both their friendship and her career were developing he was taking her at face value, which was what she wanted.

As she checked her looks in the compact she had taken from her handbag she very much hoped this would be the case. It was very important for Jack Ward to see her as ordinary straightforward Helen Maddox, deserted wife and still grieving mother. She would not want it any other way. She could not have it any other way.

'So,' Jack said finally, after he had settled them both into a secluded corner of the utterly unprepossessing hotel. 'You think you have some news, eh?'

He now lit his pipe in preference to another cigarette, slowly drawing the flame of the match down into the bowl with each inhalation as he got the tobacco burning. 'What I'd really like you to find out for me is where to get some decent baccy—but I suppose that'll have to wait.'

Helen smiled, opened her bag and produced a tin of Balkan Sobranie. Jack frowned for once in open astonishment as he looked first at the tin and then at Helen.

'Railway stations are useful places to be in more ways than one,' she said. 'I can't promise a regular supply, but every now and then—'

'I imagine this isn't exactly altogether correct,' Jack replied, lifting the tin and turning it round and round in his hand as if it were some sort of valuable antique. 'But then on the other hand there is a war on. Much obliged,' he added in the slightly facetious tone he used to cover up his shyness. 'Very much obliged, I must say.'

Helen concealed her pleasure, happy to believe that this would be a very positive point in her favour, if push ever came to shove.

'There are two people in particular who meet regularly in the tea bar, sir,' she said, returning to business but keeping her voice good and low. 'She comes up on the Hastings line, so possibly even from the target station, same day, same time. Always a Thursday, always early afternoon, arriving at the station at two fifty, and leaving on the down line on the three thirty-three, which is never at three thirty-three but there or thereabouts.'

'The man?'

Helen shrugged. 'Nondescript, like her. Middle-aged, thin, average height, grey raincoat, grey trilby—large beak-like nose,' she recalled, 'but no other distinguishing characteristics. She's early middle age, I'd say. Slightly plump, average height,

348

perhaps no more than five four, five five, but always wears a hat, which I think is unusual, seeing that hardly anyone wears a hat nowadays—women, that is—because you can't get hats, and everyone's saving the hats they do have for something special, rather than day to day wear—'

'Yes, yes,' Jack interrupted. 'I get the point. Do they talk, or what? What attracted your attention? Besides the famous hat.'

'The fact they don't talk, I suppose. She has a cup of tea, he reads the paper. She smokes one cigarette, then gets up and leaves.'

'They're certainly not having an affair then. What else?'

'Well, when she goes—usually with quarter of an hour to kill before she has to get her train back—he picks something up she's left on the table. Usually a magazine. In fact I think it's always a magazine, which he then folds up, slips in his pocket and goes. He always pays, incidentally, never her. When he arrives he calls over a waitress, orders for her without asking her, then pays. And she goes back and catches her train.'

'Wonder what's in the magazine,' Jack mused. 'Could be money, of course. Could be information.'

'She doesn't look like the sort of woman who'd be blackmailed.'

'Who does?'

'I'd have thought someone more glamorous. This woman—from what I can see of her—certainly isn't glamorous.'

'She could be a murderer. Most unlikely-looking females murder their spouses—poison usually. Women love poison as their MO. Modus operandi,' he explained in answer to her look. 'What colour is this famous hat, as a matter of interest?'

'Peacock blue.'

'Always the same hat?'

'Yes. Why?'

'Just curious. How close have you got to them?'

'Not close enough. They always sit by the door and my station is behind the bar.'

'Can you get to serve them?'

'Not without permission, which I won't get, because the manageress doesn't like me. Thinks I'm too posh, would you believe?' Helen laughed. 'And if I break ranks to get closer I'll arouse their suspicions because I'll have Brünnhilde on my heels.'

'She isn't someone known to you, obviously. What I'm saying is no one from Baker Street?'

'There are an awful lot of us at Baker Street, sir.'

'Worth a try. You never know. Point is you're going to have to get close enough to get an ID, just in case. Same goes for him,' Jack said as he finished his drink. 'That's an order.'

He went out ahead of her, as was prearranged, making sure as always never to be seen arriving and leaving with the same person, just in case there was someone watching.

As indeed there was—a tall, elegant man well hidden in the dark of the doorway of a bombed-out building opposite. When he saw Jack leaving he noted the time down in his notebook and waited for the imminent departure of Jack's guest, which would also be duly noted, just for the record. In the meantime, in what little light there was, he checked the state of his carefully manicured nails.

*   *   *

Within her first week at the aerodrome, which was all anyone ever called it, Poppy could dismantle a six-cylinder engine, name all the parts and reassemble it, leaving it in perfect running order. Trafford assured her such a depth of knowledge was not altogether necessary if all she was going to do was—as she called it—*budger them up*, but agreed with Poppy's assertion that while a little knowledge was a dangerous thing, a lot wouldn't ever come amiss.

'Anyway, who knows?' Poppy said. 'One might be asked to pose as an engineer—in fact one probably will—which would require a full knowledge of working engines.'

'A female engineer?' Trafford wondered, cutting a small black cheroot into halves and offering one to Poppy. 'Yes, of course, Jerry does like to put the female of the species to work, doesn't he? So they might well drop you out of a plane disguised as a femmy oilhand, eh? Yes, yes—see what you're getting at, and very good too—if one's going to do a job, do the fudging thing proper like, right? Now then, day's work done, time to recreate. What'd you like to do? Get blotto? Get even more blotto? Or get totally blotto?'

Poppy laughed with delight as always at her new friend's outrageousness. Even though they had done nothing but work hard, the week had been endless fun, since Trafford managed to turn everything and everyone on their heads and back to front, yet still teach them what they had come to learn. Early on in the week Poppy had learned to her astonishment that the gang of Australians she had met when she first arrived had all been sent to

Trafford to learn how to fly. Far from being the aces they had professed themselves the first evening Poppy had spent in their company, it emerged that they were all complete greenhorns who had been given up on by their flying instructor down south as totally unsuitable material. Five days in Trafford's company and they were all flying like air show experts.

'How come?' Poppy had asked Trafford when she had learned the truth.

'Only one way to teach someone how to fly,' Trafford had answered obliquely. 'And that's to put 'em up there.'

'Yes, of course. With an instructor.'

'Nonsense. To hell with instructors yelling in your ear. Only way you learn to fly is when you blotting well have to! Want to learn?'

'If I had the time I wouldn't mind,' an emboldened Poppy had replied. 'Might come in useful one day.'

'When we've a day off, I'll teach you.'

'A *day*?'

'Tell you what!' Trafford had said with a grin, picking her pug up and cuddling him. 'Take the manual for your bedtime reading. Read it, mark it, learn it and all that sort of claptrap—and I bet you'll be in the air solo by day two!'

Normally it wasn't the sort of challenge Poppy would have dreamed of accepting, not being the kind of person ever to be rushed or dared into anything. Poppy far preferred to approach things pragmatically, to view things coolly, to make her judgements in her own time and arrive at any decisions once everything had been properly considered. But there was something entirely

352

unrealistic and preposterous in Trafford Perkins's wager that made her pick up the gauntlet she had thrown down.

'When?'

'Soon as done,' Trafford had replied. 'Day after you finish your course, we'll have you up in the air.'

* * *

Now that day had dawned, Poppy no longer felt quite so sure. For a start it was good and wintry, with a strong northeasterly blowing hard across the Fens, sharp and cold enough to bring tears to the eyes, and second there was the matter of the machine that was sitting out on the tarmac waiting for them—a single-seater yellow Tiger Moth.

'There has to be some mistake,' Poppy said over the wind that was fast turning into a gale when Trafford arrived beside her dressed in full flying rig, as indeed was Poppy. 'Shouldn't that have two seats?'

'Life of me can't see why!' Trafford roared with laughter. 'Two people can't fly one of those things!'

'Why ever not?' Poppy wondered, falling straight into the trap.

''Cos it's only got one blotting seat, ducky! That's why!'

Poppy wondered, not without good reason, how anyone could learn to fly without an instructor on board. She was about to find out.

'It's OK, little one!' Trafford led Poppy back towards the hangar behind them. 'That's for later.'

'I have to say I'm relieved to hear it.'

'Not much later, duck—only a bit. The boys have been working on the two-seater.'

Inside the hangar stood a bright red Tiger Moth, this time a twin-seater biplane. The gang of Australian flyers had been fine-tuning it, to judge from the amount of grease on them, and now they wheeled it out on to the one serviceable runway they had left.

'All aboard!' Trafford cried, getting a leg-up from a couple of her pupils, followed a little too quickly for her liking by Poppy.

The handsome blond Australian swung the propeller over, the engine kicked into life, and even more quickly, much to Poppy's consternation, they were airborne.

'Bit choppy today!' Trafford yelled at Poppy from behind her. 'Good for the old equilibrium!'

For the next two hours Trafford kept up a non-stop tutorial at the top of her voice on how to fly a small aircraft. Poppy had always been lost in admiration for Trafford's ability to talk without apparently drawing breath, but this was a *tour de force* to cap all her previous *tours de force*. On top of that there was a howling gale blowing around them, buffeting the small aeroplane all over the sky but none the less and blithely Trafford demonstrated spins, stalls, twirls, tips, plunges, climbs, glides, tumbles and finally—and not before time, Poppy thought to herself—landings. But that wasn't the end. Having touched down, Trafford immediately accelerated and took off again to show Poppy how to land another three times, coming in from different angles and from different heights, each time making a perfect three-pointer, regardless of the gale.

'See?' Trafford shouted, as they taxied in towards the hangar. 'Nothing to it! Log falling off time!'

'I'd prefer to be standing on a twig actually!' Poppy called back, taking off her goggles and trying to come back to earth in a more metaphysical way. 'Even so,' she said, once they had alighted from the plane, 'I must say I'm looking forward to my next lesson, because I have to admit that was pretty damn' exciting.'

'Next lesson?' Trafford guffawed, searching for her cheroots. 'Next lesson be budgered! I only ever give one, and one's all you're getting, too! Ask the boys here!'

Poppy had no need to ask them. She could see by the grins on their faces that the truth had been told, just as she could see the looks of absolute disbelief that she, a mere girl, was going to be able to do what they had done, namely fly a Tiger Moth after one lesson at the hands of Ace Perkins—and a week with the manual, a book that Poppy now knew off by heart.

'Remind me of what you're staring at,' she said, putting her hands slowly on her hips. 'I've forgotten.'

'Nothing, Sheila,' Blond Ace No. 1 smiled back. 'Just we got a little book going on how long before we see you in the skies. Solo.'

'What do you reckon? Bruce?' Poppy asked pointedly. 'I'd love to hear.'

'Certainly not within twenty-four hours, if that's a clue, sweetheart.'

'That's a very big clue,' Poppy replied. 'See you boys later.'

The good thing, as Poppy saw, sweating over the manual in the top room of the control tower while George chased his long tail, was that at least the

355

gale had blown itself well and truly out, leaving skies so clear that it would be no surprise if frost followed shortly. The bad thing was her blood was up, and as Poppy knew that was not always the best state to be in when meeting a new challenge.

Even so, she had picked up the gauntlet, and having done so, being Poppy, she was going to run with it and see the challenge through, if it was the last thing she did.

'Which I sincerely hope, George, will not prove to be the case,' she said to her little dog as, reluctantly, she closed the manual for the last time and prepared to leave the building. As she went out of the door she changed her mind and hurried back to pick up the manual.

'Just in case,' she said to George again, stuffing the book inside her flying jacket. 'You never know.'

The boys were waiting around the hangar, idly smoking and chatting as if they hadn't a care in the world. What they were really doing, as Poppy well knew, was waiting for her, to see if she was going to take up their dare.

'Don't you boys have *anything* to do?' she wondered. 'Worthwhile, that is.'

'Tomorrow we're going off to collect some new Spits and deliver 'em out to Sicily. That do you?' her tall blond friend remarked.

'What really will do me is if you boys would be good enough to wheel that yellow plane out for me—that is if she's ready to go up.'

'She is, Sheila. Are you?'

'Absolutely, Bruce. Ready as I'll ever be. And if one of you would be kind enough to hold George and keep him safe till I land. Thank you.'

She smiled at a very tall, rather shy young man

who came forward to take George from her.

'I hope you like dogs,' she said.

'We've got four of the tykes at home,' he confessed. 'I love 'em.'

'Good. Then wagons roll, as I believe they say.'

The gang of young men, except for the one holding George, pushed the yellow Tiger Moth on to the hard standing outside the hangar and prepared to help Poppy aboard.

'Sure you know what you're doing?' the blond one asked, trying to keep any trace of anxiety out of his voice.

'Let's hope so,' Poppy replied, buttoning up her flying jacket and helmet. 'The name's Poppy, by the way. Not Sheila.'

'Mine's Derek,' he replied. 'Not Bruce. You don't have to do this, you know,' he added quietly. 'We were only joshing you.'

'I do have to do it, Derek. And not only do I have to, I actually quite want to do it. OK?'

'Whatever you say, Poppy. Just take care.'

'I fully intend to.'

'You aren't wearing a 'chute,' he said suddenly. 'That really is just plum daft.'

Before Poppy could reply, Derek had ordered one of his mates to collect a parachute from inside the hangar. He then helped Poppy strap it on.

'That's the ripcord,' he said, indicating the ring hanging down on the front of the harness. 'If you have to—which pray God you don't—jump, count to five, and pull. Remember—wait to pull. Don't panic. If you pull it too soon you could get tangled in your machine, and you don't want that.'

'Heavens no.' Poppy laughed. 'I've got to come back in one piece. George hasn't had his dinner yet.'

With a final shrug and a lot of good luck wishes, Derek gave her a leg-up on to a wing and Poppy scrambled into the cockpit. She spent a good moment adjusting her goggles and familiarising herself with the array of instruments and switches in front of her before sticking one arm in the air.

'Chocks away!' she yelled, as they spun the propeller and the engine roared into life. 'Don't go away now!'

'You neither, Poppy!' Derek yelled back. 'I'll have a stiff drink ready on the bar!'

She taxied the plane gingerly to the end of the runway, facing a very slight headwind of not more than eight knots. Ahead of her lay the long strip of concrete, its potholes repaired as best the boys could manage with a mix of sand, earth and what little cement they could scrounge. It was plenty long enough, big enough in fact for a heavy bomber to take off, for which fact Poppy was deeply grateful as she sat preparing to throttle up for take-off, since she considered she might need every inch. She also considered simply turning the plane to the left, taxiing back to the hangar, disembarking and giving the boys best—except they weren't the reason for her undertaking this crazy, foolish, mad, exhilarating challenge. Poppy was doing this for herself. Not to prove anything, but to see whether she was really capable of stretching herself and becoming a singular individual, or whether she would just have to settle finally for being the Poppy her mother had so despised, a fundamentally decent but obviously dull girl with little ambition and precious little ability or talent.

She was allowing herself to be driven this far

358

because of something else as well—a disturbing suspicion that she had exaggerated the importance of her part in the Churchill plot. That in fact it had been Scott and Eugene who had made all the running and she had really only been a passenger. Her infiltration of the British Fascists had been brave enough, she realised that, just as she realised that anyone in her section would have been capable of doing the same thing, with a few of them no doubt carrying it off even better than she had. So she had to do this. She had to find out whether or not the Poppy she hoped and believed existed underneath all the veneer she had so carefully built up since her disastrous meeting and marriage to Basil Tetherington really did live, or whether in fact there was no other Poppy than the unexceptional and untalented daughter to whom her mother was so convinced she had given birth.

That was why she was now taxiing down the runway, increasing her speed towards the number of knots required to achieve take-off. So far she had held the little plane absolutely steady, accelerating smoothly and finally reaching the required sixty-five knots, and still—she was happy to see—with plenty of runway left, enough in fact even to abort in perfect safety.

But abort she did not. Instead—pulling a face of the grimmest determination and half closing her eyes—she injected even more speed, gently eased the joystick back, checked her trim, and found herself airborne—and climbing.

She felt she could hear cheers in her head as she rose higher and higher in the clear sky. Certainly she was cheering herself for having got over what she considered one of the worst two bits of the

359

entire exercise: taking off and landing. The actual flying, she had decided in advance, was the easy bit, or rather the *easier* bit. Once she had levelled the plane out, she was determined to stick to her game plan, which was to reach a sane and sensible height of no more than a thousand feet, and simply to circle the airfield half a dozen times at a speed no greater than a hundred and five knots, not trying to do anything fancy, in fact not trying to do anything other than hold her steady and level, and then—hopefully—bring her in to land.

That was the bit she was dreading. She had almost taken the take-off for granted, knowing that if she hit the right speed with the aircraft steady, as long as she lifted the nose at the right moment, aeronautical science would take over after that. She'd read her manual of flying carefully, that was for sure, and one thing her studies had taught her was that provided an aeroplane was travelling with sufficient impetus to fly, once the nose was lifted and even more thrust applied, the air pressure under the craft's wings would simply lift it skywards. Then all you had to do was keep climbing until you reached the required height, in no circumstances allowing your airspeed to dip or the craft to become unstable. There were waves in the air that kept you afloat, Poppy realised as she studied the diagrams and drawings, just like a boat on the sea. You were buoyant and airborne, rather than afloat, but in a way the principle of flying was the same as that of sailing. Launch your plane on to the waves and keep it riding them.

She had now reached nearly one thousand feet according to her altimeter, so carefully and gingerly she nudged the joystick away from her until she thought she was level—only to discover to her sudden horror that she was not. The nose of the plane was dipping sharply, Poppy having eased the stick a little too far forward. At once she tried to adjust it, but in her sudden anxiety she had obviously pulled the joystick too hard since the plane bucked under her almost like a horse, its nose going from dive position to climb. The Moth's engine began to scream its own protest at being asked all at once to climb out of what had been just about to be a dive, and for one heart-stopping moment Poppy thought she had stalled, the engine choking, spluttering, and actually it seemed dying on her, only to cough itself back into life, urged on by Poppy's increasing the airspeed and mercifully finding the exact right spot for the joystick. After reaching an all but upright position in the sky, the Moth was now flying absolutely level, albeit with its right wing tipping dangerously low, causing the little yellow aircraft to bank and circle in a much tighter loop than Poppy had intended. For a moment she thought about pulling the manual out from her skeepskin-lined flying jacket in order to remind herself of what to do in such a situation, but thought better of doing so when she realised that what with her thick flying gloves, and not exactly crystal clear goggles, she wouldn't be able to make out much of what the manual said anyway, even if she could keep the plane steady enough for long enough to give her sufficient time to swot up the facts.

Instead, she held steady and simply put her brain on recall. In front of her eyes appeared chapter and verse from the manual, her intense study paying life-saving dividends. It was all there: how to trim

361

the plane out of too steep a bank if the occasion should arise, adjusting flaps and rudder with her feet while keeping the aircraft absolutely level by the lightest of adjustments on the stick. *Don't ever snatch!* she heard Trafford yelling at her as they spun round the sky on her one flying lesson. *Don't ever snatch, grab or do anything fast! Think slow— and act slow! One wrong yank and you're down, sweetie! And you ain't going to be hot enough to pull out of a spin!*

So slowly did it, easily did it, and moments later the boys on the ground, shading their eyes against the sun, were relieved to see the bright yellow Tiger Moth above them flying steadily on an even keel with a perfect and healthy engine note.

'Now all the poor darling has to do is bloomin' land,' Derek observed. 'So, everyone—cross fingers!'

Poppy, having mastered the trick of circling steadily and evenly, was now loath to break the pattern, wishing she could stay up there for ever, even contemplating baling out and dropping safely to land, until she realised the plane might crash on an inhabited part of the countryside below her with terrible consequences. She found herself also idly wondering to whom the plane actually belonged, concluding that whoever was the rightful owner would not be best pleased to find it had been wilfully jettisoned by an unlicensed woman who had no right to be flying it. With a relectant burst of laughter, Poppy realised she would probably end up in court not to mention having her name splashed all over the papers for perpetrating an act of such idiocy. She could also certainly kiss goodbye to any future work for the Intelligence service and most likely Scott too.

'You certainly don't want that, Poppy!' she shouted at herself as she began to straighten the plane out preparatory to making her descent. 'That is not what you are up here doing this for! To make an idiot of yourself! So get a grip and pull yourself together!'

Far below her, once she had straightened the aircraft, she could see the airfield, the landing strip and a tiny group of men looking up at the sky. Once again panic gripped her, freezing her into inaction, the plane flying by itself for a moment without any help from its young pilot. Then the next thing Poppy knew was that the Tiger Moth was descending slowly but surely towards the airstrip, guided by her own hands, both of which were lightly on the joystick as all of a sudden she was filled with the joy of flying. It seemed impossible, at that moment, that a fragile little single-engine winged vehicle should be able to defy the elements and stay airborne, still less be *made* to fly, least of all by a tyro such as herself. Yet here it was, and here she was, flying now at five hundred feet and making what seemed like a perfect approach.

Back came the relevant pages of the manual in her mind's eye—angle of descent and speed, the moment to raise the nose, throttle back hard, let the nose back down as the wheels hit the strip— *bounce! Once! Twice! Keep it cool, keep it slow, throttle back—back—all three wheels down, tail level, nose level—slower, slower—reverse throttle—more! More—once more—that's all, swing to the right, kill the engine, slow it down nicely, slowly now—and stop. Down!*

Poppy hardly dared to open the eyes she had closed once she had swung the aircraft round to taxi it slowly back towards the hangar. Not until the plane had stopped completely did she open them, looking around in absolute wonder and then up to the skies where she had only moments ago been flying—she, Poppy! She had defied the element of air and flown a craft made of wood and canvas up to over one thousand feet and stayed aloft for twenty minutes before bringing the little plane down to make what felt—but probably only felt— like a perfect three-pointer.

Then she heard the shouts—and saw the gang of them running towards her, the tall shy one holding George safely aloft, the lot of them led by Derek who was waving his flying helmet round and round his head in triumph like a flag.

'Fantastic, Poppy baby! Just bloomin' well *fantastic*!' Derek yelled, a paean of praise picked up at once by the rest of them, who whooped and hollered, yelled and cheered themselves hoarse.

Poppy was hardly aware she was being carried shoulder high from the moment she stepped on to the wing of the plane prior to disembarking, but she was. Derek and one of his colleagues were chairing her back to the hangar, her hands holding tight to their shoulders as the rest of the gang circled their heroine, still cheering and jumping up and down with excitement.

'Not only was your lift-off a beaut, hon!' Derek cried. 'But what about that for a landing!'

'It was all right, was it?' Poppy called down to him. 'I really don't remember much about it, actually.'

'Three point perfection, hon! Now I only have

one question for you!' Derek stated as he swung her down, still with his arms round her. 'Will you marry me?'

His friends and colleagues at once shouted him down, claiming they had first call, a freckle-faced ginger-haired young man dropping to his knees, sweeping off his helmet and demanding not one of her hands in marriage but both of them. Before she knew what was happening, Poppy was surrounded by half a dozen kneeling Australians all beseeching her to be their wife.

'What is all this?' a voice suddenly demanded out of the blue, as from nowhere the tall and as always elegent figure of Trafford Perkins arrived on the scene. 'What on earth is all this brouhaha, shilly-shallying and assorted nonsense will someone tell me, please?'

'You mean you didn't *see*?' Derek gasped. 'You don't mean you missed the air show?'

'Of course I didn't, you silly boy,' Trafford replied, smacking him lightly on the head. 'I saw every single moment. I simply wondered what all the fuss was about, that's all.'

'Because she only did it, Traffy! She only bloomin' well *did* it! She only bloomin' took Tiger up and round and round and then down again after only one bloomin' lesson, that's what the fuss is all about!'

'You surely didn't imagine it would be otherwise, Derek, did you? Just remember whom Poppy had as her teacher. Just remember whom you *all* had. So now let's all go and get absolutely rotten blotto, shall we?'

*　　*　　*

365

For the rest of her spell at the aerodrome, Poppy spent less time learning about engines than she did flying. She flew whenever possible, and whatever was put her way, spending hours in the air with Derek whom Trafford grudgingly allowed to give her star pupil her final polish in a dual-control deHavilland, Derek finding no need to use the controls other than to teach Poppy how to get out of a stalled spin, an experience that Poppy found exhilarating. By the time it came for her to return to base, as she put it, she had a full pilot's licence, dexterously arranged for her by Trafford with one of what she called her *tame ones*.

'It's all perfectly clean and above board, dear girl,' Trafford assured her. 'We just had to speed the process along a little. There's no knowing when this piece of paper might come in handy,' she added, handing it to Poppy. 'There's always a shortage of flyers—not necessarily in the RAF, you understand, because I imagine one would have to have one of those sex changes we keep reading about in order to join that little mob, but in the civil quarter. Awful lot of us ferry craft all over the place, you know. Test 'em too—I was asked to try out some new hush-hush bit of balsa and sticky paper the other day—flew like a porker, too. Not me, I assure you. The aforesaid wonder plane. Never flown such a crate. Could have built it better myself—but there's always a call out, you know. Deliveries mainly, but the odd test does come up. If you want, dear thing, I can put your name forward at such times, although I imagine the boss has other plans for you. You could always let me know if you have any free time anyway—and spend some leave up here flying stuff round the shop. You'd enjoy that, I imagine, and I have to say you're a neat bit of a flyer, too—well taught, natch. But then that's the main thing. I'm a bit of a Flying Jesuit like that, you know. Give me a girl and I'll give you a pilot in a week. Have to say—' She stopped, lit her half cheroot, then smiled her wonderful crooked smile at Poppy. 'Have to say—though keep this one close to the bosom—you're the quickest so far, whatever the boys tell you. And I'll tell you something else, sweetheart. Derek lost not only his heart that day—he lost quite a large chunk of his pay packet, too. About three months' worth, I hear—but you know something else? First time I haven't heard him whinge about losing. Pity you're hitched—he'd have flown off with you.'

Oddly enough, that made Poppy feel even better about herself.

Chapter Ten

Harvey sighed, put his feet in their highly polished handmade shoes on to the desk in front of him, and took another look into his metaphorical net.

Still only tiddlers, he mused privately. *Where are the big boys, one wonders? Where oh where oh where?*

In spite of his intense effort to unearth the *caochán* all roads seemed to be turning into cul-de-sacs. *Yes*, he reminded himself this very morning when he was assessing the situation, *one has had plenty of good leads and some of them looked as though they were going to prove to be very productive.* Yet they had not—they had all ended in apparent

367

dead ends, leaving Harvey Constable as nonplussed as he had been when he embarked on his covert investigation. People meeting people was all very well, but unless he could produce hard evidence that they were involved in sedition and treachery such people remained simply on the suspects list.

Admiring the craftmanship that had gone into making such a perfect pair of brogues, he turned his toes first inwards and then slowly outwards as if his feet were enjoying a private dance of their own while he ran an imaginary finger down his imaginary list of not so imaginary suspects, only to find himself sighing again with deep internal dismay. All the connections he had tried to make between certain parties were specious and based purely on supposition. That was his major disappointment. He had—as was his way—been utterly diligent in his detective work, not only examining the histories of all persons who had access to Top Secret information but following so many of them that he had practically gone round in circles. He had genuinely supposed that by now he would have come up with the culprit or culprits. Such was not the case. At the moment, other than having a list of several suspects, he was empty-handed and apparently no nearer the truth.

He had therefore decided to broaden the scope of his enquiries and take a look at people he considered to be above suspicion. After all, he reasoned, those closest to the throne are often those with the most reason to betray, because sometimes they feel that they should be the ones wearing the crown.

He began with Anthony Folkestone, although, of all the people he was about to put under scrutiny, in his personal consideration the major and Jack Ward had to be the least likely to be involved in any treachery. That, however, was not the impression Anthony got when he found himself at the end of one of what Harvey Constable called his *little chats*.

'That thing on your wall behind you, Major,' Harvey said, nodding at Anthony's map cabinet. 'One has to assume, from the locking device on the front and the substance of what can only be described as a third rate piece of woodwork, that it contains highly confidential information.'

'You would be perfectly correct in your assumption, Captain,' Anthony replied, deliberately using Harvey's army rank in order to maintain the proper protocol, a device that also enabled him not to be visibly or audibly riled by his interviewer's overtly sarcastic tone. 'I being the only person with a key.'

Harvey looked at him, raised one quizzical eyebrow, took something from the top pocket of his jacket and positioned himself so that he stood in front of the locked cupboard with his back to Anthony.

'Not a very good lock I'd say, wouldn't you agree?'

He stood aside to reveal the doors of the cupboard swinging open, exposing all the highly confidential information within.

'You have a skeleton key, Captain?'

'I have a piece of wire, Major. As used by professional burglars. The sort of lock you've employed is child's play to them.'

'Perhaps so, Captain. But then we're not in the habit of employing professional burglars in MI5.'

'On the contrary, Major. It is part of many an

369

agent's training. The ignoble art of pilfering. I should imagine that a very high percentage of bogeys, as the Colonel will insist on calling them, who sit here being briefed by your good self could open and close this cupboard the minute your back was turned.'

'When I am not present in my offices, Captain, they are kept locked at all times, particularly this one—the inner sanctum, if you will.'

'The very same criticism applies, Major. It would take one of your fully trained agents but a moment to be in and out of here with what they need to know. If they weren't able to do so, then I would question their necessary skills very closely.'

Anthony regarded him steadily, but was unable to comment on an observation with which he found he had fully to agree.

'I shall have maintenance build a much more secure cabinet, Captain. I shall commission it today.'

'I should not mount or keep any visible display at all, if I were you, Major. Other than in your head, or in a properly secured filing cabinet. I am sure you understand?'

'Filing cabinets are also lockable devices, Captain, if you recall,' Anthony said, containing the small smile of triumph that threatened to appear. 'So the selfsame criticism would govern them too, I should imagine.'

Harvey glanced at him briefly then strolled to the window to look out, hands clasped behind his back, fingers flapping up and down like a butterfly's wings. Then he suddenly laughed, and shook his head.

'The trouble with anything like this is that all the

time one lives on the very cusp of farce, don't you find?' he said, turning back to Anthony and strolling across the room to retake his seat by the desk. 'You're absolutely right, of course. If my dedicated thief can get into your map cupboard he can just as easily get into your filing cabinet, or even—although with a lot more difficulty—possibly into your safe, since I imagine that like everyone else you keep the papers you finally don't want anyone to see under proper lock and key.'

'I'm not really prepared to answer that question, Captain. I think you understand the reason why.'

'If it's a matter of discretion—'

'It's a matter of protocol, Captain. As I am sure you will appreciate.'

'It's a matter of you trying to put me in my place, I'm beginning to think, Major.'

'I can't say I enjoy having my integrity questioned. Nor my loyalty.'

'I am simply doing what is required of me. What is required of you—as you are quite well aware, Major—is that you will say nothing of this interview afterwards. Because this interview has not happened.'

'I am perfectly well aware of that, Captain. But that does not prevent me from expressing my opinion. And my feeling is that I strongly resent being under this sort of suspicion.'

'And I assure you that you are not alone in your sense of righteous indignation, Major. There is not one single person under the roof of this wonderful house who is not *under suspicion*.'

'Does that include your good self, I wonder? Captain?'

'Knowing the ways of the Colonel, Major, I am

371

quite sure I come pretty high on his list. After all, in some departments and by certain people I am not regarded as the right sort of material myself. Certain parties would be only too happy if they could build a case against me and have me removed from the Service. But that is really neither here nor there. We have to leave aside any sense of grievance. I am quite sure the Colonel has already informed you that we have a very serious breach of security here, and we must discover how this information is being leaked. It is vital. More than vital.'

'Rather you than me, Captain. Now if that will be all, I have some rather important work to get on with.'

'*Moi aussi*, Major. And quite off the record—at this stage of proceedings, any help would be most welcome. Good day.'

Harvey collected his notes, files and books and with a polite smile to Anthony left him to get on with the business he had in hand. In the outer office Miss Budge wished him a polite good day, which Harvey acknowledged with a nod before placing his files on her desk and pulling up a chair to sit down opposite her.

'A few general questions, Miss Budge,' he explained. 'We haven't really talked to each other, have we? If you would be kind enough to spare me a little of your precious time?'

Harvey deliberately gave her no chance to reply, since the question was academic, Miss Budge having no choice in the matter. He then explained that everything they discussed was of course highly confidential and covered by the OS Act, and forbade her to talk to anyone else about these matters after he had finished with her. He also informed her in general terms of the enquiry he was conducting, without specifying the exact reason for the investigation.

'I have asked that we are not disturbed during this interview,' Harvey told her, opening a file in front of him. 'Marjorie is in full charge of affairs while we're talking, so you don't have to worry yourself with any administration. I see from your records that before the outbreak of war you worked for the Service in the field, as an active agent operating in Spain, Germany and France. That is correct, is it?'

'Yes, sir,' Miss Budge replied, her hands folded neatly in her lap. 'I worked undercover in all three countries.'

'Spending most of your time in France.'

'I had quite a long term in Germany too, sir. Trying to identify any possible sympathisers.'

'Dangerous work.'

'I think most field work is that, sir. Although oddly enough I felt more at risk in France, since I was never utterly sure quite whose side certain of the French bourgeoisie were really on.'

'I know just what you mean,' Harvey agreed with a polite smile. 'Although once you make friends in France, you make them for life.'

'Yes, sir.'

'Did you make any friends in France?'

'Not really, sir. But then I'm not a very gregarious type. I don't have many friends. In fact I sometimes think I prefer dogs, sir. Been like that ever since I was a little girl.'

'Quite right too, Miss Budge. I'm a cat person myself.' Harvey smiled again and then consulted his file once more. 'You were a highly regarded agent, Miss Budge. All sorts of good mentions here—and recommendations.'

'Thank you, sir.'

'If you hadn't been so badly injured in the field . . . ?'

'I hope I would still be active, sir,' Miss Budge replied without hesitation. 'In fact I would very much hope so, sir.'

'It was your idea to apply for a desk job?'

'I was recommended, as it happened.'

'Says here you applied.'

'I had to make a formal application, sir. That's perfectly correct. But I was recommended to do so by my Section Head.'

'None other than our Miss Lavington, I see.'

'Sir.'

'You were pretty badly hurt in that scrap, were you not?'

'I mended, sir.'

'Broken leg, shot twice, once through the chest, once in the back. Took a bit of mending, I'd say. In fact I see here you were off games for nearly a year.'

'I suffered some problems, sir. So I was told. Took some time to mend.'

'Yes,' Harvey agreed. 'That's in your report as well. Hardly surprising. Being betrayed isn't the most comfortable of experiences. Nor I imagine is being shot in the back.'

'My fault really. I should have seen that one coming, sir.'

'Your betrayer. He was—as the French have it— a *copain*?'

'He was someone I had been working with for

374

some time, yes. Although this wasn't in France, sir. This was in Germany.'

'But your companion in arms was a Frenchman. Was he not?'

'Quite correct, sir. Hervé Dumas.'

'Working undercover—like yourself—as a German.'

'Yes, sir.'

Harvey sat back for a moment to stare intentionally into space, lighting himself a cigarette as he did so.

'How come he got to shoot you in the back, Miss Budge?'

'Because he was a rat, sir. It happened at a rendezvous—a meeting I had with someone—a German—someone I was quite sure was a British sympathiser—and it was a trap. I had no idea Hervé was even there. But he was—and I was caught between them both, one in front, one behind. And then Hervé shot my contact— betrayed us both, in fact.'

'You were lucky to escape.'

'I only escaped because I killed Dumas.'

'Even though he had shot you first. From behind.'

'He came round in front of me, sir. After I had fallen. I fell all the way down the stairs.'

'Ah,' Harvey said. 'It doesn't say anything about that here. It's a little bare—as these reports are inclined to be. It simply says you sustained two bullet wounds and a broken leg in an engagement with the enemy.'

'I understand, sir.'

Harvey noted that Miss Budge had turned quite white at the recollection, and that her whole body seemed to be trembling.

'I'm sorry,' he said quietly. 'I know this must be quite wretched for you.'

'It's all right, sir. It's just that I haven't really spoken about it since my return to the fold. As I was saying, Dumas came down the stairs and round in front of me, as I was lying on the floor. I think he assumed I was dead—and to make sure he was going to put another bullet into me anyway. He can't have seen my gun or he'd have delivered his *coup de grâce*. As it was he gave me just enough time to shoot him, which I did.'

'And well done too,' Harvey said, closing the folder. 'Little wonder you came to your desk job so highly recommended.'

'Thank you, sir. But it's no substitute for the real thing,' she replied, permitting herself a smile for the first time. 'I've always been a bit of a loner, sir.' She stopped. 'It can be a little too social at Eden Park.'

'I'm sure. But my advice to you is to stick it out, because although I'm quite sure you find your job boring compared to being in the field, we're not going to be able to win this wretched war without a bit of pen pushing. I know what I'm talking about. They've stuck me behind a desk indefinitely as well. So I know how you feel.'

'Thank you, sir.'

Harvey reopened her file as if to check something.

'You went home to convalesce, right? Oop north?'

'My parents live in Lancashire, sir. Little spot called Whitewell. Do you know the Trough of Bowland, sir? One of the loveliest places in

376

England, I say.'

'I've fished there many times, Miss Budge. Couldn't agree with you more. So—thank you for your time,' Harvey said, rising. 'You've been most helpful.'

'I don't see how, sir. With respect.'

'By answering so very truthfully, Miss Budge. And economically.' Harvey sighed, tapping his files into order on the desk. 'I can't tell you how long-winded some people can be. You can always tell the people who aren't quite telling the truth, because they do go on so. So thank you again—for your economy, and accuracy.'

'Thank you, sir.'

Miss Budge got up to open the door for her interviewer.

'I see you had a dog when you were in Germany,' Harvey said, stopping in the open doorway. 'You had to leave him behind, did you?'

It was the only time in the entire interview Harvey actually saw Miss Budge left speechless. She blinked her eyes hard, a frown clouding her brow as if she was searching for exactly the right words to say, hurt in her eyes.

'Yes, sir,' she finally replied after clearing her throat nervously. 'I'm afraid I did. It was something I regretted very much, but there was no alternative.'

'Of course not,' Harvey agreed, noting the pain still visible in her eyes. 'How could there be? Again, my thanks—and perhaps one day soon you'll be able to get yourself another little dog. When this *wretched* war is over.'

'Absolutely, sir,' Miss Budge replied, her composure restored. 'Peace can't come a day too soon.'

*   *   *

After a cup of insipid tea taken in his private office, Harvey considered his next move. There were four names he needed to look at, two of them being Eugene Hackett and Jack Ward himself, who even though already marked down by Harvey as an AS (Above Suspicion) Harvey knew still had to be included in the investigation for it to be said that he had done a thorough job. Besides, Harvey had actually noted a couple of blips in the Colonel's record that merited further investigation, particularly since one of those blips linked him directly to one of the two other names on his list.

Harvey cleared his desk and prepared to enter what he hoped might be the last phase of his enquiry.

*   *   *

To Scott—and to Lily too—it seemed there was only one way their task could have gone so terribly wrong. They had been betrayed.

How they had escaped with their lives neither of them knew; nor did they understand, as they lay in silence in the dark at the very top of a remote hay barn in the middle of what Scott described as *France nowhere*, how they were still at liberty. It had been such a simple operation, or so it had seemed. They were to collect the latest drop from home. Two debutante agents had been sent to take their places, and a safe return to England organised for Lily and Scott. They were to escort them to their safe house, introduce them to the

378

team of Resistance fighters with whom Scott and Lily were now heavily involved, and help them plan the next campaign of sabotage against the enemy stationed in Valognes, southeast of Cherbourg, in the Manche. The team with which Scott and Lily were associated was regarded as one of the crack Resistance units operating in the northwestern sector of France, where they had fought a long and on the whole highly successful campaign against the Germans with the loss of only three members of the twenty-strong group.

Fortunately, given the circumstances of the war and the knowledge of what happened to those who fell into the hands of the Gestapo, all three had been killed in a running gunfight with the enemy, the rest of the group happily escaping with only minimal damage. Furthermore, they had shaken off their pursuers with predictable ease since this was their country, disappearing into the vast countryside without leaving a trace, disbanding as was their habit whenever they ran into difficulties, and taking flight to various bolt-holes in Calvados, Orne or even a couple of them as far south as Maine-et-Loire.

But this time, with this new drop, things went badly wrong from the very outset. First of all, at the very last minute the location was changed. After frantic messaging back and forth to HQ it was discovered that this information was false and had obviously been fed to them by a double agent. The drop was postponed for a week until a new and safe location could be organised. In fact it took less than a week, and four days later ten of the team were in position round the perimeter of a field in the middle of a large stretch of farmland fifteen miles inland from Coutances, awaiting the arrival of what Scott had dubbed the *new bugs*.

The plane bringing them over arrived three minutes late, dropping two parachuted people and four parachuted sets of fresh supplies right on target.

The two agents were shot when they were still a good twenty feet in the air, their dead bullet-riddled bodies crashing to the ground, to be covered by their slowly collapsing parachutes. At the same time as the sudden burst of lethal gunfire the whole dropping area was set alight by flares and hand-held floodlights, the latter being used to search the field and its immediate environs in slow sweeping movements. Once the lights had temporarily passed him by Scott had been able to see that they were surrounded on all four sides by Germans who outnumbered them, Scott roughly guessed, by ten to one at the very least. Not only that, but the Germans had crept up from behind them, unheard and unseen, having obviously successfully removed the sentries the Resistance group had posted against such a contingency, thus cutting them off it would seem from any line of retreat.

'The ditch!' Lily whispered at Scott, who was preparing to fight what he considered was very definitely going to be his last fight. 'We might be able to make it back through the ditch!'

Lily had remembered the long, filthy, stinking, but deep irrigation ditch that they had used on their way to take up their waiting positions hidden in the high banks and hedgerows that surrounded the field. Where it ran to she had no idea, other than that it ran away from the field and the heart of the farmland. It was deep enough to hide a person at full height, and if they managed to stay concealed there was an outside chance that they could make their escape that way, always provided the enemy was ignorant of its existence and its disposition.

'How many of us can we alert?' Scott had to shout back to her now, so cacophonous was the sudden outbreak of rifle fire. 'Can we all get out that way?'

Lily had no idea—all she knew was that there were six of them on that side of the field and if she could pass the message on to her nearest companion, who was a good fifty feet away, he might be able to get word to his closest colleague. That was not only the best she could hope; it was all. She said nothing of course to Scott, whom she left to concentrate on his self-defence while she scrambled under heavy fire along the bank until she could shout to Yves who was fighting next to her. There was no time to wait for any reply or signal since the line of fire was becoming more and more concentrated on the area where she was, as well as getting uncomfortably nearer. Instead Lily somersaulted three or four times along the bottom of the bank, before crawling as fast as she could for the next few feet and finally standing up and running to where she could still see Scott, up on one knee and firing as fast as he could with his rifle at the ever closing enemy.

The next moment she had bundled him into the ditch with her, both of them flattening themselves in the mud and filth at the very bottom. Seconds later another body crashed down, half on top of Scott and burying him even more deeply in the mud.

The three fighters lay as still as they could until they heard the gunfire receding, then stopping, only to start up again as other targets were suddenly spotted. When it was clear that the enemy's attention was engaged elsewhere, Scott, Lily and Yves began to crawl through the mud and debris, away from the sound of the ambush, until they were a good quarter of a mile away. Then they risked standing up in order to hasten the last part of their flight and ran as fast as they could along the deep cutting, their heads still well out of sight, until so distant had any noise of the handfight become that they felt it safe to stop and assess their situation.

They found themselves at what was obviously the end of a track, a lane that was terminated by the deep ditch that continued to run away into the darkness on either side. Yves pulled out his pocket compass and peered at it in the moonlight, the luminous figures giving him a position he then checked by the stars in the clear night sky above them.

'I would say we are very well placed,' he remarked. 'We have come in the opposite direction to the nearest town, so we are facing due south. What we must now do is split up and find somewhere to lie low until those that are left of us can regroup—God willing—back at base.'

'I don't think so,' Scott disagreed. 'I don't think we should return to base—in case they have taken any of us alive.'

'No one will talk!' Yves protested. 'But no one!'

'Just in case, my good friend. We cannot rely altogether on the undoubted courage of our colleagues. All the Gestapo have to do is find a way to make you talk—and they do. Not necessarily by torture, but by the involvement of innocents. We know that, Yves. We have seen it too often.'

Yves thought, then nodded. Just as Scott said, battle-scarred as they all were now, they had indeed seen and heard of things that they had never imagined they would witness. Just the threat of the execution of six totally innocent civilians, often women and children, would be enough to make any of their colleagues reveal the location of a base that they hoped and believed would now be both empty and deserted. No one could be blamed even if the place whose location they betrayed was still in use. Pain could be tolerated. The death of innocent women and children was an altogether harder thing to take. So they reasoned, while in all three hearts lay the heavy dread that in fact they might actually be the only survivors.

Before they parted, Yves promised to let them know, via one of the safe third parties their group used as messengers, what had happened to his cousin Rolande, who had been among the ill-fated reception committee at the landing field.

'If anyone comes through this it'll be Rolande,' Lily assured him. 'And even if he doesn't, you can bet the German army's going to be short of an awful lot of its soldiers.'

Yves grinned, kissed Lily a fond farewell and embraced Scott.

'Whatever happens,' he said before he disappeared into the night, 'when peace comes we shall meet in Paris and get fiercely drunk, my friends! *Au revoir!*'

Lily and Scott thought long and hard about whether or not they should separate, finally deciding that the best plan would be to wait and see. They knew how intense the search for them would be, since their group had been hunted hard and endlessly ever since the Germans discovered how much damage they were doing. There was a big price on all their heads, and while they knew they were in a fiercely loyal part of France, they also knew that as in any country there were always informers and rats, people who would sell their birthright to the enemy for a guarantee of their own safety. So they knew it was useless just to hide up. They had to keep low but keep moving, always not one but half a dozen steps ahead of their pursuers, who were experienced hunters dressed in civilian clothes and often driving French cars, but always when seen on the move unmistakably German—and not only German but Gestapo.

So throughout December Scott and Lily stayed together but kept on the move. They were protected whenever possible by members of the Underground, put up at great risk to their courageous hosts, although they always made sure they moved in under cover of dark and out again before sunup, criss-crossing the country until finally they found themselves exhausted and all but at their wits' ends. What finally brought them to their senses was the first sight of a poster bearing both their more than recognisable images. Not just one, but suddenly a whole plethora of posters stuck it seemed everywhere they went. Most of them were torn down as soon as they were posted, or so badly defaced that subsequent identification of Scott and Lily would have been miraculous. Not that the Gestapo would mind, as Scott pointed out when first they saw the posters. The idea was to let Scott and Lily know that the Gestapo knew what they looked like, which perhaps might be enough to disconcert them and throw them off balance. A secondary aim was to spread the word a lot more widely that there was good money to be claimed for their betrayal.

'Time to split,' Scott decided some time into January when they were huddled under rough blankets in an old abandoned hen house of a farm on the outskirts of a tiny village ten miles east of Ernée in the Mayenne district. Scott had already dyed his blond hair black as well as growing an equally blackened moustache, while Lily had cut her hair so short that she looked like a boy. But they both knew that however good their immediate disguises the time had passed for them to stay together on the run. As it was they felt they had taken unnecessary risks by staying together, jeopardising each other's safety as well as the possible security of their Resistance colleagues by making it easier for themselves to be identified and picked up. The plan was that they would make their separate ways up to Isigny on the Calvados coast, where Rolande and Yves had originally set up their group's first base. The house had been unoccupied by anyone known to belong to the Underground since the group had decanted itself to carry out its sabotages on the Cherbourg peninsula, but had always been kept ready for any member who became detached from his colleagues, or needed safe housing. How Scott and Lily got there would be entirely up to their own inventiveness and resourcefulness.

'But to make it more fun,' Scott suggested, 'how about a little side bet? As to who gets there first.'

'Great idea,' Lily said, trying to stop her teeth from chattering. 'What's the pot?'

'Fifty quid to first runner home.'

'Fifty quid?' Lily laughed. 'I ain't got fifty quid, Captain Stuffy! Tell you what I could do, though— if by any chance I lose.'

She looked at him by the light of a candle stub in an old food tin and then softly whispered in his ear.

Scott smiled and raised an eyebrow. 'I'd better make sure you win then,' he whispered back. 'Hadn't I?'

*   *   *

Eugene failed to make it home in time for Christmas, as Kate expected. He failed to make it home through January either, being moved from Burleigh Hospital up to Bristol where they were pioneering new treatments for broken backs and necks. After further treatment there he was finally allowed to return to Eden Park at the beginning of February, coinciding with the failure of the Allies to win the second battle of Monte Cassino.

'I don't know what to make of it,' Eugene growled at Kate from over the top of the latest neck brace they had fitted him with a week before he had finally left hospital. 'When I left Italy we were winning the damned war hand over fist. Now we're stuck at the bottom of some blessed monastery fighting for our lives.'

'It'll be OK, Eugene,' Kate comforted him,

386

settling him into his chair by the window of his flat so that he could look out over the stable yard, only to be met with one of Eugene's blackest looks.

'You think I want to sit here?' he demanded. 'And watch Micky riding my fellow out every day? And wish I was up in the saddle again? No thank you, Katie—I'm not sitting stuck in front of a damn window like some old war relic! I'll sit by the fire and read, if you don't mind.'

'I thought you said you still found reading difficult? Holding the book up in front of your face for ages—'

'Let me be the judge of that, will you! Now hand me over *Portrait of the Artist*, there's a good girl. And that bottle of whisky too, while you're at it.'

'You're not meant to drink. At least I didn't think you were—because of the medicines they've put you on.'

'Jesus, woman! You'll be telling me what to think next! I'm allowed one drink, of course. So pass over the damn' bottle and a glass and take your scolding elsewhere.'

'One drink.'

'I said one drink, didn't I?' Eugene retorted, settling himself in his repositioned chair. 'And that's all I'll be having. One drink.'

'At a time,' Kate smiled. 'Knowing you.'

For a second Eugene regarded her without a smile. Then, unable to resist, he clicked his tongue, rolled his eyes heavenwards and held out a hand.

'Come here,' he commanded. 'Sit on me knee but mind me blessed neck.'

'I will not sit on your knee because I'm far too concerned about your blessed neck, Eugene, thanks all the same. I shall put a kiss on my finger,

387

put my finger to your lips, then I shall sit here like the obedient little two-shoes you want me to be, and watch you having your one drink.'

'You can read to me if you'd rather,' Eugene growled. 'Because you're damn' well right about it being tiring holding the book up. So unless you've something better to do—'

'I have nothing better to do for at least a couple of hours,' Kate replied, opening the book at the appointed place. 'Then I have to go out.'

'What do you mean, you have to go out?'

'Sit down, Eugene, will you? Sit *down*!' Kate gave a great big sigh and gently eased Eugene back down in his chair. 'It's not the end of the world if I go out, you know. When you were in hospital you didn't know what I was up to and you didn't mind.'

'That's all you know, precious.'

'You couldn't mind because you didn't know because I wasn't up to anything. But I did go out— not with anyone, I just went out. For drinks with my friends, for walks with Poppy and George, to go and have tea with my mother sometimes—but occasionally I do admit I did walk out with a member of the opposite sex.'

'I suppose you think this is funny, do you?'

'Mind you,' Kate continued, 'I'm not quite sure you'd think of him as a member of the opposite sex. I made friends with Captain Constable.'

'Oh you did, did you?' Eugene frowned.

There was a pause as he mulled over the idea.

'He's not interested in women, so I will lift my embargo on him, anyway.' Eugene regarded her bleakly.

'What's wrong with him in any case? One of your great literary heroes, Oscar Wilde—'

'Yes, all right! All right!' Eugene interrupted. 'I'm jealous of anyone you go out with. So who are you going out with tonight?'

'No one,' Kate replied. 'My mother's coming down for the weekend. Apparently she's got things she wants to talk to me about, and since I can't get up to town, and she has a bit of leave due—'

'I'll forgive you your mother. I forgive anyone who had anything to do with the creation of you.' He sighed.

'Hurry up and mend, will you? I'm not a great one for just blowing kisses.' Kate too sighed.

*   *   *

Anthony thought long and hard about his proposition, long before he voiced it. He agonised over whether or not he should discuss it with Marjorie, before finally realising that were he to do so he would without a doubt be talked out of it, and thus be deprived of the chance of seeing a particularly bold dodge that Jack and he had thought up through to its conclusion.

'Billy,' he said one morning, when he had finally made up his mind. 'I need a word with you, in complete confidence.'

Billy made sure the door was firmly shut before crossing to the desk that was situated well out of earshot of the office next door. Ever since he had begun working directly for Major Folkestone he had become totally obsessed with security, developing a routine of checking and double-checking that was beginning to drive Marjorie half mad. Before he went to bed the entire cottage would be checked, with Billy making sure all the

389

doors were properly bolted and the windows secured, and he insisted on vetting any mail that came directly to the cottage itself, often even checking the contents of private letters with his famous spying instrument in case there should be something volatile.

Marjorie often confronted him, demanding to know where he imagined the dangers might be coming from, but all Billy would do was shake his head and mutter, 'OS Act, Marge. You should know better than that.' For of course now that he was actually working in security, Billy saw himself as a walking information centre, someone full to the brim with classified information and therefore a ready target for enemy spies and the like. Marjorie twigged this without being told, and first of all tried teasing Billy out of it, only to find that he greatly resented not being taken seriously. Next she tried to reason with him, as gently as Marjorie was capable of reasoning, only to find herself likewise rebuked and rebuffed. Finally she gave up and just took to sighing and expostulating whenever Billy indulged himself in one of what he called his Security Checks.

'I have a job for you, Billy,' Anthony told him as Billy stood smartly in front of his desk, at ease, but not easy. 'If you don't think you're—' The major just stopped himself in time, having been about to say if Billy didn't think he was quite up to it. 'If you don't think it's right for you,' he corrected himself, 'just say. I'll quite understand since you're relatively new to this game and this could be quite an undertaking.'

'Understood, sir,' Billy replied, having mentally already accepted the challenge. 'Fire ahead.'

390

Anthony looked down at the papers on his desk in order to hide his smile of genuine pleasure, albeit one tinged with an undercurrent of anxiety. He had grown very fond of Billy, seeing him now not so much as a son figure but as a possible brother-in-law—if he found out that Marjorie felt the same way about him as he felt about her. Then he stopped smiling when the reality of what he was about to propose hit him once again. It was a highly dangerous mission, one that could endanger the young man's very existence. Billy, of course, came to his rescue, as usual.

'If you're having second thoughts, sir, don't,' he said. 'I'm game for anything, sir. You know that. I wouldn't have been so bloomin' keen to sign up, would I, sir? If I hadn't calculated the risks.'

'You're quite right, Billy,' Anthony replied. 'And I'm having no second thoughts whatsoever. I know perfectly well that not only will you be game for what I'm about to propose to you but you'll succeed triumphantly. This is something right up your street, young man.'

When Billy heard what was planned for him, he was thrilled, excited and proud. The major was right. It was something right up his street.

*   *   *

'You can't tell me anything *at all*?' Marjorie echoed in dismay, even though she knew perfectly well just how sealed Billy's lips were. 'You could give me *some* sort of indication, surely?'

'You know better than that, Marge,' Billy replied, checking through the items he would need and was allowed to take. 'All I can tell you is I have to go away for a while, and that is it. Sorry.'

'Oh, God, Billy,' Marjorie suddenly sighed. 'What have I got you into?'

'You in't—you *haven't* got me into anything, sis,' Billy said, sitting down beside her and putting his arm round her shoulder. 'You didn't start this bloomin' war, did you? So why make yourself responsible for everything that happens in it? People have to fight wars, and this is one war where we really do have to fight back or else we're done for. You know that better than anyone 'cos that's something you've always believed in. I believe in it too, sis—and I'm doing what I'm doing 'cos it's something I can do, and because I can do it I have to do it, right? So chin up, sis—you know me. I'm dead crafty. I won't get into no scrapes, don't you worry. I can handle meself, and I can handle anything I'm asked to do. I'm not little Billy no longer. I'm great big Billy, OK? If I hadn't got this dicky pulse thing, I'd be over there fighting hand to hand, wouldn't I? So don't you worry about a thing, 'cos this is going to be a doddle, promise.'

He gave her a quick hug and a playful punch on the arm, and since she knew there was nothing she could do to dissuade him, Marjorie went and made them both a cup of tea.

*   *   *

Just before she left on her own mission, Poppy found herself going to the sewing box and taking out the old diary. It seemed wrong, but it proved somehow irresistible since hardly had the owner of the beautifully gold embossed diary been married before her beloved husband too was called away to

392

fight Napoleon.

Ben the carpenter came from the big house yesterday. We are all to have new iron bars set across the shutters to keep out Napoleon's invading army. Being so near to the coast as we are, I tremble at the idea of troops outside the windows, of being forced to admit them to the House of Flowers. Rather than that I shall fight to the death, so with that in mind have asked one of my brothers to bring across a gun for me when he next visits—something I must not tell Mother . . .

There was a later entry that quite touched Poppy's heart, because she knew exactly how the former chatelaine of the House of Flowers felt.

Nothing from my dearest dear now for months. I know nothing of where he is, or how he is. Every night I pray to God that he may come back to me, that I may yet again hold him in my arms, the most beloved of men. The army has had great losses on the Peninsula, but I know we shall prevail under the leadership of our great General Wellington. I must not think of my beloved—I must only continue to pray for the safety of us all, and for victory, which I know must come. My brother delivered the necessary old blunderbuss for my protection. He gave it as his opinion that one look at myself armed to the hilt with such a weapon and Bonaparte would run for miles. Even so, I remain firm in my determination to use my weapon should the need arise, which please God it shall not. For we

393

will never surrender, none of us. Not ever!

Poppy put the diary down for a few minutes, staring into the fire. There was comfort in the fact that it had all gone on before, the fighting and the threat of invasion and then the subsequent victory, yet she found herself reluctant to read on in case the diarist's beloved husband failed finally to return from the war. Somehow she felt that if that was what had happened, Scott would not return to her. So rather than read it to the end as had been her intention, Poppy closed the diary, retied the ribbon, and put it back into the little old mahogany chest where she had found it.

Chapter Eleven

Jack Ward's state of mind was the very opposite of that of the young woman whom he was about to despatch into occupied France on a highly dangerous mission. While Poppy sat with hope in her heart Jack was suffering from exactly the same malaise from which their Prime Minister often suffered, a visit from the Black Dog of despair.

As a younger man Jack had never suffered from any form of mental malaise, always firmly believing that whatever life threw at you, you simply had to jolly well get on with it. Even after the loss of his young wife and baby he had managed to keep himself on an even keel without once resorting to any of the props generally used by people in such emotional predicaments. He had got through it, he told himself at the time, by getting on with it. The

Black Dog only began to visit him much later, and at moments when he least expected it. At times when he felt quite buoyant and optimistic about his affairs he would suddenly wake up in the middle of the night with the Black Dog sitting on his chest. Nothing would shake it, nothing would get rid of it, nothing would encourage the creature to leap off and disappear back into the dark recesses of the night whence it had first appeared. Jack would lie in his bed sinking under the deepest of despairs, or he would pace the floor, smoking a cigarette and drinking a large glass of whisky in the hope that when he had finished both the Dog would have gone. But it never had. As soon as he lay back in bed there the beast was, pressing him down with its unutterable weight, rendering him physically and mentally paralysed, until at last when dawn broke the creature would slink quietly away and Jack would be able to fall into a shallow, fevered sleep.

Worse followed. Now when the Dog visited it didn't disappear at dawn but sometimes stayed with him not just all day, but for days at a time. Jack being Jack never let it show, but inside his nerves became so raw and his mentality so depressed that he thought his judgement was in danger of becoming impaired. When things got to this dangerous state, Jack had to take himself carefully in hand to ensure that no wrong decisions were made and no one's security or indeed life was threatened. He coped, as Jack always coped, but only because of his strength of character and purpose. Where lesser men would have given in to self-indulgence, Jack fought back. Where others would have crumbled under the psychological pressure, Jack rebuilt. Where the weak would have become even weaker, Jack became strong, so much so that as things now stood he looked forward to doing battle with the Dog, not because he got anything out of his despair, but simply because Jack Ward liked a challenge, and to him there were few things more challenging than having to fight one's own psychological corner.

But something else had made a difference to him, or rather more precisely some*one* else. Jack had always made it a firm principle not to get involved with anyone with whom he worked, since to him that would mean losing the proper perspective. He simply could not risk endangering lives by concentrating his emotions on one person in his organisation more than any other. He had always told his agents that they would only be able to do their job properly as long as they retained their objectivity, and the same went for himself. It was only common sense, but since Jack was a traditionalist he liked lines to be clearly marked so that anyone working with him knew exactly what the limits were. Jack Ward valued simplicity, and clarity, above all, most of all for himself.

Yet he was too honest not to realise that he was in danger of becoming emotionally involved. When he was alone in the evenings he would convince himself that it was the war. War had strange effects. He was so often alone in his thoughts, so solitary in his habits, he was bound to start feeling vulnerable.

When he was away from Helen he noticed that he had begun to miss her; so much so that he found himself inventing reasons for them to have yet another meeting, even when he knew they were going to draw a blank. The problem was—and it was one that exacerbated his dilemma rather than helped alleviate it—Jack didn't know how Helen felt about him. He knew she had to show up when he told her to because he was the Colonel. He was running her. She was one of his agents. If she failed to appear he could take her off the case—or, worse, he could relegate her to a desk job, to endless filing and minor secretarial duties, the sort of work she would hate after the excitement of being in the field.

So here he was again, face to face over a glass of warm beer in the corner of yet another of his nondescript hostelries, places specially chosen for their very lack of distinction, with Helen dutifully reporting on her week while Jack just as dutifully listened. But the fact was there was absolutely no reason for their meeting since the trail had long ago gone cold. The woman in the peacock blue hat had never reappeared since Jack and Helen's first discussion about her. It was as if she had been standing behind them, listening to every word, and then realising she had been spotted had disappeared totally from view. And since she had never been given a chance to get near the suspect Helen had never been able to give a better description of her. All she could say was what she had said before, about her possible age and her build. Because of her hat, Helen had never once seen her face clearly, certainly not well enough to recognise her again, particularly if she had seen her hatless.

'Someone must have tipped her off,' Jack remarked, staring moodily into the bowl of his empty pipe. 'It's too much of a coincidence that after we had spotted her, she just vanished.'

'She could have been someone totally innocent

could she not?' Helen asked. 'Or if not innocent in the true meaning of the word, someone involved in some sort of skulduggery that was not treason, but adulterous perhaps, as you first suggested. A woman simply being blackmailed.'

'She was our bogey woman, Helen. I know it,' Jack replied. 'I'm like a dog. I have a damn' good nose. And the scent I picked up from that one was positive, I can tell you.'

'You only had my word for it, Colonel. You never saw her yourself, so you never really had the chance for a personal assessment.'

'I know,' Jack growled. 'But I have a sixth sense. Rather like the sort of instinct women are meant to have.' Jack glanced up at her over his unlit pipe. As sometimes happened when he looked at her, Helen was surprised by the expression in the eyes behind the horn-rimmed spectacles. 'In this job you have to work on instinct. You have to substantiate your initial assumption—provide the proof, down to the last dot, in triplicate, et cetera, et cetera. But sometimes *all* you have to work from is instinct— and something told me the woman in the hat was just the lead we wanted.'

'I'm sorry. I feel I let you down.'

'Don't be ridiculous. You have nothing to be sorry for.'

'She might have picked something up from me. Caught me staring at her. I imagine that people when they're doing wrong are rather jumpy, aren't they? Very aware of people looking at them. They'd have to be. Wouldn't they?'

'I imagine so, Helen. But I don't think you could have alerted her. I can't see you as the sort of person who's ever caught staring. You're too well brought up.'

Jack smiled at her so warmly that Helen dropped her eyes and stared into her glass. The Colonel hardly ever made a personal statement; it took her by surprise. More than that, it disconcerted her.

'I just hope it wasn't anything I did, sir, that scared her away,' she said quietly, suspecting that in fact that could well be the very reason for the woman in the peacock blue hat's disappearance, since she couldn't imagine any other.

*   *   *

Jack had so much wanted to lay business aside for just one moment and ask Helen to go for a walk with him in Hyde Park. It was a fine day in late February, with the milky winter sun about to warm into a warmer spring glow. Already there was more than a hint of spring with a full show of bulbs, early narcissi and late crocuses prevailing in spite of the mayhem of the world around them, the sudden splurge of colour giving a lift to ground that had lain dead and grey since early November, its colour reminding the survivors of the last great war that they had endured, only to find themselves under siege once again; the sacrifices of so many millions of young men seemingly wasted as the very same enemy, once again, tried to obliterate their tiny island home into submission. But with the promised advent of spring everyone's heart lifted and their hopes rose, as is the way when winter finally allows spring best, and all at once not only the ground but the trees too burst back into a life that had been saved for this moment of renaissance. So, too, the spirit of the people of Britain waited for a spring of its own, one glorious sunny day in the not too distant future when this madness would finally be over, when mothers could welcome home their sons, wives embrace their husbands and sweethearts hold their sweethearts for ever more; safe at long, long last.

Jack walked slowly through the park alone, having denied himself the undoubted pleasure of Helen Maddox's company on this warm and gentle February day. No air raid sirens shrieked their warning against the presence of enemy bombers over the capital; there was just the hum and rumble of a vast city going about its business as Jack continued his progress round the Serpentine, stopping on the bridge to watch the ducks paddling round in wide circles and the pigeons flapping down from the trees in search of crumbs and titbits from the distant figures seated on park benches eating their picnic lunches on their laps.

Jack would have liked to be sitting in the mild sunshine with Helen, down there at the edge of one of London's prettiest ponds, not eating a picnic lunch perhaps, but looking into each other's minds and beings, searching for that little bit more to know, the extra discovery that would consolidate the feelings they had for each other. But it was not to be and rightly so, Jack reminded himself. The war was far from won. They had a traitor in their midst, and the security of the nation itself could be at risk. There was no time for enjoyment, least of all the deep pleasure and happiness that comes with love. Someone, somewhere, hated them all so much they were willing to betray their fellow countrymen and send them to their deaths, either at the hands of the enemy in the field, or against a cold stone wall shot by a firing squad.

The weight of undiscovered treachery always stopped Jack in his tracks. He was about to authorise the mission of two young agents on two particularly difficult dodges, and if the *caochán* was still active, as he was sure it was, then they were in danger of being betrayed before their feet even touched French soil. As his sixth sense once again kicked in, he turned on his heel, found a taxi and urged it back along up to Baker Street as quickly as it was possible for it to go.

*   *   *

He was too late to abort Billy's mission. The young man had been dropped into France the night before and was now to all intents and purposes lost to them until he had fulfilled his allotted task. He managed, however, to stop Poppy from being despatched at the eleventh hour, much to Anthony's astonishment and Poppy's utter dismay.

'You're only postponed,' Anthony told her, after he had summoned her to his office late that same afternoon. 'The Colonel's convinced you might have already been betrayed and doesn't want to risk you. We're going back to the drawing board on this one, and if the target is still in place when we've done the redesign then we'll recommission. But since this is a major one, you'll have to be held in reserve—which might mean cooling your heels a bit for the next few days.'

Poppy dutifully accepted her fate, while inwardly boiling. She had just got herself to exactly the right stage of mental and physical preparation for her drop, like a racehorse after its last gallop prior to a race. But now she was going to have to go off the boil, only to work herself back up into the right state of edginess and fervour needed to fuel this sort of work when required to do so. So to let off a bit of steam she went down to the shooting range that had been set up in the basement of the great house and fired off twenty-four rounds with her pistol. All of them scored bulls.

*   *   *

Billy knew everything about the region, everything about the people, and everything about the family of which he was to be a part. He had known all that well in advance of his leaving, but now he was actually here—in France—everything he had learned had to be put into a different perspective. A foreign countryside looked very different in reality as opposed to on the page, as Billy soon discovered. Maps were flat and neat; the countryside was sprawling, alien and untidy. Languages might come easily to the tongue, but when people spoke to you not only in their regional dialect but also, as most French people were prone to do, at great speed, it wasn't always as easy to understand as it had seemed in the classrooms or round the breakfast table at Eden Park. Then there was the reality of the war itself. Billy, having survived air raids, having been to London and seen the damage, and having devoured every bit of information he could about the war from the newspapers, thought he was not only well informed but a bit of an expert when it came to what was happening, where and to whom. But nothing could have prepared him for the actual sight and the sound of war.

The small town of Nantelle to which he had been sent had suffered extensive and brutal damage in the previous world war, having been all but razed to the ground. Painstakingly it had been rebuilt, not fully but satisfactorily enough for trading to be resumed by the mid-nineteen twenties and farming to be re-established after that, agriculture having been hit hardest of all due to the rape of the land by the big guns and the non-stop trench warfare. The people too had suffered personally at the hands of the Germans, the women having been raped and many of the men murdered for allegedly passing on information to the enemy, so it was neither a happy nor a particularly welcoming place in which Billy now found himself. The Goncourt family was a large, argumentative and truculent brood, a clutch of eight headed by a father who barely spoke a word to anyone and a mother who used the back of her hand like a fly swat on any child that got in her path regardless of their age or sex. The children were five boys and three girls. The boys had all been too young to fight when war had first broken out, but were now plenty old enough to work on the vast, depressing farm whose buildings looked as if they had been put up in the Dark Ages and left untouched since, and whose semi-cultivated land seemed to stretch into the next province. The three girls were all still at school, none of them pretty and all of them rude and unpleasant to all and sundry as long as they were out of sight of their mother. As soon as Maman came near, however, they turned into little Sisters of Mercy, perfect

403

angels who would do anything for anybody, polite and concerned, quiet and demure. Their abrupt change of manner, however, did not seem to save them from their mother's constant scolding or slapping, which they put up with like the pretend saints they were.

They did not know what to make of Billy, since Billy was an idiot. Only Jacques, the father, knew who Billy really was and what he was doing here, something he would never reveal to his family even if it had been permitted, being a man of such great suspicion and privacy that he fully believed at least two if not three of his own children were capable of being collaborators. Maurice Goncourt was an old contact of Jack Ward himself, Jack's own father having stayed with the Goncourts for several years running when he had taken to holidaying in that part of France, a habit Jack himself had continued until as a sensitive young man he grew appalled and tired of the noisy children being so readily spawned in the great farmhouse of Nantelle and decided to take his holidays elsewhere.

But Maurice and he had always kept in touch, because Jack knew how much his father had liked the taciturn Breton. He also knew Maurice was a man to be trusted, not only because of his very distinguished record in the previous war—a history to which he simply never referred—but because his heart and sympathies lay immutably with la belle France and her fight for survival under German occupation. That was why Jack had so carefully handpicked the place where Billy was to be sent, and why Maurice and Maurice alone had been informed of the reason both for Billy's visit and for his apparent state of mental simplicity.

404

The idea had come to Jack not long after the Christmas pantomime where Billy had given such a memorable performance as the village simpleton. He couldn't actually put hand on heart and say the notion occurred to him as swiftly as Archimedes had been struck by the principle that came to be named after him, but he did always like to think that the idea was sown the evening he sat chuckling away at Billy's wonderfully funny performance.

Then, when Anthony and he had been trying to think up a dodge that would help them gain information about the German defences preparatory to the D-day landing already pencilled in for June of that year, Jack was for no apparent reason suddenly put in mind of Billy's performance as the Simpleton.

'The one person who has the entrée practically everywhere,' Jack had explained in the ultra-slow, over-cautious manner he adopted when considering or discussing matters of great importance. 'The Simpleton. The Village Idiot, as he's so unkindly called. Because he has a childlike behaviour pattern, and because he can't seem to communicate with anyone properly, people tend to disregard him completely. They say anything they feel like in front of him, indiscretions, lies, secrets, anything you like. He can go almost anywhere, as well, following along like a child again, enjoying just being with people, trying to make them laugh, sometimes making a damned nuisance of himself but rarely ever being sent packing or punished for it.'

'Unless he runs foul of the village bullies, of course,' Anthony remarked. 'Terrible things used to happen to the poor lad in our village when I was

405

a kid, just to amuse the bully boys.'

'There is that risk, granted, but when you hear what I have to say I think you'll agree it's a risk worth taking. Besides, the person who is going to be exposed to it is very good at looking after himself.'

Jack had then laid down his plan. Billy should be dropped into France to a designated family that would adopt him as the child of relatives who had been killed in the war. Billy would play the Simpleton, right from the moment he left the aeroplane to the moment he came home, trying to work his way into places where no one else could go, where he might be able to gather information that no one else could get.

Anthony was intrigued by the notion, then appalled when he realised what danger it would put Billy in. Jack contradicted him, saying that if Billy played his part right—which Jack was absolutely sure he would, because they had seen him do it— no one would pay him any attention, particularly the Germans who would be so busy looking out for what they considered to be bona fide Underground fighters that they would quite overlook one who was actually attaching himself to them.

Jack was so persuasive that he soon won Anthony over to his side. Not that it would have mattered had he not, because Jack was already so determined on his dodge that he would have commissioned Billy anyway, with or without Anthony's agreement. But it was better that Anthony should agree since, as Jack well knew, the major was very fond of the young man. Should anything happen to Billy on a mission such as this with which Anthony had not concurred, Jack knew he would have an awful lot to answer for.

So it was that Billy found himself on the streets of the small town of Nantelle, acting the Simpleton. The first week was a nightmare because he had to be escorted into town by the two youngest Goncourt boys, ill-mannered youths who as soon as they arrived in the town square at once set about organising the dunking of their idiot cousin in the fountain that stood in traditional pride of place in the centre of the square. Other kids with nothing better to do joined in the fun and games, an initiation ceremony that Billy was forced to endure daily for over a week until the bullies bored of it and returned to more productive pastimes, such as trying to steal some of the little produce that was in the shops or breaking the windows of anyone suspected of collaborating with the enemy.

The latter activity could only take place at certain times of day when the occupying soldiers were off at their work, which as Billy soon learned from listening was the installation of new defences along the seaboard against the rumoured landings as well as the reinforcement of the existing ones. After a few days Billy began to make his presence felt in front of the German soldiers as they assembled in the square prior to being trucked off to work on the coastline twelve miles north of the village. As they paraded in the morning, Billy would parade as well, mimicking the soldiers' drill in his Simpleton way, with a broom as his rifle. At first some of the soldiers had been ready to take offence until the more affable of their number pointed out what a card the boy was, and how comic were his little manoeuvres. So successful was Billy's daily cabaret that it was only a matter of days before the Germans made him perform for them while they were waiting for their trucks.

Billy was only too delighted to obey, grinning daftly and talking absolute gibberish as he marched up and down with his broom, shouldering arms, presenting arms, standing to attention, standing at ease, shouting unintelligible orders all the while and even finally daring to goose-step in front of the enemy, a move he made sure always ended with a crashing pratfall in a puddle whenever possible. The soldiers would roar with laughter, applaud, and even reward him with sweets, prizes that Billy was careful to dole out immediately to the bully boys who were now his chums, so completely in thrall were they to his wonderfully funny routines.

But Billy knew perfectly well that if he made the slightest mistake, if he once slipped up, the game would be over. Someone in this odd, ill-tempered village would be bound to report him in return for a small sum of money and that would be that. That would be the end of his mission. Not for one moment did it occur to Billy that it would be the end of him—that was the last thought in his head. All he thought about was succeeding at what he had been set to do, and on top of that perhaps even doing something that he was not expected to do.

He did have one long stop, however, a safety net that both the Colonel and Major Folkestone insisted upon, and that was the contact numbers for Rolande and Yves, both of whom so far had miraculously survived the whole occupation while remaining fully employed in the Resistance. If he ran into any real trouble that did not end in an arrest, Billy was ordered to make contact with one or both, and they would see to his safety. At the back of his mind Billy was glad of that, for while he had no worries as to how he would behave in action or concerns as to what might happen to him if things went wrong, he still would prefer to get home in one piece, for Marjorie's sake more than for his own of course.

But so far so good. By the end of his third week in residence, Billy had been not only accepted by the youth of Nantelle but adopted by the Germans, who now treated him like a mascot. At first, when Billy realised what was happening, he worried that his new friends in the little town might see him as some sort of collaborator. But because his character as the Simpleton was so sweet and harmless, and because he was so innocently funny, everyone seemed to accept the fact that a young man without the benefit of proper mental faculties wouldn't know left from right, let alone German from Frenchman. So while they would have seriously beaten up any one of their own number who was befriended by the hated foe, they excused Billy by reason of his simplicity.

Billy now marched with the Germans up and down the road, escorted them to their trucks, and was there waiting for their return in the evening to escort them back to their billets. A week later his greatest admirer, a corpulent corporal named Otto, suddenly pulled him up into the back of his truck and allowed him to travel with them all the way to the coast. He was not, of course, allowed any further than that; he had to remain in or around the truck all day and keep himself amused while the engineers went to work. For the first few days Billy never strayed from his post, sitting by the wheel of the truck and eating the food the soldiers shared with him when they stopped for their breaks. In return, he would do funny walks, sing nonsense songs, or perform appalling gymnastics, falling all over the place until he had all the soldiers falling over as well.

At the beginning of the next week, in all 'innocence' he followed his favourite corporal—albeit at a distance—to the defence works. A sentry spotted him and raised his rifle, sighting the barrel straight at his head. Billy immediately responded by trying to stand on his head and falling in a heap, buying enough time for Corporal Otto to explain his presence. The corporal then hurried back to him and tried to shoo him back to the truck. Billy copied him, shooing him in return back to the gate, and the mutual shooing continued for a good few minutes until Billy had not only his friends in hysterics as usual, but also—he noted with inner satisfaction—the sentry too, who had put down his rifle to mop his eyes with his handkerchief.

The following day the sentry waved the corporal's puppy dog through, an act that Billy rewarded by doing his best backward walk, while doing his best to look to the front by turning his head as far round as he could. By the time he arrived on a clifftop bristling with machine-gun dugouts, gun posts, mortar batteries and radar equipment, he had won a whole host of new admirers from regular soldiers he passed en route.

By the next week Billy was an established feature of life on the clifftop, so much so that he thought he would be ill for a couple of days to see whether or not they missed him enough to drop their guard altogether.

He lay at home feigning a terrible pain in his

410

head, a performance that won only laughter from his so-called cousins, although Madame Goncourt showed her true nature by nursing him and caring for him as if he was one of her own. While he lay in bed he thought a lot about the soldiers he was duping, and now that he was away from them he felt a sudden terrible pang of guilt. While he knew they were using him in a way for their own entertainment, not one of them had been unkind to him, jeered at him, or done anything deliberately to hurt him. They had laughed at him, yes, but then Billy had been inviting them to do just that. But they had also fed him, watered him, allowed him to sleep peacefully when he wanted to, and lent him a coat to wear in the evening when it turned cold one day when they were late home. More than that, he had seen in many pairs of young eyes, eyes not much older than his, a look that he understood because he knew he had worn the very same expression himself all those years ago at the Dump, that terrible school where he had been abandoned before he was rescued by Marjorie's love. The eyes he saw had that same look of loneliness and of fear, except the fear they showed was not just at being in some place totally alien to them, but fear that they might not survive the next episode in their young lives, the invasion of France by the mighty Allied forces that would almost certainly end the war, at the cost of many thousands of German lives.

Before he went to sleep, he prayed with all his might that what he was doing might help to bring a quicker end to the hostilities that were decimating the youth of Europe.

*　　　*　　　*

On his return he was treated like the prodigal son, given special treats by his soldier friends, of chocolate and cake, cigarettes and biscuits, while those who could speak a little French tried to find out what had been the matter. Billy of course could not answer them sensibly, so instead he pantomimed a terrible pain in his head that made him spin and tumble, play-acting the frightful affliction that had made him writhe and faint, until his large audience's good humour was restored. Even the stern-faced officers who at first had tried to get rid of this new nuisance had been won over, and at lunchtimes he was now often required to go and do his famous gymnastic show for the cadre of top brass who, although they took their specially cooked meals in a fairly luxuriously equipped hut, were all too obviously bored with the works that were being carried out and only too happy to be entertained by some chump from the local village.

By the end of his third week on the clifftops, Billy had the run of them, an apparent freedom to go wheresoever he chose. He could hardly believe his good fortune and wondered at the brilliance of the Colonel in concocting such a plan. Sometimes he was stopped when faced by a soldier who had no idea who he was, but there was always someone close at hand to explain, and as soon as Billy turned up the gibberish act an extra notch, he had any putative enemy quickly won over.

Every evening, back home at the great farmhouse in Nantelle, under the pretext of trying to teach him some sense, Maurice would take Billy off into a room far away from the occupied ones where he would bolt them both in and allow Billy

412

to sit at a vast desk strewn with clean sheets of paper and an abundant supply of freshly sharpened pencils. Here Billy would draw and detail everything he had seen that day, down to the size and make of the guns, their calibres, and their positions, as well as any new defences he had noticed: dugouts, pillboxes, machine-gun nests, anything and everything that might be of use. When he had finished, each drawing would be carefully rolled up inside another and they would all be inserted into a long cardboard tube that was then shut and firmly sealed at both ends. In turn the tube would be shut away in a drawer, the drawer locked and the key hung back around Maurice Goncourt's massive neck.

Finally, the two of them would smoke one cigarette each, a habit Billy had started on his sixteenth birthday along with most of his contemporaries. When they had finished Monsieur Goncourt would take what was left of the candle to light them both back to the main part of the house, and Billy would then retire to his bed.

During the length of the evening, not a word would be exchanged, never once. All Monsieur Goncourt would do would be to nod while Billy was transferring his vital information on to paper, or fall asleep if the session was a long one, which it normally was. When Billy was finished he would wake the old man up, hand him a cigarette and they would smoke. In all the time he was at the farmhouse Maurice Goncourt barely said one comprehensible word to him, yet Billy felt as safe with him as he did with the Colonel and Major Folkestone.

As for Maurice Goncourt, he admired the young

Englishman more than he could say. His feelings were such that he only had two wishes—first that Billy would manage to get home safely—and second that one of his own sons might learn from Billy's example and perhaps turn into something like this young Englishman who was so willing to risk everything.

*   *   *

'What on earth is Hackett doing out here?' Jack wondered as he and Harvey Constable rounded the corner of the west wing of the great house to find themselves almost face to face with Eugene who was standing in the middle of the main lawn shaking his fists at the heavens.

'Fulminating, as usual,' Harvey said, coming to a halt and staring. 'It seems he hasn't taken at all to wearing a brace on his neck.'

'Hasn't taken to being sidelined, you mean. Does he do this often?'

'In some form or another, yes. We get some sort of visual protest regularly, but more often than not it takes the form of railing against the gods for being so unfair. Luckily he and we have the redoubtable Kate, who seems somehow to be able to keep the lid on him most of the time—although I wouldn't want to be in her shoes.'

'I imagine that fall probably saved Hackett's neck, if you'll excuse the pun,' Jack murmured, watching the antics of the man he still considered to be one of his top agents. 'He was defying the law of averages already, so although I miss him, I'm more than happy to see him still alive. I'm actually astonished.'

'Alive *and* kicking,' Harvey added with a smile. He pointed to the opposite wing of the house. 'He kicked a very large cabbage at the orangery over there the other day—broke a window.'

'So I see.'

Jack nodded, and changed direction, not wishing at this particular moment to find himself involved in one of Eugene's long and convoluted exchanges. He hadn't the time for that. Jack Ward was concentrating only on catching Eugene's *caochán*.

'As you know, I put a stop on the Meynell girl,' he said. 'My sixth sense if you like, but whatever, something was telling me it wasn't right. I know young Billy made it into France safely, but maybe that was luck—or maybe it wasn't. You can't tell until someone's down. But we wasted a lot of time after we found that rogue file.'

'So godchild is off the hook, is she?'

'Off the hook and on her way to the Bahamas,' Jack replied. 'Someone definitely used her as their fall guy.'

'Are we any closer to naming a name, boss?' Harvey enquired, clasping his hands neatly behind his back. 'I can't say that I am.'

'Hmmm,' Jack said, stopping to relight his pipe. 'Sometimes I think we're getting very close, and other times it goes way out of focus. So what I do then is an Agatha.'

'An Agatha,' Harvey sighed. 'As in an aunt of yours, perhaps? Or as in la Christie?'

'Right second time, old boy. I do an Agatha Christie summary—you know the sort of thing. A run through the list of suspects with the whys and why nots.'

'Let's start with—I don't know, boss—who shall

we start with?'

'Let's start with you,' Jack replied, walking on now that his pipe was well alight. 'You're the nearest. You have an impeccable track record as far as the firm goes—undoubted heroism, practically a hundred per cent result rate in the field . . . in fact eveything about you is above suspicion—except your sexuality. As you know without me reminding you, one false step could land you in gaol. Worse than that, your sexual predilection leaves you open to blackmail, and anyone who is open to blackmail has to be suspect.'

'Couldn't agree more,' Harvey replied. 'I'd put me high up any list, if I wasn't me. But it isn't I.'

'I know that,' Jack said. 'Don't ask me why—I just do. And I'd better be right.'

'You're telling me you had better,' Harvey retorted. 'I'll say. My turn to do you in.' He glanced at Jack, then fell to a long silence.

'Come on,' Jack said. 'We haven't got all day.'

'Zero,' Harvey sighed finally. 'Can't think of one good reason for you to turn your coat.'

'I could be schizophrenic.'

'You could. But you're not. And neither are you.'

'Very good.' Jack allowed himself a grim smile, even though their subject matter was highly serious. 'I don't think I have a good enough reason either. I could be bitter over what happened to my wife—but I'm not really. Not any longer. And anyway, what happened to her has little bearing on matters of national security. It hardly affected my patriotism.'

'I can't imagine anything that would, boss.'

It was Jack's turn to glance at Harvey, privately grateful for the compliment. 'Marjorie Hendry,' he

416

said, sticking his pipe back in his mouth. 'The quiet one. Her aunt—whom she adored—used to work for us. Damn' good she was too—the most unlikely people usually are. She got killed in a so-called road accident, which we all think was engineered by Poppy Tetherington's traitorous first husband. Poppy Meynell as she is now. Young Marjorie didn't take that too well and always swore she'd avenge her aunt.'

'So that lets her off the hook, surely?'

'I think so—but one can never be certain. Suppose she thinks we didn't try hard enough? That we finally let her down. Would that be enough to turn her?'

'I don't think so.'

'Neither do I. Billy—her half-brother—is certainly above suspicion.'

'I'll *say*,' Harvey interrupted.

'So is Scott Meynell, so too is Poppy—although I imagine my picture's been taken down at the moment, first of all for sidelining her, then for postponing her dodge.'

'Eugene? Mmm?' Harvey said. 'Our very own lunatic Celt.'

'Hackett? One man I never suspected,' Jack replied calmly. 'Even when I had jolly good reason to do so. He'd almost be too obvious a choice—Irishman working for British Intelligence, born in the south, grandmother a well-known Nationalist—but no, not Eugene Hackett. Of all the men working for us at the moment I would bet my life on Hackett above anyone else. He has a record even better than yours in the field.'

'He drinks stronger drinks,' Harvey said, mock huffily.

417

'I doubt that.' Jack nodded. 'Having spent a few nights on the toot with you, Harvey. What about Tony's assistant? The Miss Budge person? You interrogated her, I seem to remember.'

'Mmm. Wanted to bury her, ended up admiring her,' Harvey replied. 'I have to say she's the sort of woman I just don't understand, but that's neither here nor there. I think the bewilderment is mutual. But if you're talking track records, hers is impeccable.'

'True,' Jack cut in. 'I agree with everything you say. But what we have to do—somehow—is narrow all this down.'

'Kate Maddox has to be ruled out, she's just not the type. But.' He paused. 'What about her mother?'

Jack glanced round at Harvey, breathed in deeply, then shook his head, walking on steadily towards the lake.

'When we were last reviewing this, Colonel, if you remember—' Harvey called after him, before hurrying to catch up. 'When last discussed, you painted a picture of a woman betrayed, scorned, deserted by her husband—cast down by the death of her son, a woman alone, in other words—'

'She still has Kate,' Jack interrupted gruffly.

'She lost her son,' Harvey stated firmly. 'Then just as she was coming to terms with her loss, her husband walks out on her, leaving her quite alone.'

'She's fine. Really. Believe me. She's coping.'

'Because you gave her a job? Sir?'

'I gave her *back* her job.'

'Was it your idea? Or hers?'

'Six of one and half a dozen of the other.'

'She has to be on the list,' Harvey insisted. 'Sir.'

'I know, I know.' Jack glared at him and sat down heavily on a bench by the side of the lake. 'Everyone has to be. She is no exception.'

'How high up on the list?' Harvey wondered, sitting down next to him. 'Sir?'

'High enough, dammit. Plenty high enough.'

'At the moment she'd be quite near the top of mine, Jack,' Harvey stated quietly. 'Really quite near.'

'Then perhaps I'd better prove you wrong.'

'Perhaps you had better—sir,' Harvey replied, his mouth tightening. 'Perhaps that is exactly what you had better do.'

*   *   *

Knowing that Harvey had only talked sense, and that he had to sort out the situation with Helen Maddox one way or the other, the following day Jack returned to London. Since their last meeting, Helen had been instructed to work out a week's notice behind the tea bar at Charing Cross Station before returning to her desk in the Baker Street HQ of the SOE. Jack contrived to meet her outside her office one Friday evening, just as she was preparing to leave.

'Well, well,' he said, smiling in greeting. 'The very person I was hoping to see.'

'I had no idea,' Helen replied. 'No one told me you wished to see me, Colonel.'

'Perhaps not on business,' Jack said, falling into step alongside her as she walked down the corridor to the stairs. 'I thought we might go and have a quiet drink.'

Helen frowned at him as Jack held the door he

had opened for her at the top of the stairs to allow her through. They descended to the street where Jack immediately hailed a cab.

'Not somewhere local, I take it,' Helen observed as they settled into the back of the taxi.

'I'm fed up with those dreary places we have to frequent. Since you're not doing anything this evening—'

'Forgive me, Colonel.'

'Jack this evening, Helen. We're off duty now.'

'How do you know I'm not doing anything this evening?'

'I had my secretary check.' Jack glanced at her to see whether or not Helen was objecting.

'I don't put everything down in my diary, you know.'

'I should hope not. But at least you're free for a drink, otherwise you wouldn't be here. And if you're still free after a drink, I have two tickets for *Sweeter and Lower*. With Hermione Gingold.'

'I love Hermione Gingold.'

'I'm told it's very funny,' Jack remarked. 'I gather there's a skit with her as the queen of all stirrup-pumpers that's said to be hilarious.'

Helen smiled back at him and readily accepted such an attractive invitation, but only on condition that they could first stop off at the flat she had started to rent since working in London so that she could change out of her work clothes. While she washed and dressed Jack drank a pink gin and gazed down on the life outside in the street below, not seeing it at all, his mind being fully concentrated on the vital problem that he was more determined than ever to solve. His single-mindedness did not stop him appreciating Helen's change from office worker in plain blouse and dark skirt into a highly attractive woman in a deep red silk dress with a matching short jacket, nor did it lessen his enjoyment of first their drink together and then the hilariously funny revue which continued to play without interruption when a siren sounded its air raid warning halfway through the first act. No one left their seat.

'I can't remember when I last enjoyed a show so much,' Helen confided as Jack walked her to the door of her block of flats. 'Thank you very much. It was a lovely evening.'

'Thank you, Helen. It wouldn't have been in any way as—as good,' Jack replied, 'if you'd decided not to come.'

They looked at each other for a moment, before Helen began the search for her door key in her bag.

'I have a bit of gin left,' she said. 'If you'd like a drink?'

'Who can say no to such an offer in times like these?' Jack smiled. 'If that's all right, I'd love a drink.'

'I wouldn't have asked you if it hadn't been all right,' Helen replied, opening the door and letting them both in. 'After you, Claude.'

'No, after *you*, Cecil.'

They both laughed at the repetition of jokes from ITMA, the nation's favourite radio show of the moment, as Jack followed Helen up the stairs and into her little apartment.

'I met a man the other day who doesn't think ITMA's the slightest bit funny,' Jack said dolefully. 'It beggars belief, not finding ITMA funny.'

'Probably just trying to be different,' Helen replied, pouring them both a drink. 'Some people can only ever draw any attention to themselves by trying to be different.'

'You don't seem to have that trouble,' Jack remarked.

'He probably wouldn't have found Hermione Gingold funny this evening either,' Helen continued, glancing at Jack. 'I can't get on with anyone who doesn't laugh. Mind you, Harold—my ex-husband. He had absolutely no sense of humour whatsoever.'

'How come you married him?'

'How come indeed. Oh to be blessed with foresight rather than hindsight.'

'Here's to this damn' war being over soon,' Jack said, switching the subject and raising his glass. 'I'm looking forward to being able to do things we haven't been able to enjoy for such a long time now. I never thought I'd miss cricket, you know— but I do. I haven't seen a decent cricket match since 1939—because of course there hasn't been one. No county matches, nothing. Only one-day games between scratch sides on private pitches. I shall look forward to going back to Lords, and the Oval. What will you look forward to doing, Helen?'

'I don't know, Jack,' Helen replied, suddenly serious. 'Probably because before the war I didn't do very much. When I was married all I did really was that. I was married. I had my children, I brought them up as best I could, made as good a home for them as I could, but I didn't *do* anything. Nothing that wasn't centred round the family. There was Kate's tennis, of course, but her father was so against that. Her father was so against Kate altogether, really. He was determined she would have no life of her own.'

'You weren't,' Jack interposed. 'Which was why you sent her to me.'

'I don't know what I would have done without you, Jack,' Helen replied truthfully. 'First of all you gave me work, then you took Kate under your wing; then, after—after everything else that happened, you took me back again. I can't thank you enough.'

'It means that much to you, Helen, does it?' Jack wondered quietly. 'Your work? Or is it just the fact that you've got something to do?'

'Fair enough.' Helen smiled, getting the implication. 'You're at perfect liberty to ask that, because when I began to work for you I had no idea how much of a patriot I was, or wasn't. Now I can say—hand on heart—that it isn't just working that matters to me, Jack. It's very much the sort of work I do. There isn't anything I wouldn't do for this country of ours. I just wish I was young enough to be of more use.'

'Why does it matter that much to you, Helen?' Jack said, offering her a cigarette and then lighting it and his own. 'You don't mind me asking, do you? But not everybody feels the way you do. In fact many people who've been through—' he stopped. 'Who've had your sort of experience, shared that kind of thing—'

'Yes?' Helen suddenly leaned forward in her chair to stare at Jack. 'Yes? Yes? What? Many people who've shared my sort of experience of *what* exactly?'

'What's that phrase?' Jack wondered, looking straight back at her. 'You know. Something about always hurting the thing you love.'

Helen continued to stare at him for a moment;

423

then, stubbing out the cigarette she had barely smoked, she got to her feet.

'It's been a lovely evening,' she said. 'But I think you ought to go now.'

'I'm afraid I can't, Helen,' Jack replied. 'I have a job to do. It's not a job I always like doing, but it's a job that has to be done.'

'If you're suggesting what I think you're suggesting?'

'My turn to ask what,' Jack cut in. 'So yes, Helen? What?'

'I really think you had better go.' Helen turned her back on him and walked towards the door.

'I have to examine every contingency.'

'Yes. I realise that, but surely not to suspect me, surely not?'

'I have to suspect everyone.'

'If you think I am capable of treachery then you are not the man I thought you were. Hoped you were.' She turned to look at him. 'I'm not capable of treason, Jack,' she continued steadily. 'I love this country more than anything. And to betray it would be to betray everything I have always believed in. And other things that I have come to believe in—more than ever.'

Jack frowned, looking at her wondering fleetingly what she meant.

'You don't understand, do you?' she went on quietly. 'Nothing occurs to you, nothing matters to you outside your work I don't suppose.'

'Not true as it happens, Helen,' Jack interrupted. 'Not true at all. Other things do matter, *will* matter.'

'It is true, Jack. It would never occur to you that someone might be—' She stopped. 'Let me put it another way, if I may. I don't think you realise, because of the sort of person you are—I don't think you imagine for one moment that someone like me—who has had the things happen to them that have happened to me—rather than becoming sour and bitter—some people can have their whole lives altered—maybe even be actually saved—by kindness.'

Helen could hardly get the last words out. She sat down quickly on the sofa staring ahead of her, suddenly dejected beyond words. Silent.

Jack watched her without saying anything, smoking his cigarette, immobile.

The room fell to silence, a silence that seemed to grow and grow until it was broken by the slight sound of Jack stubbing out his cigarette in the glass ashtray.

'Now that's out of the way,' he said quietly. 'To work. The first thing we have to talk about is the matter of a certain peacock blue hat.'

*   *   *

Two hours later, at the dead of night, Jack Ward finally left Helen Maddox's flat.

As he walked down the deserted street with his pipe clenched in the corner of his mouth he nodded to himself and smacked one fist into the palm of the other hand.

'Gotcha,' he said to himself. '*Gotcha.*'

*   *   *

The following morning from a private office in Baker Street on his scrambler telephone he put an urgent call through to Harvey Constable at Eden Park.

'You're to organise a false drop,' he instructed Harvey. 'You're to invent a whole new mission, delegate an agent, and issue the necessary map reference for the drop, which you will then arrange to be observed by our friends in the area. If they find the enemy ready and waiting for our non-existent drop, then we're home and hosed. If not, my head is on the block, so keep praying. Naturally you will make sure all this information is put on Tony Folkestone's desk and that the orders are issued by him through the usual channels.'

Chapter Twelve

There was very little more now for Billy to do as far as his mission was concerned. He had plotted and described practically every defence and gun position along the stretch of the Cherbourg clifftop which he had been allowed to wander more or less at will, and that information was now safely in the hands of his superiors, transported to them by the Underground along a route invented two years previously and as yet happily still undiscovered. But that was not Billy's concern. He had done the job he had been sent to do, and now he must try to obey the next part of his orders, namely to return himself safely to base.

He knew that in a way this would be the most difficult part of his mission, since it was the part Major Folkestone had explained in the simplest terms. He was simply to make his way to Isigny and

426

contact either Rolande or Yves. They would take him to the safe house, from where an escape route would be organised along which he was to travel home with a different identity, one that would be created and papered for him in Isigny when he reached it.

First he had to get to the town. Since it was known that he belonged to a family in Nantelle, he could not simply disappear. Even though Monsieur Goncourt knew the truth, others did not, and someone was bound to report the absence of a person as extraordinary as the Simpleton stranger who had suddenly landed in their midst. They might do it purely out of concern in case something had happened to the poor young man, or someone might suspect a ruse. Whatever the possibilities, Billy could not take the chance of inadvertently raising an alarm against himself.

He had to find a way of getting to Isigny without arousing suspicions or triggering a final alarm. So while he was still amusing himself and his German admirers high above the very beaches where the Allies were soon to land he looked, and above all he listened, something Billy had always been good at doing. He eavesdropped on the transport crew, an easy task since none of them suspected for a moment that their simple young jester was all but fluent now in German. The poor lad could hardly get his tongue round his own language, let alone speak a word of theirs. When Billy was around no one bothered to shoo him away even if they were talking confidentially, which was how he soon learned that none other than his favourite corporal, Herr Otto, was to drive to Isigny the following morning to pick up some vital fuses for some equally vital piece of communications equipment. He was to take one of the smaller trucks, collect the materials, and return to the site by midday. This would suit Billy admirably, since it was Corporal Otto who chauffeured him to the clifftops every day. Billy's only problem would be how to stay in the truck without raising the corporal's suspicions.

Fortunately, Billy got the break he required. Corporal Otto had not the best of waterworks, it emerged, and so before making the long drive to the town he hopped out of his driving seat and disappeared into the latrines. Billy, having already disembarked, wondering how he was going to effect his stowing away, saw his chance. All the other soldiers having dispersed to go about their work, Billy simply slipped himself under the tarpaulin in the back of the vehicle, well out of sight of Corporal Otto when he finally returned to his truck. He stayed there undiscovered until they reached Isigny where Corporal Otto parked and disappeared inside a small warehouse on the outskirts of the town. When the coast was clear, Billy slipped out of the back of the truck and disappeared up the deserted road that led into the centre.

It could not have worked better. He had thought he might have to wheedle and cajole Corporal Otto into giving him a lift, that is if he could have got the fat soldier to understand what he wanted without giving himself away. Failing that, he would have had to find some other mode of transport, but as it happened Fate could not have been kinder. The corporal did not know he had carried young Billy in and therefore would not notice he was missing until

428

it was time for the troops to return to Nantelle. With luck they might imagine that Billy had simply wandered off somewhere, and maybe wouldn't give him a second thought until the following morning. Even then his absence was not going to bring the whole German army to a stop while they searched for him. Billy finally was flotsam, and if he disappeared he would soon be forgotten. What was important was that he got to Isigny without raising alarms or suspicions.

Since no one was on the lookout for him, no one took very much notice of the apparently simple youth wandering through their streets, staring at house after house. One or two idle youths threw stones at him, and a few more shouted rude jibes as he grinned at them inanely. Otherwise he was unbothered, and after an hour's careful searching he finally found the safe house, where he was discreetly welcomed by a young woman called Nina, a little brunette with a rather full and sensuous mouth to whom Billy found himself immediately attracted.

She was a Resistance fighter herself, her job at that time being the organisation of escape routes out of her area to wheresoever the fugitives wished. She already understood Billy's needs and immediately set about reforming his appearance so that it would be in line with the description on his new papers. She had clothes ready for him, hair dye, a pair of spectacles with plain lenses, and a change of shoes. She also had money for him, as well as a set of most authentic-looking papers. His new occupation was that of house painter, which allowed him to be as peripatetic as the occupying laws allowed.

But first he had to get bathed, washed and shaved. He had to expunge all trace of the Simpleton and become his new character. As Billy the Simpleton he had had to endure remaining dirty and generally unkempt, but now he had to wash that role right out of himself in order to adopt his new personality.

Nina filled a hip bath in the kitchen with jugs of hot water she had ready on the range, and laid a big thick white folded towel on a chair nearby.

'Would you like me to scrub your back, young man?' she asked as Billy began shyly to loosen his clothing.

Billy shrugged, turning away from her in order to hide his blushes.

'If you want me to scrub your back, just call. I shall only be in the scullery here, getting our lunch ready.'

Nina disappeared into an adjoining room where Billy heard her busying herself chopping vegetables. When he felt he was quite safe he slipped out of his dirty clothes and gratefully into the bath where for ten minutes he soaped himself into a state of utter cleanliness. Then he lay back and shut his eyes, wallowing in the luxury of the hot water and the sweet smell of fresh soap.

When he opened his eyes he saw Nina looking down at him.

'I thought I heard you call,' she said with a frown. 'Did you call?'

'I don't think so,' Billy mumbled. 'Unless I fell asleep, that is. And called out in my sleep.'

'So sorry,' Nina apologised, although, Billy noted, without moving from the spot. 'But while I'm here? Would you not say yes to my scrubbing your back? It is always so difficult, is it not? Trying to get one's back clean? Here . . .'

She produced a large brush and dipped it in the water, too close to Billy for comfort. He swallowed hard and tried to speak, but found himself struck dumb. Since he was not saying anything, Nina took it for granted that she might indeed scrub his back and so she did, smiling to herself as she stood soaping her brush behind the handsome young man, before gently but firmly beginning to scrub him down.

Billy had often thought about kisses. He had dreamed about kisses, and wondered about kisses—how a girl's lips might taste, what her kisses might be like, how indeed even to kiss her back. Now he was finding out, and what he was finding out exceeded his wildest dreams. Nina kissed him sweetly, she kissed him softly, she kissed him gently. She kissed him carefully and tenderly, and her kisses showed him what his kisses should be like, so Billy kissed her back. He kissed her sweetly, and softly—he kissed her gently and he kissed her tenderly, and as he did so she ran her fingers through his wild wet hair, dexterously, skilfully, easing his head closer to her, and when he came closer she kissed him with more passion, Billy with one foot still in the bath and one foot out, Billy with both feet out, following her across the room as she pulled him to her, still kissing him, laughing a little between kisses, teasing him with her touches, burning his wet skin with her gentle caresses, hugging his firm, fit body to her small soft one, soaking her clothes with his bath water, still kissing him while she unbuttoned the front of her own blouse to reveal just herself beneath, slipping out

431

of her cotton skirt and nothing else, as if she had
been waiting for him, expecting the arrival of her
young lover, easing him now to her, pulling him
gently down on to her unmade bed, a place of
heaven that smelt of warmth and of flesh, of
woman, of hair—the wonderful intoxicating smell
of a young woman's tresses—hair that Billy's face
was buried in as she took him down on top of her,
into white sheets that had wrapped her body that
night, that still held her scent, her being. They
tumbled as two and became as one, enveloped in
linen, enveloped in each other, lost in the
sweetness of love.

*   *   *

At midday Yves burst in, disturbed, angry.
'They have him,' he told Nina who was sitting
with Billy now, eating the repast she had so lovingly
prepared. 'They caught him last night on his way
through—someone must have informed against
him.'
Billy looked anxiously from the stranger who
had burst in to Nina, who put her hand over his.
'Yves,' she said. 'This is Billy.'
'I know. Forgive me, Billy. I thought it must be
you—who else? But I am so angry! Bah!'
He grabbed the bottle of red wine by the neck
and poured half its contents down his throat while
Billy watched in admiration. He had never heard
anyone actually say *Bah!* before—let alone a
dashing handsome Frenchman who looked as
though he had just strolled out of Dumas—and
while he sensed that the news he had brought was
not good, he was still in a state of fierce

432

intoxication induced by his introduction and welcome to life as effected by his now beloved Nina.

'They have one of yours,' Yves growled at Billy, wiping his mouth on his sleeve. 'We were ready for him days ago but he did not show—and now when he arrived in town last night the sons of bastards were waiting for him.'

'Where is he, Yves?' Nina asked. 'Have the Gestapo got him?'

'That is the good part. Not yet.'

'Yves is my brother, by the way, Billy.'

'Ah,' Billy said, pushing his plate to one side to attend to what was being said.

'The police have him. Locked up in the little gaol in rue St-Paul. The Gestapo won't be long in coming—they'll be here by this evening, knowing them—so we're going to have to organise something.'

'I have an idea,' Billy said. Had Nina and Yves known him better they would not have been the slightest bit surprised by this disclosure, but since Billy was a stranger to them they were hardly interested in anything he had to say, since they both considered him a little on the callow side to be coming up with anything seriously constructive.

'It will mean my having to be Simple Billy again,' he explained to Nina. 'But then that's not too difficult. The problem is how to get me arrested. Yeah—yeah, I know. I just give myself up.'

Billy grinned at them, and they stared back at him. Finally, Yves sat down and listened in silence as Billy explained his plan.

*   *   *

At first one of the two policemen in charge of the tiny gaol was not in the slightest interested in Billy. In fact he was visibly irked by his presence as Billy danced and jogged round his desk, trying to explain his plight in all but unintelligible French—that he was a mascot of the German engineers, that he had got a lift in with Corporal Otto and then had missed his lift home because he had got out from his hiding place to have a look at where he was.

At one point the policeman took him by the scruff of his neck and dumped him unceremoniously outside the police station, only for Billy to bounce back in and start all over again. By now his partner, who had been half asleep in a chair in the corner of the office, had begun to listen, able it seemed to pick up the gist of what Billy was saying, particularly now that he was explaining how cross his German friends would be if he went missing and no one had helped him.

'OK,' the second policeman said, stopping Billy. 'I get your drift, son. And I think much the best thing would be if you stayed here? With us? For a while?'

Billy nodded with intense enthusiasm at this suggestion.

'Good,' the policeman continued. 'Then tomorrow, when I have to go out that way, I can return you to your friends?'

More enthusiastic nodding followed from Billy.

'Who I dare say will be well pleased to see both you—and me.'

The policeman grinned, winked at his colleague who was now in the picture, and patted Billy on the

434

head. Billy patted him back. The policeman wasn't so sure he liked that, and held up a warning finger at Billy. Billy held one up at him. Then he pushed the policeman in the shoulder, hard, so that he almost fell back. The policeman went to punch Billy, and was only stopped from doing so by his colleague, who jumped up from his desk to keep them apart.

'He's soft, Louis—don't go hitting him,' he said. 'We'll put him away in a cell out of harm's way till you take him back tomorrow. Best place for him, because God knows the sort of mischief he'd get up to in here. Come on, you.'

He grabbed Billy by the collar, too hard for Billy's liking, so Billy kicked him hard on the shins. For his reward he was hurled with unnecessary force into the cell bang next door to their other prisoner, who protested at the manhandling of the youth. He was told to shut up or take the consequences, while they prepared to lock Billy's door.

Whereupon Billy threw a fit.

It was a very convincing one, too. It was also very frightening, as he lay thrashing helplessly and violently on the floor, his face contorted and his limbs wildly out of control.

'Water,' the patient in the next cell advised through the bars. 'You'll have to get him some water and one of you loosen his clothes. Unless you want him dying on you.'

The two policemen regarded their important prisoner carefully, then one nodded to the other to do as advised. As his companion hurried back to the outer room to fetch water, the remaining policeman bent over Billy to start loosening his clothes.

Whereupon Billy punched him in the throat, so hard that he began to choke, clasping his neck with both hands, allowing Billy to grab his pistol from his belt and then knock him cold with the butt. As the policeman keeled over, Billy grabbed the keys he had long ago spotted hanging from his belt and jumped to his feet, hiding behind the intercommunicating door to wait for his colleague.

'Quickly, you fool!' the other prisoner shouted. 'The poor kid's choking to death!'

The moment the second policeman appeared at the door with a jug of water, Billy struck, crashing the pistol butt down on his head and knocking him out cold as well. Then he let the other prisoner out.

'I recognised you the moment I saw you,' Scott said. 'I very nearly said something. I very nearly gave the game away.'

'Not you, sir,' Billy grinned. 'Never.'

He handed Scott the pistol, and the two of them dragged the unconscious policemen into the cell he had just vacated, tying their feet and hands with their belts and ties, and stuffing their mouths with their own handkerchiefs, fixing the gags in place with some tape Billy found in the desk. Then Billy pocketed the second policeman's pistol and they left the cell, locking the door behind them and taking the keys.

They hurried out, locking the inter-communicating door as they went, before locking up the whole station and strolling out on to the main street.

On their way back to the safe house, they threw the ring of keys into the canal.

*　　　*　　　*

Poppy had been told nothing about the drop's being a false one. She had simply been given her instructions just as if the whole mission was utterly bona fide, a set of orders given to her as usual after briefings by Cissie Lavington and Anthony Folkestone in his office. Poppy was code-named Armistice and the mission she was to embark upon was called Field Day. After her briefing, Poppy returned to her house to prepare herself for the departure she believed was scheduled for the following night.

The only difference in the routine was that Jack Ward had been present during the whole of her briefing with Cissie, and then with Anthony. Other than acknowledging her arrival and departure, he had not addressed anything directly to his agent.

Early the following evening, still in spring sunlight, Poppy was driven to the airfield from which Billy had departed on his first mission behind enemy lines. As they approached the row of small anonymous buildings and she saw the aircraft ready and waiting out on the tarmac, Poppy felt a deep thrill of excitement. While they waited for cover of darkness, Cissie and she checked and double-checked her papers and all the rest of her equipment. Then they sat smoking and chatting together as if waiting to be asked for a dance at some smart ball while the maintenance and flight crew prepared to leave.

At ten to midnight all was ready. At eight minutes to midnight, as Poppy was buckling on her parachute, the telephone on the desk in the corner of the office rang. Cissie answered it at once,

437

listened, said nothing, nodded and replaced the receiver. Then she walked across the room and closed the door.

'Something the matter?' Poppy wondered. 'No last minutes hitches, surely?'

'You're not going, dear,' Cissie said. 'Nothing personal, but you're grounded.'

Poppy looked at her in open astonishment, about to protest. Cissie pre-empted her. 'There's absolutely no point, dear. Save your breath, because these are orders from the top. You're not going and that's it. So sit down, have another fag and cool your heels.'

Poppy turned away, wanting to do anything and everything other than sit down, smoke a cigarette and cool her heels. She couldn't believe Fate should conspire so cruelly against her that both her missions should be aborted, but she had and they had, so far from sitting down and cooling off Poppy felt like going round and smashing every single piece of furniture in the drab little office, breaking every pane of glass in the windows and then setting fire to the entire place.

Instead, she stood by the window and watched with ever increasing bewilderment as the aircrew hurried out to the waiting aircraft.

'I thought you said the mission had been aborted?' she said angrily to Cissie.

'It has, ducks, it has. This is something else altogether, believe you me. And something tells me it's not just for your good, but for the general good.'

Still baffled and angry, Poppy stood and watched the plane accelerate down the runway and disappear into the night.

'You're to disappear for a while too, I understand,' Cissie said to her, as she escorted Poppy out of the back of the building to a small anonymous car that was ready and waiting for them in the alleyway. 'The driver here will take you to a safe house where you are to remain until you are recalled. That's an order. Cheerio.'

Cissie slammed the passenger door on Poppy and banged on the roof of the car for the driver to leave. As the car bumped away down the uneven surface, Poppy sat back in her seat and swore long and roundly under her breath.

'Beg pardon, miss?' the driver said, half turning round to her. 'Did you say something?'

'Yes I did, as a matter of fact,' Poppy replied. 'Want to know what?'

In response to his agreement, Poppy told him exactly what she had said. The driver said nothing for the rest of the journey.

*   *   *

Exactly fifty minutes later the aircraft was over the dropping zone. They had flown through one light flak bombardment as they were crossing the French coast, then a surprisingly heavy one just when they thought they were well in the clear, but fortunately the enemy scored no hits.

The pilot circled the zone once, as arranged, then dropped his dummy followed by some cases of what should have been vital equipment but was in fact nothing but fresh pig manure, thoughtfully collected and packed by someone with a ready sense of humour. As the plane departed, one of the crew looked back to see if all the parachutes had

439

opened on their automatic rig, and saw the first flashes of gunfire as the ambush was sprung.

'Good show!' he called to his pilot. 'Jerry's there and taken the bait!'

'Pity we didn't booby trap those cases!' the pilot returned. 'Then he really would have got a nice little surprise!'

On the home run not one anti-aircraft gun picked them up, so that two hours and ten minutes after departure the pilot landed his plane safe and unmarked back at the little airfield.

*   *   *

Jack and Harvey examined the pilot's report and a transcript of the French agent's eyewitness account of the predicted ambush. They then reassessed the reports in the files before them on the desk in Jack's private office high up in the attics of Eden Park before coming to their conclusion.

'Good,' Jack said finally, opening a brand new tin of tobacco he had purchased the day before in London. 'Time to pull the net in, I'd say.'

'Good work, boss,' Harvey said, lighting up his own smoke having closed his files. 'Want to tell me what finally persuaded you?'

'The hat,' Jack said, carefully lighting his pipe. 'The peacock blue hat. We joke about women and their hats, probably because they take them so seriously.'

'I take hats *very* seriously,' Harvey replied. 'But I'm not quite sure about peacock blue. That depends. It would certainly never be my first choice, except perhaps worn with black.'

'I don't want anything going wrong,' Jack said,

440

getting up from his chair to go and stare out of the attic window. 'I don't want to have this one jump out of the landing net.'

'Everything should be in place by tomorrow, as you want, sir,' Harvey assured him, neatly tapping his cigarette ash into his tin ashtray.

'The longer I'm in this game the more I wonder,' Jack mused, staring down at the parkland far below him. 'Why, Harvey, why. It's always the whys I find so difficult. It's usually the last thing you suspect, too, when you're trying to find a reason. If they don't tell you, and you're left guessing, now that really can mess a chap up.'

'What do you think the why is in this one then?'

'Search me, chum,' Jack sighed. 'Search me. Let's just hope we find out.'

*   *   *

Lily was beached, and she knew it. With the help of the Resistance she had been making steady if slow progress towards her northern destination, but then almost inexplicably all forward routes became impassable or unusable. Several sorties by bands of helpers she encountered during her travels had quickly to be aborted as they kept encountering German road blocks, new defences and worst of all a constant stream of incoming troops and armaments, all headed it seemed for the northern coastline and the defences immediately behind.

She soon gathered it had to be because of the impending invasion by the Allied armies. Of course Lily had known this was on the drawing board, but the plan had been to keep ahead of the Germans as they moved their forces up into new positions,

441

dodging the emplacements with which they were already familiar and utilising several new routes opened up by the French Underground fighters. It had all gone according to plan, until May when wherever they went or in whatever direction they turned either Lily and a small band of guerrillas came to a standstill, or Lily by herself found herself alone and stranded, just as she did now.

Nor could she get back to her last position, having been cut off overnight by the arrival of battalions of infantry and artillery who were now busy beginning to dig in what must be a secondary line of defences. Unable to move forwards or backwards, Lily used her initiative and began to scout laterally, spying out the new points of occupation and noting the rough size of the forces and the deployment of their heavy guns. Her head already contained information of paramount importance that needed to be relayed back to base so that it could be passed on to the designated receivers in both the British and the American forces as they prepared to invade Europe. Much of the information she had been sent to collect had already been transmitted back to base, but since she had begun her peregrinations through France, Lily had made it her job to learn as much as she could about the movements and positioning of the German forces.

Now she was stuck, and well and truly so. Hiding out in a deserted house in a small town fifty miles inland from the Calvados coastline, consulting her map, she concluded that the whole of the northwest seaboard was going to be a no-go area, since that was where the invading armies were rumoured to be going to land. In fact it had to be more than a rumour from the way the Germans were preparing the defences along that coastline, so Lily had to look either to escape east across France and Belgium and into the Low Countries, or else to find a way to get lifted out of the area she was in now, which would mean someone having to fly in over the coastal defences and pick her up in front of the German's second line of defence, a near impossibility. Or she could keep going laterally until she got to the Somme or Pas de Calais, districts that although still heavily occupied would not be quite so frenetically busy as the newly defended regions further west.

But in order to get out she would have to make contact with base, and to do that she needed to re-establish contact with the Resistance. Most of those with whom she had been working lay south of where she was now, or north or even west. The further east she ventured the fewer contacts she had, and she might find herself depending on help from parties totally unknown and not recommended to her.

In the end Lily decided on a much more ambitious plan of action, one that she chose because after a continuing series of non-starts and aborts every time she planned to make some ground, it seemed the only way she was going to survive.

Lily decided to become a double agent.

*   *   *

The day after Jack had announced his findings to Harvey in the attic office at Eden Park, Harvey set the agreed procedures in motion. On the stroke of ten thirty a.m. he was informed that the two women had arrived on the second floor as expected, and he at once telephoned through to Marjorie's desk to give his next set of instructions. Having heard what she was to do Marjorie knocked on Miss Budge's door to tell her that the two visitors expected by Major Folkestone were waiting with her in her office and would Miss Budge be good enough to inform the major.

'There are two visitors to see you, Major,' Miss Budge said, after being admitted into the inner sanctum. 'I don't have any appointments in your diary for this morning, sir.'

'Who are they, Miss Budge? It might have been something we overlooked in our haste,' Anthony said, looking up from his work. 'There has been a bit of a panic on of late, as you know.'

'Miss Hendry said it's Kate Maddox, sir—and her mother?'

Anthony glanced at his secretary again, tapping one of his famously sharp pencils in a tattoo on his desk. 'Do we know what they want, Budgie?'

'Confidential apparently, sir. I can easily stave them off, sir, make another appointment.'

'No,' Anthony said after a moment. 'No, I don't see why. I'm sure it won't take long. And after all as I understand it Mrs Maddox works for us as well—albeit in Baker Street. No—have Miss Hendry show them in, please, Budgie, and perhaps you can organise us all some tea.'

Miss Budge closed the door and returned to her intercom to instruct Marjorie to show the Maddoxes through.

A moment later Kate put her head round the outer door.

'Come through, Miss Maddox,' Miss Budge said with a smile. 'The major's expecting you.'

Kate entered as bidden, and crossed the small room towards the inner door being held open by Anthony Folkestone. A moment later her mother followed, wearing a smart grey topcoat and a bright peacock blue felt hat.

Miss Budge watched them go into the inner office and Major Folkestone close the door. For a moment she stood quite still by her desk before finally turning and making for the outer door, which she carefully opened.

Outside on duty stood two large military policemen.

*　　　*　　　*

As soon as he had closed the doors behind him Anthony put a finger to his lips to indicate to his visitors that they were to say nothing for the moment. Then, talking only the merest small talk, he made his way round behind his desk and handed some papers to Helen and Kate.

He continued to chat while the two women read what was on the sheets of paper in their hands, talk that contained no important information but none the less was being directly overheard by an invisible third party—invisible to them, that is, but not to anyone who might have been in the outer office where they would have seen Anthony's trusted assistant listening to every word that was being said by way of a small earpiece attached to the intercom on her desk, a device adapted like the one on Major Anthony Folkestone's desk by Miss Budge herself to pick up any conversation being held within the inner office, a secret outlet controlled only by the one switch on Miss Budge's machine.

So far she had heard nothing that was of any interest, nothing that would tell her what she wanted to hear or indeed needed so desperately to hear, such as how Helen Maddox had come by such a remarkable piece of millinery.

Just in time she saw the outer door opening, enough time for her to drop the earpiece back into its nest of cotton wool in the top drawer of her desk that faced that outer door. Jack Ward stepped into her domain, with a nod and a polite smile.

'Good morning, Miss Budge,' he said. 'Don't bother to announce me—the major is expecting me.'

Jack let himself into the inner office, carefully closing the door behind him. Immediately Miss Budge retrieved her listening device and tuned back in.

How did I come by it? she heard Helen Maddox saying, with a laugh. *You had best ask the Colonel that, I think.*

Bit of burglary, Jack Ward growled. *Personally effected as it happens. I've always enjoyed that side of it, you know—the burglaring.*

Should imagine you're very good at it, sir, Anthony replied. *Like most things you do.*

I have to say I find it oddly exciting. Although in this case . . .

Yes, sir?

A little sad really.

Miss Budge sat down slowly at her desk, staring across the room, the listening device still held to her ear.

You always hope against hope, you know, Jack

446

Ward said. *At least I do. Times like this I find myself hoping I'm wrong, but the sad thing is I rarely am.*

So who does the hat belong to? Kate was now asking. *Are you saying whoever owned this hat—*

Someone hushed her. Miss Budge definitely heard someone make a hushing noise. Now there was silence in the room.

Now there was whispering. Miss Budge pushed the device more tightly against her ear, trying to hear what was being said.

Come on, she whispered to herself. *Come on, damn you! Come on!*

After all, she had been able to hear everything before—every single detail of every single drop, and dodge; the names of every single agent, new or experienced, as well as all the map references, the reports on the missions, the statistics, the future plans. She had heard everything so clearly that she had soon stopped bothering opening the major's wall map to make sure of the placings. It had been as easy as that—no need to access files, no need to try to learn the combinations of the safes—just use the bugging skills she had been taught when she was an active agent herself. It was as easy as that—

She eyed the inner door, just in case it burst open and they confronted her—but to judge from all the whispering that was still going on they were too busy to bother about her.

She knew they must know. Jack Ward must know. It was Jack Ward who had burgled her flat. Blast that hat. Damn and blast that stupid hat. But who had seen her in it? She had only ever worn it to the station to meet the informant. Kurt. Kurt— who had said he loved her—sworn he loved her and would love her for ever—that bastard to whom

447

she had entrusted her beloved Tansy.

The whispering had stopped. Miss Budge glanced backwards towards the door behind her, her free hand clasping the locket round her neck, the locket she now opened, the locket that held her favourite picture of Tansy—Tansy sitting on the lawn in the sunshine, as good as gold, as sweet as any angel. What had happened to her?

She heard voices.

What will happen? What will they do?
What they have to do, I'm afraid.
My God.
The poor girl.
The poor wretched woman.

No. Oh no they wouldn't. They wouldn't do that to her. She had decided long ago that if and when this moment came, she would know just what to do. She reached quickly for the key to her desk drawer and in seconds had unlocked it and pulled it open.

The door behind her was opening now, and as she turned she could see Jack Ward. She could see his face. And she could see the question in his eyes.

But it was too late. Too late for Jack to find out why she had done it. As he moved towards her all he could smell was the acrid scent, the never to be forgotten smell of cyanide.

*   *   *

Later that morning, another of Jack's people was trying on a hat in a smart little shop in the centre of Rouen, watched by an admiring German captain who was sitting on a chair smoking a black Sobranie cigarette with one hand and tapping the side of his shining black jackboots with a swagger

448

stick held in the other.

'What do you think, Eric?' Lily wondered, turning her elegantly clad figure round so that the officer could see her head on.

'Captivating, my dear. The very picture of French chic.'

'Do you want me to have it?'

'You may have anything you like, my sweet. Up to a point, of course, yes?' The officer laughed, as did Lily, as did the shop assistant, even though there was nothing remotely funny.

'But you have been so generous already, dear Eric. This dress. This jacket—the shoes—and now this hat.'

'A woman as beautiful as you must be allowed to show off her beauty. And I could not bear this story of how you lose everything in this fire. The fortunes of war, alas, are not always good fortunes.'

'At least I escaped with my life, Eric. My poor husband was not so lucky.'

'He might not have been—and for that I am so sorry,' the officer remarked as he paid for Lily's latest purchase. 'But then one man's misfortune?'

Eric smiled at her. As Lily smiled back she considered that if there was not a war on, and if Eric had not been her enemy, she might—but only might *just*—have found him attractive enough to allow him to buy her the fineries she now wore. As it happened, her plan had been easier to put into operation than she could have dared hope. In Lisieux, she had set out her stall to find a woman her size and shape who was well dressed and obviously living a comfortable enough life under occupation by some means or other. This would not prove difficult, as Lily had long ago realised. It

449

seemed to her that it was a whole lot easier to live fairly well in Occupied France than it was in Unoccupied Britain. Here in France there were few if any shortages. There was food and drink in abundance and apart from the curfew there were few restrictions imposed on daily life. Of course, loss of freedom of movement and speech was one of the greatest handicaps, but as Lily had observed, provided you kept your nose clean and obeyed the basic rules, you not only survived but could survive very well, particularly if you were a pretty unattached woman.

So once she had targeted a woman of her own physical disposition Lily waited till she had left her house and then she burgled her. She took just the number of clothes and shoes she needed as well as the necessary cosmetics, all of which she packed neatly into one of the woman's expensive suitcases. She took two handbags, some stockings and lingerie, a few pieces of small but valuable-looking silverware which she immediately sold in the very next town, and, as a lucky bonus, four hundred francs that she found in a sock under the mattress.

In the town where she sold the silver she checked into a small *pension* in the back streets and changed into her new personality. Looking like the proverbial million dollars she then sought out the cafés and restaurants frequented by the German officers and sat at the bar looking aloof and unobtainable. So successful was her apparent reserve that she had offers of drinks within her first ten minutes.

Eric had seemed the most susceptible of all the young officers she met at the Café Montmorency. He was a languid soul, much given to striking poses and admiring himself whenever possible in looking-glasses. That was the nice bit. The rest of him was all Nazi storm troop officer, cold grey eyes, a mouth that curled in permanent disdain, and a set to his whole physique that suggested only arrogance. Yet Lily spotted a weakness, one that lay as ever in conceit. As long as someone was conceited someone else could pander to them, flatter them, sweet-talk them into indiscretions, and Eric was going to prove the perfect example of that rule.

Lily had to do nothing—at least as yet—to get him dancing attendance. In fact the less she did the more he sought her company and her approval. In order deliberately to irk him she would often in the early part of the evenings she spent in the café flirt more with his colleagues than with him, always however returning her attention to him just when he was about to become disenchanted. Her problem was that she did not have very much time, so she had to hurry, but she had to do so without making it look as though that were the case.

But before she could put her stratagem into play she needed some vital information, specifics she could only get from the Underground. She had one number she could call, but only once, and only in absolute extremis. Considering the danger to her life, she decided this had to qualify as that sort of case and so she made the call.

'Brown mouse,' she said. 'I need names from a dead cell—the nearer to Rouen the better.'

'How many beans in a can, brown mouse?'

'Seven hundred and five.'

There followed a short silence while a decision was obviously being made. Lily stayed patiently

451

silent in return, not wishing to hurry or worry.

'You need an exit?'

'I think I have one—and can do better than that. I think I can bring down a tree.'

There was no hesitation now. A list of eight names, a location, the cell code name and its most recent missions followed, all of which Lily took down quickly in shorthand.

Then she hung up. She hoped the line was clear the other end and that she had not been long enough on the line anyway for a trace to be made. She would never forgive herself if, in order to save her own life, she had endangered the lives of others—or, worse, caused them to lose their lives, however unwittingly.

Chapter Thirteen

For once Lily was dining alone with Eric. This was what she had most wanted to happen, although it was also something that she feared since she knew he was bound to make a move on her sooner or later. But that was a risk she had to take, because without it she had absolutely no chance of succeeding. Besides, she knew that if she was not prepared to take risks she should have stayed behind a desk.

'Don't you so hate the Jews?' he wondered, picking up a conversation Lily had hoped would not be rekindled, although she knew that if she could see this one through and convince him of her sympathy, she would win his trust in her completely.

'What do you think?' she said as disparagingly as she could. 'My father's import export business was quite ruined by the Jews. They bled him dry.'

'They are an intolerable people altogether,' Eric sighed, wiping the corners of his mouth delicately on his linen napkin. 'The Führer is so absolutely right in wishing to cleanse the world of them. Do you not agree?'

'If I was a man I would help him do it,' Lily replied, privately begging her Jewish grandmother for forgiveness.

Eric laughed. 'You are the most delicious woman, Lily,' he said. 'You are definitely someone I wish to be on our side. So you agree that we are the master race, yes? That the world will be a better place when we can control the sort of people who breed.'

'If they turn out anything like you—and me,' Lily said, sipping her wine, 'then of course the world will not only be a better place but a much lovelier one.'

'I would like to kiss you now, Lily. In fact I think I shall.' He pulled her face towards him with one hand and kissed her full on the mouth. 'You taste good. I look forward even more now to later tonight.'

Lily smiled back at him, wishing she could feel the same. But she had no alternative. He was her only way out.

He took her to his hotel, a place the Germans had requisitioned, formerly one of the best hotels in the city. He took her straight up to his huge and luxurious bedroom on the first floor, where he poured them both a large brandy.

'Are you assuming I'm going to sleep with you,

Eric?' Lily asked as he handed her the cognac.

'I never work on assumptions, Lily,' he replied. 'I only ever act on certainties.'

'Is that a compliment?'

'It is certainly no insult. But in one way it is a compliment—to you. I mean that I should wish to sleep with you. I can have any woman in this town—more or less—and not only in this town. Sometimes I have to apply a little pressure, you know? Some small reminder of what might happen to them or to someone else should they not find me as desirable as I am finding them. They always say yes. In the end.'

'You know,' Lily said, putting her head to one side, 'I think one of the most attractive things about you is your complete and utter arrogance.'

'And one of the most attractive things about you are your breasts. Now please come here—I think I have done with talking.'

As he undressed her, Lily thought soulfully of the things she was required to do for England. She had not wanted to sleep with him; she had not intended to do so. She had in fact prepared all sorts of female excuses and reasons for not doing so, but somehow she felt that if she tried anything like that on this dangerous and deeply unpleasant man, he would either sit it out and wait, or else he would simply rape her. Besides, she needed vital information from him, and what better way to get it than to sleep with the enemy?

Oddly enough, when it was all finally over and Eric lay deeply asleep beside her, Lily reflected that it hadn't been quite such a terrible ordeal as she had feared. Storm-Trooping Eric had turned out to be a more than adequate lover.

'Do you always sleep with your pistol under your pillow?' Lily asked him in the morning as they sat up in bed, trying to find the energy to get up.

'I only ever sleep with it under my pillow for good reason,' Eric replied.

'And what was last night's good reason?'

'If you hadn't slept with me I was going to kill you.'

'Thanks.'

'If you hadn't slept with me I would have known you were not what you said you were. And so I would have killed you.'

He had breakfast sent up to the room, fresh croissants and very good coffee. They sat at a table in the window watching the sun rise over the beautiful city.

'Anyway,' Lily began as idly as she could, knowing this was possibly the last chance she would have. 'As I told you when we met, I used to work for the Resistance.'

'I thought you still did?' he replied, looking up quickly.

'Yes, of course, I explained that. I just am not so involved with them as I was. It's very hard since I began working for you lot as well to put in the same hours.'

Eric found this hilarious and roared with laughter.

'How I wish there were more like you, Lily! In fact I would look more kindly on those French scum if they had a few more fighters like you. Anyhow—the reason you changed sides was

455

because they killed your lover.'

'Don't look like that. As if it was something only the French would do! You tell me a better reason! No, don't bother—you are all pragmatic German and I am all emotional French! But when they accuse your lover of being a double agent, and then without a proper trial or hearing take him out and shoot him in the back of the head—you think you stay enamoured of the Resistance? Besides, now they are all Communist pigs, and I am no Communist.'

'Thank God.'

'Enough of that,' Lily said, pretending to try to control her mock outrage. 'Let's talk about today. Today you tell me the Gestapo go and seek revenge on Cell Blue in—where is it? In the caves in the St-Estèphe area they use as their base?'

'No, no, Lily, that is not what I said. I said nothing of the sort.'

'But that is who you are after, surely? Cell Blue? The most potent cell here—in this area? They were responsible for—I can hardly tell—it might be easier to tell you what they were *not* responsible for! Guy Rochfort? He killed what—ten of your men! Pierre Dupont? He blew up four tanks last week alone! You must remember the tanks you lost?'

Eric nodded, about to interrupt but not yet allowed.

'If you're not going after Cell Blue, what are you doing? Who are you going after? You're not going to let them slip through your fingers, surely?'

She was glad to see Eric visibly disconcerted for the first time. So now she let him have his go, cocking her head on one side while she waited for illumination.

'I have issued instructions for a unit called the Red Birds to be rounded up.'

'The Red Birds?' Lily said aghast. *'The Red Birds?'*

'They work from Dumeaux. They're led by someone called Chantal—and someone called Gérard the Great—'

Lily frowned as if she had misheard. 'Gérard was killed three weeks ago. Chantal fled to Spain, so I heard. But go on. Go on.'

'You are sure?'

'Eric—darling man—I have the right information. I have much better information than you, my dear. Gérard was killed in a skirmish one night when they were trying to bring in an English drop. They probably tried to cover it up because he was a very important guy—he was the area leader and very high up altogether in the Resistance—and if they know you know he is dead . . .' Lily shrugged tellingly. 'But you know what I think? I say you are barking up the wrong tree, and worse—you are about to make a terrible fool of yourself.'

Eric didn't like that, just as Lily hoped he would not.

'What was this other cell you were talking about?'

Lily told him. She told him the names of all the members, the exact location and their track record. She could do that with impunity because she knew the cell had been disbanded and that the members had moved on to pastures new under new identities, some of them hopefully to Dumeaux.

When she had finished Eric got on the telephone at once to his headquarters to inform them of the information that had come to hand and to recommend an immediate change of plan and target. Half an hour later his telephone rang and it was confirmed that the raiding party had been redirected to search the caves and mountains of the St-Estèphe area in search of a group called Cell Blue, led by two men called Rochfort and Dupont.

'I shall have to leave now, alas,' Eric said, much to Lily's vast but well concealed relief. 'I have much to thank you for.'

'No, no.' She laughed. 'I have much to thank you for. Perhaps tonight you will give me something for which I shall be even more grateful?'

'I shall give the matter considerable thought during the day,' Eric agreed. 'And if today we are successful in rounding up these *cochons*, I may even let *you* treat *me*.'

As soon as he was well and truly gone, Lily dressed and departed, leaving the hotel as if she was a resident about to return, and disappearing into the backways and alleys of the town.

She needed transport desperately, having consulted her little book of maps and seeing how far away Dumeaux was. What she had to find was a small garage with a petrol supply, and a motor car.

She asked around, with as much innocence as she could, pretending she knew the name of the garage but not the location, then the location but not the name of the garage, before being directed to a small Citroën workshop in the back streets. There were a couple of two-door Citroëns parked out the front, the sort favoured by the Gestapo when making one of their flying raids, fast, nimble cars, one of which would suit Lily's purposes admirably. She was happy to see there was also a gasoline pump.

The proprietor was bent over the open bonnet of some other car which he was busy servicing. The first thing he knew about having a visitor was the feel of a gun barrel in his neck.

Lily told him not to say anything, just to move quietly to his office and get the keys for one of the Citroëns. She stayed behind him all the time, the gun barrel now in his back and concealed under her jacket, which she had taken off specifically for the purpose.

Once he had the keys, she walked him to the car and the pump, and ordered him to fill the car to the brim. He was about to say something but Lily stopped him by pressing the gun barrel even harder into his back. The car was duly filled. Then she walked the proprietor back to his office, opened the heavy door of a closet at the back and pushed him in. He still had his back to her for which Lily was grateful since she had no wish to see his face as she crashed what he had thought was a gun barrel but in fact was a length of heavy small-calibre lead piping down on the back of his head. As he fell unconscious to the floor, Lily locked the closet, threw the key in the rubbish bin, and getting into the Citroën drove at a steady pace out of the city.

*   *   *

Once on the open road she could drive as fast as she liked. There was next to no traffic and what there was seemed largely agricultural. Dumeaux lay nearly twenty miles north of Rouen, and she was there in half an hour, once she had got free of the city. It was a pretty little town, a place that seemed all but deserted when Lily parked the Citroën in the square and wondered where to start looking.

On the far side of the square she noticed a blacksmith at work, shoeing a large farm horse. Like most farriers he was a strong man, built like an ox, nut brown from the sun and covered in a slick of perspiration. Working on what she liked to call her theory that such a man generally was a typical Resistance fighter, which she privately admitted was more guesswork than constructive conjecture, she approached him, admiring his skill and the fine animal on which he was working.

Then she asked him where she might find Gérard le Grand. As she did so, the thought suddenly dawned on her that if anyone was going to be called Gérard le Grand it was possibly this giant of a man.

He didn't even look up.

'Who is asking?'

'A friend of Pierre Dupont. And Guy Rochfort.'

'So? Why are you interested?'

'I am an ornithologist, monsieur. I have come to see your famous Red Birds.'

Again he didn't look up. He simply continued nailing the shoe on to one vast hoof held in the crook of his lap.

'There is a very good little bar over there, m'selle,' he said. 'Chantal's. The proprietor is a friend of mine. She should be able to help you. Tell her Gérard sent you.'

The first thing Lily told Chantal was of the activities of the Gestapo back in Rouen, alerting her to the fact that they were after both her and Gérard in person, as well as their cell whose code name was also known to them, as was its location.

460

There was little doubt in either of their minds that once they had drawn a blank in St-Estèphe, or someone had double-checked their records, the Gestapo would set off post haste for Dumeaux, so the cell must disband and escape as fast as possible.

But first Lily needed the use of a radio transmitter. Since it was deemed too dangerous for her to use the one in the village belonging to the Red Birds, Lily was directed to a tiny hamlet up in the hills eight miles to the east where she was to ask for Father Roman. He would allow her to use the transmitter hidden behind the altar of his tiny church. What was more, there was a large farm on the outskirts of the hill village that might well be ideal for landing and taking off a small aircraft.

*   *   *

Billy and Scott had been forced to take the long route. Owing to the activities in the Channel both of the Allies and of the Germans, few merchant boats were leaving the ports along the northern French coast and no small fishing boat was willing to take the risk of making a run across the minefield that particular stretch of water had become. Nor was there any chance of an airlift since not only were they badly positioned but they also no longer had access to a radio. So they made their way home via the long and still very dangerous escape route that wound up through the very northern tip of France, through Belgium and finally into the Low Countries, the liberation of Brussels itself still a good three months away. But like many others before them, thanks to the unending help afforded them by Resistance

461

fighters everywhere, the two men made it, finally finding berths on a merchant ship headed for Harwich that was sailing under a neutral flag.

The day they set sail, the Allied armies chose also to take to the seas, crossing the English Channel in their thousands to begin a series of terrible battles that would finally herald the end of the war in Europe. One infantry unit of the US First Division landing on Omaha Beach had cause to be particularly grateful to the unsung hero who was crossing the Channel in the opposite direction, the young man who had discovered and depicted all the enemy fortifications and gun positions along a particularly important position on top of the very cliff under which they had landed, thus arming them with the sort of advance knowledge that enabled them to surprise and knock out these resolute defences, creating an all important throughway for their following troops.

*　　　*　　　*

The message soon made its way to Anthony's desk. As soon as he read it, he set about finding a way to facilitate the request it contained.

It was Cissie who came up with the answer.

'Obviously,' she drawled, looking at the map Anthony had spread out before him. 'Obviously Blackbird can't move from where she is, first because Jerry is going to be looking for her and second because he's going to be very busy in that particular area.'

'One has to imagine the Red Birds did as told and scooted,' Anthony remarked. 'If any of them fell into Gestapo hands and one of them cracked

462

on the wheel, then our own little bird's chances would go down to near zero. I think she's going to have to sit this one out.'

'I don't think so, if you don't mind me saying, duck,' Cissie replied. 'I don't think she'll be able to sit it out because they're going to comb that jolly old landscape with a fine-tooth. No one pulls the wool over the Gestapo's eyes and gets away with it—not if they can help it. And if they don't find her themselves, you can bet yer bottom someone will blow the whistle on her. No, I think one simply has to go in and get her.'

'Got enough petrol in the Austin, Cissie?'

'I wasn't thinking cars, Tony, you oaf. I was thinking planes. 'Ickle planes.'

'Any ideas for 'ickle pilots? Everyone's awfully busy, I'm afraid, as you've probably noticed.'

'As it happens,' Cissie said, 'I think I know the very person.'

*　　　*　　　*

Poppy went to collect the plane herself, for the very good reason that she wanted to see Trafford again in order to get all tips she could for the dangerous mission she had readily agreed to undertake.

'Any news 'bout the old man, sweetie?' Trafford wondered after she had greeted her friend. 'Or is it still a case of no news being good news?'

'That's it, I'm afraid, Traffy. But actually I do believe that. They do have a habit of telling one the worst PDQ at the office. So I have this feeling . . .' Poppy smiled, holding up crossed fingers.

'You betcha, Pop,' Trafford agreed. 'And won't there be a party when he touches terra firma, eh?

463

Now, to the matter in hand this—er dodge of yours. Obviously you're going to have to try to miss their blooming radar, sweetie, which means going in very low where poss, because in Tiger Tim you won't be able to go très high. Since most of the ballyhoo's going on west at the moment, one hopes Jerry's eye won't be quite so on the ball over the northern coast—but even so they'll take a pot-shot at you if you get in their sights. Best way to avoid that sort of nonsense is to bunny hop—as if you were hedgehopping, really. Fly in over the coast in a series of hops, up and down, up and down—should keep you off their screens because they won't be able to get a good line on you for long enough to pick you up as an enemy aircraft. Same goes for the flak—just keep flying at various altitudes. In a way, dear girl, the lower the better, but then of course they'll have the weather ears on and they'll hear you if you're too fudging low. Whatever you do, and however you do it, when you reach target—which I'm too damn' sure you will—your very bestest bet is to touch down, but don't stop. Keep Tiger Tim moving and get your pickup to run like stink and jump on board while you're still motoring. You can get them those instructions before you go, roger? Because when Jerry gets wind of some beastly little antique flying in over his head he'll run his fat little legs off after you in order to shoot you out of the sky, so get in and out FAYFC. Fast as you fudging can. When you're flying back, as you leave the airfield, keep low. Oddly enough it's harder to hit a low flying aircraft at speed when it's right over head than higher up when you can take its measure. You've simply got to make it *très, très difficile* to take a pop at you,

464

then just fly like budgery till you see the White Cliffs de Dover and hear dear Vera singing. I have an even better idea. Why don't I make the flight? I'm a lot older and much more disposable than you are, so why don't I make the flight? Yes, that's settled—I shall make the flight and you shall stay here and go to the ball.'

'If you try any of that nonsense, Traffy,' Poppy warned her, 'the boys have promised to help me lock you up in the hangar until I get back. Got that?'

'Should never have taught you how to fly, dear thing,' Trafford sighed. 'Because this is just the sort of lark I was born for.'

* * *

Once it had been confirmed that Blackbird had received her orders and would be ready to be collected at 0130 hours the following morning, Poppy was given the green light. Anthony drove her personally to the airstrip from which Billy had taken off on his mission and at which Poppy had discovered hers had been aborted. Now she had the chance to make good the terrible disappointment she had suffered that night by performing one of the most difficult collection jobs undertaken by the Service during the entire war. She had of course no idea of the identity of the Blackbird, other than that the agent was one of the Colonel's most valiant bogeys who simply had to be collected, not only to save the agent's life but because of vital information the Blackbird had collected.

Poppy mentally prepared herself for the ordeal facing her, hers not to reason why. It was hers to do

465

and hopefully not to die. She had been sick with nerves all the previous night, spending the dark hours hugging her little dog to her in her bed as, unable to sleep, she tried to imagine everything that could and possibly would happen to her so that she would be ready for all contingencies. But in the small hours the more she thought about it the more absolutely terrified she became, until abandoning hope of any further sleep altogether she decided to get up, make herself something hot to drink and sit by the fire until dawn came up when she knew her sanity would be restored.

It was restored long before the sun began to rise in the east, gently flooding the woodlands round her little house with a magic light that fingered through the trees like long dazzling golden wands, filling the first hours of the new day with gentle brilliance, a shining that seemed to bring with it a new sense of hope, which in its turn brought fortitude and restored the confidence of those whose belief had wavered during the troubled hours of the night. But Poppy's calm and confidence was finally restored before the rise of the sun. It came back to her when once again she found herself taking the diary from the little mahogany sewing box beside her chair, and when she had finished reading it she knew without a doubt that she would prevail.

'At least at night all planes are grey.' Anthony smiled as he walked Poppy towards what in daylight would have been a bright yellow aircraft. 'I just wish we could have got you something a little nippier. A little more up to date.'

'I'm actually happier with Tiger Tim, sir,' Poppy replied, doing up her flying jacket and checking the straps on her parachute. 'I don't suppose my pickup will have had time to put on something as sensible as a parachute?'

'Doubt it very much, Poppy. But then we hope you won't have reason to need parachutes.'

'Not with me driving, sir,' Poppy grinned. 'Particularly at the heights I intend to travel. Wouldn't have time to open.'

The ground crew, having finished their last pre-flight checks, legged the pilot on to the wing and stood ready to spin the engine into life.

'Good luck!' Anthony called. 'Safe home!'

'Mine's a brandy!' Poppy called back. 'As in large!'

Then she was off, speeding down the runway, taking off perfectly and disappearing into the darkness of the skies above them.

* * *

She flew over South Foreland, north of Dover, and thence just south of Ostend where she understood the defences were more suspect. Her information was perfectly correct since over the Belgian coastline her plane did not come under fire once. In fact she had a completely clear passage as far south as Ypres where she experienced her first flak. At once she dropped to an even lower altitude than she had been keeping, flying now at two hundred and fifty feet while zigzagging across the night sky, until crossing the border of Belgium and France she turned her little plane north of Lille to head due southwest across Picardy, again to fly unmolested south of Amiens and thence to her destination east of Rouen.

She had expected to meet more flak around Amiens, but it appeared no one had either spotted or heard her tiny craft as it battled across the night sky. She was now back at her proper cruising level, the plane was flying perfectly, and her time was spot on. Poppy took several deep breaths and then plotted the rest of her course, estimating that she had twenty-five minutes' flying time left before touching down in a mown field eight miles east of Dumeaux, a field that would be temporarily lit by a flare the moment those waiting heard the sound of her aircraft.

One minute ahead of schedule Poppy began her descent, aiming only for a map reference, unable to see anything but darkness down below ahead of her. Fifteen seconds later the field was suddenly lit by the vivid glaring light of a flare, allowing Poppy to see the strip that had been prepared and to make a vital life-saving last minute adjustment to her approach, an approach that otherwise would have had her crash straight into a huge oak tree that stood slap bang in the middle of the field.

'Nobody thought to mention the blasted tree, of course,' she muttered through clenched teeth, as the wheels below her touched down and the plane took a violent upward bounce, owing to the rough terrain.

Holding level and steady, Poppy endured three more hops of diminishing proportions before the aircraft had in her estimation properly landed, whereupon in line with her orders she kept travelling at speed towards the end of the allotted runway, before throttling back enough to allow her to swing the plane round one hundred and eighty degrees ready for immediate take-off. Again in line with her orders, she began to taxi back along the field, intending to hit the throttle a hundred yards from her turning point.

At first she thought there was no one out there, but then, after thirty yards of taxiing, she saw a figure break cover and begin to run as fast as possible towards the side of the plane. The person was about fifty yards from the Tiger Moth, which would allow just about enough time to grab hold of the rope they had left tied on the struts of the right hand wing for this very purpose, and haul themselves up and on board in one neat but demanding move.

'I hope whoever it is, is fit,' Poppy remarked to the plane, watching her land speed. 'Because they're only going to have one crack at it.'

Looking over the side of her cockpit, Poppy could see her passenger, dressed in a flying suit, a helmet already on and buckled tight, grabbing for the trailing rope.

'Come on!' Poppy yelled over the noise of the engine. 'Grab it! Grab it and pull!'

Her passenger could not possibly have heard in the mayhem, but now the flying-suited figure had grabbed the rope and to Poppy's delight and relief had pulled themselves expertly on to the wing and then equally expertly into the seat in the open cockpit in front of Poppy.

'Well done!' Poppy screamed. 'Now hold tight!'

Giving the plane full throttle, Poppy turned her full concentration to getting them back airborne. As the plane accelerated down the field, she heard the first shots, and saw the flashes from the muzzles of some of the guns now trained on them. A bullet crashed through the fuselage in front of her, followed seconds later by another that tore through the fabric just behind her seat, but the plane was still stable and accelerating fast.

The only trouble was they seemed to be running out of runway.

Poppy tried her best to make out how much field she had left but with the flare having long since died it was sheer guesswork. If she had done her job properly she knew she should have about fifty yards to spare before she needed to be wheels off the ground, yet at the back of her mind she suspected that because she had been concentrating so hard on getting her passenger on board she might have taken her eye off the ball for just a little too long, hitting the throttle five seconds later perhaps than she should have done, and thus sacrificing those precious fifty yards.

She was right. Those fifty yards had gone.

Yet somehow, miraculously, thanks probably to the little extra purchase Poppy had on the joystick as she went for lift-off, the Tiger Moth was off the ground and up in the air, although if Poppy could have seen by how little its wheels missed first the huge hedge at the end of the field and then the roof of the enormous barn over which it had to climb she might possibly have fainted. None the less they were airborne and flying, Poppy wheeling hard right at once to try to disconcert the gunmen on the ground who were still determined to bring the little aircraft down. The Resistance were playing their usual brave role, staying in place to shoot it out with the Germans rather than fleeing to safety once the plane was in the air and their job done, an heroic act that by taking out four of the ten German guns without doubt saved Poppy and her passenger from a fatal hit.

In another half a minute they were both out of range and out of sight, banking in the opposite direction now before climbing up high into the night sky. Below them the little band of Resistance fighters stole away in their own darkness, with only one injury and that a nowhere near fatal one. They left behind them five dead Germans and three wounded ones, after a small valiant battle of great importance won by yet more unsung heroes.

Poppy knew she would not have enough fuel to return the way she had come, so instead of flying northeast she turned the biplane north to head for the Dieppe coastline, an area she knew to be well defended but one that offered the shortest run home, directly over the Channel and Beachy Head where as long as they didn't hit any trouble she intended to land somewhere in the Downs behind the cliffs. Unfortunately they flew almost straight into trouble.

It happened well before they reached Dieppe. After half an hour of uninterrupted flight the sky was suddenly ablaze with the flak of anti-aircraft fire. Looking around her, Poppy at once realised it was not directed at them at all, but at a squadron of bombers to the east of them, a dozen huge aircraft lit up by the brilliance of the ack-ack and silhouetted against the night sky like a school of enormous flying whales. They were flying alone with no fighter escort, obviously on the home run after a mission. Even as she was watching one of the bombers took a direct hit and began to spiral out of control spinning slowly and inevitably to a fatal crash below.

The next thing they knew the sky was full of

German fighters, homing in on the squadron for what looked like a duck shoot. As yet it seemed no one had spotted the tiny biplane on the very outskirts of the action as Poppy tried to hold a steady course north, and because so far they were both safe and unnoticed Poppy decided to lose height, to drop down as far as it was safe to do so, hoping to be able to hide away in the darkness as well as the cloud cover below. But then, in the mirror she had fixed in her cockpit, she saw the flare of guns behind her, guns aimed right at the Tiger Moth.

Bullets tore and screamed past her, some—how many Poppy had no idea—tearing into the lower wing on the starboard side. Knowing that one moment more of hesitation would spell death, Poppy dipped the nose of the aircraft, killed the engine and dropped it straight into what she hoped would look like a fatal spin.

It seemed to work since the pilot of the Messerschmitt, having circled to come back and finish the job, must have seen what he thought was a death hit as the biplane spun apparently out of control to disappear into the clouds below, for instead of pursuing his victim to make sure of a strike he banked hard and fast to join the rest of his comrades in attacking the bombers.

There was no time to scream. Whatever Poppy's passenger was thinking, they certainly did not seem to be panicking. Not that Poppy had any free time to study the habits of her fellow traveller—but she could see a pair of gloved hands gripping the edge of the cockpit as the Tiger Moth spun deliriously earthwards.

'Traffy,' Poppy muttered to herself. 'All I can say

to you at this moment, Traffy, is that you had better have done your stuff—and you too, Bruce!'

If the engine didn't kick back into life at once they were dead. Poppy knew that, but then she also knew that if she had not killed the engine and deliberately spun the plane they would both be dead anyway, or if not dead as yet, burning slowly and horribly as the biplane spun faster and faster out of control.

But they were still alive, and while they were still alive there was hope—particularly once the engine coughed and spluttered into life at Poppy's second attempt. Now all she had to do was control the spin and pull out of the dive.

'That's all,' Poppy thought as she began to go through the procedures as taught to her in her crash course of flying at the aerodrome. 'I simply have to control the spin, get the nose up and kick on. Child's play really, compared with being on a mad Arab mare bolting out of control.'

Derek and Trafford had both done their job. But then as both Derek and Trafford would have readily volunteered they had a star pupil, someone who was a naturally gifted pilot. Not many tyro pilots could have survived the spin and stall Poppy had encouraged; in fact a lot of experienced pilots would have encountered great difficulty in saving themselves from such a situation. Yet within a quarter of a minute Poppy had pulled the plane out of its death spin and had it back flying on an even keel.

By way of thanks her passenger half turned round in front of her and gave a double thumbs up. Poppy responded by thumbing up in return, while privately thinking they weren't out of the woods yet. Even so, now they were far below the cloud cover it became plain and level flying until they reached the Dieppe coastline where Poppy once again anticipated trouble.

Expecting more anti-aircraft fire she dropped down even lower, hoping to fly over the coast at not much more than one hundred feet. Her only problem might be encountering some lethal object of the same height or higher than her plane. But having carefully charted her approach along the flatlands before arriving at the low lying coastline itself, Poppy reckoned the risk was minimal, so from a hundred and fifty feet she took the plane fifty feet lower and hoped for the best.

Again her luck held until she was over the dunes and heading for the sea—but then just as she hoped she had made it to relative safety she heard a burst of high-powered shooting break out from below and then behind the plane. Easing the joystick back she felt the plane begin to climb at once, only for it suddenly to shudder as a hail of bullets ripped into its tail area.

'Damn, damn,' Poppy swore as she felt the plane begin to falter. 'Damn, damn and double damn.'

Checking both flaps and rudder she got the impression that she still had control; at least, enough control to fly the aircraft in a straight line, as long as the enemy scored no more hits from what she imagined had to be a heavy machine-gun nest somewhere in the sands over which she had just flown.

Next she breathed in briefly to see if she could smell fuel, but again mercifully she drew a blank. To judge from the signals Poppy was getting from the figure in the front seat, her passenger was also

474

unharmed. Hoping they had escaped relatively unscathed, she eased the stick back in an attempt to climb higher, but the little plane faltered, failing to respond. Poppy eased the stick back even further and at last the nose rose and the plane began to climb, though how high she had no idea since when she checked her instruments she found the altimeter was no longer functioning, along with all the rest.

Understanding that as a result of the hit she had lost her instruments, Poppy took stock and thought ahead. As long as the plane had suffered no other serious damage, particularly to flaps and rudder, then provided she made enough height they might just be able to limp home. She could only guess at their height, which was worrying since the course she had plotted was designed to take them in right over the massive cliffs at Beachy Head. It would therefore seem only sensible to replot their route and try to get home by diverting west to come in over the relative levels of Brighton Beach, hoping they had either enough height to clear the Down directly behind the town or enough aircraft left to make an emergency landing there.

But when she tried to steer the plane left she got no response, only a drop in height. Quickly she eased the plane back up to the height she hoped she had been maintaining, only for the engine to splutter, miss and splutter again. At once she adjusted the fuel feed, and, miraculously, seconds after doing so—seconds that felt like minutes—she felt the engine begin to fire again on all cylinders, although now when she asked it to climb it stayed resolutely level.

Again she tried to turn to the left, and again the

same thing happened. The same thing happened when she tried to steer to her right, although at least when she tried this direction the loss of height was not accompanied by any loss of power. Even so, there was no way Poppy was going to be able to change the direction in which she was headed without going down in the drink. She was faced with Hobson's choice. Swallowing hard, Poppy flew straight on at her present altitude.

Guessing at both her airspeed and the distance, Poppy calculated they were still about twenty-five miles from the English coastline. Even though her instrumentation was down, she knew they were travelling a long way short of full speed, estimating from the sound of the engine and from the difficulty she had in gaining altitude that their speed was probably no greater than eighty knots, which meant they should be arriving at Beachy Head in between fifteen and eighteen minutes' time, provided she could sustain her current rate of velocity. The fact that she saw the huge cliffs looming up in front of her in the pale light of a moon that was at last clear of the cloud cover that had earlier saved their lives meant she had miscalculated.

It also terrified the life out of her, as well as suddenly giving her heart. For although they were much nearer the cliffs than she had estimated, the fact that they had arrived there sooner than her calculations had suggested could only mean that somehow they had picked up air speed, which in turn meant that Poppy might now be able to get the plane's nose up. She was going to have to do so, because as she stared ahead of her at the cliffs that seemed to be rushing towards her, she realised they were flying in at a height of at least fifty feet below their top. If she couldn't gain height, and quickly, they were dead.

Checking that she had the throttle set to maximum, which indeed she had, Poppy prayed hard and set her hands either side of the joystick. Her passenger was unmoving, all attention seemingly fixed on the mountain of white chalk and stone ahead of them. Checking the distance and able only to guess at it, Poppy reckoned the distance that lay between them and certain death could be no more than a quarter of a mile, and given that they must be travelling at nearly one hundred miles an hour that gave them approximately a quarter of a minute to gain sixty feet, in a plane that seemed unwilling to rise another sixty inches.

She pulled the joystick back, not hard but with utter determination, the sort of purpose designed to will Tiger Tim not to fail her. For two, three, four, five seconds there was no response at all, other than the chilling sound of a splutter as all at once it seemed the engine was about to cut out altogether and the plane, simply glide silently into the cliffs to explode with a shattering concussion and a life-enveloping ball of flame.

But it didn't. Instead the splutter seemed to galvanise the engine into stronger life, and suddenly Poppy saw the nose start to lift. She eased the joystick back even more, knowing that she was running the risk of over-cooking the climb yet having to take that risk since it was the only chance left for survival. And as the nose lifted so the plane climbed slowly, inexorably and then with a sudden surge as if the plane had got inspiration from a vortex of air beneath its wings. Whatever the explanation it was now climbing surely and steadily, and as Poppy dared to look directly forward at the solid mass of cliffs that had been about to take away two lives, she saw it falling away beneath the Tiger Moth, at first by only a matter of feet as the little plane cleared the very edge of the stone and chalk massif, so near in fact that Poppy swore the undercarriage was about to catch and bring them down head first; yet on the plane climbed until now they were flying a good thirty to forty feet over the grassland below, when it could climb no more. Then, once it had reached its safe height, it began to falter the way a winged bird sometimes does, fluttering and tipping before it crashes to the ground.

The moment she felt the plane begin to fail Poppy hit her internal emergency button, knocking back her airspeed instead of panicking and trying to increase it. The Tiger Moth steadied, just long enough for Poppy to trim the craft sufficiently to get her level; then she dropped the nose by a matter of a few degrees, just enough to begin an uncontrolled descent towards the downland that was now coming up to meet them, but not so much that they would nosedive into the ground. Enough in fact to leave her some control over the descending plane, enough to lift the nose, which she did, just enough for the plane to level itself— which it did—then to cut the engine—which she did—and for the plane to glide in to do an emergency landing—which it did.

Poppy closed her eyes, held on to the side of the cockpit, prayed and sat out the bounces. The Tiger Moth, brilliant little plane that it was, bounced six times, each bounce lower than the preceding one, but never tipped and never nosedived. It kept its equilibrium, landing and running in a long uncontrolled semicircle on top of the cliffs until finally it hit a shelf of grass, a ledge firm enough and strong enough to halt its progress and to tip the plane slowly up on to its nose so that it rested on its now shattered propeller, its rear wheel spinning slowly and silently while the occupants sat at first too stunned to move.

They jumped even though there was no smell of fuel. Having got themselves unstrapped they stood up in their tipped up cockpits and leaped sideways out, landing on the wings and sliding forward. As soon as their feet hit the ground they ran. They ran harder than they had perhaps ever run until they were a good hundred yards from the crashed plane, where they threw themselves face down on the ground to await the inevitable explosion.

There was none. Whatever had happened to the plane—and judging from the amount of bullet holes in the rear fuselage plenty had happened to the plane, including half a dozen entry points not six inches behind Poppy's seat—the fuel lines had remained intact. Wires must have been damaged, broken in all probability—the same with any electrics and with pressure lines—but the fuel supply was intact, and, since the electrical system had failed, there were no sparks to ignite any possible fire.

Poppy stood up, still gloved and helmeted, put her hands on her hips and surveyed the little plane with love and pride. If it had been smaller she would have gone and hugged it.

Next to her, her passenger was also staring at the

crash site, before turning to Poppy and removing
goggles and helmet, throwing her arms around her.
'I don't care who you are, you're a blasted genius.
Marry me, please? *Please!*'

Poppy, seeing who her passenger was, took her
own goggles and helmet off and smiled back.

'You might just want to reconsider the last part
of your statement.'

'Poppy?' Lily stared at her. '*Poppy!*'

Chapter Fourteen

By D-day, Anthony Folkestone had quite made up
his mind that Marjorie was the girl for him, and
having come to that particularly difficult decision
he now had to find the right way to tell her so. It
just did not seem good enough simply to take her
out for yet another drink in a public house that,
like everyone else locked up in Eden, he was
beginning to find more than a little dreary and
certainly most unromantic. The trouble was, with
no leave in immediate prospect for either of them
and so much work on their desks, it was all but
impossible to get up to London, or indeed
anywhere else. Then Marjorie inadvertently came
to his rescue by learning how to jitterbug.

In fact both she and Kate had been learning to
jitterbug for quite some time now. It had come to
them a little later than to most other young women
of their age since they were not so exposed to the
whims and trends of fashion as their urban
contemporaries, but they had both been to a local
hop six months earlier where many of the

American soldiers posted nearby used to go to dance. And they had all heard about the jitterbug.

When Kate and Marjorie first saw it being expertly danced by a couple who looked professional they were so good, it quite took their breath away. The man moved rhythmically and constantly, shifting his weight from one foot to the other as he spun his partner round him, her feet beating out double time to the music; the woman switching from left hand to right hand as her partner turned her then turned her again, being lifted and dipped over his shoulders, being spun round him with both feet off the floor, and finally, as a sort of *coup de grâce*, being thrown in the air above his head, caught, held aloft, turned and then dropped to the floor to slide through his open legs and out the other side. Then she was caught once more by her partner, who had swiftly turned to grab her hands and turn her for one last spin— whereupon she performed the perfect splits to land on the floor with one arm up in the air.

The whole dance floor had come to a stop to watch them, and when the demonstration was over they had applauded and cheered the couple to the echo.

'We have to learn how to do that.' Kate had laughed. 'I can't wait to teach Eugene and have him twirling me round his head like that!'

The two young women had spent many happy evenings in the cottage patiently learning the basic moves of what was also known as jiving, they discovered. They listened to the wireless endlessly, waiting for the right tunes to be played, and were soon on their way to becoming very polished performers. All they needed now was their partners.

But with Eugene out of action for so long, and Marjorie still technically unattached, they found themselves dancing with each other more often than not until Marjorie saw a 'Jitterbug Hop' advertised one night when they were in the local pub. It was to be held the following weekend at the local fire station of all places, but then since the outbreak of war women all over the country had got very used to dancing in the most unlikely places, from deserted ballrooms in crumbling country houses that had been taken over by the army to huge echoing Nissen huts on busy RAF stations, and even between the aisles of department stores after closing time. But neither Kate nor Marjorie had ever been to a dance in the local fire station.

'I wonder what you two are so busy laughing about,' Anthony wondered as he joined them and peered over their shoulders at the hand-painted poster. 'Gracious me—what's a jitterbug hop in heaven's name? And in the fire station?'

'Don't be such a *grandfather*, Tony!' Marjorie teased, taking his hand. 'Why don't you come and see for yourself? Kate and I are going—as I should imagine are the rest of the section.'

'*Jitterbugging?*' Anthony had persisted. 'Don't you have to be a Yank to jitterbug?'

When they got to the dance the following Saturday they found the fire station already packed and jumping, one set of the station doors having been thrown wide open so that the overspill could dance on the concrete apron outside to the music of a great-sounding six-piece band that came from the local US Army base. And everyone was already jitterbugging with various degrees of experience and skill.

'Hey!' Kate laughed. 'This looks great! I just wish Eugene was well and fit enough to be here.'

'I should think Eugene does, too,' Anthony agreed. 'The wonder is he let you come by yourself.'

'He hadn't any choice,' Kate replied. 'I said I'd wring his neck if he said no. Seriously—he was very good about it. After he'd stood outside roaring like a bull for ten minutes.'

'Actually, you know, looking at it, I'm not sure this would be Eugene's thing exactly, are you?' Marjorie wondered. 'Isn't he inclined to get all romantic?'

'So come on—who's going to ask me to dance, I wonder?' Kate enquired generally. Within seconds she had half a dozen offers, finally selecting a tall, well-built GI who whisked her on to the floor and at once began to jive with tremendous skill and speed. When last seen Kate had one arm stuck high in the air and was whooping with unbridled delight.

Anthony sat out the first number, and then the next, until Marjorie wondered whether he would ever ask her on to the floor.

'Look,' he said finally. 'This isn't very fair on you. Why don't you do what Kate's done and find yourself a partner? I'll have one of these Coca-Colas that are on offer and try and pick up a few hints. Go on, Marjorie—you're here to enjoy yourself.'

Reluctantly Marjorie allowed herself to be escorted on to the floor by one of the local firemen. He was not a good dancer; enthusiastic certainly, but devoid of any sense of rhythm and co-

483

ordination, condemning poor Marjorie to five minutes of dancing from hell. Thanking him politely she hurried back to Anthony, who encouraged her to enjoy the singular lack of dancing talent of another couple of local young men before suddenly surprising her by leading her on to the floor at the start of a very up-tempo number.

'You don't have to do this, you know!' she called to him above the band. 'This isn't in the line of duty sort of thing at all!'

'Save your comments for afterwards, miss,' Anthony smiled before proceeding—as Marjorie later put it—to dance her socks off.

He was not just good, he was very good: light on his feet, beautifully balanced and with a tremendous sense of rhythm and invention. In fact he was so good that Marjorie spent most of the hectic jive with a deeply puzzled frown on her face. When the number was over Anthony said nothing, but just bowed, while she said nothing to him because she was speechless. Before she knew it the next dance had begun and they were off again, this time to a slower beat but with no loss of expertise. They danced three times in a row before the band took a break, whereupon Anthony took her outside for a breather, walking her away from the station until they found a bit of peace and quiet under the shade of a huge mature chestnut tree.

'They call people like you dark horses, you know that, don't you?' Marjorie said after she'd got her breath back.

'They call people like me all sorts of things,' Anthony replied, producing his silver cigarette case and offering her a smoke. Marjorie took it and then wondered why. The last thing she suddenly found herself wanting was to have a cigarette in her hand or mouth should Anthony suddenly decide to kiss her, but then she realised he wouldn't be thinking of kissing her if he himself was also smoking a cigarette. 'When you achieve the rank of major, people call you all sorts of names, and you can't blame them. There's something that comes with the rank of major that makes people want to stick their tongues out at you. I don't know what it is. But there you are.'

'It's not something I want to do, I promise you.'

'There is something I want to do,' Anthony said matter-of-factly. 'Something I've wanted and been meaning to do for some time, as it happens.'

He kissed her. Although they had both lit their cigarettes he simply leaned over and kissed her, his free hand on her waist, the hand holding his cigarette held to one side. A moment later and simultaneously they both dropped their cigarettes to embrace each other properly.

'You're as good a kisser as you are a dancer,' Marjorie whispered, her arms round his neck. 'You're also full of surprises.'

'Well, that's one thing my mother didn't teach me,' Anthony replied, with a half-smile.

'What did she teach you?'

'How to dance. My mother was a ballet dancer.'

'Was?'

'She died when I was fourteen. I still miss her. She was a wonderful person and my father misses her too, more than he can say.'

Marjorie stared at him. This was not at all the sort of thing she had expected to hear from Major Anthony Folkestone.

'You're looking puzzled, Marjorie. Do tell why.'

'Your father's a general, isn't he?'

'So? Soldiers aren't all tanks and guns, you know. Sometimes they're rather the reverse of the famous description of Chopin. You know—cannons in roses and all that.'

'All what?' Marjorie enquired.

'Well, in as much as Chopin's music can very often be described as cannons hidden in roses, so some soldiers may be found to be roses hidden behind cannons. My father's a case in point. He's a wonderful amateur painter and an absolutely first rate pianist.'

'And your mother was a ballet dancer.'

'Prettiest woman you'd ever see. Light as down, sweet as an angel, and a wonderful dancer. She'd have loved you. What a pity you won't get to meet her.'

'I *am* getting to meet her, Tony.' She smiled. 'Through you.'

'Do you know, Marjorie, that's the nicest thing anyone has ever said to me. Thank you.'

'You deserve it. You're the nicest man I ever met.'

'I want you to marry me, Marjorie. Or rather I want to marry you. Blow me, I don't know which the right way round is now, I'm in such a state of confusion. Let me put it another way—'

'Yes.'

'Let me put it this way—what did you say?'

'I said yes. Yes I will marry you, Tony. I can't think of anything I want more. So if you haven't asked me properly, ask me again so that I can say yes again. Because I love saying yes to you.'

'Will you marry me, Marjorie?' Anthony asked

again, dropping down to one knee. 'Will you really marry me?'

'Yes, Anthony Folkestone,' Marjorie replied. 'Yes I really will.'

They kissed again, and then again. Then as they kissed for the fourth time, or was it the fifth time they were interrupted by a strange droning noise in the sky above them. Both of them looked up, disturbed and puzzled by the ominous sound.

'What on earth do you think that is?' Marjorie wondered, looking for something in the sky to explain it.

'I don't know, Marjorie,' he replied. 'It's not a noise I can put an aircraft to. Not any aircraft that I know, anyway.'

All at once the strange drone cut out, leaving an ominous silence. Others had heard it as well, those outside the fire station at any rate, since they could be seen looking upwards as they too tried to identify the noise. Then, after the silence, came the sound—the now unmistakable sound—of a bomb exploding.

'My God,' Anthony said, frowning deeply in the direction of the explosion, and seeing the light of flames licking up into the sky. 'Whatever it was has crashed. And blown up.'

Minutes later, the station having been cleared of dancers, the fire engines roared out, some of the firemen still pulling on their jackets in the cabs, accelerating away to fight a fire caused by the crash of an unknown and so far unidentified missile.

Anthony and Marjorie stood hand in hand, watching the huge machines disappearing into the distance as beyond them the flames reached higher and higher into the night sky.

Of course, Billy had heard nothing about this latest development. All he knew was that he was safe, he had completed his mission successfully, he had rescued Scott, and they had got home in one piece. So when his homecoming train reached Maidstone where he changed to pick up the branch line to Goudhurst where Marjorie was to meet him, he was still innocent of the fact that something he had thought up so long ago had actually come to fruition. How he missed reading about it he never knew; possibly because once he and Scott had gleaned what the main news was, their only determination was to go out and get roisteringly drunk before having to report back to HQ. Consequently both men slept for most of the journey down to Maidstone and idly flicked through magazines for the branch line run down to the local station. By now, of course, they were the firmest of friends, Scott admiring of Billy's invention and imagination as well as grateful to him for ever more for saving his life, while in return Billy's hero-worship of Scott, which had been quite substantial before his own adventure, once he had learned of Scott's own adventures in Occupied France now knew no bounds. Best of all they enjoyed laughing together, Scott constantly teasing Billy, while Billy took great delight in setting all sorts of traps, both physical and psychological, for his hero.

So it was in the very best of moods that they finally alighted at Goudhurst where they found Marjorie and Poppy waiting for them in Kate's pony and trap. Had the girls been five minutes late, the terrible incident would never have happened; had they not come by trap but by car the same would have applied. But as it was, they were there on time, perched up high in the trap, happier than any of them had been for as long as they could remember.

After Scott and Poppy's reconciliation, a reunion so sweet and so passionate that Marjorie and Billy, themselves both thrilled and delighted to see each other again, had to take a turn around the little country station in order to give the sweethearts a bit of time to themselves, Scott—being an excellent driver—took the ribbons and so began the longed-for journey home.

They were so full of happiness and sheer joie de vivre that had they all been talking and laughing as much as they had been they might none of them have heard the dreadful warning. As it was, an angel passed overhead and they all fell suddenly to silence. And in that silence came the dreadful droning roar in the skies above that the people of Britain had come to so hate and fear. Billy stared up at the sky, not having any idea what it might be, and Scott pulled the pony to a walk while he stared up in amazement.

Not the girls—in a second Marjorie and Poppy were on their feet in the back of the trap, searching the skies for the tell-tale shape they had come to know and to fear. At that very moment the roar cut out, and the air was full of silence.

'Quick!' Marjorie yelled, grabbing Billy by an arm. 'Get down! Quickly! *Get down, Billy! Run!*'

Poppy was doing the same to Scott, urging him to jump down from his seat and take cover, but both young men shook them off to stare instead at what they had seen in the sky—and what they could still see. The next thing either of them knew was that they were both being knocked bodily from the front of the trap and dragged along the road.

'For God's sake hurry!' Poppy was screaming. 'Run! Hurry! If you don't you'll be killed!'

If they hadn't listened to the girls, if they hadn't suddenly got the message, they would have been killed, too. In fact it was a miracle that none of them were killed, and had they been killed it would have been the fault, indirectly, of an RAF pilot flying high above them, who spotting the V1 and, guessing that it might be headed directly for the great house and its outbuildings that he could see below him, set about using a defence technique the bravest flyers had developed to try to deflect Hitler's latest dirty weapons from their targets. He had flown his Hurricane up alongside the pilotless V1 until he could get the wingtip of his fighter under the nearside wing of the flying bomb, which he then tilted off course by banking his own plane just enough to change the bomb's trajectory. There was always a chance of course that the bomb, once its timer cut the engine out, would still crash into somewhere inhabited, but more often than not, thanks to the skill and courage of the pilots, they managed to steer the bombs towards open, uninhabited countryside.

Such was the case exactly with the bomb that had been headed for Eden, no doubt deliberately targeted there thanks to information previously leaked by the now dead *caochán*. Had it scored the direct hit that was intended, the Intelligence forces and MI5 would have been devastated, losing not only so many top agents who were awaiting their next mission, but invaluable information. As it was, thanks to the Hurricane pilot's courage and skill, he tipped the V1 just at the right moment, pushing it way off course so that it would land, so he hoped, bang in the middle of one of the enormous exposed tracts of Kent countryside he could see below. What he could not see was the tiny pony and trap far, far below him, carrying not one but three of Eden Park's heroes.

It was the hole that saved them. Running and stumbling across the tracks beside the lane, not half a mile from Gibbet Cross, they fled into the woods, pursued closely—had they known—by a now silent V1 that was closing in on them ominously fast. Then the ground simply opened up under their feet and all four disappeared with shouts and screams into a passageway far below them, fortunately—unlike most of the passageways cut below ground to serve the catacomb of caves that ran under Eden Park—a grass-floored and not a concreted corridor.

They fell in a heap, one on top of the other, and as a terrible whistling noise near deafened them from above, they covered their heads with their arms and crushed themselves as tightly together as they could.

Seconds later, the V1 crashed through the trees and exploded with a huge detonation a hundred yards into the woods. It was clear that had they been anywhere above ground they would all have been killed by the blast, but lying as they were twenty feet below ground and insulated from the explosion by the solid rock formations of the caves around them, the only access being an already weakened air vent that had collapsed beneath their weights, they escaped with cuts, bruises and, in Marjorie's case, one broken wrist.

'What the hell was that?' Scott wondered once the noise had subsided and the dust and dirt had settled. 'What in the name of God was that?'

Billy knew.

He knew when he had heard the engine cut out. He knew, because that was the way he had designed his own flying bomb to work, with a timer cutting out the engine once the target distance had been achieved, so that the unpiloted aircraft would then glide down in deadly silence to explode on its intended target.

For the rest of his life he would often wonder quite how the enemy got hold of the idea in the first place? He would lie awake arguing with himself. *I know it's possible for two people to think of the same idea at more or less the same time, but in this instance I just think that it must be a little too coincidental ...*

But any answer he might have received now lay with the *caochán* in an unmarked grave in unconsecrated ground, a round silver locket around her neck, within it enclosed a photograph of a golden-coated dog staring up devotedly at the photographer.

Epilogue

The last pages of the old diary she had found were something that Poppy always liked to reread on the anniversary of the day that Scott had returned safe to her. It was a moment she saved for herself, refusing to share it with anyone lest the slightest remark, well-meaning comment, or off-hand observation would destroy something which had meant so much to her for so long. It was as if, during the dark days of the war, the writer of the diary had become her secret friend, providing Poppy with the reassurance that times like this had passed before, that similar perils had been survived, and that finally against all odds great victories had finally been won.

I am exhausted from all the anxiety, knowing that if by God's grace my beloved is returned to me it will be a miracle beyond all imagining. Then early this very morning there was a great belting on my door, so loud that I feared it would cave in, but when I opened it, it was to one of the sights I shall always treasure, young Billy Cosworth from the rectory, his grandfather's old forage cap set back on his thick head of curls, his face wreathed in smiles.

'Boney is defeated, ma'am!' he cries. 'Boney is done for! Father sends to tell you that the battle at Waterloo is won and Boney is defeated!'

Quickly I snatch up my bonnet and shawl and follow Billy down through the woods, past the lake and on to the big house. We are only halfway across the lawns that run beside the lake when the church bells start to ring—the sound we all most longed to hear, the very peals of victory. Billy turns to me and says, 'I bet they're ringing out all over England ma'am! Imagine that!' and indeed I do. I think of that, and feel near to fainting at the very idea of every bell in England sounding for this wonderful day, this great victory, this time of joy that now must follow so much sadness and despair. There cannot be a house or a family in the land that has not suffered the loss of a loved one, not a village that has no memory of some bright handsome boy who has been taken, in the long campaign against the villain Napoleon, not a place anywhere in this land that because of him has not had to learn to live with grief, tears and a sorrow that will never be allayed.

Yet through it all we have always surely known that the tyrant must be defeated, and that we alone had the courage to do it. And because of this great day I swear as we all must do that no enemy shall ever invade this blessed island of ours, not ever. I know we all feel the same. I can tell from the faces all around me—we are determined no one shall ever threaten us again in such a way, but if they do then we shall repel them in just the same way as we repelled Bonaparte. I say to young Billy, 'You will always remember this day, won't you, Billy?' which he will. I can tell from the look in his bright eyes, and from the joy etched on his face that this is a moment he will never forget. Then after the prayers of thanksgiving in the church, and many tears of gratitude shed as we speak them, I quickly leave the congregation and hurry home, where I now sit and await the return of my beloved, for him to return to me and to our little House of Flowers, with God's grace, I know he most surely will.

Nowadays Poppy always looked up at this moment, because although she knew that the writer's husband does indeed return safely and heroically, she never read beyond the words *Home at last—praise be!* So touching were the entries subsequent to the return of the writer's soldier husband that, after she had read them once, Poppy felt as if she was intruding into a moment that should be utterly private, just like the moment Scott had finally returned to her, and together they had closed out the rest of the world as they shut the doors of the House of Flowers to retire to their bliss within.

So Poppy would always close the diary at this point, retie the faded ribbon that kept it shut and intact and carefully replace it in its hidey-hole at the bottom of the ancient little mahogany box where she had found it. England was at peace, those who would invade her had been repelled, husbands and lovers were returned, and so Poppy would lock the mahogany box back up, hide the key away and quietly leave her little drawing room, as if she was leaving someone she had woken to fall back asleep once more, until the following year.

Postscript

Anthony married Marjorie at St Michael's Church in Little Midfield, the village adjacent to Eden Park. Billy was their best man. They both continued to work for Intelligence until they began a family.

Eugene Hackett married Kate Maddox in the Church of Our Lady in Ashbrook. Billy was their best man too. Eugene made a full recovery but was still considered not fit enough to continue active service. He retired to breed thoroughbred horses in Wicklow. The best horse he bred was an Irish Derby winner. It was called The Dodge.

Jack Ward married Helen Maddox in the Kensington Register Office, London. Harvey Constable was his best man. They moved home to the Cotswolds and adopted two children.

Scott and Poppy Meynell finally went on honeymoon, first to Brighton, and then on to Devon. George went too. Scott remained working for Intelligence while Poppy founded a training school for pilots.

Billy went to look for Nina after the war was over, only to find she had married a Communist film director who had also been a member of the Underground. Billy himself became an actor, while continuing to work part time for Intelligence.

Yves and Lily married after a long engagement that was broken off four times. They live in the Loire Valley, have five children and run a restaurant that was awarded two Michelin stars seven years after they opened it.

Poppy's dachshund George married a redhead, who bore him four puppies. Scott and Poppy have the pick of the litter.

Cissie Lavington was offered the post as head of MI5 but refused, preferring early retirement to breed roses in her now famous garden in Somerset.

Harvey Constable became one of the top international couturiers. He never married.

THE END

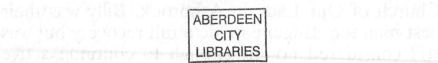